EDWARD MARSTON was born and brought up in South Wales. A full-time writer for over forty years, he has worked in radio, film, television and theatre and is a former chairman of the Crime Writers' Association. Prolific and highly successful, he is equally at home writing children's books or literary criticism, plays or biographies.

www.edwardmarston.com

a&b

The Devil's Apprentice

An Elizabethan Mystery

EDWARD MARSTON

Allison & Busby Limited
12 Fitzroy Mews
London W1T 6DW
www.allisonandbusby.com

First published in 2001.
This paperback edition published by Allison & Busby in 2014.

A CIP catalogue record for this book is available from
the British Library.

ISBN 978-0-7490-1687-6

10 9 8 7 6 5 4 3 2 1

Typeset in 10.5/15.5 pt Sabon by
Allison & Busby Ltd.

The paper used for this Allison & Busby publication
has been produced from trees that have been legally sourced
from well-managed and credibly certified forests.

Printed and bound by
CPI Group (UK) Ltd, Croydon, CR0 4YY

*To my beloved daughter, Helena,
not forgetting Milton, the faithful hound
and Mad Max, the amazing cat.*

A witch is one that worketh by the Devill, or by some devilish or curious art, either hurting or healing, revealing or foretelling things to come, which the devil hath devised to entangle and snare men's souls withal unto damnation.

George Giffard : *A Discourse on the Subtill Practices of Devilles by Witches and Sorcerers,* 1587.

Chapter One

Nicholas Bracewell had walked only fifty yards from the house when he saw the dead body. Covered in frost and spattered with mud, the old man lay in a narrow lane, huddled against a wall in a vain attempt to ward off the severe cold. Nicholas had seen death too many times to be shocked by its handiwork but he heaved a sigh of compassion at this latest example of its random cruelty. Its victim had been defenceless, an elderly beggar with no home to shelter him, no family to protect him, no warm food to sustain him and no clothing beyond a few pitiful rags to keep the icy fangs of winter at bay. When he bent over the corpse, Nicholas was surprised to see a farewell smile etched into the haggard face. Here was a willing sacrifice, a creature so tormented by the miseries of his life and the extremities of the weather that he could not endure them another day. The grotesque, toothless, frozen smile signalled his escape and added a poignancy to his grim demise. Closing his eyes, Nicholas offered up a silent prayer for the soul of the dead man.

London had known cold winters before but this one seemed to be unusually harsh. It was as if nature were exacting punishment for its earlier bounty. Having allowed the capital to bask in a hot summer then enjoy a remarkably mild autumn, it made amends for its kindness by sending wind, rain, snow, ice and fog to attack the city. Christmas had been celebrated in a blizzard. New Year's Day was pelted with hailstones. Twelfth Night was disturbed by a howling gale. A frozen river brought the cheering diversion of a Frost Fair on the broad back of the Thames but the mood of elation soon passed as treacherous ice began to crack up indiscriminately, causing panic, injury and an occasional drowning. There was no relief. When the snow thawed, it was quickly replaced with frost, colder, sharper and more insidious in its effects. The very young or the dangerously old were the first to be cut down by its chill scythe. As he set off again, Nicholas knew that the beggar with the congealed smile would not be the last corpse to litter the streets of Bankside.

He found the watchmen at the Black Horse, drinking ale and keeping as close to the fire as they could, grumbling about the weather and complaining that honest men could hardly be expected to do their duty in such hostile conditions. It was a dank, dark inn, frequented by prostitutes and other low life in the area. Forsaking their roles, the two watchmen were making common cause with the very people they were appointed to keep under observation and, from time to time, arrest. It was not untypical behaviour. Nicholas reported the death and described the location of the corpse but his words elicited no sympathy. The tall watchman with the straggly beard was merely irritated.

'Another one?' he protested, rubbing his hands before the flames. 'Why don't these old fools have the grace to die in someone else's parish? He's the third this week to be snared by Jack Frost under our noses.'

'Then he deserves some consideration,' said Nicholas.

'So do we, good sir.'

'One thing,' said his companion, a short, smirking stoat of a man. 'He's in a warmer place than we are, that's for sure. This cold has turned my pizzle to an icicle.'

Nicholas was blunt. 'Is that why you bring it into a leaping house instead of patrolling the streets as you're enjoined to do? If you had less concern for yourselves and more devotion to your work, you might be able to save a few lives for a change.'

'You've no cause to scold us,' said the stoat, defensively.

'I've every cause. Now, show some respect for the dead. I've told you where his body lies. Arrange to have it removed. If it's still there when I return to Bankside, I'll come looking for the pair of you to know the reason why.'

'What business is it of yours?'

'I live here.'

'So do we.'

'Then prove yourselves worthy neighbours.'

Turning on his heel, Nicholas left the fetid taproom and stepped out into the fresh air. The icy wind plucked mischievously at him. He gave an involuntary shudder. He adjusted his cap and pulled his cloak more tightly around him. Swift movement was the best way to defeat the cold. Setting off at a brisk pace, he walked purposefully in the direction of the bridge, preferring to cross the river on foot rather than brave the rigours of a cold journey by boat. When he reached the corner of the street, he paused to look back. Shamed by his words, the two watchmen tumbled out of the Black Horse and slowly headed for the lane where the dead body had been discovered. Nicholas was satisfied. He continued on his way.

London Bridge was seething with activity. Parallel lines of shops and houses stretched the entire length of the structure, narrowing it to such an extent that there was barely room for wagons and coaches to pass each other. Nicholas pushed his way through the crowd, ignoring the brush of a horse's flanks against his shoulder or the harder caress of the cart that it was towing. His mind was still on the frozen figure in Bankside. It was not simply that he felt guilty about having slept in a warm bed while a man was shivering to death nearby. The sight had a deeper significance for him. In one tragic death, he saw the potential of several. Westfield's Men, his beloved theatre company, was also a casualty of winter. Driven from its inn yard venue by the malignant weather, its life was gradually ebbing away, its members thrown into the wilderness of unemployment, its work fading into distant memories, its willpower eroded to the point where it might soon just lie down, turn its face to the wall and quietly expire.

Westfield's Men had endured many crises in the past. Plague and fire had driven them from the city, Privy

Council and Puritans had threatened them within it. Rival companies had done everything in their power to destroy them. Nicholas was only the book holder, a hired man with no financial investment in the troupe, but he had led the fight against every enemy that threatened them. Even he, however, was powerless against the vagaries of the English climate. The ugly truth had to be faced. If the austerities of winter continued for much longer, Westfield's Men would be starved into submission and frozen into a mass grave. Nicholas felt a pang of regret that made him catch his breath. Gritting his teeth, he quickened his step.

When he made his way to the other side of the bridge, Nicholas plunged into an even more turbulent sea of humanity. Gracechurch Street was given over to its market, a lively, sprawling free-for-all in which dozens of pungent odours competed to invade the nostrils and where the noise was deafening as traders yelled, customers haggled, horses neighed and foraging dogs tried to outdo them all with a cacophony of snarling, yapping and barking. Only the scavengers and pickpockets worked in silence. There was no room for calm reflection in such a throng. Nicholas had to watch where he was going and use his strong shoulders to force his way through the press of bodies. He was relieved when he ducked in through the gateway of the Queen's Head and left the frenzy behind him. His relief quickly changed into sadness. He came to an abrupt halt.

The inn yard was empty. The venue where Westfield's Men had given their finest performances was cold, deserted and neglected. Pools of ice glistened on the cobbles. The stables were uninhabited, the galleries vacant and the roofs sprinkled with frost. It was disheartening. A yard that had witnessed stirring drama, echoed to the sound of mighty lines or listened to the strains of expert musicians was now bereft of life or sound. Nicholas found it impossible to believe that he was standing on the very spot where the makeshift stage was erected. Had those bare galleries really been crammed with cheering spectators? Was that place of honour up above once occupied by their patron, Lord Westfield? Did hundreds of people actually stand shoulder to shoulder in that yard? Where had they all gone? Why had they left no sign of their passing? It was eerie.

One thing about the Queen's Head, however, did not change. Its landlord, Alexander Marwood, was the same miserable, mean-spirited ghoul that he had always been. As soon as the book holder stepped into the taproom, Marwood was at his shoulder.

'This weather will be the ruination of me!' he complained.

'It serves none of us well,' said Nicholas wearily.

'But I suffer more than most, Master Bracewell. This damnable cold keeps the coaches away and my beds empty of custom. All that I get in here are the sweepings of the streets,' he went on, extending an arm to take in the whole room. 'Look at them. Not a gentlemen among them. Not a full purse in the whole establishment. Here we have nothing but knaves and rascals, buying a niggardly cup of ale in order to sit out the whole day in front of my fire. Where's the profit in that? The cost of logs is crippling. And this evil company drives out good custom. T'was ever thus.'

Nicholas let him moan on for several minutes before cutting his litany short.

'Master Firethorn sent word that I should meet him here,' he said.

Marwood nodded. 'He's taken a private room. I'm to send you there.'

'Direct my feet.'

'First, let me tell you how oppressed I've been.'

'Later,' said Nicholas firmly. 'I'll hear all later, I promise. Master Firethorn does not like to be kept waiting. Tell me where he is and I'll trouble you no further.'

Peeved to be losing a sympathetic ear, Marwood sniffed noisily and explained where to find the room. Nicholas thanked him. He went up a flight of rickety stairs and along a passageway worn smooth by the tread of many feet. The landlord's directions were superfluous. From behind the door at the far end came a sound so deep, rich and expressive that it could only have issued from the throat of Lawrence Firethorn.

'No, no, no, you idiot! That is not what I said at all!'

Deprived of his rightful place on stage at the head of his company, Firethorn was taking out his frustration on Barnaby Gill, his old adversary. Nicholas tapped on the door then opened it to walk in on a familiar scene. Firethorn was on his feet, gesticulating wildly, Gill was perched on a chair, arms folded and head turned away in disdain, and Edmund Hoode was flapping ineffectually between them like a dove of peace whose wings have been comprehensively clipped. Nicholas's arrival brought the argument to a sudden end. Hoode lurched across to embrace his friend.

'Nick!' he exclaimed. 'Thank heaven you've come! Lawrence and Barnaby are at each other's throats again.

There'll be bloodshed soon if we don't stop them.'

'Nonsense,' said Firethorn with a ripe chuckle. 'Barnaby and I had a slight difference of opinion, that is all. I was merely pointing out the stupidity of his argument.'

'It pales beside the lunacy of your own,' retorted Gill.

'You're both as bad as the other,' chided Hoode. 'Two squabbling children.'

'Nick, dear heart,' said Firethorn, closing the door and shepherding the newcomer towards a chair. 'Come in and take your ease. It's a long, cold walk from Bankside but I've news that might warm you up. Sit down, good friend.'

Slipping off his cloak, Nicholas took the chair in the corner while Firethorn and Hoode resumed their own seats. The atmosphere was fraught. An exchange of civilities helped to ease the tension slightly but it was not dispelled. Nicholas looked around his companions. Firethorn, the manager and leading actor of the company, was resplendent in his close-fitting Italian doublet, his beard well-groomed, his eyes aflame. Gill, by contrast, shorter and slighter of build, was still wrapped up in his fur-trimmed cloak, brooding sulkily. A gifted clown on stage, he was morose and capricious when he quit the boards, qualities that were intensified by his keen rivalry with Firethorn. Edmund Hoode was the resident playwright, a pale, thin, self-effacing man who all too often found himself being ground helplessly between the mill wheels of Firethorn and Gill. Hoode's attire was more sober and far less expensive than that of his two colleagues. Because there was no heat in the room, all three of them still wore their hats.

16

'Thus it stands, Nick,' said Firethorn, seriously. 'Winter has done its best to kill our occupation. Snow and ice have turned us out of the Queen's Head and made the roads too impassable for us to tour. We could do nothing but sit, shiver and pray to God for deliverance. Our prayer,' he announced, brightening, 'has finally been answered.'

'I disagree,' said Gill.

'That is taken for granted.'

'The whole notion is ridiculous.'

'Let Nick be the judge of that,' said Firethorn, impatiently. He turned back to the book holder. 'Our esteemed patron, Lord Westfield, has received an offer on our behalf that may be construed as manna from heaven.'

Gill snorted. 'Manna, indeed! I see it as one more snowstorm descending out of the sky to bury us up to our waists.'

'I'll bury you up to the top of that ridiculous hat of yours, if you dare to interrupt me again, Barnaby. Hold your tongue, man. Is that beyond your competence?'

'What exactly is this offer?' asked Nicholas, anxious to head off another spat between the two men. 'If it comes from Lord Westfield, it must have some worth.'

'It does, Nick.'

'I beg leave to doubt that,' said Hoode, diffidently.

'You see?' said Gill, triumphantly. 'Edmund agrees with me.'

'Not entirely, Barnaby.'

'Let's hear what Nick has to say,' insisted Firethorn, making an effort to rein in his irritation. 'And he cannot do that until he has learnt the facts of the case. Though he may not be a sharer, I value his thoughts above those of anyone in the company.' He distributed a punitive glare between Gill and Hoode to ensure their silence. 'In brief,' he continued, 'the situation is this. We are invited to Silvermere, the home of Sir Michael Greenleaf, there to reside for ten days, during which time we are to stage six plays for the entertainment of Sir Michael and his guests. The fee is handsome, the welcome cordial. What more could we ask?'

'Very little, at face value,' said Nicholas. 'Where is Silvermere?'

'In Essex, no more than a day's ride away.'

'This news is indeed excellent.'

'I jumped for joy when I first heard it.'

'That's understandable.' He looked across at the others. 'I'm cheered by these tidings. What possible objection can there be?'

'You have not yet heard the conditions,' said Gill, sourly.

'Conditions?'

'Yes, Nick,' added Hoode. 'Two of them. Tell him, Lawrence.'

'They're not so much conditions as trifling requests,' said Firethorn, airily, trying to make light of them. 'The first is that one of the plays we present must be entirely new. That's hardly an unjust stipulation. Sir Michael is paying well and expects the best. He wishes to offer some newly-minted masterpiece to his guests.'

'And who is to be the author of this piece?' asked Hoode.

'Who but you, Edmund?'

'Impossible!'

'Inevitable.'

18

'There's no time to write a new play.'

'Then refurbish an old one and change its title.'

'That's villainy, Lawrence. I'll not stoop to deception.'

'Theatre is one great deception, man. We practise on the minds of our spectators. How is Sir Michael Greenleaf to know that his new drama is but an ageing body in a fresh suit of clothes?'

'He may not know,' replied Hoode, indignantly, 'but I will. It would turn my stomach to be party to such a low trick and our reputation would be sorely damaged if the truth were to come out. Did you not say that Lord Westfield might be present?'

'Yes,' admitted Firethorn, 'but only for a few days.'

'Should he chance to be there when we perform, he'll uncover our device at once. Drunk as he usually is, our patron knows when he has seen a play before, however well we disguise it. No, Lawrence, this condition cannot be met. We are bidden to Silvermere at the end of this month. I cannot conjure a play out of the air in so short a time. You must thank Sir Michael for his kind invitation but refuse it nevertheless.'

'Why be so hasty?' intervened Nicholas. 'I see your dilemma, Edmund, and I think it wrong to put you in such an unfair position. Our best work comes from you, it is true, but surely we can look elsewhere on this occasion. Another pen might answer our needs here.'

'Not in less than a fortnight, Nick. What hand could work so speedily?'

'None that would produce a play worthy of our company, perhaps, but I'm not speaking of a piece that must be grown from seed in its author's mind. I talk of a play already written but untried in performance. It's called *The Witch of Rochester*.'

'By heaven, you're right!' said Firethorn, slapping his thigh. 'It went clear out of my mind. The play had many faults but enormous promise. That's why I gave it to you to read, Nick.'

Gill was outraged. 'You showed a play to a mere book holder before I cast my eyes on it? That's unforgivable, Lawrence. Nicholas may do his duty behind the scenes but it is I who have to transmute the written word into life on the stage. I've never even heard of *The Witch of Rochester*.'

'No more have I until this moment,' said Hoode with mild annoyance.

'I was keeping it as a pleasant surprise for the both of you,' lied Firethorn.

'You'd forgotten all about it until Nicholas jogged your elbow,' observed Gill, testily. 'If it can be so easily mislaid in your memory, it can hardly have a strong purchase there. Many faults, you say. I do not like the sound of that. Be warned, Lawrence. I'll not risk my art on some base brown-paper stuff written by a floundering author. What arrant fool puts his name to this witches' brew?'

'Egidius Pye,' said Nicholas, 'and he's no arrant fool.'

'Nor is he a poet of any repute.'

'No, Master Gill,' confessed the other, 'but he's a talented playwright who will learn much from seeing his work translated to the stage. Master Pye is a lawyer, an educated man with a ready wit. One of his plays saw the light of day at the Inns of Court and he has a commission to write another. He's no raw newcomer but a man whose pen we should nurture and encourage.'

'That's a decision for the sharers to make,' said Gill, loftily. 'Only an actor can make a true judgement of a play.'

'I disagree,' said Hoode, loyally. 'Nick has a keener eye than any of us.'

Firethorn nodded. 'Precisely why I first showed this piece of witchcraft to him. When you read a play, Barnaby, you see only the part intended for you. Because he lacks your overweening vanity, Nick can view a drama in its entirety. And I agree with him. *The Witch of Rochester* may cast the very spell we require.'

'In time,' warned Nicholas. 'It needs work on it still.'

'Edmund can help there. It's much easier to polish an existing play than to labour over a new one. All that Master Pye needs is the benefit of a guiding hand.'

Hoode was sceptical. 'If he'll accept it, Lawrence.'

'No question but that he will.'

'Some authors tolerate no interference with their work.'

'Egidius Pye will do as he's told.'

'The first thing you might advise him to do is to amend his title,' said Nicholas. 'Since we are to perform at Silvermere, it might make sense to shift his witch from Kent to Essex, a county more seasoned in sorcery. Lose one letter, substitute two and Master Pye's work becomes *The Witch of Colchester*. That might appeal to Sir Michael.'

'It certainly appeals to me, Nick,' said Firethorn, clapping his hands. 'It shall be done. There, my friends. One condition is already met.'

'Not until I've read the play myself,' said Hoode.

'You'll appreciate its rare quality at once, Edmund.'

'That still leaves the second condition,' Gill reminded him, 'and it remains quite insurmountable. A dozen new plays would not make me sanction that.'

'It's a bold demand,' agreed Hoode.

'A suggestion,' emphasised Firethorn, 'not a demand. We may yet find some happy compromise. What Sir Michael Greenleaf is asking,' he said to Nicholas, 'is that Westfield's Men take a new apprentice into the fold.'

'Madness!' decided Gill.

'Not necessarily.'

'We have enough mouths to feed, as it is,' argued Hoode.

'I'll take responsibility for feeding one more,' volunteered Firethorn. 'Our boys have been happy enough under my roof and they have not gone hungry with a wife like Margery to do the cooking. I think that we should consider the request.'

'Who is the boy in question?' wondered Nicholas.

'His name is Davy Stratton.'

'What do we know about him?'

'Precious little beyond the fact that he is eleven years old and desirous of entering this verminous profession of ours. Davy is the son of Jerome Stratton, a rich merchant and close friend of our host in Essex. Lord Westfield gave me to understand that Sir Michael would regard it as a great favour if we could accept the boy.'

'And if we do not?' challenged Gill.

'The invitation to his home loses some of its warmth.'

'It crumbles, Lawrence. Take the lad or stay away from Essex. That's the offer. In exchange for ten days' employment, we may be saddled with a useless boy for years on end. It's a monstrous bargain and we should reject it outright.'

'There's room in the company for one more apprentice.'

'When we have no work for the boys already indentured? Spurn this Davy Stratton. We'll not have him thrust upon us in this way.'

'Hold there, Master Gill,' said Nicholas, thinking it through. 'This offer may be unlooked for but it comes at an apposite time. John Tallis can no longer carry a young woman's part with any success. His voice has broken and his features coarsened.'

'Do not mention the rogue to me!' growled Firethorn as an old wound reopened. 'I was there at the fateful hour when John Tallis betrayed us. *The Maids of Honour* was the play. In the person of the King of France, I asked the blushing Marie to accept the hand of the Prince of Navarre in marriage. And what happens? John Tallis chooses that moment to change his sex. His maid of honour turned into a croaking bullfrog who all but ruined the play. I could have gelded him on the spot!'

Nicholas was tactful. 'John is more suited to the roles of older ladies now. Nurses or grandmothers are still within his compass. A younger voice is required. I thought to have found it in Philip Robinson but he preferred to remain at the Chapel Royal. It may just be that Davy Stratton is a better deputy.'

'He's an imposition we can do without,' said Gill, vehemently.

'I incline to the same view,' added Hoode. 'We can manage without a new boy.'

'When he brings employment in his wake?' said

23

Firethorn. 'Would you kiss away ten days' of work in a private house? Think of the fee we would forfeit and of the new friends we might make for our art. Remember that this Jerome Stratton is a wealthy merchant, eager to place his son among us. We can set a high price on such eagerness. There's ready profit in this for Westfield's Men.'

'Only if the boy is an apt pupil,' said Hoode.

'I'm sure that he will be, Edmund.' His voice took on a sharper edge. 'Are you not vexed by this enforced idleness? Do you not fear that your art will desert you? A moment ago, Nick mentioned the Chapel Royal. Does it not gall you that boy actors perform each day at Blackfriars while we languish here?'

'Of course, Lawrence.'

'Do you feel no sense of injustice that the indoor playhouses thrive while those of us at the mercy of the elements are thrown out of work?'

'It wounds me to the quick.'

'Then do something about it. Seize this offer with both hands. Sir Michael Greenleaf is our host but there may be some among his guests who will also see fit to employ us in time. Ten days in Essex may gain us tempting invitations elsewhere.'

'That's true,' conceded Hoode, warming to the idea.

Gill was unconvinced. 'It still does not solve the problem of an unwanted boy,' he said, testily. 'I refuse to let a complete stranger foist his son upon us.'

'Sage advice, Master Gill,' said Nicholas.

Firethorn bridled. 'Will *you* turn against me as well, Nick?'

'By no means,' returned the other. 'I support all that you've said but I also accept the contrary view. Whatever the lure, no company should be compelled to take an unknown quantity into its midst. The remedy, therefore, is simple. Meet this Jerome Stratton and question him closely. Examine his son to see if he is fit for the demands of the stage. Davy and his father will not be complete strangers then. We'll know them for what they are. If the boy proves unequal to the task, turn him politely away.'

'If he shows talent,' said Firethorn, beaming happily, 'we take the lad into the company and pocket the money from his father. This is the wisest counsel of all, Nick. I knew that you should be part of these deliberations. Is it agreed, then?' he asked, looking at the others. 'We put Davy Stratton to the sternest test?'

'As soon as possible,' said Hoode.

'But against my better judgement,' sighed Gill.

'Come, Barnaby,' teased Firethorn. 'I would have thought you'd be the first to welcome a new boy into the company. You consort more with the youth of London than any of us. And however plain and pimply young Davy turns out to be, he'll be ten times prettier than John Tallis. Will that not content you?'

Firethorn chuckled and Gill retreated into a hurt silence. Though he still had reservations about the new play, Hoode was pleased that the decision had been made. Nicholas, too, was glad, delighted with the unexpected invitation from Sir Michael Greenleaf and hoping that it was possible to accept it. Their reputations were a matter of great pride to his three companions. To the lesser mortals in the company, however, work was simply a means of survival. Employment at a fine house in Essex would be a godsend to them. Food, lodging and an appreciative audience would be guaranteed. Nicholas longed to have the pleasure of spreading the good news among his fellows.

'Thank you, gentlemen,' declared Firethorn, rising to his feet. 'We'll have that death's head of a landlord fetch us a bottle of Canary wine to celebrate.' He squinted as a shaft of sunlight came in through the window. 'Look, my friends,' he said, pointing. 'A change in the weather at last. The sun is shining to bless our enterprise. It's an omen.'

'Yes,' murmured Gill, 'of the worst possible kind.'

It was a pity that none of them heard his dire warning.

Chapter Two

'Well, my boy,' said Jerome Stratton, beaming complacently, 'what do you think of it?'

'It's very nice, Father,' replied Davy.

'Nice? Nice?' chided the other. 'Is that all you can say? The Royal Exchange is one of the great sights of London and you simply dub it 'nice'. Look properly, Davy. And *listen*. That excited buzz you hear is the sealing of a thousand contracts. This is the very heart of the city, the place where goods are bought and sold, fortunes made or lost and commercial dynasties forged. To merchants like me, the Royal Exchange is home.'

'Yes, Father.'

'That's why I brought you here. To feast your eyes on its magnificence.'

'Thank you,' said the boy. 'It's very big.'

'Nice? Big? You're too miserly with your adjectives,

lad. The Exchange is a true phenomenon. It may resemble the bourses at Antwerp and Venice but, in my view, it surpasses both. I was little above your own age when the first brick was laid by Sir Thomas Gresham some thirty odd years ago. Do you see that huge grasshopper atop the bell tower?' he went on, pointing upwards. 'An emblem from the Gresham crest. The memory of Sir Thomas is kept fresh in our minds.'

'Yes, Father.'

Davy Stratton's dutiful answer concealed his doubts. Whatever else the merchants and bankers were doing as they milled about in the piazza, they were not thinking about the late founder of the Royal Exchange. They were too busy wrangling over contractual details, considering new investments, soliciting loans or trading gossip. It was the same whenever merchants came to stay at their house. Jerome Stratton would speak to them for hours on end in their private language and the boy would be left on the periphery of the conversation, present but completely disregarded, reduced to the status of a piece of furniture in the room. It did not endear Davy to the merchant class in which his father flourished. The Exchange was overwhelming in its size and crushing in its exclusivity. Davy felt more alienated than ever. It might be home to his father but it was a species of torture chamber to him.

'Most of the materials came from abroad,' said Stratton, resuming his lecture. 'The slates were imported from Dort, the wainscoting and glass from Amsterdam. And, of course, the architecture is inspired by the Italian masters so it has a truly international feel, as befits the trading centre of our wonderful city.' He gave a teasing grin. 'Or do you think that London itself is merely 'nice' or 'very big'? I hold that it's the finest city in Christendom. What's your opinion, Davy?'

'It frightens me a little.'

'Does it not also dazzle you and make your blood run?'

'No, Father. There are so many people.'

'You'll soon get used to that, lad. If you come to live here, that is,' he added, shooting a glance at the boy. 'You do *want* to move to London, don't you?'

'I believe so,' said Davy uncertainly.

'It will be the making of you.'

Davy Stratton had grave doubts about that as well. What both he and his father had agreed was that the boy's future did not lie in the commercial realm. He lacked interest and showed no aptitude for business. Small for his age, Davy had a slightness of build and delicacy of feature that seemed ill suited for the cut-and-thrust world inhabited by his father. Though he was an intelligent boy, he was too reserved and uncompetitive to follow in Jerome Stratton's footsteps. Where the father was big, fleshy and confident, the son was short, thin and withdrawn. Yet Davy was not without an innate toughness. A quiet determination that shone in his eyes.

'Have you seen enough?' asked Stratton.

'I think so, Father.'

'Then you are no merchant, Davy. I never have enough of the Exchange. Would you not like to take another turn around the courtyard?'

'If you wish.'

'It's a question of what *you* wish, lad.'

'I'm cold, Father,' admitted the boy. 'My teeth are chattering.'

Stratton slipped an arm around his shoulder. 'Then we'll keep on the move,' he said cheerily. 'Let me show you the shops. I'll wager that one of them will arouse your curiosity.'

Davy allowed himself to be led towards the steps. As they made their way slowly through the crowd, Jerome Stratton dispensed smiles and greetings on both sides. He was in his element. Smartly attired in a padded doublet of a purple hue, he kept out the pinch of winter with a thick, fur-trimmed cloak and a velvet hat. Stratton had a red, round face that was lit with a professional geniality. He had been eager to show off the Royal Exchange to his son and was disappointed by the latter's reaction. Expecting him to be enthralled on his first visit to London, he instead found Davy subdued and defensive.

'I hope that you're not having second thoughts,' he warned.

'About what, Father?' asked Davy.

'The reason that brought us here in the first place.'

'Oh, no.'

'Are you sure?'

'Yes, Father.'

Stratton was unconvinced by the boy's lacklustre response. When they reached the upper level, they strolled past a series of small shops where milliners, apothecaries, goldsmiths, booksellers and others plied their trade. Not even the glittering display in the armourer's shop drew more than a cursory glance from Davy.

His concerned father took him aside.

'What ails you, lad?'

'Nothing, Father.'

'You can't deceive me,' said Stratton. 'When I came to London for the first time, I walked around with my mouth agape. So many awesome sights to see. It was one of the happiest days of my life. But you've hardly lifted an eyebrow, still less given a gasp of surprise or a grin of appreciation. We've been to St Paul's, the Tower and everywhere in between yet none of them fired you with enthusiasm. Why not?'

'I told you, Father. I'm cold.'

'It was even colder in Essex but that didn't stop you playing in the garden when the snow was a foot deep. You can't blame all this on the winter. Unless,' he probed, leaning in close, 'your shivers are nothing to do with the weather.'

The boy nodded. 'They're not.'

'Are you nervous?'

'A trifle, Father.'

'There's no need to be, Davy,' said the other reassuringly.

'But what if I fail?'

'Out of the question. I know that you face an important test but you'll come through it with flying colours. You bear the name of Stratton. We never fail. Just think, Davy,' he said, touching the boy's arm. 'This afternoon, you're going to meet Lawrence Firethorn, the most famous actor in England. I've seen him on stage a dozen times and been amazed on each occasion. A signal honour awaits you today.'

31

Davy bit his lip. 'Will he *like* me, Father?' he said.

'Of course, he'll like you.'

'Supposing that he does not?'

'He will, Davy. Master Firethorn will adore you.'

'I'm not so sure of that.'

'*Make* him like you!' ordered Stratton, tightening his grip on the boy's arm. 'Play-acting is not so different from business. Look at me. The reason I've been so successful is that I force people to like me. I gain their confidence. It's the first step towards parting them from the contents of their purses. Sparkle, Davy!' he urged. 'Win over Lawrence Firethorn and a whole new life beckons.'

'Yes, Father.'

'That's what you want isn't it?'

'I believe so.'

'Then prove it. Live up to the name of Stratton. I'd hate to think that you were going to let me down. This is your opportunity, lad. Take it while you can. Make me proud of you.' He released his grip. 'It's what your poor dear mother would have wished. Keep her in your thoughts, Davy. Your mother doted on you.'

The boy bit his lip again and stared at an invisible object on the ground. It took him a full minute to compose himself. When he looked up again, his voice was firm.

'I'll do my very best, Father,' he said. 'I promise.'

Nicholas Bracewell turned into Chancery Lane and lengthened his stride. As soon as he reached the Middle Temple, he was reminded why he had such a distrust of lawyers. There were dozens of them, all dressed alike, scurrying off to court or holding impromptu disputes with colleagues in the open air, each one exuding that mixture of arrogance and smugness that he found so unappealing. Bruised by occasional dealings with the legal profession, Nicholas made a point of keeping well away from its denizens but, in this instance, he had no choice in the matter. The one redeeming feature of this visit was that he was representing Westfield's Men rather than seeking advice on his own account. A legal contract would be involved but it would cost him nothing but his congratulations.

Though he had never met Egidius Pye, he could glean something of the man's character from his work. *The Witch of Rochester*, as it was still called, was an unlikely play to issue from the pen of a lawyer. It was rich with incident, steeped in the mysteries of witchcraft, abounding in humour, sprinkled with bawdy and shot through with wry comments on the human condition. All that betrayed its author's profession was the extended trial with which it concluded though even that had a comical impetus. Imperfect as it was, the play had intrigued Nicholas and, now that he had read it, impressed Edmund Hoode as well. It was original, incisive and throbbing with life. Since the playwright now had to be sounded out in person, Nicholas had been dispatched to the Middle Temple.

Notwithstanding his discomfort at being surrounded by lawyers, it was a welcome assignment for the book holder. Egidius Pye, he decided, was highly untypical of the breed, a gifted author with a questing mind, a keen sense of the ridiculous and a healthy irreverence for the law and its practitioners. Nicholas pictured him as a tall, fair, fearless young man with an independent streak, a natural rebel whose histrionic talent seemed to be quite instinctive. When he located Pye's chambers, however, he came in for a severe shock. The lawyer was nothing whatsoever like the man he has envisaged.

'Master Pye?' he enquired.

'Yes,' said the other cautiously.

'My name is Nicholas Bracewell and I'm here on behalf of Westfield's Men. I believe that you submitted a play to Master Firethorn for his consideration.'

'Why, so I did.'

'If you can spare the time, I need to discuss it with you.'

'By all means, my friend. Come in, come in.'

Nicholas stepped into a large, low, cluttered room with a musty smell. Ancient leather-bound tomes stood on the shelves. Piles of documents littered every available surface. A plate of abandoned food lay half-hidden beneath a satchel. A pewter mug had fallen to the floor and taken up residence beneath the table. Other forgotten items filled every corner of the room. Egidius Pye was at one with his surroundings. Tall, scrawny and stooping, he had an air of sustained neglect about him. Though he was still in his late thirties, the receding hair, the greying beard and the ponderous movements made him seem twenty years older. A white ruff offset his black apparel but Nicholas observed that both were stained by food and flecked with dirt. So close were the eyes, nose and mouth that it looked as if all four had retreated to the centre of the face out of sudden fright on the principle that there was safety in numbers.

After shutting the door, the lawyer waved Nicholas to a

seat beside a fire that was producing far more smoke than heat. He lowered himself gingerly onto a stool opposite his unexpected visitor.

'You're a member of the company?' he asked reverentially.

'Merely its book holder, Master Pye,' explained Nicholas, 'but I was fortunate enough to be allowed to read *The Witch of Rochester*. It's a remarkable play.'

'Oh, thank you, thank you!'

'It was a pleasure from start to finish.'

'And does Master Firethorn share that opinion?'

'He does, sir. That's why he sent me to speak to you.'

'Do you mean,' said Pye in a hoarse whisper, 'that there's a faint hope my work might actually be presented on stage?'

'More than a faint hope. A distinct possibility.'

'Praise God!'

Egidius Pye clapped his hands together as if about to pray. Torn between joy and disbelief, he inched so close to the edge of the stool that he all but fell off it. He opened his mouth to emit a noiseless laugh, exposing a row of uneven teeth and a large pink tongue. Nicholas marvelled that such an apparently staid, slovenly, pallid, middle-aged man could have created a work of such manic frivolity. Evidently, there was more to the lawyer than met the eye.

As instructed by Firethorn, the book holder introduced a cautionary note.

'Everything, of course,' he said, 'is subject to certain conditions.'

'Make what conditions you like, dear sir. I accept them all.'

'That's hardly the stance of a lawyer, Master Pye. A

contract will need to be drawn up. Given your profession, we expect you to question every detail.'

'I bow willingly to Master Firethorn's demands.'

'But an author has certain rights, enforceable by law.'

'What care have I for the law?' said the other with a hint of recklessness. 'It has brought me misery and boredom. Do you see these chambers, Master Bracewell? They were built at the request of my father in order that his only son could join him in the Middle Temple. And what happened? No sooner had the place been finished than my father – God bless him – died, leaving poor, unworthy, unwilling me to carry on the family tradition. Ha!' he exclaimed with a hollow laugh. 'It's no tradition. It's a curse. The law is a great rock that I'm doomed to roll up a hill like a second Sisyphus. I loathe the profession.'

'That comes through in your play.'

'It was not always so,' confessed the other sadly. 'The Inns of Court do have their appeal. When I first entered the Middle Temple as an Inner Barrister, it was like being an undergraduate at Oxford all over again. There was much jollity amid the hard work. There was a measure of light in the gloom. Then I became an Utter Barrister and most of the jollity ceased. Now that I'm a Bencher and in a position of some authority, I find it hard to remember that there was a time when I practiced the law instead of being imprisoned by it. Forgive me,' he said, moving perilously closer to the edge of the stool. 'You did not come to hear the story of my wasted life.'

'I'm interested in anything you have to tell me.'

'Then let me just say this. Lawyers drive me to distraction. What has kept me sane is the company of those who live in the Middle Temple while having nothing whatsoever to do with the law. There are many such people. Sir Walter Raleigh is one. When he is in London, he often resides here. I have had the honour of dining with him. Sir Francis Drake, too, has connections with us though we see precious little of him.'

Nicholas smiled fondly. 'Sir Francis was ever ubiquitous.'

'You speak as if you know him, Master Bracewell.'

'I do, indeed. I had the privilege of sailing with him around the world. Not that it seemed like a privilege at the time,' he added with a slight grimace, 'but it was an unforgettable experience. Life aboard the *Golden Hind* was an education.'

'Tell me about it,' encouraged the other.

'Oh, I'm not here to talk about myself, Master Pye.'

'But I worship Sir Francis – and Sir Walter. They are proper men while I am just another mealy-mouthed barrister, practicing the black arts of the law. What was your voyage like? What countries did you see? What marvels did you behold?'

'I'll tell you another time,' promised Nicholas, too conscious of his duty to permit much digression of a personal nature. 'I'm here simply to acquaint you with the way in which your play has been received and to see how amenable you are to some suggested changes.'

'Changes?'

'Improvements and refinements.'

'Ah, I see.'

'The piece still has too many rough edges before it can be performed. With your permission, they can be cunningly removed.'

'Teach me the way to do it and I'll happily oblige.'

'Good,' said Nicholas, pleased to find such a cooperative attitude. 'I take it that you've watched the company perform?'

'Many times,' said Pye, presenting the uneven teeth for inspection once more. 'I've spent endless happy hours at the Queen's Head.'

'Then you must be familiar with the work of Edmund Hoode.'

'My inspiration!'

'I'm glad to hear that, Master Pye, because he has offered to work with you on the play to bring out the very best in it. If you agree, that is.'

'Agree!' repeated the lawyer, jerking forward so sharply that he slipped off the stool and landed on the floor. 'It's my dearest wish. I can think of no finer tutor than Edmund Hoode. I'll sit at his feet and prove a conscientious pupil.'

'There's not much that you need to be taught,' said Nicholas, helping him up. 'Besides, time is against us. Such changes as are necessary will have to be made with a degree of speed. Let me explain.'

Omitting any mention of a new apprentice, Nicholas gave him a brief account of the invitation from Sir Michael Greenleaf and the place that *The Witch of Rochester* might occupy in their repertoire. Egidius Pye quivered with pleasure throughout. The book holder was relieved. Other authors had caused untold problems for Westfield's Men, too egotistic to take advice, too possessive to allow the slightest alteration to their plays and too vindictive when their work failed before an audience. Pye had none of these faults. Nicholas was satisfied that the renegade lawyer would form a sound partnership with Edmund Hoode. Together they would improve the play beyond recognition. Nicholas put the man's congeniality to the test.

'How would you feel about a different title?' he asked tentatively.

'Title?'

'Yes, Master Pye. In view of the fact that we may perform in Essex, we felt it more appropriate if your witch came, perhaps, from Colchester.'

'Why not?' said Pye readily. '*The Witch of Colchester* is as good a title as my own and an apposite one. I concur. Move the witch anywhere from Portsmouth to Perth and I'll raise no objection. Whatever the location, my drama still holds its shape.'

'True enough.'

'*The Witch of Colchester*, eh? I like it.'

'That's a relief.'

Nicholas explained in outline the terms of the contract that Westfield's Men would offer him but Pye was not really listening. Overcome with joy at the prospect of seeing his play performed by one of the leading troupes, his mind was not attuned to fine detail. All that he wanted was confirmation that the visit to Essex would take place. The more they talked, the more Nicholas grew to like him. Egidius Pye was, in many ways, an unprepossessing character and he would inevitably encounter mockery from some of the actors but he had a number of good qualities. He was modest, intelligent, eager to learn, well versed in theatre and generous in his comments about Westfield's

Men. He had written his play as a labour of love, not to win fame or financial reward. Nicholas warmed to him. He asked a question that formed in his mind when he first read the man's play.

'Do you *believe* in witchcraft, Master Pye?'

The lawyer was shocked. He looked like an archbishop who has just been asked to deny the existence of God. Righteous indignation welled up in his eyes. He clicked his tongue and shook his head disapprovingly.

'You seem to know so much about the subject,' said Nicholas.

'Knowledge comes from careful study.'

'Have you ever met a witch?'

'Not exactly.'

'But you believe that such people exist?'

'Of course,' said Pye with burning sincerity. 'Don't you?'

It was a tiring walk to Shoreditch but Nicholas was too preoccupied to notice either the distance or the biting wind. The meeting with Egidius Pye had been a revelation. As he reflected on their conversation, he began to wonder if he had at last met a member of the legal profession whom he could befriend. One thing was certain. If the play were to be performed by Westfield's Men, its dishevelled author would have need of a friend in the company. Actors were robust individuals who expressed their feelings in warm language. They would show little respect for the sensibilities of Egidius Pye. When sparks began to fly during rehearsal, as they assuredly would, the newcomer would need support and protection. Nicholas was ready to offer both.

By the time he finally got to the house in Old Street, they were all there. Margery Firethorn fell on him with her usual affection, clutching him to her surging bosom while she planted a kiss on his cheeks. She stood back to appraise him.

'You look cold and famished, Nicholas,' she said.

'I am neither,' he replied.

'Are you sure that you would not like to come into the kitchen for moment? There's a fire to warm you up and food to take away the pangs of hunger.'

'No, thank you.'

'Is Anne looking after you properly?'

'In every way.'

Margery cackled. 'That's what I like to hear. Take her a message from me. When Anne tires of you, I'll take you in myself and spoil you even more.' She guided him across to the parlour. 'Lawrence said I was to show you straight in. The visitors have not long been here. I tell you, Nicholas,' she said with a roll of her eyes, 'I'd rather feed the son than the father. Jerome Stratton would eat me out of house and home.'

Margery bustled off to the kitchen, leaving Nicholas to knock on the door on the parlour. He went in to be greeted by Lawrence Firethorn, standing in the middle of the room while his guests were all seated. The actor spread his arms wide.

'Nick, dear heart!' he declared. 'You've come upon your cue. Allow me to introduce Master Stratton and his son. This is Nicholas Bracewell, young Davy,' he went on, moving over to the boy. 'If you join the company, you'll have no better tutor. The rest of us may strut upon the stage, but it's Nick who builds it for us in the first place. In every sense, he's the scaffold on which Westfield's Men stand.'

Nicholas exchanged greetings with the two strangers before being conducted to a seat in the window by his host. Firethorn lowered his voice to a whisper.

'Did you transact your business at the Middle Temple?'

'I did,' said Nicholas.

'Satisfactorily?'

'Extremely so.'

'Then one success precedes another,' announced Firethorn, turning to the others, 'because I'm confident that Davy will be an asset to the company. I knew it the moment I clapped eyes on him. Have you ever seen a boy more suited to our needs than this young gentleman? He has the look of the perfect apprentice.'

'My son is ideal for your purposes,' said Stratton expansively. 'I'd not place him with anyone other than Westfield's Men. You choose the best, we require no less.'

Nicholas was struck by the boy's features and impressed by his bearing. Even with a solemn expression on it, Davy Stratton's face had an undeniable prettiness. A neat wig and a costly dress would transform him instantly into a beautiful young woman. The book holder was less enamoured of the father, however, noting how Stratton kept his son under close surveillance to ensure that the lad gave a good account of himself. Nicholas was not certain if he was witnessing excessive paternalism or a form of polite menace. At all events, Davy was impervious to both, ignoring his father altogether and sitting there with a self-possession that was surprising in one so young.

The would-be apprentice was winning admiration elsewhere as well. Edmund Hoode was watching him with a contented smile while Barnaby Gill, shedding his earlier resistance to the notion of a new apprentice, was positively gloating over the boy, letting his gaze travel slowly over every detail of his face and frame. Nicholas was glad that the boy was too innocent to realise the true nature of Gill's interest in him. Crucial as it was, appearance was not the only factor in the choice of an apprentice. Other qualities had to be considered, as Firethorn knew only too well. Nicholas was glad when the actor strode across to the boy and became more businesslike.

'Can you read and write, Davy?' he asked.

'Yes, sir,' replied the boy.

'He's had an excellent education,' said Stratton. 'His Greek and Latin are above reproach. You'll not be able to fault him on those, Master Firethorn.'

'Davy is more likely to fault me, sir, for I'm no classicist. There'll be little call for Latin, however, and none at all for Greek. Plain English is our preferred language. Tell me, lad,' he said, crouching before the boy, 'can you sing?'

'As sweetly as a nightingale,' said Stratton, patting his son's leg.

'Is that so, Davy?'

'He's worthy of a place in the Chapel Royal.'

'Let him speak for himself, Master Stratton, I beg you.'

'A full room makes him shy.'

'You only compound that shyness by supplying answers for him,' said Firethorn with forced politeness. 'Pray, desist, sir. If your son is shy in front of four strangers, how will he fare in an inn yard with hundreds of spectators?'

'Davy will cope easily with all that confronts him,' asserted Stratton.

'Will you, Davy?' asked Firethorn, hiding his exasperation at the father behind a kind smile. 'Do you want to be up there on a high stage?'

'Oh, he does, he does,' continued the father. 'He yearns for nothing else.'

Firethorn rose to his feet. 'What I yearn for, Master Stratton, is the opportunity to hear your son's voice. We appreciate the fact that you brought him to us but we can hardly judge his true merit when he is not permitted to open his mouth.'

'A thousand apologies. I'll hold my tongue.'

'Thank you. Now, then, Davy,' said Firethorn, making one more attempt to establish direct contact with the boy, 'why do you wish to join Westfield's Men?'

'Because they are the finest company in England, sir,' replied Davy.

'You have good taste. Have you ever seen us perform?'

'Unhappily, no, sir, but your reputation goes before you.'

'A reputation for what?'

'Good quality, Master Firethorn. Fine drama, well acted.'

'Have you any idea what life in the theatre is like?' asked Firethorn.

'Very exciting, sir.'

'Excitement is part of it, I grant you, but there are many frustrations as well. It's a hard life, Davy, but a rewarding one. Though we cannot offer you the security another profession might bestow, we guarantee you experiences that will thrill you to the marrow. Begin as a humble apprentice and you may soon be performing at Court in front of the Queen herself. How does that sound?'

'Nothing would delight me more.'

'Are you prepared to commit yourself to Westfield's Men?'

'With all my heart, sir.'

Delighted with the answers, Firethorn looked across at his colleagues, collecting a smile of approval from Hoode and a nod of assent from Gill whose gaze never left the boy. Nicholas indicated his own approbation though it was not unmixed with doubt. Davy Stratton had spoken well but his replies had been too glib for the book holder's liking. It was as if the son had been carefully rehearsed beforehand to say exactly what they would wish to hear. To get a clearer idea of the lad's character, it was imperative to separate him from Jerome Stratton.

'Might I make a suggestion?' asked Nicholas.

'By all means,' said Firethorn.

'Davy is patently the sort of boy you seek. Only one thing remains to convince you of his suitability and that's to hear him read a part. Could he not be given a few minutes to study a short speech while you and Master Stratton discuss the terms of an apprenticeship?'

'A most sensible notion, Nick.'

'So it is,' said Gill, rising to his feet. 'Find me some lines and I'll take the lad into the next room to school him in how they should be delivered.'

'Thank you, Barnaby,' said Firethorn, quelling him with a glare, 'but you're not the teacher for this lesson. Since the play we choose will probably have been written by Edmund, he is the best person to instruct young Davy.'

'I'd value Nick's help,' insisted Hoode, getting up as Gill slumped back into his seat. 'Between us, I'm sure we can coax a performance from the boy.'

'So could I!' said Gill under his breath.

'It's settled,' declared Firethorn, crossing to a large cupboard. 'Step into the next room with Davy. I've a hundred scraps of plays in here,' he continued, opening a door and burrowing inside. 'The very thing!' he said, reappearing with a scroll in his hand. 'A speech from *The Merchant of Calais*, a role that was tailored for me from the best cloth that Edmund Hoode ever provided. The son of one merchant will counterfeit the lover of another. Here, Nick. Have the piece.'

Nicholas took the parchment from him then went into the adjoining room with Davy Stratton and Edmund Hoode. The boy gave a shudder as they left a warm fire to enter the cold chamber where the family ate their meals. It was a long narrow room with a window at the far end. After glancing at the speech, Nicholas handed it to Davy.

'Here, lad,' he said softly. 'Stand over there where you get the best of the light and read the lines to yourself. If there's anything you do not understand, ask the author for he is here beside me.'

Davy did as he was told, face puckered with concentration as he read the lines.

'I seem to remember that you helped greatly in the play's

creation,' said Hoode in a confiding whisper, always ready to give credit where it was due. 'There's something of your own father in my merchant, Nick. Robert Bracewell casts a long and welcome shadow. You and Davy have something in common. Both of you were brought up in merchant households.'

Nicholas winced slightly at the reminder. 'Let's give him time to study the piece before we hear it,' he advised. 'It's a speech that will test him.'

'Where is it from?'

'Act Five. Mary fears that she has lost him forever.'

'Dick Honeydew squeezed tears out of the lines when he played the part.'

'We must expect a little less from Davy.'

'I'm ready, sirs,' said the boy.

Hoode was impressed. 'That was quick.'

'The speech is not difficult, only a little mawkish.'

'Mary is speaking from the heart,' said the playwright, stung by the comment.

'I meant no offence, Master Hoode. I like the verse.'

'Then let's hear it,' said Nicholas, concealing his amusement at Hoode's mild upset. 'And take your time, Davy. They are fine words. Don't gabble them.'

Davy Stratton nodded, cleared his throat then read the lines.

'*Where can he be? To whom should I complain?*
What hope remains for me, his cherished love,
If he is cast adrift upon the sea
Or wrecked upon some distant, hostile shore
Where merchants' bones but thicken up the stew

To feed some wild and heathen cannibal?
If he be swallowed by the ocean deep
A thousand miles from home, then I am lost,
Bereft of all that helps to keep the flame
Of life alive. Why does my lover hide
From one who is his designated bride?'

He had a good, if reedy, voice and gave a competent performance. What it lacked was any real expression or sense of character. Hoode was a kind critic.

'Well done, Davy!' he said. 'Considering that you've never seen them before, it was brave stab at the lines. The lady who speaks them in the play is called Mary and she is agonising over her lover's long absence. Since he's a merchant whose ship has gone astray, she begins to suspect all kinds of horrors. Mary is in a state of panic. If you can, try to show us her anguish.'

'Yes, Master Hoode.'

'Say the lines as if you really *mean* them,' said Nicholas.

'I will,' promised the boy.

He took a deep breath before launching himself into the speech once more. There was much more emotion in his voice this time even though it was uncontrolled. Nicholas exchanged a glance with the playwright. Both reached the same conclusion.

'That was markedly better,' said Hoode.

'Yes,' added Nicholas. 'But don't let your voice get too shrill or the words will be lost. And listen to the rhythm of the verse. You must keep to that at all costs.'

'Shall I try it again?' volunteered the boy.

'In a moment.' He regarded him shrewdly before speaking. 'Do you really wish to join the company, Davy?'

'Yes, sir.'

'Is that your idea or your father's?'

There was an awkward pause. 'We both agreed on it,' he said at length.

'Did you not wish to become a merchant like your father?'

'Not in a hundred years!'

'You seem determined on that point. Life in the playhouse is dogged by all kinds of problems. You'd have a softer time in trade and it would be more profitable. Why do you turn your back so decisively on your father's profession?'

'It's no more than you did, Master Bracewell.'

Nicholas was taken aback, unaware that he had overheard his earlier exchange with Hoode. The playwright burst out laughing and gave him a nudge.

'A tidy answer, Nick. You stand rebuffed. Now, let's hear the piece again.'

A third reading showed a definite improvement, a fourth gave the speech power and definition. Keen to show how easily the boy took direction, they escorted him back into the parlour where Firethorn was discussing the financial implications with Stratton.

'Back so soon?' he said.

'The speech is in a fit state to be heard, Lawrence,' said Hoode.

'Then let's have it. Take a seat, gentlemen,' he invited, moving across to a chair himself. 'Now, Davy. You have a captive audience. Imagine that you're on stage in front of hundreds of spectators, all needing to pick up every word you say. When you're ready, let's hear you pine for your missing lover.'

Davy looked at almost all of them in turn, avoiding only Jerome Stratton whose face was wreathed in smiles. After running his tongue over his lips, the boy began

'Where can he be? To whom should I complain?
What hopes remain for me, his cherished love . . .'

Firethorn was delighted, Gill was entranced and Stratton's smile became a grin of triumph. Nicholas and Hoode were pleased to see that the boy had heeded their advice. Davy put much more feeling into the speech, overdoing it at times but nevertheless turning lines on a page into something akin to a performance. When it was over, the father clapped appreciatively and Firethorn leapt to his feet.

'You're a born actor, Davy!' he declared.

'Thank you, Master Firethorn,' said the boy modestly.

'What did the rest of you think?'

Hoode spoke without hesitation. 'Davy would be a gift to us.'

'Nick?'

'I agree,' said Nicholas. 'He learns quickly.'

'Barnaby?'

'Davy has a natural charm, it's true,' said Gill slowly, 'but he'll need more than that to hold the spectators at the Queen's Head. Can he sing, I wonder? Can he dance? Perhaps I should teach him a little jig so that we may judge his movement?'

50

'That won't be necessary,' said Firethorn heavily. 'I think that we've seen all that we need to. It's merely a question of getting our lawyer to draw up the contract and Davy Stratton becomes a member of Westfield's Men.'

'You didn't specify the length of his apprenticeship,' noted Stratton.

'That's because it varies with each boy. Some take six or seven years before they grow to maturity, others, like John Tallis,' said Firethorn with rancour, 'arrive at that stage much earlier. We'll have it entered in the contract that Davy is bound to us for three years, a period that can be extended as soon as it's expired. Will that content you, sir?'

'Admirably.'

Firethorn turned back to the boy. 'What about you, Davy? Are you ready to pledge yourself to us for the next three years?'

Stratton was peremptory. 'He'll do as I tell him, Master Firethorn.'

'I'd prefer to hear it from his own lips. Well, Davy?'

Ignoring his father once again, the boy looked around the other faces. Firethorn beamed at him, Gill produced his first smile, Hoode gave him a wink of encouragement and Nicholas nodded a welcome. Davy Stratton made his decision.

'I'm yours,' he said boldly.

Chapter Three

Anne Hendrik was delighted at the news. Even though it meant that they would be apart for a while, she was genuinely pleased on his behalf. She knew from experience just how depressing it was for Nicholas Bracewell when the company had a lengthy period of unemployment.

'These are good tidings, Nick,' she said happily. 'A new apprentice, a new play and a new venue. Fortune is smiling on you at last.'

'Thank heaven!' he sighed.

'But it's a pity that you had the apprentice and the play forced upon you.'

'Not necessarily, Anne. Both may turn out to be prime assets to the company. Davy Stratton has enormous promise and *The Witch of Colchester*, as it is now entitled, has won everyone's approval. When he read the part assigned to him, even Barnaby Gill was overjoyed and he's the most difficult person to satisfy.'

'What does he think of the new boy?'

Nicholas arched an eyebrow. 'Need you ask?'

'Keep him well clear of the lad,' she counselled. 'As an actor, Barnaby Gill is a genius; as a man, he has serious shortcomings.'

'That's a discreet way of putting it, Anne,' he said with a smile. 'But have no fear. There are enough friendly eyes to watch over Davy Stratton. Besides, the other apprentices will soon warn him. They know Master Gill of old.'

Nicholas was having breakfast with her at the house in Bankside where he lodged. Anne Hendrik was no typical landlady. The English widow of a Dutch hat maker, she took charge of the business after his death and ran it with great efficiency in the premises adjoining her house. Anne had taken a lodger in the interests of security rather than from financial necessity. Nicholas Bracewell proved an ideal choice. Considerate and reliable, he became her close friend and, in due course, her lover. They had drifted apart at one stage but, reunited again, found that the bond between them was stronger than ever.

'When will you leave for Essex?' she asked.

'Tomorrow.'

'So soon?'

'The company will not set out then,' he explained, finishing his drink. 'I'm being sent on ahead to take a look at the house where we'll perform. Measurements have to be taken, decisions made. Sir Michael Greenleaf has invited us to play in the Great Hall of his home but, until we actually see the place, it's impossible to know how to make best use of it. We've no idea, for instance, what scenery we should take.'

'I hope that you're not going alone,' she said with concern. 'A solitary rider would be a certain target for robbers.'

'Oh, I don't think so, Anne. Winter has put paid to most highwaymen. It's far too cold to lurk among the trees in case a traveller rides past. In any case, I'll not be on my own. Owen Elias has volunteered to come with me. If we should meet trouble, there's nobody in the company more skilled with a sword than Owen.'

'Except their book holder.'

'That was one more advantage of sailing with Drake,' he said, wistfully. We were drilled in the use of weapons of all kinds. And the voyage itself toughened us beyond measure. Only the most robust managed to survive.'

Anne touched his hand softly. 'I'm glad that you were one of them.'

'So am I.'

Their eyes locked as mutual affection surged but the moment soon passed. The maidservant came in to clear the table. Anne withdrew her hand and sat upright. She waited until the girl had gone before she spoke again.

'It will be a cold journey for you, Nick.'

'Not with that new hat you kindly made for me,' he said. 'When I'm wearing that, I feel snug and warm. Then there's the cloak that Lawrence Firethorn gave me.'

'It suits you.'

'He used it in dozens of plays until it faded and wore thin. Our tireman, Hugh Wegges, sewed on a patch or two for me and the cloak is as good as new.'

'You should have let me use my needle on it.'

'No, Anne. You do enough for me as it is.'

'I wish that I could do more.'

'Thank you.'

He reached across the table to squeeze her hand in gratitude. The maidservant entered again to disturb a tender moment. She was carrying a few logs. When she had put them on the fire, she went out again.

'You'll have to train that girl better,' said Nicholas with a grin.

'The house has to be kept warm.'

'It's always warm when you are in it, Anne.'

She acknowledged the compliment with a smile. 'I'll miss you,' she said.

'And I'll miss you,' he replied. 'I'm sorry that we'll be separated for a while. On the other hand, I'm glad that Westfield's Men will at last have employment. It irks me when we are forced to stand idle.'

'Nobody could accuse you of being idle, Nick. You've found a hundred things to keep you occupied during this long wait and I've been the beneficiary. Think of all the repairs you made to the house.'

'I prefer to think of those who are not so well placed, Anne. Hired men like Ned Rankin or Caleb Smythe or little George Dart. They've suffered mightily. Then there's old Thomas Skillen, our stagekeeper. I'm not even sure if he's made it through the winter. Peter Digby and his musicians have had a desperate time as well.'

'What of the sharers themselves?'

'Most have other professions to fall back on, Anne. Walter Fenby, for example, was a silversmith before he turned to the theatre. Rowland Carr was a scrivener. Actors of the stature of Lawrence Firethorn and Barnaby Gill, of course, are always in demand for solo performances at private houses so they've still had an income of sorts.'

'What of Edmund Hoode?'

'Poems and epitaphs.'

'Epitaphs?' she echoed.

'Winter has filled the graveyards,' he sighed. 'Both the nobility and the gentry like to send their loved ones off to heaven with an epitaph written especially for them. Edmund has a gift for penning such memorials. It grieves him that he profits from others' misfortune but even poets must eat.'

'It's good, honest, important work.'

'Not in Edmund's eyes. He thinks himself a vulture, feeding off the dead.'

'How many of the company will travel to Essex?'

'A goodly number,' he said, rising from the table. 'That's my office this morning. To find each one of them and spread the welcome news. Rehearsals begin tomorrow in earnest.'

'What plays will you take?'

'That's still to be decided, Anne. We're having the usual complaints from Master Gill who wants the whole repertoire to be built squarely around him. The one certain piece is the new one that Sir Michael Greenleaf requested.'

'*The Witch of Colchester*.'

'That's it. Our first play by Egidius Pye. Not that it's in a fit state for performance as yet. Edmund has a number of improvements to make.'

'Will the author permit radical changes to his work?'

'Gladly,' said Nicholas. 'I've never met a more obliging fellow. Master Pye raised no objection. Edmund is to call on him this very day. They'll need to work fast.'

'What manner of man is Master Pye?'

'An unusual one.'

'In what way?'

'It's difficult to say,' he admitted. 'He was so unlike the person I imagined when I read his play that I began to doubt it was indeed his work. But it certainly is.'

'How will Edmund get on with him?'

Nicholas thought of the strange creature he had met in the Middle Temple.

'I think he'll find Egidius Pye an object of profound interest,' he said.

'Come in, dear sir,' said Egidius Pye, motioning him into the room. 'This is an honour.'

'Thank you,' replied Edmund Hoode, stepping in out of the cold. 'It's good to make your acquaintance, Master Pye.'

'Shall I take your cloak and hat?'

'Thank you.'

Removing both, Hoode handed them to his host and immediately regretted doing so. The room was only marginally warmer than the street outside, its little fire issuing puffs of black smoke into the room but no discernible heat. Pye laid the cloak and hat on the table before waving his guest to the chair beside the grate. He perched precariously on the stool opposite Hoode. The lawyer's eye fell on the sheaves of parchment in his hand.

'I see that you've brought my play, Master Hoode.'

'Along with my congratulations, sir.'

'Do you mean that?'

'It's a clever piece of theatre.'

'Oh, thank you, thank you,' said the other effusively as if his life had just been saved by the intercession of a brave stranger. 'Praise from you is praise indeed. This calls for a celebration,' he decided, getting slowly to his feet and lumbering towards the door. 'Excuse me for one moment.'

He left the room and gave his visitor time to take his bearings. Edmund Hoode looked around with macabre fascination. The place was even more soiled and disorderly than Nicholas Bracewell had led him to expect. Plates of discarded food stood in the most unlikely places and the floor was awash with bundles of documents. Thick dust lay everywhere while spiders frolicked openly in their webs. Hoode wondered how the lawyer could work effectively amid such chaos. It was minutes before Pye returned. When he did so, he was carrying a pitcher of wine and two goblets.

'Allow me to offer you some of this,' he said, placing the goblets on the table so that he could pour the liquid into them. 'It has an excellent taste and was a present from a grateful client.'

'I trust that she was not a witch,' observed Hoode, attempting a little humour. 'I've never been fond of dark potions made from obscene ingredients.'

Pye let out a cackle. 'Bless you, no!' he exclaimed. 'This is no witch's brew. You'll find nothing more troubling in it than a frog's eye and a slice of rat's liver.' He saw the look of disgust on Hoode's face. 'I jest, sir, I jest,' he promised, handing one of the goblets to him. 'As you see, it's Canary wine of the finest vintage.'

'Then I raise my cup in a toast to you, Master Pye.' After lifting the goblet in the air, he sipped the wine. 'Most pleasing to the palate.'

Pye resumed his seat. 'I'm more concerned that the play is to your taste,' he said with an unctuous smile. 'It does not pretend to the quality of your own work, of course, but I like to think that it's not without merit.'

'Merit and true worth.'

'Is that the general opinion?'

'Barnaby Gill likes it and Lawrence Firethorn but a keener critic is the man you've already met. Nicholas Bracewell has sounder judgement than the lot of us. If he believes that a play will work on stage, it invariably does.'

'It was a pleasure to meet him.'

'Nick is the person who recommended *The Witch of Rochester*,' explained Hoode. 'He's also responsible for the notion of shifting the location to Essex so that it will have a deeper resonance for our audience.'

'I owe him my undying thanks.'

'You'll have far more cause to be grateful to Nick Bracewell before we're done. The play calls for a number of effects that only he could devise.' He sat back to appraise his host. 'What made you write it in the first place?'

'It wrote itself, Master Hoode.'

'That's what I sometimes say but I know the truth of it. Plays are like houses. They have to be constructed brick by patient brick. Imagination may design the shape of the house but much hard labour goes into its erection.'

'It didn't seem like labour at the time.'

'Why not?'

'Because witchcraft is a subject dear to my heart.'

'An uncommon interest for a lawyer.'

'I'm no lawyer,' retorted the other with sudden vehemence before gulping down some of his wine. 'I came into the law out of loyalty to my father rather than through natural inclination. It has vexed me ever since. Do you know how many of us there are, Master Hoode?'

'Too many, I suspect.'

'When my father entered the Middle Temple, barely fifty men a year were called to the bar. That figure is now past four hundred. As for attorneys, those who practice in the two common-law courts, their numbers have increased almost as dramatically. Two hundred or so could be counted in my father's day. And now?'

'Five hundred?' guessed Hoode.

'Well over a thousand. The city is being overrun with lawyers. They breed like flies and are just as bothersome. Please don't number me among them, sir. I've grown to detest my colleagues for their hideous uniformity.'

'Uniformity?'

'When a lawyer breaks wind, he smells the same as all the others.'

The vulgarity of the remark made Hoode blink in astonishment. Egidius Pye looked too prim and polite to venture such a comment. He was an odd character. Hoode had been warned that it was not easy to take to the man and he could now understand why. Apart from his physical peculiarities, Pye had a disconcerting manner and breath that smelt in equal parts of vinegar, onions and rancid cheese. The man's bachelor status was self-evident. No woman would let him near her. Working with him would not be without its drawbacks. After another sip of wine, Hoode tapped the play in his lap.

'We need to discuss this, Master Pye.'

'I'm all ears, sir,' said the other seriously.

'The plot is good, the characters engaging and the thrust of the piece well judged. There is, however, space for considerable improvement.'

'Show me where it is, Master Hoode.'

'I will but, before we tinker with what is already there, let's first talk about what is not. Supplying the play's deficiencies must be our initial task.'

'Please list them.'

'First, we need a Prologue, a speech of twenty lines or so that both explains what is to follow and gives the flavour of the piece.'

'It shall be done,' agreed the other.

'I'll help you with it, Master Pye,' offered the other. 'That done, we need to introduce more songs into the action. We have the witch's chants, I grant you, but they are hardly music. Softer sounds are required to lull and delight our audience. I've marked the places where such songs could be used. We've fine musicians and good singers in the company. Let's employ them to the full.'

'Willingly, sir. What else?'

'Dances. Barnaby Gill will take the role of Doctor

Putrid and he never steps upon a stage unless he can dance a jig or two. If we don't set them down, he'll put them in *extempore*. Master Gill, I fear, has a wayward streak,' cautioned Hoode. 'It's best to make allowances for his eccentricities.'

'I'll follow your advice to the letter.'

'Then I'll indicate where the dances would be most appropriate.'

'Is anything else missing, Master Hoode?'

'Only an Epilogue.'

'That's easily provided.'

'Something crisp and comical.'

'Spoken by Lord Malady?'

'No,' said Hoode firmly, 'by the witch of Colchester herself. Black Joan sits in the title of your play so let her bring it to a conclusion. The Epilogue might be a form of spell in itself. Rhyming couplets. Six or eight of them at most.'

'These are all distinct improvements,' conceded Pye.

'Once we have made those, we can turn our attention to some crucial changes.'

'Of what nature?'

'I'll explain that when we come to them, Master Pye.'

'As you wish, sir.'

'The main purpose of this visit was to establish that we can work fruitfully together, as I sense that we can, and also to fix times when we may do so.'

'I'm eager to begin, sir. We may start immediately, if you wish.'

'What of your other commitments?'

'They can wait,' said Pye, flicking a hand in the air. 'This takes precedence over all else. Give me what time you can allow today then we'll meet again tomorrow.'

'A sensible idea.'

The lawyer was about to rise. 'I'll clear a space on the table.'

'If it's all the same to you,' said Hoode, remembering the warm fire that awaited him, 'I'd prefer to work in my own lodging. I've copious notes on your play there. If we walk briskly, it's not too far away.'

'Then let us do just that.'

The two of them drank their wine then got up from their seats to put their goblets on the table. While Pye went off into the next room, Hoode put on his coat and hat. He glanced around again. The lawyer's chambers were hardly conducive to the creative impulse. Smoke and low temperature would conspire against them. The sombre atmosphere would inhibit them. There was another factor to be considered. Like Nicholas Bracewell, the playwright had a frank distrust of lawyers. From the moment he had entered the Middle Temple, he was expecting to be charged a fee, if not placed under arrest. Escape was vital.

When his host reappeared, Hoode barely recognised him. Wrapped in a moth-eaten black cloak, Egidius Pye wore a floppy hat that all but obscured his face. He stepped in close and peered out from beneath its undulating brim.

'I can hardly contain my excitement,' he said.

'As long as you don't break wind in the process.'

Hoode's jest was fatal. Pye not only let out a cackle of

amusement that was accompanied by a veritable gust of bad breath, he lost all control and emitted such a violent rasping noise beneath his cloak that it flapped about like a main sail in a tempest. A pungent odour made itself known. Clutching the play under his arm, Hoode darted for the door in sheer desperation.

'You're a true lawyer, after all, Master Pye,' he said ruefully.

Lawrence Firethorn finally gave in to the boy's entreaties. When he heard that two members of the company were to visit Essex the next day, Davy Stratton begged the actor-manager to let him go with them. He was not prompted by homesickness. In the brief time he had been with them, Davy had settled down well and made every effort to befriend Firethorn's children as well as the apprentices who lodged under his roof. Nor was the request fuelled by a desire to see his father again. From the moment that Jerome Stratton had left the house in Shoreditch, he had been neither missed nor mentioned. What Davy sought was the adventure of a ride alongside Nicholas Bracewell and Owen Elias, two people with whom he felt he had an immediate affinity. In his favour were the facts that the boy had his own pony and that he knew the way to Silvermere.

After consultation with Nicholas, and after issuing a string of warnings to the boy, Firethorn agreed to let him go, reasoning that he could come to no harm and that he would learn much simply from being in the company of the two men. On the following day, therefore, all three of them set out for Essex. The actor-manager had loaned Nicholas his own horse and the ever-resourceful Elias had acquired one from an undisclosed source.

'I hope that you didn't steal the animal, Owen,' said Nicholas.

'Not me,' said the Welshman with a throaty chuckle. 'I'm no prigger of prancers. The only thing I've ever stolen is an odd maidenhead or two. No, the horse was merely borrowed from a close friend. Her husband does not return until Friday so it will not be missed from his stable.'

'Whose husband?' asked Davy innocently.

'That needn't concern you, lad,' said Nicholas, shooting Elias a look of reproof. 'We've a young lad with us, Owen. Remember that and moderate your language.'

Elias grinned. 'I'll quote the Bible, if you prefer.'

'Polite conversation is all that's required.'

'Then you shouldn't have brought me along. Politeness is not in my character, Nick, as you well know. Besides, if Davy is to join Westfield's Men, the sooner he gets used to hot words and rude thoughts, the better for him.'

'Don't lead him astray.'

'I thought he was here to lead us.'

'I am,' said Davy. 'When we get nearer the house, I'll show you a short cut.'

'How long will it take us to get there?' asked Nicholas.

'That depends how fast we ride, sir.'

'Then let's get a move on,' decided Elias, kicking his horse into a canter.

The other followed suit and all three of them headed

north-east along the frozen road. Nicholas rode between the others, glad of the Welshman's presence on a journey that might well be fraught with danger. A stocky man of middle height, Elias was a useful ally in a fight with the strength and temper to cow most opponents. Like Nicholas, he wore both sword and dagger. The book holder also welcomed Davy's company and not merely because the boy had a good knowledge of the county to which they were riding. He liked the new apprentice and was pleased with the opportunity to get to know him better. There was still much that he did not understand about him.

'How far is Silvermere from your own home, Davy?' he asked.

'A few miles,' replied the other.

'You'll be able to call in and surprise your father.'

Davy was unequivocal. 'Oh, no!'

'Why not?'

'Because he would not wish it.'

'But you're his son. He's bound to be pleased.'

'He may not even be there,' said the boy evasively. 'I'd rather stay with you.'

'If you say so.'

'I do, Master Bracewell.'

The boy lapsed into a silence that Nicholas did not even try to disturb. The tension he had noted between father and son would only be explained in time. It was important not to browbeat Davy. The boy, he surmised, had endured enough bullying already.

'What do you know of this new play, Nick?' asked Elias.

'*The Witch of Colchester* is a lively comedy. It will serve us well.'

'Lawrence must have faith in it if he is saving it until the end of our stay. Will it prove a fitting climax to the work of Westfield's Men?'

'I believe so.'

'When can I read my part?'

'When Edmund and the author have finished polishing the piece,' said Nicholas. 'You're set down to take on the role of Sir Roderick Lawless.'

'I like the sound of that name.'

'So does the playwright. He's a lawyer with an inclination to lawlessness.'

'An outlaw, then?'

'Only in the bonfire of the mind.'

'Sir Roderick Lawless, eh? Do I get to rant and rave?'

'Constantly.'

'What traffic do I have with women?'

'You've a wife, the Lady Adeliza, and you consort with Black Joan herself.'

'Black Joan?'

'The witch.'

'There are no such things,' said Davy, coming out of his reverie.

'How do you know?' asked Nicholas.

'My father told me.'

'But I thought that Essex was crawling with witches,' said Elias.

'Not according to my father, sir,' returned the boy. 'He says that witchcraft is only a cunning deception.'

'Then he won't enjoy one of the plays we're due to present. I take it that your father will be in the audience at Silvermere.'

Davy's face clouded. 'I expect so.'

'He's bound to be there, surely?' said Nicholas. 'Master Stratton gave us the impression that he and Sir Michael Greenleaf were much more than neighbours. Your father's name was mentioned in the invitation we received. The one person I think we can count on seeing at Silvermere is your father.'

'Yes,' added Elias, 'he'll be there to watch his son taking his first steps on a stage. In his place, I certainly would be. What about you, Nick?'

'I wouldn't miss it either.' Seeing the boy's obvious discomfort, Nicholas did not press the point. 'What's the name of your own house, Davy?'

'Holly Lodge.'

'A pretty name. Is it a pretty place?'

'Silvermere is much larger and more interesting.'

'That's not what I asked.'

'Holly Lodge is a nice enough house,' conceded Davy. 'But I've left there now.'

'You have indeed,' said Elias. 'You live in Old Street, Shoreditch, at the tender mercy of Lawrence Firethorn.' He gave a short laugh. 'That house might well be called Holly Lodge as well for you'll prick yourself if you step out of place. Margery Firethorn is the soul of kindness but she has a tongue as sharp as any holly bush.'

'Only for those who misbehave,' said Nicholas.

Elias laughed again. 'Such as her husband.'

'That's between the two of them,' rebuked Nicholas. 'It's no business of ours. Davy will be well looked after in Shoreditch. It will be a true home for him.'

The apprentice said nothing but Nicholas sensed his approval. They were in open country now and maintaining a comfortable speed. Hedges and trees were still rimed with frost. Early morning sun made the fields glisten. The breeze was stiff but it was largely at their backs. Apart from the occasional cart going into market, they saw nobody. A bleak and empty horizon stretched out in front of them. It was like riding into a wilderness.

'Have you ever met Sir Michael Greenleaf?' asked Nicholas, turning to Davy.

'A number of times.'

'What sort of man is he?'

'A good one,' said the boy. 'I like Sir Michael though many think him peculiar.'

'Peculiar?'

'Yes, Master Bracewell.'

'In what way?'

The boy searched in vain for the right words and despaired of finding them.

'You'll have to judge for yourself,' he said.

Though hampered by the rutted track with its random pools of ice, they made steady progress. After hours in the saddle, they stopped at a wayside inn to rest the horses and to take refreshment. Davy Stratton had grown more talkative, seeing the chance to reap the benefit of their experience in the theatre and plying them both with questions. The apprentice had one query that obviously worried him.

'Will I only be asked to take the role of a woman?' he said with distaste.

'Yes,' replied Elias, supping his ale. 'Maids, maidservants, whores, nuns, queens and empresses. All aspects of the fairer sex, Davy, even down to scolds and seductresses. But there's ample recompense for you.'

'Is there, Master Elias?'

'You may come to play my wife and enjoy my sweetest kiss on stage.' He chuckled as the boy's face registered disgust. 'It could be worse, lad. You might have to suffer an embrace from Barnaby Gill. You'd soon come back to your husband after that.'

'Don't mislead him, Owen,' chided Nicholas. 'You'll not take any roles of significance for a long while, Davy. They fall to Dick Honeydew and the others, trained, as they all are, in presenting themselves in female guise. During our stay at Silvermere, you may not even get on stage at all or, if you do, the likelihood is that you'll be no more than a page or a humble servant.'

'Man or woman?'

'Neither. You'd play what you are – a young boy.'

Davy looked relieved. Nicholas decided that he felt embarrassed at the idea of donning female attire at Silvermere in front of his father. The book holder also believed that the reason he was peppering them with questions was to ensure that he did not have to yield up any answers on his own account. It was a curious paradox. The nearer they got to Davy Stratton's home, the less willing he was to talk about it.

On the next stage of the journey, the boy showed his value, guiding them along a track that twisted its way aimlessly through oak woodland. When they came out into open country again, the road did not improve. Churned up by the passage of many hooves then frozen hard, it meandered through fields that shimmered in the sun as the last of the frost melted away. Barley, wheat and corn were extensively cultivated throughout the area but they were hidden beneath the thick blanket of winter. Sheep were the only animals they passed, foraging in groups and scattering in mild panic whenever the travellers got close to them. Nicholas was enjoying the ride, glad to be free of the fetid air of London and taking an interest in the unfolding landscape. Davy, too, was in good spirits, handling his pony with the ease of a practiced horseman. Elias was less comfortable, troubled by the cold, bored by the surroundings and starting to suffer twinges in his buttock and thigh.

They rounded a bend at a steady trot then rode up a hill. It was surmounted by a stand of elms whose branches moved creakily in the wind. Nicholas was the first to spot movement among the trees and he drew Elias's attention to it with a nudge. Both men eased their cloaks back to free their swords.

'When I tell you,' said Nicholas, turning to Davy, 'kick your horse into a canter.'

'Why?' asked the boy.

'Just do as I say, Davy.'

'Are we in danger?'

'I'm not sure.'

Keeping up the same pace, they moved slowly up the hill. Nicholas and Elias betrayed no outward signs of caution but their eyes were scanning the summit with care. A head poked briefly out from behind a thick trunk then withdrew. The ambush was set. There were too few trees to offer cover for more than a handful of men and, since the elms stood only on one side of the road, the attack would have to come from that side. It simplified matters considerably. Nicholas waited until they were only twenty yards from the summit before reaching across to slap the pony hard on the rump.

'Now, Davy!' he ordered. 'Ride on!'

The pony scurried off at once and was safely over the crest of the hill before the outlaws emerged from their hiding places. There were four of them, all on foot, all armed with swords or spears. As Nicholas and Elias approached, a pair of sturdy robbers ran at each of them. One man tried to grab the reins of a horse while the other struck at its rider with his weapon. It was a forlorn exercise. Anticipating the ambush, both riders had their swords out in a flash, parrying the attack and inflicting sufficient wounds to leave their adversaries howling in anguish. The two men who attempted to seize the reins fared no better. Instead of dealing with the gentle gait of two horses, they were buffeted by animals that had been spurred into a fierce plunge of speed. One man was knocked to the ground by the impact. The other, who sustained a glancing blow from the horse, also received a hard kick under the jaw from Elias's foot that sent him cartwheeling along the grass verge. As the riders vanished down the other side of the hill, four dazed men were left to lick their wounds and meditate on the folly of their action.

The travellers cantered for a couple of miles until they were certain that they were not followed. When they slowed to a trot, Davy wanted to know what had happened.

'Were they robbers?' he asked, wide-eyed.

'They thought they were,' said Elias, grinning broadly. 'But they met their match in us, didn't they, Nick?' He slapped his thigh. 'Diu! That was wonderful. I needed a bit of excitement like that.'

'How many of them were there?' said Davy.

'A dozen at least.'

'Four,' corrected Nicholas. 'We caught a glimpse of one of them in advance.'

Elias chortled. 'It was probably the one I kicked under the chin,' he decided. 'I must have loosened every tooth in his head.'

'Weren't you frightened?'

'Of four foolish outlaws? Never, Davy.'

'Desperate men do desperate things,' said Nicholas. 'And they must have been desperate to be skulking on top of that hill in this weather. They'll have poor pickings today.' He turned to his friend. 'Thanks for your help, Owen. I'm very grateful that you came with me.'

'So am I,' said the Welshman. 'I thrive on action.'

'When I rode to London with my father,' volunteered Davy, 'we travelled in a large group. There were well over twenty of us.'

'That's the safest way,' said Nicholas.

'But you miss out on all the fun,' complained Elias.

Another hour brought them within reach of their destination. Davy Stratton grew increasingly nervous, glancing around with apprehension. When they came to a fork in the road, he called them to a halt and pointed ahead.

'That's the long way round to Silvermere,' he explained. 'It would take us past Holly Lodge in a great loop. If we strike off through the forest, we can reach Silvermere in half the time.'

'But we'd miss seeing your home,' said Nicholas.

'It's of no account to me.'

'Are you sure?'

'Yes,' said the boy. 'This is the way I want to go.'

'Then lead on.'

The track through the forest was so narrow that they were forced to ride in single file as they wended their way through the looming oaks and elms. Davy kept up a brisk trot, picking his way along with the confidence of someone who was very familiar with the surroundings. When they entered a clearing, it was Elias's turn to bring them to a halt.

'Hold there!' he called. 'I need to look upon the hedge.'

'You drank too much ale at that inn,' observed Nicholas.

'I could never do that, Nick.'

Elias dismounted and went behind a tree to relieve himself. Nicholas took the opportunity to get down from his own horse in order to stretch his legs. A snuffling noise made him turn around and walk towards a clump of bushes, one hand on the hilt of his sword. When he got within a few yards, there was a sudden squeal and a pig scuttled out from behind the bushes. Nicholas relaxed and watched the animal until it disappeared among the trees in search of food. He swung round to stroll back to his horse but was met with a shock. Davy Stratton had vanished. There was no sign of the boy or the pony. Tying his points, Elias came ambling out from behind the tree.

'Where's the lad?' he enquired.

'I've no idea,' admitted Nicholas, looking anxiously around.

'Perhaps he's gone off to spray the side of tree, as I did.'

'I hope so.'

'Didn't you see him go?'

'My back was turned.'

'Davy!' yelled Elias. 'Davy, where are you?'

His voice echoed through the forest, its sheer volume evicting two birds from a high branch. There was no answer. A grim silence descended.

'Davy!' shouted Nicholas, cupping his hands to his mouth. 'Davy!'

There was still no response. Elias scratched his head and gave a shrug.

'He must have wandered off when you weren't looking, Nick,' he said.

'I'm afraid not.'

'What do you mean?'

'Davy didn't wander off,' said Nicholas. 'He deliberately ran away.'

It took them some time to find their way back to the fork in the road. Deciding that a search would be futile, Nicholas instead suggested that they make for Holly Lodge, the boy's home and therefore his most likely destination. The wider track allowed them to ride side by side at a canter.

'I think he may have had second thoughts,' said Elias.

'About what?' asked Nicholas.

'Life in the theatre. Underneath that puny exterior, Davy Stratton is a red-blooded young man. He's insulted by the idea of dressing up as a woman. I would be.'

'That's no reason to abandon us like that, Owen.'

'Maybe he was just playing a game with us.'

'He is,' said Nicholas, 'but it's a deeper one than I thought. Now I realise why he was so eager to act as our guide. It offered him a chance of escape.'

'From what?'

'From us, from the company, from London itself.'

'Why was he so keen to join us in the first place?'

'I'm not convinced that he was. His father made that decision.'

'On what grounds?'

'That remains a mystery.'

They were both relieved when the house eventually came into sight. Holly Lodge was a large, sprawling, timber-framed house with a thatched roof. Smoke curled up from its chimneys. A brick wall and a clutch of outbuildings gave it protection from the wind on one side. They rode up a drive that bisected the formal garden and dismounted. A servant admitted them into a draughty hall before going to fetch his master. It was not long before the portly figure of Jerome Stratton came strutting across the oak boards. Nicholas exchanged greetings with him then introduced Owen Elias.

'I did not expect visitors,' said Stratton brusquely, 'so I'm not at liberty to entertain you, I fear. You are on your way to Silvermere, I take it?'

'Yes, sir,' replied Nicholas.

'It is not too far distant. My servant will teach you the way.'

'We already have a guide, Master Stratton. At least, we did until we lost him in the forest. We wondered if he had come back here.'

'Of course not. Why on earth should he come to Holly Lodge?'

'Because our pathfinder was your son.'

Stratton was astonished. 'Davy?'

'He insisted on coming with us,' said Elias. 'We thought he was homesick.'

'I doubt that,' growled Stratton. 'You lost him in the forest, you say?'

'Yes,' confessed Nicholas. 'The truth is that he gave us the slip.'

He explained the circumstances of the boy's disappearance and saw Jerome Stratton's irritation turn to anger. When he was in Shoreditch, the merchant was relentlessly good-natured. The affable manner was now hidden beneath a smouldering rage. He tightened both fists and glared at his guests.

'You let him get away from you?' he demanded.

'We had no reason to suppose he wanted to go,' said Nicholas.

'It could be that he simply went astray,' suggested Elias.

Stratton was bitter. 'No question of that, sir! I own that forest and use it to supply timber. Davy often went there. He played with friends among the trees and loved to watch the woodcutters at work. He didn't go astray,' he emphasised. 'Davy knows that forest better than anyone. He ran off.'

'Why?' said Elias.

'That's what I intend to find out.'

'Where could he have gone?'

'Not to Holly Lodge, that's for sure.'

'But this is his home, Master Stratton.'

'He's an apprentice with Westfield's Men now,' retorted the other. 'When you have the sense to keep hold of him. Why did you let him go, you idiots?'

The Welshmen tensed and Nicholas stepped in before Elias lost his temper.

'We're as sorry as you are, Master Stratton,' he said evenly, 'and we'll do all we can to retrieve the boy. When someone expresses a desire to join the company, it never occurs to us that he will take flight at the earliest opportunity. And if you really take us to be idiots, you should not have entrusted your son to us.'

'No,' added Elias testily. 'We were ambushed on the road and saved Davy's life. If that be idiocy, then have the pair of us locked up in Bedlam.'

'I spoke too hastily,' said Stratton, eyes darting as his mind grappled with the problem. 'Forgive me, gentlemen. This is sorry news but it's wrong to blame it on you.'

'Perhaps Davy is not suited to the theatre,' said Nicholas, probing gently.

'He is, he is. The lad spoke of nothing else.'

'Who first put the notion into his head?'

'I did, of course.'

'Even though it meant that he would leave home?'

'Davy's a restless boy. He wanted to spread his wings.'

'Was your wife equally ready to lose a son?'

Stratton coloured slightly and he gritted his teeth. 'My dear wife passed away last autumn,' he said. 'Were she here, she would have wanted for Davy exactly what I want.'

'Then it was your decision to have him indentured?'

'It was a decision my son and I reached together.'

Elias was blunt. 'Why has the little devil gone back on it?'

It took Stratton a few moments to rein in his anger. Summoning up his last reserves of bonhomie, he gave a flabby smile and crossed to open the front door.

'Thank you for coming, gentlemen,' he said cheerily. 'I am indebted to you both. But this is a domestic matter and I'll resolve it as quickly as possible.'

'But we're concerned for Davy,' said Nicholas.

'Yes,' said Elias. 'We'd hate any harm to come to the lad. Although he deserves a box on the ear for the way he left us stranded in the middle of the forest. We need the imp back, if only to guide us home to London.'

'You shall have him back,' Stratton assured him.

'Then you know where he is?'

'Forget about Davy. Ride on to Silvermere to meet Sir Michael. I daresay you have come to see the Great Hall before you play in it. Discharge the duty that brought you to Essex in the first place, gentlemen. Sir Michael will be expecting you,' he continued, opening the door even wider.

'I bid you farewell. Continue on the road and you cannot miss the house.'

The visitors traded a look then went out past him. Nicholas turned back.

'What about Davy?' he asked.

'I'll find him for you,' said Stratton.

'Where?'

'That's my business, sir.'

And he closed the door firmly in their faces.

Chapter Four

Silvermere lived up to its name. Standing at the very heart of the Greenleaf estate, it was a vast house built of a light-coloured brick that took on a silver hue in the afternoon sun. Visitors first had to skirt the kidney-shaped lake that fronted it, an expanse of water that added to the beauty of the property and acted as a kind of moat. Fringed by reeds and frozen solid, the lake was a silver mirror in which Nicholas Bracewell and Owen Elias could see their reflections as they rode around its edge. It had a fairy tale sheen to it. They were pleased to observe that someone had cleared away the ice at the far end to give the wildfowl access to the water. Two ducks paddled their way bravely across their depleted habitat. A large black swan waddled uncertainly down the bank towards the water.

The house itself made Holly Lodge look modest by comparison. Its central feature was a high turreted gate-tower that rose up defiantly and gave the place the fleeting appearance of a castle. Wings stretched out on either side then turned back to form a courtyard at the rear. Silvermere comprised a Great Hall, a small dining parlour, a chapel, family apartments, guests' lodgings, steward's lodgings, porter's quarters, servants' quarters, great kitchens, brew house, bake house, larders and cellars. The stable block stood off to the right of the property, linked to a series of outbuildings and a few small cottages. Out of sight at the back of the house was a walled garden with a small pond and a collection of statuary that was covered in moss and pitted with age. There was no hint of timber or thatch in the exterior of Silvermere. Brick and slate predominated.

'Look at the size of those chimneys!' said Elias, gaping. 'They're enormous.'

'All the better to warm up the house, Owen.'

'How many servants would you need to run a place like this?'

'None,' said Nicholas, 'for I'd never covet such a home.'

'I would. I'd invite the entire population of Wales to stay with me and still have a few rooms left empty. It'll be a positive joy to perform our work here. Silvermere puts the Queen's Head in the shade.'

'Don't you miss our friendly landlord?'

'Yes!' said Elias with feeling. 'I miss Alexander Marwood with pleasure.'

Nicholas grinned. 'I fancy that we'll have a kinder reception here.'

'I hope that it's kinder than the one we had at Holly

Lodge. If he has a father like Jerome Stratton, I'm not surprised that Davy took to his heels.'

'But he ran away from *us*, Owen.'

'I know and I can't understand why.'

'You frightened him off by threatening to kiss him on stage,' teased Nicholas.

'Where on earth could he have gone?'

'His father knows.'

'Does he?'

'Yes. I saw it in his eyes.'

When they dismounted at the front entrance, an ostler came to lead their horses off to the stables. A servant admitted them and took their cloaks and hats. The visitors then found themselves confronted by the household steward. Romball Taylard was a tall, stately man in his early forties with an impassively handsome face and watchful eyes. Black hair rose in curls from the high forehead and the beard was meticulously trimmed. Taylard was so immaculately dressed and exuded such an air of quiet confidence that he seemed more like an occupant of the house than someone who was merely employed there. After introducing himself and his companion, Nicholas explained why they had come and asked if they could meet Sir Michael Greenleaf. The steward's voice was deep and melodious.

'That will not be possible at the moment, sir,' he said.

'Is Sir Michael not at home?' enquired Nicholas.

'He's otherwise engaged. You'll have to wait until he's finished. Sir Michael will brook no interruption when he's working on one of his experiments.'

'Experiments?' repeated Elias. 'Of what kind?'

'A private nature.'

Taylard managed to make a polite reply sound like a rebuff. Elias smarted under the man's searching gaze and bit back the sarcastic remark he felt impelled to make. Nicholas, too, caught the faint whiff of disapproval that emanated from the steward. Whoever had conceived the idea of inviting Westfield's Men to perform at the house, it had evidently not been Romball Taylard but, since they would need to work closely with the man, Nicholas made an effort to win him over.

'You have a magnificent house here,' he noted. 'I suspect that you run it with commendable efficiency.'

'It's a huge undertaking,' said Taylard, grandly. 'I strive to serve.'

'We'd be grateful for your help and advice.'

'Call on me whenever you wish.'

'We'll do that immediately,' said Elias, tiring of the man's disdain. 'Show us to the Great Hall, if you will. Nick and I can take stock of it while we wait for your master to finish this experiment of a private nature.'

'I'm not at liberty to do so,' replied the steward loftily.

'Why not?'

'Sir Michael does not allow complete strangers to wander about his house.'

'But we're not strangers,' argued Nicholas, using a more reasonable tone than Elias. 'We're here at the direct invitation of Sir Michael himself. If you won't conduct us to the Great Hall, can you at least tell us where the company will be housed during our stay in Essex?'

'Not in Silvermere itself,' said Taylard crisply. 'We'll

have guests enough in here when the time comes. The players will have to be lodged elsewhere.'

'Players?' echoed a voice. 'Did I hear mention of the players?'

They turned to see an elegant woman of middle years, smiling graciously and descending the staircase in a dress of almost regal splendour. Lady Eleanor Greenleaf may have lost some of her beauty but she had retained all of her poise and charm. When the steward introduced the visitors to her, Nicholas gave a polite nod and Owen Elias produced the extravagant bow he reserved for audiences at the end of a play. The Welshman discovered that he had an admirer.

'Owen Elias!' cooed Lady Eleanor. 'Of course! I recognise you now. I've seen you many a time at the Queen's Head. And I once watched you perform at Lord Westfield's house. You played in *The Corrupt Bargain*, did you not?'

'I did, indeed, Lady Eleanor,' said Elias, glowing with delight.

'Excellently well, as I recall.'

'Thank you, thank you.'

'But I liked you best in *Love's Sacrifice*. The piece moved me to tears. Shall we have that played here when you come to entertain us?'

'That's something I have to discuss with Sir Michael,' said Nicholas. 'We need your husband's approval before we make our final choice.'

'Oh, he'll be no help to you,' she said with a fond smile. 'I'm the playgoer in the family, not my husband. He only likes the theatre. I adore it. All that he insists is that you give one play its first performance within these walls.' She turned to the steward. 'Why keep the visitors waiting, Romball?' she asked. 'Please fetch Sir Michael.'

'He's involved with his experiment, Lady Eleanor,' he warned.

'Then prise him away from it and tell him to come at once.'

'Yes, Lady Eleanor.'

After inclining his head slightly, Taylard went off into the recesses of the house, moving at a dignified pace and managing to convey both obedience and mild censure. Lady Eleanor ignored him, crossing instead to the south wing to stand before a pair of double doors with ornate brass handles that gleamed as if polished only a second before.

'I daresay that you would like to view the Great Hall,' she said.

'If we may, Lady Eleanor,' said Nicholas courteously.

'Then here it is.'

Taking hold of the two handles, she flung open the doors and strode into the room as if making an entrance on stage. Nicholas and Elias went after her, pleased to have exchanged a haughty steward for the benevolent lady of the house. Moving to the middle of the Great Hall, she spread her arms and pirouetted on her toes.

'This is your playhouse, sirs,' she declared. 'Will it serve?'

'Extremely well,' replied Nicholas.

Elias nodded enthusiastically. 'It'll be a joy to perform in here.'

'That's why I urged my husband to invite you,' she said. As soon as they entered, Nicholas knew that the place could be easily adapted for their purposes. The major decision of where to set their stage made itself. The Great Hall was a long rectangular room with oak panelling on the walls and a high ceiling that was supported by a series of beams into which the Greenleaf coat of arms had been expertly carved. At the far end was a minstrels' gallery where the company's musicians could sit and which could also be used for certain scenes in the plays. Curtains could be hung from the balustrade. Doors at either end of the wall beneath the gallery made it the ideal place of entry. Enough light streamed in through tall windows to make afternoon performance feasible without any additional illumination. Candelabra would be needed if a play were requested for an evening show.

'Well?' said Lady Eleanor.

'We've never had a finer playhouse,' complimented Nicholas.

'It does not match The Rose.'

'It surpasses it,' said Elias with gallantry. 'When we play at The Rose, we have to endure the vulgar manners of the Bankside spectators and the foul breaths of the ruffians who fill the pit. Here we perform to a select audience in conditions that any actor would envy. When I die and go to heaven, Lady Eleanor,' he said with a dramatic gesture, 'this is what I expect to find.'

'I trust that you'll favour us with your presence before you go,' she said.

Elias gave a chuckle and strode around the room to get a feel of it. Nicholas was measuring the place with his eye, arranging the seating, wondering how high the stage needed to be built and envisaging how scenery could best be employed. Lady Eleanor looked on with a contented smile as the two of them explored the space in which they were to present their six plays. Both men were patently well satisfied. They met beneath the gallery to have a silent conversation but it was short lived.

A loud explosion suddenly went off somewhere close by and the floor seemed to shake. Elias reacted with a yelp of surprise and Nicholas looked around in bewilderment. Lady Eleanor remained as serene and imperturbable as ever.

'That will be my husband,' she said sweetly. 'His experiment is completed.'

Close confinement with Egidius Pye was not something that Edmund Hoode either sought or relished but, in the interests of Westfield's Men, he endured it manfully. It was not merely the lawyer's bad breath and irritating manner that made him an unlovely companion. Pye also revealed a passion for debate that slowed down the creative process until it almost came to a halt. Acceding to all of Hoode's suggestions, the novice author nevertheless insisted on arguing over each new line that was inserted, finding at least a dozen variations of it before reaching a conclusion. Hoode's career as a playwright had been long and testing. He had never been allowed the luxury of time to reflect and refine. Plots had to be devised within a strict time limit. Characters had to spring instantly into life, verse had to flow like a fountain. Last minute changes had to be accommodated. It was, in every sense, drama on the hoof. Pairing a comparative beginner with a practical man of the theatre only served to widen the gulf between them. Hoode did his best to stave off exasperation. After another interminable quarrel, he sat back in his chair.

'We must strive to work more quickly, Master Pye,' he sighed.

'Speed is the enemy of felicity.'

'I'd sooner be infelicitous than late with the delivery of a play. Whatever we write, it will probably be amended in rehearsal. Leave room for the actors to act. You must not expect to make all their decisions for them.'

Pye was horrified. 'Won't they speak the lines we set down for them?'

'To a certain degree.'

'But I laboured so hard over the piece.'

'It's still a play,' Hoode reminded him, 'and not Holy Writ.'

'But it took me well over a year to write it.'

Another sigh. 'I feel that we've already spent as long trying to improve it.'

'To good effect, Master Hoode.'

'More or less.'

'Shall we move on to the next scene?' asked the lawyer eagerly.

Hoode raised a palm. 'No, Master Pye. I think not. We've gone as far as we decently can today. Let's start again in the morning and see if we can't at least break into a respectable trot.' He got up from the table. 'Let me show you out.'

After showering him with apologies and thanks, Pye put on the moth-eaten cloak and the floppy hat. He followed his host out of the room and down the staircase. As the two men stepped out into the street, evening shadows were just beginning to fall. Hoode was blatantly anxious to send his visitor on his way. Before the lawyer could depart, however, a familiar figure bore down on them. Lawrence Firethorn's voice boomed inimitably along the street.

'Do I spy a brace of happy poets?' he said, arriving to clap both men on the shoulders. 'Well met, sirs.' He stood back to look closely at Egidius Pye. 'Every inch a playwright! Welcome to the company, Master Pye! We owe you thanks.'

'It's I who should express gratitude,' said the lawyer, quivering nervously as if in the presence of royalty. 'You have no peer as an actor, Master Firethorn.'

Firethorn grinned. 'I'm glad that we agree on that point.'

'When you step out upon a stage, it's like Zeus descending from Mount Olympus to grace us with your genius. Oh, sir,' he said obsequiously, 'this is a signal honour. I'm quite lost for words.'

'I wish you had been so inside my lodging!' murmured Hoode.

Firethorn introduced himself properly, exchanged a few pleasantries with Pye then sent him on his way. He was always careful not to fraternise too much with a playwright until his work had proved itself in performance and he was, in any case, convinced that actors of his standing were naturally superior to the clever scribblers who provided their lines. Edmund Hoode, a competent actor as well as an author, was the exception to the rule, the only playwright whom Firethorn allowed close to him. He invited himself into his friend's lodging and the two of them were soon sharing a cup of wine. Hoode's desperation was etched deeply into his brow.

'What ails you, man?' asked Firethorn. 'Another disastrous love affair?'

'Not this time, Lawrence.'

'Then what?' His eye ignited. 'Unlooked for fatherhood?'

'Not even that,' said Hoode mournfully. 'At least some pleasure would have been involved in that instance.'

'Pleasure and repentance.'

'It's all repentance here. I bitterly regret my lunacy in agreeing to it. Pregnancy of a kind is indeed the root of my misery. I wish that I'd never been persuaded to act as midwife to Egidius Pye's play.'

'I thought that you admired the piece.'

'I did, Lawrence. I still do.'

'Then where's the problem?'

'Walking home to the Middle Temple with that ridiculous hat on his head.'

'The fellow's a lawyer,' said Firethorn contemptuously. 'He deserves ridicule.'

'Pye is insufferable,' wailed Hoode. 'He disputes every vowel and defends every consonant as if they were brought down from Mount Sinai on a stone tablet. And the worst of it is that he does it without rancour or spleen. Master Pye is Politeness itself. He doesn't even grant me an excuse to lose my temper with him.'

'What's the import of all this?'

'The brace of happy poets you spied are really a pair of bickering snails.'

'Has the play not been improved, Edmund?'

'Only with painful slowness.'

'That will not do,' said Firethorn warningly. 'Let me speak to Master Pye. I'll light such a fire beneath that arse of his that he'll burn with zeal to work faster. *The Witch of Colchester* must be finished soon so that we can start rehearsals on it. Every other play we take to Silvermere has been tried and tested at the Queen's Head. We could perform some of them with our eyes closed. But not this new piece.'

'It was a mistake to accept it,' said Hoode dolefully.

'Nick Bracewell spoke up for it. So did you at first.'

'I stand by that judgement. There are parts of it I would be proud to have written, Lawrence, and I confess it freely. Had we the play without the playwright, all would be well. But we do not. The witch comes with a spell called Egidius Pye.'

Firethorn laughed. 'Leave him to me. I'll put the wretch in his place.'

'I'm coming around to the view that only a sharp sword could do that.'

'Now, now, Edmund, you were a callow author once. Spread a little forgiveness. Bake him aright and this Pye will be delicious when he comes out of the oven.' His eye fell on the pages littering the table. 'What changes have you made?'

'Only the obvious ones so far.'

'Keep the essence of the piece. It has quality. And retain the bawdy, Edmund,' he instructed. 'Master Pye is wonderfully coarse and comical at the same time.'

'That was the alteration he resisted most strenuously.'

'What was?'

'The bawdy,' said Hoode. 'I pointed out that we must bear our audience in mind. Ribaldry that would please the stinkards at the Queen's Head might only offend the more refined sensibilities we'll encounter at Silvermere.'

'I don't agree.'

'We play to the gentry, Lawrence.'

'So? The crudest laughter always comes from the gentry, not to mention the aristocracy. I'm at one with Egidius Pye on this. Leave his bawdy unmolested. Lord Westfield will also be in the audience, remember. Our patron will complain loudly if there's no base humour to set him roaring.'

'What of the other guests?'

'They'll split their sides at some of Pye's jests, I warrant you.'

Hoode shook his head. 'I still have my doubts, Lawrence.'

'Then leave the matter until Nick Bracewell returns. He means to discuss the repertoire with Sir Michael Greenleaf to see what is and what's not in demand. We'll soon know if the people of Essex enjoy some cheerful vulgarity in their drama.' He put a consoling hand on his friend's shoulder. 'Take heart, Edmund. All is well.'

'Not to my eye. I fear for the whole enterprise.'

'That's treasonable talk. Would you rather sit out the winter writing sonnets or composing epitaphs for dear departed loved ones whom you never met?'

'No.'

'Then rejoice in our good fortune.'

'I did until I met Egidius Pye.'

'He's one small part of a very large bounty,' said Firethorn. 'We have work at last, Edmund. Gainful employment. You should have seen the faces of the company when we had our first rehearsal today. They shone with happiness. It was as if they'd just been let out of the darkest dungeon in Newgate. They are actors once more. Would you deprive your colleagues of such joy?'

'I share it with them.'

'Then why these sad looks and silly fears?'

'I have a presentiment of catastrophe.'

'A hard winter was our catastrophe. It almost froze our art to death. Suddenly, a thaw has set in,' said Firethorn, swallowing the last of his wine with a gurgle. 'Our work is in demand and our finances are repaired. Six plays at Silvermere will bring in as much money as a dozen at the Queen's Head and we've no lugubrious landlord to bark at our heels. Then there is the additional benison of a new apprentice.'

'Davy Stratton has yet to show his mettle.'

'I have no qualms about the lad. Nor about his father, for that matter.'

'His father?'

'Yes, Edmund,' said Firethorn, pouring himself some more wine. 'I've more good news for you. Master Jerome Stratton not only gave us thirty pounds when the contract was signed. He has promised us another five pounds out of his own pocket when we perform at Silvermere.'

Hoode was impressed. 'That's very generous of him.'

'Generosity may break out in other places. Who knows? If we give a good account of ourselves in Essex, other spectators may be moved to put their hands in their purses. Westfield's Men are in the ascendant,' he declared, raising an arm aloft. 'We travel on the road to glory. Nothing can stop us now.'

Nicholas Bracewell paced out the Great Hall to get a more precise idea of its dimensions then he ran his eye over the gallery to estimate its distance from the floor. Owen Elias, meanwhile, was declaiming a speech from *Love's Sacrifice* at the request of Lady Eleanor, using the soliloquy both to display his vocal gifts and to test them in the new performing venue. His voice reached every corner of the room without effort. When the speech came to an end, he gave his standard bow and Lady Eleanor applauded him. Hers were not the only palms that were clapped together. Standing in the doorway with his steward beside him was Sir Michael Greenleaf.

'Well done! Well done, sir!' he congratulated.

As he walked down the hall towards them, Elias gave him a bow of his own. Romball Taylard displayed no admiration. Remaining at the door, he looked on with a mixture of curiosity and reproach.

'Ah!' said Lady Eleanor, hands outstretched. 'Here is my husband!'

Sir Michael Greenleaf took her hands in his and kissed them both before turning to regard the visitors. Introductions were performed by his wife. Sir Michael greeted both men warmly, treating them more like honoured guests at Silvermere than members of an itinerant theatre company. It was another paradox. With a social position that entitled them to condescension, Sir Michael and Lady Greenleaf were friendly and approachable. It was their household steward who gave himself the airs and graces to which he had no legitimate claim. Surprised by their host's affability, Nicholas and Owen were startled by his appearance. Sir Michael was no slave to fashion. Plain doublet and hose of a greenish hue were supplemented by a white ruff that was coming adrift from its moorings. He was a short, rotund man in his late fifties with an unusually large head that was topped with the last of his hair. The few surviving silver wisps were clogged with a dark substance, as were his beard and his ruff. Cheeks, nose and forehead were also blackened.

Lady Eleanor saw the look of astonishment on the visitors' faces.

'You must excuse my husband,' she said smoothly. 'He has been experimenting with a new gunpowder. Unsuccessfully, by the look of it.'

'Not at all, not at all, Eleanor,' he said excitedly. 'It's almost perfect.'

'Almost?'

'I still have to cure the cannon's tendency to backfire.'

Elias was amazed. 'You make your own gunpowder, Sir Michael?'

'Of course,' replied the other. 'It's vastly better than any that I could purchase and may soon be ready for use. I just need to mix the ingredients more exactly.'

'You mentioned a cannon?' said Nicholas.

'That's right. A culverin of my own design.'

'I'd be interested to see it, Sir Michael.'

'Then you shall, my friend.'

'Nick sailed around the world with Drake,' explained Elias, proud of his friend's achievement. 'He has first-hand experience of firing a cannon.'

'Wonderful!' exclaimed Sir Michael. 'I insist that you see my whole arsenal. I thought you had the look of a seafaring man about you. A voyage with Drake. What a splendid adventure. I envy you, sir. It must mean that you know how to read the stars.'

Nicholas nodded. 'There was nothing else to do through all those long nights.'

'You must see through my telescope while you're here.'

'Thank you, Sir Michael.'

'Reading the stars is another hobby of mine.'

'My husband has so many scientific interests,' said his wife indulgently.

'But why do you need a cannon, Sir Michael?' wondered Elias.

'To mount on the tower, of course,' said the other. 'As soon as the gunpowder is perfected, I'll have the servants winch the culverin up there.'

Elias was baffled. 'But why? Do you fear attack?'

'No, my good sir.'

'Then why mount a cannon on your house?'

'Because of the wildfowl.'

'Wildfowl?' gasped the Welshman. 'Am I hearing you aright, Sir Michael? You're going to shoot at birds with cannon balls?'

Sir Michael went off into a peal of laughter. 'Of course, not,' he said when he finally controlled himself. 'That would be absurd. I love wildfowl. Why else do you think I had the lake built? The problem is that, at this time of year, it freezes over. The ice is inches thick. It's a real effort to break through it so that the ducks, geese and swans have at least a portion of their water back.'

Nicholas anticipated him. 'I think I see your plan, Sir Michael. A cannon ball fired from the top of the house would smash a large hole in the ice.'

'Exactly, sir. Especially when fired at night.'

'Night?' said Elias with disbelief. 'Why, then?'

'Because that's when the temperature reaches its lowest point,' explained Sir Michael. 'Wait until morning and the ice had already hardened. Strike it when it is newly formed and you shatter it beyond repair. That, at least,' he admitted, 'is my theory.'

'I understand your reasoning, Sir Michael,' said Nicholas, careful not to smile, 'but isn't there a serious problem here? When you put your theory to the test, you'll make the most deafening noise.'

'Guests who stay at Silvermere are used to strange happenings during the night,' said Lady Eleanor airily. 'My husband has a passion for nocturnal experiments.'

'I steer by the stars, Eleanor,' he said.

'Turn your mind to more immediate matters. These gentlemen have ridden a long way in order to meet you. Put your gunpowder aside for an hour.'

'Gladly, my dear. Now,' said Sir Michael genially, 'I bid you welcome, sirs. I'm so glad that Master Firethorn and I came to composition. Westfield's Men will make a major contribution to the festivities. Is the Great Hall to your taste?'

'It's ideal, Sir Michael,' replied Nicholas.

'Ask for what you will and Romball will supply it. You've met my steward, I hear,' he said, indicating the figure still lurking at the door. 'An excellent fellow. But for Romball Taylard, we'd be in a sorry state.'

'Our first request can only be met by you, Sir Michael,' resumed Nicholas. 'It concerns the plays we offer. The new piece has been chosen but five others must be selected as well and Master Firethorn is anxious to offer you variety. He suggests comedies such as *Double Deceit* and *The Happy Malcontent* but he feels that your guests should also be given at least one harrowing tragedy.'

'Two,' insisted Lady Eleanor. 'Too much comedy will lead to boredom.'

'There's your answer,' said her husband, beaming at her. 'Four comedies and two tragedies. Though a little bit of history would not go amiss.'

'So we thought, Sir Michael. If you approve the choice, Master Firethorn would like us to present *Henry the Fifth* by Edmund Hoode, a play that has elements of comedy and tragedy in it. Will that appeal?'

'Very much,' said Sir Michael. 'Eleanor?'

'I am more than content,' she answered. 'Comedies, tragedies and a stirring history. This is wondrous fare to set before our guests. What we do need to know, however, is the name of the new play for that will have a special place.'

'Why is that, Lady Eleanor?' asked Elias.

'Because it will be the last of the six to be presented and will coincide with a highly important event.' She turned to Sir Michael. 'You explained that in your invitation, surely?'

'It slipped my mind, Eleanor.'

'Heavens!' she cried. 'Who else but you would forget his own birthday?' She squeezed his arm affectionately. 'You're going to be sixty on that very day.'

'Congratulations, Sir Michael!' said Nicholas.

'Yes,' added Elias. 'Ice or no, the cannon will have to be fired in salute that night. As to the new play, I hear that it's a riotous comedy with some darker moments in it. Nick will confirm that. He's read it from start to finish.'

'That's true,' said the book holder. 'The play will bring our visit to Silvermere to a rousing conclusion. It's not only a brilliant piece of work by a new author, it has a fortuitous link with the county of Essex.'

'What's the title?' wondered Lady Eleanor.

'*The Witch of Colchester*.'

'I love it already.'

'So do I,' said her husband, chortling happily. 'You could not have chosen anything more appropriate, gentlemen. Do you know my nickname in these parts?'

'No, Sir Michael,' said Elias. 'What is it?'

'The Wizard of Silvermere.'

'It suits you well.'

'I like to think so,' said Sir Michael, laughing gaily. 'What a fateful meeting it will be. The Witch of Colchester and the Wizard of Silvermere. We were obviously made for each other. Everything is working to our satisfaction, Eleanor,' he went on, taking her hand. 'We have our new play and Westfield's Men have a new theatre in which to perform – the Great Hall at Silvermere.'

'They also have a new apprentice,' she reminded him. 'Davy Stratton.'

'Ah, yes. Jerome's boy. How is the lad settling in?'

Nicholas shifted his feet. 'Not very well, to be honest, Sir Michael.'

'Oh?'

'We brought him with us because he knew the way to Silvermere.'

'Then where is he now?'

'We don't know,' confessed Nicholas. 'Davy ran off.'

Light was fading badly now. As he rode his pony through the woods, Davy Stratton shivered in the cold wind and grew apprehensive. He was lost. It was dark among the trees and impossible for him to recognise the paths that should have dictated his way. He thought of turning back to start again but that would only lose valuable time and render the woodland even less hospitable. Strange noises began to assault his ear. His pony, too, was frightened, jerking its head in alarm at each new sound. Davy was having difficulty controlling his mount. It was imperative to get out of the wood as soon as possible and back on a track that he knew. He dug in his heels to call for more speed but his pony simply bucked in protest. A long, loud, anguished cry then came from the throat of a nearby animal, cutting through the undergrowth like a phantom scythe and making the boy shudder. The pony reared up in terror before bolting wildly. Davy clung on to the pommel with both hands.

It was all to no avail. As the pony galloped headlong through the bushes, the overhanging branch of a tree swept the boy from the saddle like a giant hand. Davy hit the ground with a thump then rolled over. Winded by the fall and hurt by the sudden impact of the frozen earth, he needed a moment to recover. When he picked himself up with deliberate slowness, his body ached in a dozen places. The wood seemed darker and more threatening than ever now. There was no pony to take him out of it.

'Hotspur!' he bleated. 'Come back here, Hotspur!'

But the pony was fifty yards away now. Davy could not even be sure in which direction it had gone. Walking gingerly, he set off down the path in front of him.

'Hotspur!' he called with more force. 'Where are you, boy?'

The only reply came from the nameless animal whose first cry had made his pony bolt. Davy hobbled along as fast as he could, pausing only to pick up a long stick for protection. He was lost, alone and at the mercy of wild animals. Safety was a long way off now. He began to regret leaving Nicholas Bracewell and Owen Elias in the middle of the forest. With them beside him, he feared nothing. They were friends. They had even helped him to avoid an ambush. It hurt him to remember that he had let them down badly. This was his punishment for deserting them. It was no more than he deserved.

Davy steeled himself to be brave and pressed on, using the stick to push aside bushes or to support him across a ditch. He kept calling for his horse but with decreasing hope. When he stumbled into a clearing, he had the uncomfortable feeling that he had been there before and had simply travelled through the wood in a wide circle. It was galling. He rested against the trunk of an ash tree to catch his breath and consider his next move. The animal let out a third cry but it was far more distant now. As the noise died away, it was replaced by a more welcome sound. Davy heard a faint neigh off to his left. Was it Hotspur? Had the pony come to a halt at last? His spirits revived. Pushing himself away from the tree, he set off in the direction of the neigh, ears pricked to catch any repetition of the sound. When it finally came, his hopes were confirmed. It was the distinctive neigh of his pony, waiting for him not far away. Davy broke into a run, blundering through the undergrowth as quickly as his aching legs would carry him.

He had not been deceived. Hotspur was under a tree, searching the ground for a morsel of grass. Davy burst into tears when he saw him and ran towards the pony but he never reached the animal. Two men leapt out of the bushes to grab him. One of them clapped a hand over the boy's mouth to stifle his yell.

'Come on, lad,' he said grimly. 'You're going with us.'

Margery Firethorn gave her husband a warm embrace and stood back to appraise him.

'I'll miss you, Lawrence,' she sighed.

'Absence makes the heart grow fonder, my love.'

'You always say that on the eve of departure.'

'That's because it's always true, Margery,' he said, tickling her under the chin with an index finger. 'The longer I'm away from you, the more I appreciate you. It's agony for me. Being apart from my dear wife for any length of time is like losing a limb.'

'Is it?' she said sceptically. 'I know you better than that, Lawrence.'

He gave a roguish smile. 'So I should hope.'

'Marry an actor and you must suffer the consequences.'

'Travel is forced upon us. We have to go where the work beckons.'

'As long as your affections don't wander while you're away.'

'Perish the thought!'

'It would not be the first time you went astray.'

'Why ever should I do that, my love?' he said with an expression of injured innocence. 'It's madness. Why should I pick an occasional wild cherry when I have a basket of ripe strawberries waiting for me in my bed?'

'Is that all I am?' she teased. 'Something sweet to pop into your mouth?'

'No, Margery. You're much, much more. Wife, mother, lover, partner and soul mate. I tell you this,' he said impulsively, 'if you didn't have to look after the house and the children, I'd throw you over my shoulder and take you with us to Essex. Perhaps not,' he added after a pause. 'You'd only provoke the envy of the rest of the company and distract them from their work.'

'Away with you!' she said, giving him a playful push.

After a day's rehearsal and a long talk with Edmund Hoode, Firethorn had returned to his house in Shoreditch. Enticing smells from the kitchen told him that Margery had a hot meal waiting for him and she herself was a welcoming sight. Their marriage had its tempestuous moments but they were always obliterated by the passion of their reconciliations. Though his eye and hand might wander occasionally, Firethorn's heart remained firmly with his beloved wife.

'Is all well, Lawrence?' she asked.

'Exceptionally so.'

'The company must be delighted to be called to arms again.'

'Overjoyed, my love. We worked with true zeal. It's been a day of pure delight. Apart from a little petulance from Edmund, that is.'

'Edmund? That's not like him. Petulance is one of Barnaby's tricks.'

'Barnaby was in a good mood for once. Thanks to Doctor Putrid.'

'A strange name for a doctor. Has Barnaby been unwell?'

'No, Margery,' he explained. 'Doctor Putrid is the character he'll play in our new piece. A juicy role and one that cured Barnaby of his petulance. He's thrilled with *The Witch of Colchester*. The same, alas, cannot be said of Edmund Hoode.'

'Why not?'

'Because he has the task of burnishing the play for us.'

'A simple chore for someone with Edmund's skill.'

'That's what he thought until he met the author,' said Firethorn with a mirthless laugh. 'A skulking lawyer named Egidius Pye. I met him at Edmund's lodging and wondered which mouse hole he'd crawled out from. Still, enough of him!' he went on with a dismissive wave. 'Pye is only a minor irritation at worst. I'll slap him down.'

'How large a company will you take to Essex?'

'A round dozen in all.'

'Does that include the musicians?'

'Yes, Margery. I've had to be ruthless there and choose men who give me double value. Musicians who can act and actors who can play an instrument or two.'

'That must have hurt the ones you turned away.'

He heaved a sigh. 'It did but there's no remedy for it. The invitation dictated the size of the troupe. Sir Michael Greenleaf cannot accommodate unlimited numbers.'

'What about the apprentices?'

'They're additional to the twelve. Four boys only require one bed between them.'

'Four?' she said. 'Does that mean Davy Stratton is to be left behind?'

'I think not. John Tallis is the loser. He's too gruff to take a woman's role any more and too puny to play a man. I'll leave him here to kick his heels.'

'But he has far more experience than Davy.'

'Granted,' said Firethorn, 'but his father will not be sitting in the audience at Silvermere, will he? We have to play politics, Margery. Like our own dear patron, Jerome Stratton is a friend of Sir Michael Greenleaf. We must humour him. He'll want to see his son on the stage even if the lad only stands there for a second.'

'You've had to make some harsh decisions, Lawrence,' she observed.

He gave her his broadest smile. 'I made the best decision when I married you, my love.' He leant over to kiss her tenderly on the lips. 'All else pales beside the wisdom of that choice.'

'Does that mean I can have the new dress you promised?'

'In time,' he said, stepping back at once. 'In time.'

'And when will that be?'

His shrug was noncommittal. 'Who can tell?'

'You never change, Lawrence, do you?' she said with a resigned laugh. 'No matter for that. I love you as you are. Now, then. Are you hungry?'

'Close to starvation.'

'Go to the table and I'll bring the meal into you.'

'I smell beef and onions.'

'And lots more beside. Now, off with you,' she ordered, pushing him towards the dining room. 'I've work to do in the kitchen. Call in the others and we'll all eat together. I want to enjoy my family while I still have them all together.'

'Not all, Margery.'

'Who have I forgotten?'

'The smallest and youngest. Davy Stratton. Don't ask me to call him,' he warned, moving away. 'Even my voice won't reach the depths of Essex.'

Margery bustled off to the kitchen to check the contents of the pot as it hung over the fire and to chide her servant for not putting more salt into it. Too eager to make amends, the girl tipped more salt than was necessary into the soup and was chastised roundly by her mistress. When Margery called for bread, the servant fetched it from the larder then took it into the dining room. It was some time before she returned to the kitchen. Annoyed by the delay, Margery swung round to scold her once more but the girl's expression made her desist. Pale and trembling, the servant pointed to the door.

'You'd best go at once,' she stuttered.

'Go where?'

'To the dining room.'

'We'll be taking the food through in a moment.'

'Master Firethorn needs you now,' said the girl anxiously.

'What are you talking about, girl?' demanded Margery.

'Your husband, Mistress Firethorn. He's unwell.'

'That's nonsense. I saw him only a minute ago and he was a picture of health.'

'Not any more,' continued the girl. 'He begged me to send you.'

'Begged you? When he has a voice that could call me?' She eased the servant aside and walked to the open door. 'Lawrence!' she yelled. 'Did you send for me?'

The reply was so faint that she did not hear it at first. Hands on hips, she shot a stern glance at the girl then repeated her question even louder. This time his voice made itself heard from the dining room.

'Come to me, Margery,' he said hoarsely. 'Please!'

It was a cry for help and she answered it immediately, rushing out and charging into the dining room. The sight that awaited her made her gasp in dismay. Firethorn was seated in his customary place at the head of the table but he was not the robust husband who had flirted with her only minutes before. He was patently in distress. Arms on the table, he panted stertorously before being seized by a coughing fit that racked his whole body. Margery dashed forward to put an arm around him.

'What is it, Lawrence?' she asked. 'What's wrong with you?'

'I don't know, my love.'

'When did this come on?'

'The moment I sat down in here.'

'Were there no signs of illness earlier in the day?'

'None, Margery. I've never felt fitter.'

'Was it something you ate? Something you drank?'

'I've no idea.'

'Are you in pain?' she said, kissing him softly. 'Where does it hurt?'

'All over,' he moaned.

He slumped forward and her alarm grew. She crouched in front of him, taking his head in her hands to hold it up so that she could take a close look at him. The change in Firethorn was dramatic. The strapping husband who had come bounding into the house earlier on was now a weak and troubled man. His eyes were dull, his mouth agape. The room was cold yet his face and beard were glistening with sweat. When Margery put a hand to his forehead, she drew it away in fear.

'Dear God!' she exclaimed. 'You're on fire, Lawrence. You have a fever.'

Chapter Five

Nicholas Bracewell was pleased with their welcome at Silvermere. Their hosts could not have been more amenable. Sir Michael Greenleaf was kind, attentive and unfailingly obliging while his wife's admiration for Westfield's Men never faltered. They were such a gracious and engaging couple that Nicholas wondered how they had been befriended by their wayward patron. Lord Westfield's cronies tended to be in his own mould, amiable sybarites, devotees of drink and gambling, idle aristocrats who hung around the Court in search of favour or who left it in flight from scandal. Sir Michael and Lady Greenleaf did not conform to the usual pattern. Where Lord Westfield and his decadent entourage were invariably deep in debt, the Wizard of Silvermere was clearly a man of substance, able to fund continuous improvements to his estate as well as to pay for his expensive scientific interests. Yet he did not flaunt his wealth. He dressed like one of his servants and behaved with a touching humility.

Owen Elias liked the man as much as Nicholas. Not only had their host provided Westfield's Men with a worthy auditorium in his Great Hall, he gave the visitors a guided tour of the house, showed them his extensive arsenal, discussed the manufacture of his gunpowder and even offered to take them up to the top of the tower. The Welshman glanced through the window with misgivings.

'It's pitch dark out there, Sir Michael,' he said.

'Exactly, my friend. The stars will be out. Wouldn't you like to come up on the roof to look through my telescope?'

'No thank you. It'll be freezing.'

'What's a little discomfort in the interests of astrology?'

'It's a kind offer, Sir Michael,' said Nicholas, aware of the passage of time, 'and I'll be delighted to accept it on another occasion but we've already stayed longer than we intended. Master Stratton told us that Stapleford is only a mile away. Put us on the road to the village and we'll seek lodging at the inn.'

'Inn?'

'I believe that it's called The Shepherd and Shepherdess.'

'But you're going to stay here, Master Bracewell.'

'Are we?'

'Yes,' insisted Sir Michael. 'I wouldn't dream of turning you out. My wife and I will be your shepherd and shepherdess. A chambermaid is already preparing a room for you. When the whole company descends upon us, of course, you'll have to make use of those little cottages set apart from the house, perhaps even of the outbuildings as well. Tonight, however, the pair of you will lay your heads beneath the roof of Silvermere.'

'That's most generous of you, Sir Michael.'

'We accept on one condition,' said Elias.

'Condition?'

'Yes,' added the Welshman with a grin. 'Give us fair warning before you fire any cannon balls from the roof in the middle of the night.'

Sir Michael burst out laughing and clapped his hands to his side like young bird making its first clumsy attempts at flight. The three of them were alone in a room at the rear of the property that served its owner as library, laboratory and workshop all in one. Along the back wall, oak shelves stretched from floor to ceiling, filled to the last inch with hefty tomes and piles of documents. One vast table was covered with scientific instruments of every description while another looked more like a carpenter's bench. The culverin was kept beside the furnace in the adjoining outhouse. Seeing it all by the light of candelabra, Nicholas was impressed. Sir Michael was no Egidius Pye. There was a sense of order and calculation in the room. It was also impeccably clean. The scientist looked after his possessions with great care. This was his private world where he sought, in his own small way, to push forward the frontiers of science.

There was a knock on the door and Romball Taylard entered. He looked almost sinister as he emerged from the shadows but his manner towards the visitors was more pleasant now that he knew that they would be staying overnight. With good news to pass on, he even contrived a smile.

'Yes, Romball?' asked his employer.

'You have visitors, Sir Michael.'

'At this time of night?'

'Master Stratton sends his apologies for calling so late.'

'Oh, I see. It's Jerome, is it? Well, he can come at any time he likes. Does he wants to speak to me or to Lady Eleanor.'

'He's really here to see your guests, Sir Michael,' said the steward, glancing at the two of them. 'Master Stratton has brought someone with him.'

'And who might that be?'

'His son.'

'Davy?' asked Nicholas, cheered by the tidings.

'Where has the rascal been?' said Elias.

Taylard smiled again. 'Only Master Stratton will be able to tell you that.'

'Then let's go and find him at once,' urged Sir Michael, leading the way.

The four of them went off down a long corridor that was lit at regular intervals by candelabra. Dancing flames threw their profiles against the walls as they passed and gave the house a ghostly quality. When the quartet came into the entrance hall, Jerome Stratton was standing beside a marble bust of Plato, holding his son by the hand and making an effort to appear relaxed. Davy Stratton, by contrast, was sullen and subdued, his face bearing some dark scratches and his attire torn and soiled. He did not look up as the others arrived. Taylard faded quickly into the background but stayed within earshot.

'The prodigal son has returned,' said Stratton with forced

geniality. 'I'm sorry to intrude at this hour, Sir Michael, but I was hoping to catch your visitors before they went off to Stapleford.'

'But they're not going to the inn,' said Sir Michael.

'Surely they don't mean to travel back to London at night?'

'Of course not, Jerome. You must think us uncivilized even to suggest such a thing. We'd never turn out guests when we have twenty rooms or more unoccupied. They'll be staying here until morning.'

'I see,' said Stratton, adjusting swiftly to the news. 'In that case, I must request a favour, Sir Michael. Is it possible that you could find a corner where Davy might bed down as well?'

'Need you even ask? The boy is more than welcome.'

'Thank you.' He nudged his son. 'Davy?'

'Thank you, Sir Michael,' mumbled Davy without looking up.

'Perhaps I might ask a favour as well, Sir Michael,' said Nicholas politely. 'Since Davy is to stay, is there any chance that he might share the room with Owen and me?'

'A sensible notion,' said Sir Michael. 'Romball?'

The steward materialised out of the gloom. 'Yes, Sir Michael?'

'Speak to the chambermaid, will you?'

'At once, Sir Michael.'

Taylard backed away again and went silently up the stairs. Nicholas knelt down in front of Davy to inspect his face and clothing. The boy looked up guiltily for a second then lowered his eyes again.

'Those are nasty scratches you have, Davy,' said Nicholas with sympathy. 'And you've a bruise on your temple. How did you come by those?'

'His pony bolted and he was thrown,' explained Stratton before his son could open his mouth. 'That's why he didn't hear you when you called for him in the forest. Hotspur – that's his pony – took fright and bolted. Davy was knocked senseless when he hit the ground. By the time he recovered, you'd both ridden off.'

'But the lad's such a fine horseman,' said Nicholas.

'Hotspur caught him unawares.'

'And us,' said Elias. 'One moment, Davy was there; the next, he was gone.'

'Thrown from the saddle. He was still dazed when he tried to find Hotspur and stumbled into a holly bush. Hence the scratches on his face and the torn clothing. The bruise must have come from the fall.' He put a gentle hand on the back of his son's neck. 'Davy doesn't recall too much about it, do you, Davy?'

'No, Father,' said the boy dutifully.

'He'll be much better after a good night's sleep,' promised Stratton easily. 'I apologise for bringing him to you in such a state but we were much nearer to Silvermere when the search party found him. My men say that he was running blind like a startled rabbit.' He patted the boy on the head. 'I'll have fresh attire sent over first thing in the morning. We can't have him riding back to London in that state.'

Nicholas was puzzled. If the father were so concerned about his son, he wondered why Stratton did not take the boy back to Holly Lodge for the night. Word of his return could have been sent to Silvermere and Davy could have been reunited with his travelling companions the following morning. Nicholas also had grave suspicions about the account that Jerome Stratton had given of his son's disappearance. A fall from the pony and a charge through woodland might have been responsible for his wounds and his dishevelled state but several hours had passed since Davy had vanished. Where had the boy been in the interim? Nicholas was surprised that someone who was supposed to know every path in the forest managed to get himself lost for such a long time. Many questions needed to be put to Davy but not in the presence of his father. As long as Jerome Stratton was there, Nicholas saw, the boy would not dare to tell the truth.

'Well,' said Sir Michael, 'may we offer you refreshment, Jerome?'

'I think not,' said Stratton. 'I have guests of my own at Holly Lodge and they'll start to feel neglected if I stay away any longer. Thank you for taking Davy under your wing, Sir Michael. Though it grieves me to part with him,' he added, giving the boy a token embrace, 'I'll abide by the terms of the contract. He belongs to Westfield's Men now.' His eyes glinted as they turned on Nicholas. 'Please take better care of him this time. Davy is very precious to me.'

'He'll be safe in our hands, Master Stratton,' promised Nicholas.

'Yes,' said Elias. 'We won't let him out of our sight again.'

'Make sure that you don't,' said Stratton sternly. His

tone softened. 'I'm glad that you both came to Silvermere. Is the Great Hall to your liking?'

'Completely so,' replied Nicholas. 'The company will be thrilled when they see where they will stage their work. We cannot thank Sir Michael and Lady Eleanor enough for their kind invitation.'

'I had something to do with that,' hinted Stratton. He looked at his son. 'Well, Davy, we must part again. Ride your pony more carefully tomorrow and do exactly what you're told. Do you understand?'

'Yes, Father,' murmured Davy.

'I expect to hear good reports of you from now on.'

'Yes, Father.'

'The next time I see you,' he said with a smile, 'will be on stage here in a play.'

It was not a prospect that lifted the boy's spirits. He glanced up at his father with a respect that was tempered with fear. Nicholas took note of his response. After a flurry of farewells, Stratton moved off and Romball Taylard glided out of a dark corner to open the front door for him. Nobody had even heard the steward return. Stratton had a brief word with the man before going outside to his waiting horse. Closing the door, Taylard drifted quietly across to his master's side to await further orders. Sir Michael raised an inquisitive eyebrow.

'Is everything in order, Romball?'

'Yes, Sir Michael,' said Taylard smoothly. 'A meal awaits our guests when they are ready to eat it.'

'I'm ready now,' announced Elias, rubbing his stomach. 'It seems an age since we last had any food. What about you, Davy? I daresay that you're famished as well.'

Davy lifted a weary head. Sir Michael produced an avuncular chuckle.

'The lad is plainly tired and hungry,' he said. 'Who wouldn't be after all the adventures he's had today? A good meal and an early night are what I recommend. Take good care of them, Romball.'

'I will, Sir Michael,' said the steward.

After another exchange of farewells, he took the visitors off down a corridor.

Margery Firethorn sat on the edge of her chair. Racked with anxiety and unable to relax, she played nervously with the edge of her apron and gazed upwards at the low ceiling. In the bedchamber above, her husband lay in a desperate condition. She had never seen Firethorn in such a poorly state. It had taken three of them to help him to his bed and, after sending for the doctor, Margery had sat loyally beside the patient, soothing him with soft words and mopping his fevered brow with a wet cloth. Instructed by her mistress, the servant fed both the apprentices and the children of the house before packing them off to bed. Margery did not want them bothering her while Firethorn was in such distress. He needed all her attention. When the doctor finally arrived, he insisted on banning Margery from the bedchamber while he examined the sick man. The long wait below in the parlour was a trial.

Eventually, she heard footsteps on the stairs and jumped up from her seat. When the door creaked open, however, it was not the doctor who came into the room but the forlorn figure of Richard Honeydew, the youngest and most talented of the apprentices. Clad only in a thin shirt, the boy was trembling with cold and blanched by unease. His soft features allowed him to impersonate a whole range of beautiful young women on stage but he was no gorgeous damsel or impassioned princess now. He was a frightened little boy with tousled fair hair, his face marred by crow's feet of concern, his slender frame sagging with dismay. Before she could stop herself, Margery snapped at him with unnecessary harshness.

'You should be in bed, Dick Honeydew!'

'I know,' he said, recoiling slightly but holding his ground.

'Then why are you here?'

'We're very worried about Master Firethorn. We heard the doctor arrive. The others asked me to come down to see if there was any news.'

'No, Dick,' she admitted sadly. 'Not yet.'

'We prayed hard for him.'

Margery nodded. She was certain that he had included her husband in his prayers but was not persuaded that the other apprentices had done likewise. They were more unruly and less inclined to prayer until she stood over them. Knowing that she would be in a tense mood, they had sent Richard Honeydew down to make enquiries, sensing that she might berate anyone bold enough to venture out of their bed. Standing barefoot on the flagstones, the apprentice began to shiver more violently.

'Come over here,' said Margery, putting an arm around him to take him across to the fire. 'You'll catch your death of cold, lad.'

'I'm fine, Mistress Firethorn,' he said bravely.

'The others put you up to this, didn't they?'

'Yes, but I wanted to come on my own account.'

'Why?'

'Master Firethorn is kind to me. I love him like a father.'

Margery hugged him to her and kissed him. 'You're a good boy, Dick, and my husband appreciates that. You're ever his favourite.'

'What ails him?' piped the other.

'I wish I knew, lad.'

'John Tallis says that he has the ague.'

'Does he?' she said angrily. 'Well, you can tell John Tallis from me that I'll come up there to give him a sound beating if he spreads tales like that. John Tallis can mind his own business. Since when has he turned into a physician?'

'He meant no harm, Mistress Firethorn.'

'That kind of talk vexes me.'

'I'll warn him of that.'

Margery calmed down and pulled the boy closer, drawing strength from his companionship while, at the same time, offering him some comfort. She was glad that Richard Honeydew had interrupted her lonely vigil. It made the interminable wait a little easier to bear. She brushed his hair back from his forehead to reveal a frown.

'Are you warmer now, Dick?'

'Yes, thank you.' There was a considered pause. 'It's never happened before, has it, Mistress Firethorn?' he said at length.

'What?'

'An illness like this.'

'No, Dick.'

'Master Firethorn is never unwell.'

'That's so true.'

It was the reason that her husband's condition alarmed her so much. Lawrence Firethorn had such a strong constitution that she took his health for granted. Now that he had been struck down, she knew that the problem must be serious. Minor ailments that afflicted the others never even touched Firethorn. He remained what he had been when she first married him; a sturdy, powerful, virile man who went through life without being troubled by anything apart from occasional toothache. Accidents which would have laid other men low were shrugged off by the actor-manager. When he broke an arm in a fall from the stage, Firethorn continued to perform at the Queen's Head wearing a splint. When he twisted an ankle dismounting his horse, he simply equipped Hector, Pompey the Great, King John, Henry the Fifth and all the other characters he had to play with a stout walking stick until he could move freely. Margery had marvelled at his indomitability. Had his luck changed at last?

'I hope that he soon recovers,' said Honeydew.

'So do I, Dick.'

'Master Firethorn is the heart and soul of Westfield's Men.'

'You've no need to tell me that.'

'If we were to lose him—'

'We won't,' she said, interrupting him sharply and giving him a reproving squeeze. 'Don't even think such a thing, Dick Honeydew. Is that what they've been saying upstairs to you? Is that another rumour spread by John Tallis?'

'No, Mistress Firethorn,' he replied, cowering before her.

'Then put that wicked thought out of your mind.'

'I will, I will.'

She mellowed at once. 'Forgive me, Dick. I don't mean to be so cross with you. I just don't want to hear such things spoken in my house. It's winter,' she said as if trying to explain it to herself. 'People are always ill at this time of year. It just happens to be my husband's turn to suffer, that's all. We mustn't despair.'

Honeydew was not reassured. When footsteps were heard on the staircase, he stepped away from her and spun round. Margery crossed to open the door so that Doctor Whitrow could come into the room.

'How is he, doctor?' she asked breathlessly. 'May I go up?'

'In a moment,' he said.

'Do you have medicine for me to give to him?'

'I've already administered a cordial, Mistress Firethorn.'

'What's wrong with him?'

'Calm down, calm down,' he said softly.

'But I'm his wife. I've a right to know.'

Doctor Whitrow gave an understanding smile. He was a tall, spare man in his fifties with hollow cheeks and deep-set eyes. Working in Shoreditch for so many years had acquainted him with many distraught wives and he knew how to deal with them.

'The first thing you must know is that there's no danger,' he assured her. 'Your husband is one of the healthiest patients I've ever met.'

'But what about his fever?'

'It's broken. The crisis is over.'

'Thank God!' she cried.

Richard Honeydew was in tears. 'My prayers were answered.'

Margery was bewildered. 'When you first arrived, he was sweating like a roast pig. Did your cordial revive him so quickly, Doctor Whitrow?'

'He seemed to rally before I even gave it to him. In fact,' added the doctor with a sly grin, 'Master Firethorn tried to push the potion away in order to deprive me of part of my fee. That shows he has all his faculties. My advice is to keep him in bed until the morning. After a good rest, he'll be in fine fettle.'

Margery could wait no longer. Thanking him profusely, she scurried past him and ascended the stairs as if pursued by the hounds of hell. She flung open the door of the bedchamber and rushed in. The sight that presented itself to her made her stop dead. Lawrence Firethorn was just about to get out of bed. The man whom she had last seen groaning in agony under the sheets was now his usual robust self. Margery blinked at the speed of his recovery.

'What on earth are you doing, Lawrence?' she asked.

'Coming downstairs to see if those little beggars have left me any food?' he said, swinging two bare feet down on to the floor. 'I'm fainting from lack of nourishment.'

She eyed him closely. 'You look wonderful to me.'

'I'm glad that I can still strike a spark in you, Margery.'

'Stay there,' she ordered, sitting him back on the bed. 'If you want food, I'll bring it to you myself. Doctor Whitrow said that you're not to stir from here.'

'I'm not listening to that old fool. He gave me such a foul medicine that I need a cup of sack to take away the taste. Let's go downstairs. We'll sup together.'

Margery was firm. 'No, Lawrence. You need rest.'

'Who does?'

'You do,' she said, lifting his feet back on to the bed. 'You must stay here.'

'But there's nothing wrong with me, Margery.'

'That fever weakened you.'

'Only for a brief moment.'

'You were in torment not half an hour ago.'

'That's all past.'

'Stay where you are,' she ordered. 'Bed is the only place for you.'

'Then I need someone to share it with me,' he said with a laugh, pulling her down beside him then rolling on top of her. 'Weakened, am I?' he went on, kissing her full on the lips. 'The only fever that I have is the one that you always give me, Margery. Come here, my love. Restore me to full health.'

Her squeal of protest was quickly replaced by a sigh of acquiescence as she yielded to his sudden passion. Firethorn roared with delight. He started to lift her dress but the nuptials were not allowed to continue. A sharp tap behind them made the lovers stop. Framed in the open doorway were all four apprentices, watching with a blend of relief and curiosity. Doctor Whitrow was standing in the middle of them, tactfully averting his gaze.

'There is the small matter of my fee,' he said meekly.

* * *

Nicholas Bracewell finished his meal and washed it down with a mouthful of ale. Owen Elias was still munching cheerfully but Davy Stratton's food lay untouched on its platter.

'Eat up, lad,' encouraged Nicholas.

'I'm not hungry,' said the boy.

'You must be.'

'Go on, Davy,' said Elias, nudging him. 'It'll help to keep out the cold.'

But the most that the boy consented to do was to pick at his meat, putting only the smallest portion in his mouth and chewing it without relish. Eager to hear an account of his movements from Davy himself, Nicholas bided his time. The boy still seemed to be in a state of shock and the presence of two servants inhibited their conversation. Having escorted them to the kitchens, Romball Taylard had vanished, leaving instructions with the cook to feed them well before sending them off to their room. The three of them were seated at a small table in the corner of the main kitchen, inhaling a rich compound of aromas and consuming their meal in the shadow of dead game that dangled from hooks. It was not the place to discuss confidential matters.

When they had all finished, one of the servants picked up a lighted candle, took them into the adjoining kitchen and opened a small door. A rickety staircase curled upwards. The visitors were forced to recognise their appointed place in the scheme of things. Detached from their host, they were not being given the luxurious accommodation that his generosity appeared to indicate. Instead, they were conducted up the backstairs to a room in the servants' quarters, vacated to make way for them and hastily cleaned. The place was illumined by three flickering candles. When the servant departed, they closed the door behind him and took inventory.

It was a small, narrow room with a slanting floor and a superfluity of draughts. Fresh linen had been placed on the two beds that nestled side by side. Crammed into a corner was a truckle bed that had been dragged in for Davy. On a small table against one wall stood a bowl and a pitcher of water. Beneath the table was a capacious chamber pot. It was the first thing that Owen Elias noticed. He jabbed a finger at it.

'It'll take a lot of bladders to fill that,' he noted. 'How many sleep in here?'

'Two to each bed, I suspect,' said Nicholas.

'Three, more like it. There are no featherbeds for the servants here. They sleep head to toe as in other big houses. Well,' he decided, flinging himself down on one of the beds, 'this will suit me for a night. It's hard but I'm used to that. What I'm not used to is sleeping on my own.' He looked teasingly across at the apprentice. 'Would you like to curl up in here with me, Davy?'

'No, no,' said the boy quickly, standing beside the truckle bed. 'I'll stay here.'

'I won't bite you, lad,' said Elias jovially. 'Not too hard, anyway. And I promise faithfully not to kiss you – unless you kiss me first, that is.'

'Leave him be, Owen,' chided Nicholas. 'He's tired.'

'Not too tired to tell us what happened, I hope. I don't know about you, Nick, but I didn't believe a word that his

126

father said to us. Davy's pony didn't bolt.'

'He did,' said the boy defensively. 'I swear it.'

'Was your father telling us the truth?'

'Hotspur bolted and a low branch knocked me from the saddle.'

'But what caused him to bolt, Davy?' asked Nicholas.

'I don't know.'

'You've been missing for hours. Where were you?'

'I'm not sure,' said the boy evasively. 'I don't remember.'

'We thought you'd run away from us. Did you?' Davy shook his head. 'Is that why you wanted to come to Essex with us?' The boy shook his head again. Nicholas traded a glance with Elias. 'You're exhausted, lad. I can see that. Get yourself some sleep and we'll talk again in the morning.'

Relieved to be spared an interrogation, Davy nodded and began to undress. His companions also got ready for bed. Nicholas sensed that the apprentice was lying but saw no value in trying to force information out of him. The only way to get to the truth was to win the boy's confidence and convince him that he was among friends who would not sit in judgement on him. Jerome Stratton's behaviour had been eloquent. It told them much about his uneasy relationship with his son and confirmed the suspicion that Davy had not joined Westfield's Men voluntarily. However, since he was now legally a member of the company, they had a responsibility to keep him in it. They would be more vigilant in future. Before he clambered into bed, Nicholas blew out two of the candles.

'Good night, Davy,' he said gently.

There was no reply. 'He's fast asleep, Nick,' observed Elias. 'Dog tired.'

'It's been a long day for him, Owen.'

'And he's had a rough time of it, by the look of things.'

Getting into his own bed, Elias licked his thumb and forefinger before using them to sniff out the last candle. There was a long pause as he tried to get comfortable and Nicholas could hear him threshing about. Elias then settled down and seemed to go off to sleep. Nicholas was about to doze off himself when the Welshmen spoke.

'Are you still awake, Nick?'

'Yes.'

'Do you think we'll ever get to know why he went haring off like that?'

'Not from Master Stratton,' whispered Nicholas, 'that's for sure.'

'I wouldn't trust him to tell me what day of the week it was,' muttered Elias, adjusting his position in bed again. 'He'd probably charge me interest for doing so. Merchants are all the same. Cheats and liars to a man.'

'Keep your voice down, Owen.'

'Nothing I say about his father will upset Davy. You saw the pair of them together earlier. There's no love lost between them. Besides,' he added, suppressing a yawn. 'The boy's dead to the world.'

'Then don't wake him up,' hissed Nicholas.

Elias reverted to a whisper. 'What do you make of Sir Michael?'

'He's a perfect gentleman.'

'He's also completely mad. Firing a cannon at night to

128

break the ice on the lake? It was all I could do to forbear laughing. And why does he keep all those weapons?'

'They interest him.'

'Weapons are for fighting and he's the most peaceable man I've ever met.'

'He's also our host, Owen, so we must take him as we found him. Sir Michael and his wife have come to the rescue of Westfield's Men. Never forget that. If he has a few outlandish ideas, we should tolerate them happily. No,' said Nicholas, keeping his voice low, 'I have no complaints at all about our hosts. The person who worries me is their steward.'

'Why?'

'To begin with, he doesn't want us here.'

'That was my feeling, Nick.'

'If it were left to him, we'd be spending the night at that village inn. It never shows in his face but I fancy that Romball Taylard objects to the very idea of Westfield's Men performing in the Great Hall.'

'Does he think we'll steal the silver or ravish the chambermaids?'

'Who knows? But that's not the only thing that troubles me about him.'

'Isn't it?'

'No, Owen.'

'What else is there?'

'The simple fact that we've seen so much of the fellow,' said Nicholas. 'He's the steward here. In an establishment of this size, that means he has immense responsibilities. He supervises the staff, advises Sir Michael, victuals the kitchens, controls the household accounts and so on. Yet he was waiting for us as soon as we walked through the door.'

'So?'

'Why should Taylard take on the office of a butler when he could delegate it elsewhere? Why lead us off to our meal when that was an office fit for a servant? Why do chores that should rightly be beneath him? Do you take my point, Owen?' he asked. 'Isn't it odd that someone who's so unhappy to have us at Silvermere is taking such pains to stay close to us?'

Elias gave a loud yawn. 'I never thought about it that way.'

'Neither did I until now.'

'What's the reason behind it, Nick?'

'That's obvious,' said his friend quietly. 'He's watching us.'

Another yawn from Elias signalled the end of the conversation. After wishing each other good night, they snuggled under the warm sheets. Elias was the first to fall asleep, marking the event with a series of gentle snores. Nicholas lay awake for a while, thinking about Davy Stratton's sudden departure in the forest and speculating on where the boy had really gone. When his eyelids grew heavy, he surrendered to fatigue and dozed off. How long he slept he did not know but it was still dark when a creaking sound brought his awake. He thought at first that it was Elias, making his way to the chamber pot but the Welshman was still snoring happily in the next bed. Nicholas sat up in bed and peered into the gloom through bleary eyes.

'Is that you, Davy?' he asked.

The creaking stopped instantly but there was no reply to his question. Nicholas grew suspicious. Hauling himself out of bed, he groped his way to the truckle bed and put out an exploratory hand. Davy was not there yet Nicholas was certain he was still in the room. He was fully awake now. Nicholas sensed that the boy was standing by the door and he moved across to reach out for him. Holding his breath and flattened against the door, Davy let out a yelp as strong fingers closed on his arm. Nicholas put both hands on the boy and was shocked with what he found.

'You're fully dressed,' he said.

'I was . . . going for a walk,' bleated Davy.

'In the middle of the night? You were running away again, weren't you?'

'No!'

'You were,' said Nicholas with subdued anger. 'Why? Where were you going?'

'Nowhere.'

Nicholas shook him. 'Don't lie to me, Davy. You put on your clothes to sneak out. I heard you trying to open the door, didn't I?'

The boy capitulated. 'Yes,' he admitted, sobbing quietly. 'I was creeping out and I'd have got away with it if you hadn't locked the door.'

'But I didn't,' said Nicholas. 'I don't have a key.'

He reached for the handle himself and twisted it. Though he pulled hard, the door did not move an inch. All three of them were securely locked in the room.

* * *

Jared Tuke did not seem to feel the bitter cold. A burly man of middle years, he walked through the churchyard as if it were a summer's afternoon rather than an early morning in winter. His only concession to the weather was to wear his largest cap but even that was set back on his head to reveal the gnarled face. He paused beside a gravestone to offer up a silent prayer. Tuke had inherited the position of churchwarden from his father and he carried out his duties with the same plodding reliability. Reuben Tuke lay six feet beneath the earth now but his son was carrying on the family tradition and, in doing so, he was able to pay his respects daily to the old man whose name was chiselled on the stone slab in front of him. He brushed a layer of frost from the gravestone then strolled on up to the church. No light showed through the stained glass window in the west front. Tuke gave a grunt of satisfaction. He always liked to be the first there.

The parish church of St Christopher stood in a hamlet on the extreme edge of the Silvermere estate, serving two other hamlets, a village and a number of scattered farmsteads. It was a small, squat, undistinguished building that had been kept in good repair throughout the two hundred years of its existence and it had survived intact the religious crises that had afflicted the country for so long. Seating in the nave could accommodate over a hundred parishioners without undue discomfort though long sermons drew attention to the roughness of some of the benches. The chancel was large enough to house double rows of choir stalls that faced each other with wooden solidity. Three wide stone steps led up to the altar rail, three more to the altar itself. Since the tower rose out of the middle of the church, the solitary bell was rung by means of the rope that dangled below the chancel arch and which was secured, at other times, to a hook set into the side of the oak pulpit.

Having let himself into the church, Jared Tuke lit a few candles then started with the preparations. By the time he heard the latch on the vestry click, he had all but finished his work. He was still appraising the altar when the vicar came into the chancel.

'Good morning, Jared,' said the newcomer.

'Good morning,' replied the churchwarden.

'One of these days, I may actually get here before you but I haven't managed it yet. Do you never sleep, man?'

'I've always been an early riser.'

'If only I could say the same!'

Reverend Anthony Dyment was a short, wiry man in his thirties with a pleasant face and an agreeable manner. Wrapped in a thick black cloak, he was still shivering visibly. He blew on his hands then rubbed them hard together. As if realising for the first time where he was, Dyment removed his hat and gave a reverential nod in the direction of the altar. Tuke had not only discarded his hat, he had also taken off his buff jerkin. It made the vicar shiver afresh just to look at him.

'Is everything ready, Jared?' he enquired.

'I think so.'

'Nothing at all left for me to do?'

'Only to perform the ceremony.'

Dyment smiled. 'We'll have you doing that before long. You do everything else.'

'It's my duty,' said Tuke with leaden sincerity.

'No man in the parish is more cognisant of his duty than you.'

Tuke had arrived not long after dawn but the sky had now brightened appreciably and light came in through the windows to supplement the candle flames and to dapple the flagstones. Dyment walked down the aisle to the rear of the nave to stand beside the stone font. Carved into it was a representation of the Lamb of God, curled up beside a cross. The vicar ran a reflective hand around the circumference of the font.

'I hope that the water doesn't freeze in here,' he sighed.

'No chance of that,' said Tuke.

'There's one sure way to make sure that it doesn't.'

He took off his cloak and walked back to the chancel to kneel at the altar rail. Without even thinking, Jared Tuke joined him in prayer. They remained there for several minutes before they were interrupted by the sound of the door being thrown open. Both of them got to their feet at once and swung round to look at the intruder. When the vicar saw who it was, he quailed. The last person he wanted to confront was Reginald Orr. The unexpected visitor was a tall, rugged, clean-shaven man in his forties, dressed in black and glowering with resentment. His voice was like the crack of a whip.

'What's that I see?' he demanded, pointing an accusatory finger.

'Where?' asked the vicar.

'There, man. On the altar behind you. That gold plate.'

'That was a gift from Sir Michael,' explained Dyment,

glancing over his shoulder at the large plate that was propped up on the altar. 'His generosity knows no end.'

'Nor do his Popish inclination. That plate smacks too much of Rome.'

'No, it doesn't,' said Tuke, stung by the claim.

'There's none of the Old Religion here,' added Dyment, vainly attempting to put some firmness into his voice. 'As you'd know, Reginald, if you showed us the courtesy of joining us in worship here.'

'I refuse to take part in Catholic celebrations,' said Orr defiantly.

'We abide by the law of the land and hold only Protestant services here.'

'Then why deck your church out as if you're expecting a visit from the Pope himself? Look at it. Gold plate. A silver crucifix. Gold ornaments. A silk altar cloth embroidered with gold thread and a vestry full of other abominations just waiting to be brought in.' Orr strode purposefully down the aisle. 'The Pope is Antichrist! Spurn him!'

'We do,' said Dyment.

'Not to my satisfaction.'

'Nothing is ever done to your satisfaction, Reginald,' said the vicar, glad that his churchwarden was beside him and even more glad that Orr stopped in his tracks. 'We have talked theology these past couple of years and you'll not be shifted.'

'I follow the true path.'

'There's more than one way to heaven.'

'Yes,' said Tuke, keen to associate himself with the notion. 'There's more than one way to heaven, Reginald

Orr, but I doubt that we'll ever meet you there.'

The visitor bristled with anger and seemed to be about to lunge forward at the churchwarden but Tuke's broad shoulders and brawny arms dissuaded him from intemperate action. Anthony Dyment was never quite sure how to cope with Orr. The man was a zealous Puritan, too scornful of the Anglican service to attend one himself and too intolerant to let others do so in peace. The only time that the man ever came through the door of the church was when he could cause trouble. The vicar braced himself for another argument with his most recalcitrant parishioner.

'I'll have no raised voices in here, Reginald,' he warned. 'This is the Lord's house. Speak with moderation or you must leave.'

Orr curled a lip. 'Do you think I *want* to enter this Romish den?'

'It's the parish church of St Christopher in the county of Essex.'

'Filled with the stink of the Pope.'

'If that's what you believe, why force yourself to come here?'

'Because I need to speak with you.'

'Then you'll have to wait until another time,' said Dyment briskly. 'I have to conduct a service of Holy Baptism in here later on this morning. Jared and I need to prepare the church properly for that. Good day to you, sir.'

'I'll not budge till I get an answer,' warned Orr, folding his arms and spreading his feet. 'Since you're Sir Michael's lackey, you'll be able to give it to me.'

'Don't insult the vicar,' said Tuke sharply.

'I wasn't talking to you, Jared.'

'Show some respect.'

'Let him speak,' said Dyment wearily. 'If that's the only way to get rid of him.'

The Puritan nodded. 'It is, believe me. All I want to know is whether this ugly rumour is true or false?'

'Rumour?'

'They say that a troupe players will soon come to Silvermere.'

'That is so,' conceded the vicar. 'Sir Michael invited them.'

'Have you raised no protest?'

'Why should I?'

'Heavens, man!' exclaimed Orr in horror. 'It's your bounden duty. Do you want a company of vile and despicable actors to befoul this county? Do you want them to stage heathenish plays in which boys disguise themselves as women and do all manner of lewd things? You're not merely vicar of this church. You're chaplain to Sir Michael as well. Use your influence. Make him turn these rogues away.'

'But Sir Michael and Lady Eleanor hold the players in high regard.'

'Theatre is anathema. It corrupts all who touch it.'

'That's a matter of opinion, Reginald.'

Orr was shocked. 'Are you saying that you *condone* this visit?'

'Not entirely,' said Dyment, wilting slightly before the man's pulsing rage. 'But it's not my place to criticise Sir Michael or to tell him whom he can invite to his own home.

It would be a gross intrusion of his privacy.'

'Stop these actors spreading their venomous poison!'

'They're merely coming to entertain the guests at Silvermere.'

'No,' said Orr, raising a finger of doom. 'They're coming to ensnare and defile. Playhouses are steaming pits of inquity. They purvey bawdy, foolery and idolatry. They feed on virginity and sneer at decency. They steal the innocence of children. Actors are born lechers. No woman within ten miles is safe while they are here. Stop them,' he insisted, banging a fist into the palm of the other hand. 'Stop these players from coming anywhere near Silvermere. If you don't do it,' he threatened darkly, 'someone else will.'

Chapter Six

It was well after dawn before he heard the key being inserted in the door. Nicholas Bracewell was waiting. After being roused from his slumber in the night, he had had no further sleep, intent on keeping guard over Davy Stratton whom he had reprimanded as firmly as he dared without waking Owen Elias. Sent back to his own bed, the boy had retreated into a deep sleep. He was still lying there as Nicholas got up and stepped past him to open the door. A servant was walking away along the passageway.

'Wait a moment,' called Nicholas.

'Good morrow, sir,' said the man, turning back.

'We were locked in our room last night.'

'Yes, sir.'

'Why?'

'It's what I was told to do, sir.'

'By whom?'

'The steward, sir.'

'Did he give you a reason?'

'No, sir. Only an order.' He pointed a finger at the neat pile of clothing on the floor. 'Fresh apparel came from Holly Lodge for the boy. I've set it down there.'

'Thank you.'

Nicholas waved him away. Picking up the clothing, he went back into the room to put it beside Davy. There was no point in reproaching a servant for doing something that he had been instructed to do. The matter would have to be taken up with Romball Taylard himself. It was one thing for the guests to be given a key and advised to lock the door from the inside but that is not what happened. Nicholas had been deliberately imprisoned with the others in the room and he wanted to know why. Owen Elias stirred in his bed. He greeted the day with huge yawn then rubbed the sleep out of his eyes.

'Good morrow, Owen,' said Nicholas.

'Are you up already?'

'I wanted to catch the servant when he let me out.'

'What do you mean?' said Elias.

'After we went off to sleep, someone locked the door from the outside.'

The Welshman sat up. 'We were trapped in here? I don't like the sound of that at all. Is this the way they treat their guests?' he asked, his anger building. 'You expect this kind of thing in Newgate or the Marshalsea but not in a private house like Silvermere. A pox on it! This is not hospitality.'

'I'm as annoyed as you are, Owen.'

'Why did Sir Michael want us under lock and key?'

'That's what I'll demand of the steward. This was done at his behest. As it happens,' said Nicholas, looking across at their companion, 'it worked to our advantage. Davy tried to sneak away in the night.'

'Death and damnation!' cried Elias, getting out of bed. 'Let me at him. I'll flay the skin off his buttocks for this.'

'No,' said Nicholas, restraining him. 'That's not the way, Owen. Wait until we are clear of Silvermere. That's the time when we may wheedle the truth out of him.'

'Why wheedle when we can knock it out of his cunning little head?'

'Get dressed. I'll wake the lad and we'll go in search of breakfast.'

But the raised voice of Elias had already brought Davy out of his sleep. Nicholas had made him undress again before he got back into bed. In his crumpled shirt, the boy looked small and defenceless. The boldness that had prompted the attempt at escape had vanished now. Davy was frightened, fearing a further rebuke from Nicholas and more violent castigation from Elias. Avoiding their gaze, he reached for his clothes then saw that fresh apparel had been provided. He began to put it on. Nicholas poured water into the bowl and washed his face and hands before drying them on a piece of cloth. He turned back to Davy.

'Wash yourself before we leave, lad.'

'Yes,' said Davy.

'Do you need to use the chamber pot?'

'No, no.'

'When you do,' warned Elias, 'one of us will hold your

pizzle for you. We're not letting you out of our reach again. Go to the privy and Nick or I go with you.'

Davy swallowed hard and finished dressing. Fifteen minutes later they were clattering along the passageway to the backstairs. When they descended to the kitchen, a servant was waiting to show them to the table and the cook came over take orders from them. The pangs of hunger were too much for the boy to endure and he joined the others in a breakfast of cold turkey pie and bread. The two men drank watered ale but Davy settled for a cup of whey. Nicholas made no mention of events during the night and tried instead to cheer the boy up.

'You'll be back with the other apprentices this afternoon, Davy,' he said.

'I know.'

'How are you getting along with them?'

'I like them well enough,' muttered Davy.

'They'll mock you at first and make you the butt of their jests.'

Davy was rueful. 'Yes. They have.'

'Take no notice of it, lad. That's their way. They did the same to Dick Honeydew when he first joined the company and he's turned out to be the best of them.'

'Dick is a friend,' said the boy, rallying slightly.

'Does he tease you?'

'No. Only the others. I want to see Dick Honeydew again.'

It was the one positive sign that he was ready to go back to London with them to resume his life with Westfield's Men. Nicholas hoped that it was something on which they could build. The meal over, they thanked the cook and were led away by a servant who had retrieved their hats and cloaks for them. They were conducted to the hall. Romball Taylard was hovering patiently by the door to dispatch the visitors.

'Welcome to the day,' he said. 'Did you sleep well?'

'Reasonably well,' said Nicholas tartly, 'but we'd have slept much better if someone hadn't locked us in all night. Why did you arrange that?'

'I thought it needful, sir.'

'Needful!' roared Elias. 'Did you fear that we'd roam around the house in search of drink and women? Hell's teeth! We're grown men. We don't need to be shut away like dangerous animals.'

'I'm sorry if it upset you,' said Taylard calmly.

'Oh, I'm far more than upset.'

'So am I,' added Nicholas, fixing the steward with a stare. 'I think that you owe us an explanation. I can't believe that Sir Michael sanctioned this outrage.'

'No,' admitted Taylard. 'I was not acting on behalf of Sir Michael.'

'This was your invention, then?'

'Not entirely. But I readily agreed to the suggestion when it was put to me.'

'By whom?'

'Master Stratton.'

Nicholas recalled the brief exchange between the steward and the departing father on the previous night. He also understood the reasoning behind the request. To make sure that his son did not abscond from the house Jerome Stratton wanted him securely locked in. Before Nicholas could speak, the steward anticipated his question.

'Why did I not give you the key to lock the door from the inside?' he said. 'The answer is simple. I feared that you might fall deeply asleep and be unaware of someone stealing the key from you.' He glanced at Davy who reddened slightly. 'I apologise for this and take the blame without complaint.'

'Well, I've a complaint or two to make,' growled Elias.

'Another time, Owen,' decided Nicholas, cutting him off with a glance. 'Nothing will be served by hot words and wild accusations at this time in the morning. We've heard an explanation and it must suffice – though I still can't understand why we weren't told what you planned to do.'

Taylard was bland. 'On reflection, that would have been best.'

'Don't you dare play a trick like this on us again,' said Elias with vehemence.

'It was no trick, sir. It had a purpose. Nobody could leave the room.'

'Did you expect that one of us would?' pressed Nicholas.

'Master Stratton felt that it was a possibility.'

'And where did he think his son would go?'

'That's not for me to speculate,' said the steward. 'The salient point is that three of you went into that room last night and all three of you came out again together.'

'How many other occupants of the house were jailed?' said Elias.

'None, sir. This was a special case.'

144

'Dictated by Master Stratton,' observed Nicholas. 'Did Sir Michael know about this? Is he aware that his steward is taking orders from someone outside his house? I venture to suggest that the master of Holly Lodge wouldn't let Sir Michael have a say in the running of his home.' Taylard was faintly discomfited for the first time. 'Do you intend to acquaint Sir Michael with what took place?'

'Sir Michael can't be bothered with every minor detail, sir.'

Elias was enraged. 'Minor detail! Turning three guests into convicted felons?'

'All that I can do,' said Taylard, trying to mollify him with an apologetic smile, 'is to give you my word that nothing like this will ever happen again. When you return next week with the rest of your company, you'll be given the freedom of the cottages, the outbuildings and the grounds. There'll be no hint of incarceration.'

'We'll hold you to that,' said Nicholas sternly.

Continued argument with the steward was pointless. He had instigated something that had fulfilled its function. It prevented Davy's escape. In doing that, Nicholas now saw, Jerome Stratton had given himself away. The merchant's glib explanation of his son's disappearance in the forest was now exposed as a lie. Davy Stratton had fled from his two companions. In making sure that the lad did not escape a second time, the father was admitting that there had been a precedent.

Owen Elias rid himself of some ripe expletives into the steward's ear but Taylard was unruffled. Having weathered the storm of protest, he opened the front door for them to hurry them on their way.

'The office of steward is more lowly than I imagined,' said Nicholas.

Taylard stiffened. 'Lowly?'

'I would have thought you'd risen above such mundane duties as opening doors.'

'Not to mention locking them in the night!' added Elias with asperity.

'I happen to be here as you depart,' said the steward.

'Then be so good as to summon Sir Michael,' ordered Nicholas, adopting a tone he might use to an awkward servant. 'Before we take our leave, we'd like to thank him for his kind hospitality.'

'That's impossible, alas,' said Taylard.

'Why?' asked Elias. 'Is he shooting at wildfowl with cannon ball?'

'No, sir. He's talking to a visitor. The vicar arrived only a moment ago on urgent business. He and Sir Michael must not be disturbed.'

'In that case,' continued Nicholas, determined not to be sent on his way by the supercilious Taylard, 'we'll speak to Lady Eleanor or can you devise a reason why she, too, is unable to bid farewell to her guests?'

The steward hesitated. 'I suppose that I could see if Lady Eleanor is available.'

'I think that you should do that or there may be repercussions. Sir Michael and his wife will be justifiably annoyed if they learn that we left without speaking to either of them. It's common courtesy on our part.' Nicholas gave a gentle smile. 'Why not fetch Lady Eleanor yourself?'

Romball Taylard was saved the trouble of making a reply. Footsteps echoed on the oak floor and two figures came into the hall. Deep in conversation, they did not at first see the group by the front door. Sir Michael Greenleaf had regained more of his dignity now that he had cleaned himself up. His attire was also more appropriate to his position as owner of the estate. One arm around Anthony Dyment, he was clearly fretful. When Sir Michael looked up to see his guests, he brightened at once.

'Ah!' he declared. 'I'm glad that I caught you before you left. Oh, this is my chaplain, Anthony Dyment, by the way,' he said, touching his companion. Nicholas and Elias gave the vicar a nod of acknowledgement. 'I was just telling Anthony what splendid fellows you both were and how much my wife and I are looking forward to the visit of Westfield's Men. Unhappily, our enthusiasm is not shared by everyone, it seems.'

'No, Sir Michael,' said Elias with a meaningful glance at the steward.

'As well as being my chaplain, Anthony is also the vicar of St Christopher's . . .' He broke off as Dyment whispered something to him. 'Of course, of course, Anthony. Leave at once if you have a christening to perform. It was kind of you to postpone it briefly while you rode over here.'

'I felt that I had to speak to you at once, Sir Michael,' said Dyment.

'A wise decision, dear fellow. But away with you.'

Gesturing both farewell and apology, the vicar went swiftly out through the door. Sir Michael turned to the others with his brow furrowed. He shook his head sadly.

'We've encountered a problem,' he told them. 'It's not insurmountable but it's definitely a problem. Anthony is the first to catch wind of it.'

'Of what, Sir Michael?' asked Nicholas.

'Opposition to your arrival.'

'Opposition?'

'I'm afraid so,' said the old man. 'We have a small but active Puritan community nearby and they hold trenchant opinions. One of their number – Reginald Orr – has been a thorn in my flesh for years. Orr can be a confounded nuisance.'

'We fight against Puritan disapproval every day in London,' said Nicholas.

'Then I don't need to explain what an unflattering view they take of actors.'

Elias grinned. 'The kindest thing they call us is "fiends from hell."'

'Reginald Orr will not stop at calling names,' said Sir Michael solemnly. 'And it isn't only Westfield's Men who have aroused his ire. He and I have a long history. As a Justice of the Peace, it's fallen to me to fine him on several occasions for breaches of the peace and to have him twice set in the stocks. He bears grudges.'

'This narrow-minded ninny will not upset us,' said the Welshman airily. 'We're used to such madmen trying to drive us off from the stage.'

'I doubt if you've met someone quite as single-minded as this man,' continued Sir Michael, sucking on his teeth. 'Anthony Dyment was accosted in his church by the rogue this very morning. Reginald Orr issued a direct threat against you.'

'He can surely not object to our visit to a private house,' said Nicholas.

'Oh yes, he can.'

'Will he try to disrupt our performances?'

'Worse than that,' said Sir Michael.

'Worse?'

'I'm afraid so. He's vowed to stop you even reaching Silvermere.'

Having shaken off his mystery illness completely, Lawrence Firethorn was in high spirits as he arrived at Edmund Hoode's lodging. He banged on the door and was admitted by the playwright himself. Hoode looked more harassed than ever.

'Is the fellow here?' asked Firethorn.

'Yes, Lawrence. Since the crack of dawn. His enthusiasm is crippling me.'

'What progress have you made?'

'None at all.'

'What!'

'He's still having second thoughts about decisions we made yesterday.'

'Fire and brimstone!' exclaimed his visitor. 'Let me talk to the villain.'

Followed by Hoode, he went swiftly up the stairs and into the room. Egidius Pye was seated at the table in the window, quill in hand as he crossed something out on a page to replace it with different wording. He gave a chuckle of self-congratulation but it changed to a gurgle when Firethorn loomed over him.

'Good morrow, sir,' said the actor with a cold smile.

'Oh, good morrow, Master Firethorn. This is an unexpected pleasure, sir. We are working well together, as you see. In fact,' he said, indicating the page before him, 'I've just made a significant change in the Prologue.'

'*Again?*' groaned Hoode.

'It's almost finished now.'

Firethorn was horrified. 'You're still dallying with the Prologue?'

'Be glad that we've got this far, Lawrence,' said Hoode. 'Master Pye spent the first hour arguing over the title of the play.'

'Not arguing,' corrected the lawyer. 'Striving to improve, that is all.'

Firethorn glanced down at the Prologue and saw a plethora of alterations. He gritted his teeth. They had been too kind to the apprentice playwright. It was high time to acquaint him forcefully with the realities of life in the theatre. He gathered up the sheaves of parchment and thrust the whole pile into the lawyer's hands.

'Take your play away, sir,' he ordered.

Pye was shocked. 'But why?'

'Because it will not make the journey to Essex with us.'

'But it must, Master Firethorn.'

'When its author is still haggling over the title? Place your witch in Colchester, Rochester, Winchester or York, for all I care! She'll not travel with Westfield's Men.'

'This is unjust.'

'No, Master Pye. It's necessary.'

'But we have a contract,' said the lawyer. 'I'll hold you to that in court. You've agreed to buy and present my play.'

'That's true.'

'Then abide by the terms of the contract.'

'I will,' said Firethorn, 'and all that the contract obliges us to do is to stage your play. No date of performance is given. We may not be able to put it into rehearsal for a year or more. By that time, you may actually have finished improving it.'

Hoode was dubious. 'In a mere year? Allow him a decade at least.'

'But I want it staged now,' whimpered Pye. 'I've set my heart on it.'

'Then you should have been more amenable to correction.'

'I have been. Master Hoode will tell you.'

'He's been far too amenable,' confirmed the playwright. 'Master Pye wants to correct everything. A minute later, he wants to restore the original lines again.'

Firethorn was brutal. 'I've heard enough. Take the piece away.'

'No!' howled Pye. 'Please.'

'You were engaged to work *with* Edmund, not against him.'

'That's what I have been doing, sir.'

'Not to my satisfaction. Thus it stands. We leave for Essex on Monday and your play is still in tatters. How can we do it justice if we do not rehearse it properly? And how can we rehearse it,' he stressed, putting his face close to Pye's, 'unless we have the piece finished. I'm sorry, sir, but we'd wait until Doomsday for you to make up your mind.'

Egidius Pye went silent. He looked down sadly at the sheaf of pages in his hand and contemplated failure. They could see him weighing up the possibilities. Firethorn winked at Hoode. The ruse was working.

'I'm profoundly sorry,' said Pye at length. 'I suppose that I have been taking my time but that comes from my training as a lawyer, sir. Caution is everything.'

'Not on the stage,' asserted Firethorn. 'Boldness is in demand there. Who, in God's name, wants a *cautious* play? We perform in a theatre, Master Pye, not in a church. Our patrons call for action and excitement. They yearn for laughter.'

'I thought that's what I was giving them.'

'It is,' said Hoode, taking a gentler tone with him. 'Your play is bursting at the seams with all it takes to make a fine comedy into an excellent one, Master Pye, but it needs certain changes. And they'll never be made if you insist on disputing every comma and going into battle over the title.'

'Take it away and work on it at your leisure,' advised Firethorn. 'If and when we deem it ready for the stage, we'll perform it to the best of our ability.'

Pye drooped. 'But you said it would be ideal for your visit to Essex.'

'It would be if I could hand it to the scrivener today so that he could begin to copy it out. But that is plainly out of the question. You're too protective of your work,

Master Pye. It happens with all raw playwrights,' he said dismissively. 'They sit over their words like a hen sitting on eggs, pecking everyone who comes near. Words are made to be heard, sir. Eggs are laid to be broken open and eaten.'

The lawyer went off into another long period of meditation. Hoode collected another wink from Firethorn. He was sorry that the actor-manager was forced to take such drastic action but it was the only route open to them. Egidius Pye eventually came around to the suggestion that Firethorn knew he would make.

'There is one remedy,' he said meekly.

'Yes,' agreed Firethorn. 'We perform another play.'

'No, no. You take *The Witch of Colchester*. I endorse the title wholeheartedly and was foolish to question it. And I agree with everything that Master Hoode has said about the piece. His experience far outweighs mine. His instinct is far surer.' He held out the play to Hoode. 'Is there any chance that you might rescue it on your own?'

'That's asking a great deal of Edmund,' said Firethorn with mock seriousness. 'Even he might not be able to make the necessary changes in time.'

'But I was told there wouldn't be many alterations.'

'That's what I hoped, Master Pye,' said Hoode wearily. 'But you kept altering the alterations at every turn until they multiplied out of all recognition.'

'Help me, Master Hoode,' pleaded the lawyer. 'I beg you.'

'It's up to you, Edmund,' said Firethorn. 'I have grave doubts.'

Pye leapt to his feet. 'No, no. Don't say that, please.'

He looked appealingly at Hoode. It was not a commission that the playwright could enjoy. In Pye's position, he would be mortified if someone else took responsibility for making changes to his work but there were mitigating factors. The alterations would not be radical and they had already been agreed in discussion beforehand. What went on stage in *The Witch of Colchester* would be substantially the invention of Egidius Pye and all the credit would go to him. The deciding factor, however, was the one contained in the invitation from Sir Michael Greenleaf. As a condition of their visit, a new play had been requested and the only one available to them was now being held out in the clammy hands of its author. If Hoode did not take on the task of amending it at speed, Westfield's Men would have to cancel their visit and return to the miseries of unemployment. The fate of the whole company had to be set against the blow to one man's pride.

'Well, Edmund?' asked Firethorn. 'What do you say? Will you work through the night to save Master Pye's play or shall we take one of the many other new pieces we have awaiting performance?'

The lawyer winced. His situation took on new pathos. Hoode gave a nod.

'I'll take on the chore,' he agreed.

'Oh, thank you, thank you, sir!' said Pye, thrusting the play into his hands then embracing him so closely that he was hit by a veritable gust of bad breath. 'Change what you will. I have complete faith in you.'

'And I have complete faith in the play,' said Hoode with

sincerity. 'It's just a pity that it comes to us when we cannot afford time to work slowly on it.'

'Begin at once, Edmund,' ordered Firethorn, crossing to open the door. 'I'll pass on the good tidings to the company when we meet this morning.'

'I'll hold you up no longer, Master Hoode,' said Pye, gathering up his satchel. 'I merely want to thank you once again for your kindness. You've true nobility, sir.'

Firethorn hustled him out then shut the door again. He waited until he heard the lawyer going out into the street below then he burst out laughing and clapped his friend hard on the back.

'True nobility, eh?' he said. 'Arise Sir Edmund Hoode.'

'You were too cruel to him, Lawrence.'

'Cruel to him and kind to Westfield's Men. Would you have us lose this golden opportunity?' He laughed again. 'Did you notice the way he jumped when I suggested that we had many other new plays at our disposal?'

'That was the cruellest touch of all.'

'Who cares, man? It worked. Still,' he went on, 'you don't want me to waste your precious time. Every minute is important. We need at least some of the piece in the scrivener's hands today.'

'It will be,' promised Hoode. 'Act One needs little improvement. I simply have to transpose to scenes to achieve more impact. Master Pye accepted that when I pointed it out to him. The long scene with Lord Malady is stronger if it comes last.'

'Which scene is that, Edmund?'

'The one where he has his first illness. You recall it,

Lawrence. Lord Malady is struck down by a mysterious fever. I remember you telling me how much you were looking forward to playing that particular scene.'

Firethorn was pensive. 'I think that I've already done so.'

'You'll milk a lot of humour from the way he collapses in his wife's arms.'

'There was no humour in it, I assure you,' said the actor grimly. 'Remind me, Edmund. I read the play but once so my knowledge of it is less exact than your own. Does not Lord Malady get struck down by a fever that miraculously disappears before the doctor can even medicine him?'

'That's right. Barnaby will your be physician. Doctor Putrid.'

Firethorn thought of the sudden illness that afflicted him and gave a shudder.

'He was called Doctor Whitrow last night,' he murmured.

The return journey was largely uneventful. There were no robbers to evade this time and Davy Stratton made no attempt to escape from them. Instead, he offered them an apology as soon as they left Silvermere and seemed truly penitent. He was riding between the two men, his pony keeping up a brisk trot with the horses.

'I'm sorry if I caused you any concern,' he said. 'It was wrong of me.'

'That's not what I'd call it, lad,' said Owen Elias. 'It was sinful. You worried the life out of us. Why go charging off like that?'

'I couldn't help it.'

'Don't tell us that arrant lie about your pony bolting,' warned Elias, 'because you'd have cried out if that had happened. You were the one who bolted, Davy. We were fretting about you for hours.'

'I was going to come back to you, honestly,' said the boy.

'But why disappear in the first place?' wondered Nicholas Bracewell. 'You weren't acting on impulse. It was deliberate. You took us into that forest in order to shake us off. That was the whole reason for coming to Essex with us, wasn't it?'

'Yes,' admitted Davy.

'Don't you like us?'

'Of course, Master Bracewell.'

Elias glowered. 'You've a peculiar way of showing it.'

'Don't you want to be apprenticed to Westfield's Men?' asked Nicholas.

'Yes,' said Davy without conviction.

'Then why desert us like that?'

'I told you. It was only for a while. I was coming to find you at Silvermere.'

'Where did you go meanwhile?'

The boy shrugged. 'Away.'

'We want a more honest answer than that, Davy,' said Nicholas.

'It's the truth,' insisted Davy. 'I just wanted to be on my own for a while. To get away so that I could think properly. And that story about Hotspur bolting wasn't really a lie,' he said, turning to Elias. 'It may not have been exactly the way my father described it but I was knocked from the saddle later on. It grew dark and I lost my way. When some animal let out a terrible cry, Hotspur was frightened and bolted. The branch of a tree hit me to the ground. That's when I got my bruises.'

'You'd have a few more, if it was left to me,' said Elias.

'What about last night?' resumed Nicholas. 'You were running away again.'

'No,' said Davy.

'It looked like it to me. And your father had anticipated it. That's why he advised that you be locked in the room.'

'I wasn't running away, I promise. I would have come back.'

'From where?'

'I don't know.'

'I think you do, Davy.'

'I just wanted to be alone again, that's all,' explained the boy. 'I would've sneaked back while you and Master Elias were still asleep. You wouldn't have known anything about it.'

'We do now,' said Elias sternly. 'And we don't like it.'

'I'm sorry.'

'It was your fault that we got locked in that bedchamber last night, Davy.'

'Let's forget that, Owen,' said Nicholas, trying to calm his friend. 'If anyone is to blame, it's Master Stratton and he's not here to answer for his actions. His son is back with us, that's the main thing. Davy may have got off to a poor start but he may yet turn out to be worthy apprentice.' He looked at the boy. 'If he puts his mind to it, that is.'

'I'll do my best,' said the boy.

'Make sure that you do, lad. When you joined Westfield's Men, you became part of a family. We're all bonded together. We don't expect anyone to flee from us.'

'I just went away for a short while.'

'To be on your own,' said Nicholas quietly. 'I know. You told us. The question is this. *Why* did you have such an overpowering desire to get away? What was it that you needed to think about?'

'Lots of things.'

'Such as?'

Davy quivered slightly. 'What's going to happen to me.'

The boy looked so small and vulnerable that Nicholas wanted to reach out to comfort him. He saw a hint of genuine despair in Davy's eyes. It did not go unnoticed by Elias. The Welshman became more sympathetic.

'I'll tell you what's going to happen to you, Davy,' he said cheerfully. 'You're going to have the time of your life with Westfield's Men. You'll be taught to sing, dance, fence, fight, use a gesture, play a part and enjoy yourself to the full. It'll be a lot more fun than falling off your pony, I warrant you.'

'We'll look after you,' said Nicholas. 'Have no fear.'

Davy was reassured. 'Thank you,' he said. 'I'm not really afraid.'

As soon as the track widened, they increased their speed to a canter. Conditions for travel had improved. It was noticeably milder and there was no wind. When they stopped at an inn shortly after noon, Nicholas was pleased with the progress they had made. He was even more pleased with the change in Davy Stratton. Having made his apology, the boy wanted to commit himself to Westfield's Men. He talked with interest about the forthcoming visit to Silvermere and pressed for details of the plays that would be staged. By the time they set off on the next part of their journey, they had put the upsets of the previous day firmly behind them.

In spite of its proximity to the capital, Essex was curiously isolated from London. The River Lea and its many courses presented a formidable barrier and the undrained wetlands near the River Thames caused additional problems. Winter came to their aid. Marshland that would have been impassable was now frozen solid, allowing them to pick their way through to firm ground and cut off a mile or two in the process. They crossed the series of bridges at Stratford atte Bow and watched the largest city in England being conjured up ahead of them. Afternoon sun gilded the rooftops and the church spires. The sheer bulk of St Paul's dominated. The Tower was gleaming.

'Not far to go now,' said Nicholas. 'It's good to be back.'

'Yes, Nick,' added Elias with a grin. 'Back home again.'

'I'll go to the Queen's Head to seek out the company there.'

'Look for me later on. I have to return this horse to the lady who loaned it to me and her gratitude may delay me somewhat.' He chuckled with glee. 'That's the best way I know to get rid of saddle sores. The pain will be rubbed delightfully away.'

'What about you, Davy?' asked Nicholas. 'Are you happy to be back?'

Davy Stratton nodded enthusiastically but he said nothing.

A productive day left Lawrence Firethorn glowing with satisfaction. Egidius Pye had been beaten into submission, the rehearsal at the Queen's Head had been excellent and news had arrived from Edmund Hoode that the first two acts of *The Witch of Colchester* were now with the scrivener. Parts had already been assigned and work on the play could begin the following day. Only the sharers had been involved in the rehearsal, the privileged actors who invariably played the major roles. Firethorn adjourned to the taproom with them. He was emptying a cup of Canary wine when he saw Nicholas Bracewell enter.

'Nick, dear friend!' he said, leaping to his feet. 'You come upon your hour.'

'I was hoping to find you still here,' said Nicholas.

'How did you fare in Essex?' asked James Ingram.

'Did they agree to let us stage *Cupid's Folly*?' said Barnaby Gill. 'Sir Michael and his friends deserve to see me at my best.'

'Let the fellow draw breath,' ordered Firethorn. 'And make way for him on that settle, James. Nick has ridden a long way in the service of the company. He deserves a seat and a cup or two of ale.'

Nicholas exchanged greetings with the others and lowered himself on to the oak settle between Ingram and Gill. His drink soon arrived and he sipped it gratefully.

'Where are the others?' asked Firethorn.

'I left Davy with your wife in Shoreditch,' said Nicholas. 'The lad was tired.'

'Margery will have a warm meal ready for him. What of Owen?'

'He's returning his horse to a lady.'

Firethorn laughed. 'That means he'll be riding bareback by now,' he said. 'And why not? Every man to his trade. But let's forget that rampant satyr of a Welshman. Tell us about your visit, Nick? What sort of a place is Silvermere? What sort of man is Sir Michael Greenleaf? Are we truly welcome there?'

'Oh, yes,' said Nicholas. 'We're blessed in every way.'

Tactfully omitting the unpleasant aspects of the visit, he gave them a concise account of what had transpired. They were delighted to hear about the Great Hall in which they would perform and the spectators whom they would entertain. It was only when Nicholas announced the repertoire that had been agreed that he sparked off a dissentient voice. Inevitably, it came from Gill.

'You made no mention of *Cupid's Folly*,' he said sharply.

Nicholas shrugged an apology. 'It had to be left out, I fear,' he explained. 'Only three comedies could be included. Since we are bound to take *The Witch of Colchester*, that only left room for *The Happy Malcontent* and *Double Deceit*. We were not able to please everyone. Sir Michael's wife wanted *Love's Sacrifice* but that, too, was put aside. We've *The Insatiate Duke* and *Vincentio's Revenge* as our tragedies and *Henry the Fifth* to add a little history.'

'In short,' said Firethorn triumphantly, 'the very six plays we chose at the start.'

'I was promised *Cupid's Folly*,' argued Gill.

'Only to shut you up, Barnaby.'

'It's a better play than *Double Deceit*.'

'But too crude and simple for the audience we are likely to find.'

'A rustic comedy would sit happily in a country house.'

'Not in the case of Silvermere,' said Nicholas persuasively. '*Cupid's Folly* would have been my own choice, perhaps, but the Great Hall is not the place to stage it. We could never set up the maypole there and that's essential to the piece. Besides,' he went on, using flattery to placate the actor, 'the play they really wished to see you in was *The Happy Malcontent*. Lady Eleanor could not stop talking about your performance in that. She told me that you had flights of genius.'

Gill smiled. 'It's true that I scale the heights in that,' he said vainly.

'It atones for the way you plumb the depths in other dramas,' teased Firethorn.

'Jealousy does not become you, Lawrence.'

'Oh, I agree. You have a monopoly on that emotion, Barnaby.'

'There's one thing more,' said Nicholas, heading off another row between the two rivals. 'Sir Michael is a scientist and inventor. He's working on a new kind of gunpowder and offered to let us have use of it for our new play. I think I can devise an explosion that will bring us great benefit.'

'So could I,' said Firethorn, grinning provocatively at Gill.

'Mock on, mock on,' said Gill, rising up with dignity. 'I am needed elsewhere.'

'Be early tomorrow, Barnaby. We begin our witchcraft.'

As soon as Gill had left, the others began to drift slowly away. Nicholas was left alone with Firethorn. After calling for more drinks, the actor moved in close to him.

'Now, then, Nick,' he said. 'Let's have the truth.'

'You've heard it already.'

'But not every scrap of it, I fancy. You're holding something back.'

'I am,' confessed Nicholas, 'because I didn't want to disturb the others.'

'Go on.'

'We were set on by highwaymen on the way there.'

Firethorn was alarmed. 'Was anyone injured? Owen? Davy?'

'The only ones who suffered were the rogues themselves. We gave them a few wounds to lick and they didn't stay around to wait for us to return. There were only four of them. When we travel as a company, we'll frighten off twice that number.'

'Is this all that you kept from us?'

'I fear not. We have to contend with two unforeseen problems.'

'What are they?'

'The first goes by the name of Reginald Orr,' explained Nicholas. 'He's a fiery Puritan who is the bane of Sir Michael's life. According to the vicar, this truculent

Christian has somehow heard of our arrival and threatens to repel us.'

'Puritans are always repellent. This is no problem to vex us.'

'It could be. Sir Michael says that the man is desperate.'

'What will he do?' said Firethorn contemptuously. 'Wave banners and hurl insults at us? We've suffered so much of that here at the Queen's Head that we no longer even notice it. Reginald Orr can be discounted. Let the fool rant on.'

'I hope that's the height of his protest,' said Nicholas.

'What's the second problem?'

'A more serious one, alas.'

'Oh?'

'Davy Stratton.'

Space was severely restricted at the house in Old Street and none of the occupants had the luxury of a bedchamber to themselves. Three of the apprentices shared the same bed in a room at the back of the house. The fourth, Richard Honeydew, had been put in with Firethorn's own children but the arrival of Davy Stratton had altered the sleeping arrangements. The two servants were evicted from their room in the attic and moved down to the cellar. Davy found himself sharing the tiny bedchamber under the roof timbers with Honeydew. When they retired for the night, the latter was full of questions.

'Tell me all, Davy,' he urged.

'There's nothing to tell.'

'You rode all the way to Silvermere and back. Something must have happened.'

'We saw the house, slept there overnight and came back.'

Honeydew was disappointed. 'Were there no adventures?'

'None to speak of,' said Davy off-handedly. 'Except for the robbers.'

'Robbers!'

'They tried to attack us but Nicholas Bracewell and Owen Elias beat them off.'

'How exciting!'

'It was over in seconds.'

'Were you frightened, Davy?'

'Not really.'

'I would've been,' admitted the other. 'Will we enjoy it at the house?'

'I think so. The Wizard and his wife are very hospitable.'

'Wizard?'

'That's what they call Sir Michael Greenleaf. He has a laboratory where he does strange experiments. Some people laugh at him for that but he's a kind man and a very generous one. His nickname is the Wizard of Silvermere.'

Honeydew laughed. 'I've never met a Wizard before.'

'You've certainly never met one like Sir Michael.'

Curled up in the same bed, they talked in the darkness until tiredness got the better of Honeydew. When he was sure that his friend was fast asleep, Davy slipped out of bed and moved towards the door. His eyes had grown accustomed to the gloom now and he knew exactly what he was going to do. Opening the door, he left it slightly ajar then reached for the little stool on which he had left his clothes. When he found that, he groped around for the chamber pot.

Richard Honeydew showed a keen interest in his friend's visit to Essex but the other apprentices were more envious, resenting the fact that Davy had gone while they had remained under the watchful eye of Margery Firethorn. Envy was bound to lead to spite. In the short time he had been back, Davy had already been the victim of several jests and a few sly punches but he knew that there would be worse to come. John Tallis was the most likely attacker. He had more cause than either Martin Yeo or Stephen Judd, the other apprentices, to strike out at the newcomer. Davy had dispossessed him. It rankled with Tallis. Only four of the boys were being taken to Silvermere and he was the one to be excluded. Davy Stratton was to blame and Tallis wanted his revenge.

The new apprentice got back silently into bed but remained awake. He did not have long to wait before he heard the telltale sound of a foot on the stair. He also heard a squeaking noise. The footsteps came nearer then paused outside the door. An eye was applied to the gap. Davy lay under the sheets and pretended to be asleep. The nocturnal intruder took one more fatal step. The result was ear-splitting. As he opened the door, John Tallis dislodged both the stool that was balanced upside down on it and the full chamber pot that was cradled within the three legs. Both suddenly landed on his head with astonishing accuracy. Taken by surprise and hurt by the heavy objects, Tallis emitted a yell of pain and fell to the floor, kicking over a small table and releasing the live mouse he had brought to slip down Davy Stratton's neck.

Margery Firethorn was the first to react. She came thundering up the stairs with a lighted candle to see what had caused the commotion. John Tallis was humiliated. Seated on the floor and soaked by the contents of the chamber pot, he rubbed the lump that was already sprouting on his skull and let out a long cry of despair. Margery lifted the candle in the direction of the bed where two pale-faced apprentices were sitting up with surprise.

Davy Stratton spoke with a voice of pure innocence.

'I think that John had an accident,' he said.

Chapter Seven

Notwithstanding its erratic landlord and its many defects, the Queen's Head was the spiritual home of Westfield's Men and they were delighted to be back there, albeit in such adverse conditions. Early rehearsals involving only the sharers had been held in a hired room at the inn but, now that the entire company was assembled, a larger space was required so they steeled themselves against the cold and went out into the deserted yard. Priority was given to *The Witch of Colchester*. The others five plays to be staged at Silvermere were stock dramas from their repertoire, works that needed only a limited amount of rehearsal. Egidius Pye's comedy, however, required the close attention they paid to every new play as they explored its potentialities. Edmund Hoode had worked throughout two whole nights to make the necessary changes to the play and was now able to join the others at the Queen's Head to rehearse his own role in it. While one scrivener hastened to finish a single complete copy of the play, another had copied out the sides for individual actors.

As the book holder, Nicholas Bracewell was the only person who had a copy of the whole play and he marvelled at the way that Hoode transformed it. Fearing that he would interfere and impede, Lawrence Firethorn had banned Pye from the rehearsals but promised him that he could attend its premiere at Silvermere. Nicholas felt sure that the lawyer would be pleased with what he witnessed, relieved to observe that his play was largely intact yet markedly improved by Hoode's deft professional touches. Since it was the last of the six dramas to be presented, *The Witch of Colchester* could be rehearsed throughout their entire stay there, enabling the company to give a confident performance. Actors swooped happily on their parts and went through their scenes with relish. There was none of the insecurity and bickering that usually attended work on a new piece.

Nicholas was thrilled to be back at the helm again. Westfield's Men had come out of their winter hibernation and their joy was touching. Even those hired men who would not be travelling with the company came to watch the rehearsal to warm their hands at the fire of a lively new drama and to share in the general pleasure. Davy Stratton was also there. He made only two fleeting appearances in the play as a servant and spoke only one line but he took it all very seriously. Davy had mixed feelings when he watched the other apprentices, taking the women's roles with such persuasive skill, wondering when he would suffer the indignity of wearing female attire. Absorbed as he was in what was going on, the boy kept a wary eye out for John Tallis, who, ousted and humiliated by the newcomer, was prowling vengefully on the fringes.

At the end of a full day, Firethorn strolled across to the book holder.

'We owe you our thanks, Nick,' he said, patting his shoulder.

'Why?' said Nicholas.

'For reminding us that we had such a splendid new play available.'

'It's even more splendid now that Edmund has worked his magic on it.'

'Yes,' agreed Firethorn with a chuckle, 'but he was not above bowing to self-interest. The role he enlarged most substantially was the one he takes himself, that of Longshaft, the lawyer. Shortshrift, the other lawyer, was given short shrift.'

'They're both excellent parts.'

'There's no dull character in the whole play, Nick, even though it's written by that very personification of dullness, the quibbling Master Pye.'

'Give him his due,' said Nicholas with admiration. 'He has an acute mind.'

'Too acute for Edmund's liking!'

'Don't be harsh on him. Master Pye has many virtues. But you've no need to thank me for recommending his play,' Nicholas continued. 'I stand to benefit from it as much as anyone else. It's a delight to be employed again and to see the happy faces of our fellows. The jollity even seems to have touched Davy at last.'

'Yes,' said Firethorn with reservation in his voice, 'he's acquitted himself well in his tiny role here. I just wish that he didn't cause so many problems under my roof.'

'That incident you told me about was clearly John Tallis's fault. He went up to the attic to give Davy a fright and got one himself instead.'

'Oh, I agree. John Tallis was deservedly baptised by a full chamber pot. But the boyish antics didn't end there, Nick. Our new apprentice has been stirring up trouble on his own account. He baited Martin Yeo, hid Stephen Judd's clothes, swore at one of the servants and stamped on the other's toe.'

'Did your wife remonstrate with him?'

'Only when she finally caught him,' said Firethorn bitterly. 'The little devil did his favourite trick and disappeared. It took Margery an hour to find him.'

'Where was he?'

'On the roof. He'd climbed out through the window.'

'In this weather?' said Nicholas in alarm. 'Frost has made the thatch treacherous. The lad might have fallen and injured himself.'

'I almost wish that he had, Nick. It would have taught him a lesson.'

'Why is Davy being so mischievous?'

'I wish I knew. I warned him that, if it goes on like this, he'll get the thrashing of his young life from Margery. But even that doesn't seem to have stopped the imp.' He sighed wearily. 'Honestly, Nick, I never thought I'd say this but I'm beginning to wish I hadn't taken him in. He's upsetting the whole house.'

Nicholas was surprised. When he looked across at Davy, the apprentice was talking earnestly to Richard Honeydew. There was no hint of devilment in either of them. Davy Stratton, in particular, had an almost angelic expression on his face.

'Let me have a word with him,' volunteered Nicholas.

'Please do,' said Firethorn. 'He has a great respect for you.'

'It didn't stop him abandoning me in the middle of that forest.'

'I'm starting to see why his father was so eager to get rid of the lad. If Davy behaves like that at home, he must be an absolute menace. Margery and I are bracing ourselves for another difficult night with him.'

'Is it that serious?'

'Yes, Nick. Martin, Stephen and John Tallis are all out for his blood and there's no telling what Davy will get up to next.'

Nicholas grew thoughtful. 'Perhaps he needs time away from the house.'

'Either he does or *we* do.'

'How would you feel if he stayed in Bankside for a night or two?'

'Profoundly guilty.'

'Why?'

'Because it would be unfair to inflict Davy on you and Anne.'

'He'll behave himself with us, I'm sure,' said Nicholas. 'Being with the other apprentices is what sets him off. Divide and rule. It's the sensible way.'

'I'd be eternally grateful to you and Anne.'

'I'll have to speak to her first, of course, because it's Anne's house but I don't think she'll object. Besides,' said Nicholas, 'I like Davy. If we spend some time together, I may be able to find out why he's misbehaving so badly like this.'

Further discussion was halted by the arrival of Barnaby Gill who wanted to argue for some changes in his lines and petition for an additional dance in Act Three. Edmund Hoode soon joined the debate. Nicholas took the opportunity to detach the troublesome apprentice from the others.

'Come on, Davy,' he said.

'Where are we going?' asked the boy, trotting across to him.

'To teach you something about taking the company on tour. It's easy enough when we play here at the Queen's Head where we keep our costumes, properties and scenery. If we travel outside London, we have to ensure that we take only what we need.'

'I see.'

'George!' called Nicholas.

'Coming!' replied a voice from within a melee of actors.

'We must check the properties.'

'At once.'

The diminutive figure of George Dart emerged from the group to join them. As assistant stagekeeper, Dart was able and conscientious. As an actor, however, he was intermittently disastrous and, even though shielded by Nicholas, often became the company's whipping boy. The book holder led Dart and Davy off to the room where the properties were stored, drawing a gasp of astonishment from the apprentice when he unlocked the door. Objects of all colour and description were piled high. The place was so crammed with the accumulated properties of Westfield's Men that there was barely enough room for all three of them to enter.

'You can help George,' instructed Nicholas.

'Yes, Master Bracewell,' said Davy.

'And be careful while you're about it. We don't want anything to be damaged.'

'We'll need the small throne for *The Insatiate Duke*,' said Dart, anxious to impress with his knowledge of the plays, 'and the larger one for *Henry the Fifth*.'

'One throne will suffice for both plays,' decided Nicholas. 'It will save space in the cart. King Henry will have to make do with the small throne on this occasion. We'll set it up high for him so that it seems larger than it is.'

George Dart nodded. 'Shall we get it out now?'

'No, we'll work through this list I've prepared. Are you ready, Davy?'

'Yes,' said the boy, staring in horror at a human skull.

'Item, Cupid's bow and quiver; the cloth of the Sun and Moon. Put them out in the passageway for the time being,' said Nicholas, pointing. 'We'll load them into the cart and lock it in the stables for safety.'

Helped by the apprentice, Dart searched for the required items. When they were found, Nicholas consulted the long list that he had so patiently written out, taking care to select items that could serve in more than one play.

'Item, four wooden targets; one breastplate of armour and three foils.' They were swiftly retrieved from the mass of properties. 'Item, one lion skin, one bear skin and one snake.'

'A snake?' said Davy, anxiously. 'Is it a live one?'

'Only when it's on stage in *The Happy Malcontent*,' said Nicholas.

'I don't like snakes.'

'Wait until you see our serpent,' said Dart, finding the items requested. 'It scares me every time even though I know that it's only made out of painted cloth.'

'Item,' continued Nicholas, 'two coffins, a boar's head and a cauldron.'

'What play will they be in?' wondered Davy.

'*The Witch of Colchester*.'

'It's the wildest comedy I know,' said Dart, giggling. 'I could hardly stop laughing when we rehearsed it today.'

'Yes, George,' chided Nicholas, gently, 'you were so busy shaking with mirth that you missed your own entrance. Plays are there to make the spectators laugh, not the actors performing them. Take especial care with that cauldron. It's heavy.'

Locating the cauldron under a wooden canopy and a pile of assorted crowns, they rolled it out into the passageway. Davy was struck by its enormous size.

'What is the witch of Colchester going to put in there?' he said.

'All sorts of things,' replied Nicholas with a smile. 'Herbs, flowers, wine, water, bits of dead animals and any new apprentice who doesn't behave himself properly.'

His light-hearted remark struck home in a way he had not intended. Blushing a bright crimson, Davy let out a cry, backed away in embarrassment then charged quickly out of the room. Nicholas was almost as surprised as the open-mouthed George Dart.

Reginald Orr was not a man to make idle threats or to be deflected from a course of action once he had committed himself to it. Though he was highly respected in the small Puritan community of which he was the acknowledged head, he was privately feared by a number of his sect who felt that his beliefs were too extreme and his inclination to violence very worrying. Nothing seemed to deter Orr, a man sufficiently wealthy to be untroubled by any fines imposed on him and sufficiently robust to withstand being set in the stocks. He lived in a sizeable house on the edge of Stapleford, a meeting hall for his fellow Puritans and, more often than not, their place of worship. Only one person called on him that evening and he was given a most cordial welcome.

'Come in, come in, Isaac,' invited Orr.

'Thank you, Reginald,' said the other, breathless from the long ride.

'Did you find anything out in London?'

'Eventually.'

'Then take a seat and tell me all.'

Isaac Upchard was grateful to slump into the high-backed wooden chair beside the fire. He was a swarthy young man in his early twenties whose ugly features were exaggerated by his habit of grimacing frequently and inappropriately as if in pain.

'It was not a task I could enjoy,' he admitted. 'Like you, I never cross the threshold of an inn but necessity compelled me to lurk at the Queen's Head for hours. It's a foul establishment, Reginald, full of roaring men and lewd women who drank and sported in the most heathen way.'

'Such places should be burnt to the ground,' said Orr.

Upchard nodded in agreement. 'What made it worse for me was that I had to discard the sober attire I wear with such pride and don the kind of clothing that would allow me to enter the inn freely. It was an effort to do so.'

'But not without results, it seems.'

'No. Actors are very talkative. I got close enough to listen.'

'But not close enough to fall in with them, I hope.'

'Oh, no!'

'That would have been a gross error,' warned Orr. 'Apart from the corruption with which you'd have been threatened, there's the question of safety. They mustn't know that you spied on them, Isaac. We don't want any of them recognising you and finding a link to me.'

'I was very discreet,' said Upchard, pulling a face as if suddenly impaled on a sharp spear. 'Luckily, the actors were not. Their boasting filled the whole taproom.'

'What you heard was the voice of the Devil incarnate.'

'That came from the throats of women, Reginald. I've never met such brazen creatures. They made vile suggestions in my ear of a kind that no decent man should ever have to endure. It was an ordeal.'

'I'm sorry that you had to go through with it, my

friend, but the truth is that I could not. Had I been in the middle of such lecherous company, I would've risen up and condemned them in the sternest tones. You, fortunately,' he said, sitting opposite his visitor as the latter produced an alarming series of grimaces, 'were able to control yourself enough to mingle unseen by them. Now, Isaac. Tell me what you discovered.'

'Everything you asked.'

'Good fellow!'

'Westfield's Men will leave London early on Monday morning. They'll be twelve in number with four apprentices besides.' He clicked his tongue in disapproval. 'Young boys, doomed to be dragged down into the mire by their elders.'

'How will they travel?'

'By the main road for most of the way. Then they strike off for Silvermere. Some will ride horses but others will travel with their costumes and scenery on a big cart.'

Orr raised an eyebrow. 'A cart, you say? That may play into our hands.'

'How?'

'I'll explain later. Go on with your tale.'

'I come to the worst part of it, Reginald.'

'In what way?'

'They're due to spend ten days as guests of Sir Michael Greenleaf.'

Orr was scandalised. 'Ten!'

'Excluding the day when they travel.'

'This is intolerable! In ten days, they could infect the whole of Essex. I'll not let them contaminate this beautiful county, Isaac.' He waved an angry fist. 'I'll make them wish they'd never set foot in it.'

'Someone has to do it or we will suffer the consequences.'

'What do you mean?'

'Six plays are to be performed during their stay,' explained Upchard, 'the last being one that was expressly requested by Sir Michael. It's very title will be enough to wound you to the quick. It's called *The Witch of Colchester*.'

'Horror of horrors!' yelled Orr. 'They mean to practice witchcraft?'

'They bragged about nothing else, Reginald. The play contains spells, secret potions and a black boar that is the witch's familiar. It's unspeakable.'

'Are demons represented on the stage?'

'Satan himself is conjured up at one point.'

'Never!' exclaimed Orr, leaping from his seat. 'This is evil of the worst kind and a threat to every Christian soul within miles. We'll allow no hideous witches to fly over our houses to cast their wicked spells. Nor will we let Satan come to Silvermere. I praise you heartily for the work you've done on our behalf, Isaac,' he said, putting a congratulatory hand on the other's shoulder. 'It was an odious task but a valuable one.'

'Had I stayed any longer in their company, I'd have been polluted myself.'

'Profanity and desecration! That's all they bring in this cart of theirs. Well, we'll be ready for them. Sir Michael Greenleaf may wish to give these heathen rogues licence to seduce and corrupt but I'll teach him some moral responsibility. Let's ride out together at first light tomorrow,' he suggested. 'We'll get the lie of the land so that we can devise a fitting welcome for these devils in human guise called Westfield's Men.'

Sunday morning found Anne Hendrik in her parlour, peering into the mirror while she adjusted her hat. Nicholas Bracewell, also dressed to go out, stood behind her.

'I can't tell you how grateful I am,' he said.

'Then don't even try,' she replied, turning to face him. 'I'm glad to have Davy here. After all you've told me about him, I was interested to meet the boy. He certainly doesn't look like the mischief-maker that Lawrence seems to think he is.'

'Davy was on his best behaviour.'

'Only because you frighten him more than Margery Firethorn.'

Nicholas laughed. 'Nobody could spread more terror than her when she's roused. Even her husband runs for cover when Margery starts breathing fire. No, I think that it was you who made the difference, Anne.'

'Me?'

'You were so kind and welcoming to the lad,' he said. 'You didn't stand over him or issue any warnings. Davy didn't feel threatened.'

'I've employed apprentices of my own, remember, Nick. In my experience, the best way to deal with them is to talk to them on their own level. Waving a big stick only makes the weak ones cower and the strong ones rebellious.' She glanced upwards. 'How did Davy sleep?'

'Extremely well. I heard him wheezing contentedly before I dropped off.'

'No attempt to sneak out of the house?'

'None, as far as I know,' said Nicholas. 'And no merry pranks with the other boys. That's one reason he's been so quiet, of course. He's not fighting a constant battle here with John Tallis and his friends. I'm sorry I had to let him share my room with me,' he said, stepping in close to plant an apologetic kiss on her cheek, 'but I wanted to make sure that nothing untoward happened.'

'Nothing untoward happened in my bedchamber, I fear,' she teased.

'The boy's needs came first, Anne.'

'Of course. I appreciate that. It would have been wrong for him to see how close we are when we're not legally married. That's why I went to some pains to treat you like a lodger in front of him.'

It was his turn to tease. 'But that's exactly what I am, isn't it?'

'From time to time.'

'I'll give him a shout. Davy!' he called, moving to the bottom of the stairs. 'Hurry up, lad. We'll be late.'

'One moment!' replied a distant voice.

'At least, he's still in the house,' said Anne.

'Not necessarily,' Nicholas pointed out. 'He could be on the roof.'

Footsteps came tripping down the stairs and Davy Stratton entered the room. There was no sign of strain in him. Nicholas noted how relaxed and happy the boy seemed. After greetings were exchanged, Anne stepped in to straighten his collar for him and to brush aside a few stray hairs that peeped out from under his cap.

'We'll have breakfast when we get back,' she said.

'Yes, Mistress Hendrik.'

'Do you like church, Davy?'

'Sometimes.'

'Do you go regularly at home?'

'Oh, yes,' he said with a rueful smile 'We have to. My father makes sure that we never miss a service on Sundays. Some of the people he does business with also go to St Christopher's.'

'What sort of man is the vicar?' asked Nicholas.

'Reverend Dyment is a devout man.'

'He seemed rather harassed when we met him at Silvermere.'

'He has a lot of trouble from some parishioners.'

'Do they include this infamous Reginald Orr?'

'I think so.'

'Have you met the man yourself, Davy?'

'No, but my father has,' said the boy. 'He had Master Orr arrested.'

'Why?' said Anne.

'For causing a disturbance in the village.'

'It's time to be on our way,' suggested Nicholas as a sonorous bell began to toll in the distance. 'We don't want to be late.'

They let themselves out and walked briskly along the street. The sun was out but it was still decidedly cold. Nicholas hoped that they would not see any more victims of the winter, frozen to death in lanes or alleyways. Several other people were heading towards the church for matins and they joined the swelling congregation. Anne was plainly enjoying Davy's company, chatting easily to him about his home life and making him feel that someone was taking an interest in him. Nicholas could still not understand why the boy had misbehaved so much at Firethorn's house and put it down to the proximity of the other apprentices. Attacking three of the other boys was Davy's form of defence. They had mocked him continuously since his arrival. He could take no more.

'Do you like being with Westfield's Men?' asked Anne.

'Oh, yes,' said Davy. 'I love it at the rehearsals.'

'What sort of an actor do you want to be when you grow up?'

'I want to be like Master Firethorn.'

'Nobody is quite like him, Davy,' said Nicholas, fondly. 'Lawrence Firethorn is the best actor in London. Even his rivals concede that.'

'Then I'll try to be more like Master Gill.'

Anne suppressed a smile. 'He, too, would be very difficult to imitate.'

'But he makes me laugh so,' said Davy, 'and he's a wonderful dancer.'

'You'll learn a lot from simply watching Barnaby Gill,' said Nicholas. 'And the rest of the players, for that matter. Owen Elias is a fine actor. So is Edmund Hoode when he has the right part.'

'What about George Dart?'

'George *tries*. He may never actually succeed, but he never stops trying.'

'Why does everyone make fun of him?'

'Because they don't appreciate him, Davy. George Dart loves the company so much that he'd die for Westfield's Men. Get to know him better,' advised Nicholas. 'In his own quiet way, George has a lot to teach you as well.'

They walked on until the church came into sight. People were converging on it from all directions and they had to slow right down when they reached the porch. As they shuffled forward in the queue, Davy was ahead of them, allowing Nicholas to have a private word with Anne. He leant over to whisper to her.

'I think you've tamed him, Anne.'

'He doesn't seem to need any taming.'

'You should speak to Lawrence Firethorn.'

'Was the boy really that bad?' she said.

'Apparently.'

'I hope that they had a quieter night out in Shoreditch last night.'

'I'm sure that they did,' said Nicholas. 'Without young Davy to set them all by the heels, they'll have had no problems. I expect that they're kneeling down in church at this moment to offer up a prayer to the Almighty for sending them Anne Hendrik.' He gave her a warm smile. 'I intend to do the same thing myself.'

Religion had only an uncertain hold on Lawrence Firethorn. Though he could be seized with Christian zeal on rare occasions, he could also blithely forget some of the Ten Commandments at times and lapse unthinkingly into sinful behaviour without any compunction. Guilt and repentance invariably followed but they were only temporary restraints.

Sunday, however, brought out the spiritual side of him and not merely because his company were unable to play on the Sabbath by virtue of the fact that the Queen's Head was within the city limits. The Theatre and The Curtain, both in Shoreditch, enjoyed the freedom of being outside city jurisdiction and performed regularly on Sundays. Turning his back on his rivals, Firethorn preferred to celebrate it as a day of rest.

Marshalled by his wife, the whole household, ten of them in all, set off for the parish church in strict formation. The apprentices led the way, the children came next, Firethorn and his wife were on their tail and the two servants brought up the rear. They took up a whole bench in the freezing cold knave, squeezing tightly up against each other in the interests of warmth. After he had said his prayers, Firethorn, seated by the aisle, glanced along the row at juvenile faces that were either drawn with fatigue or glazed with boredom. He was content. Order had been restored. The absence of Davy Stratton had allowed the house to resume its quiet, normal, unhurried pace. Margery Firethorn was thinking the same thing.

'Where do you imagine he is now, Lawrence?' she hissed.

'Davy?' he said. 'He's probably making Anne's life a misery.'

'Nick would never allow that.'

'No, Margery. On second thoughts, I think you're right. If anyone can control him, it's Nick. Maybe the fault isn't in Davy at all but in us.'

'Us?' she repeated, bridling. 'Are you criticising me, Lawrence?'

He grinned. 'I'd never dare do that, my love. Least of all in a church.'

'Good.'

'Shoreditch is not the ideal place for Davy to be. That's all I meant. Trapped inside a small house in this dreadful weather where we're all falling over each other. The lad will be fine once we're out on the road.'

'That wasn't what Nick and Owen Elias found.'

'True,' he conceded.

'Davy ran away from them.'

'But he came back in due course.'

'From what you told me, it sounded as if his father dragged him back.'

'That was Nick's feeling.'

'I trust in his instinct, Lawrence. What's to stop the boy vanishing again?'

'Loyalty to the company. He'll soon settle down.'

Margery was sad. 'I hope so. I do so want to like young Davy.'

A hush fell on the congregation as some chords on the organ announced the entrance of the vicar who came walking down the aisle with stately tread to begin the service. Firethorn was involved from the start, nestling into the familiar ritual as into a favourite chair. It was only when the sermon began that his mind wandered. The text was taken from an obscure part of Deuteronomy, the sermon was contradictory rather than explanatory, and it was delivered in such a monotonous drone that it inspired none of the parishioners and eased a few into a blissful slumber.

Lawrence Firethorn was not among the sleepers. In his

mind, he was already at Silvermere, thrilling an audience as Henry the Fifth, working on their emotions as the tragic Vincentio and rendering them helpless with laughter by his portrayal of Lord Malady in *The Witch of Colchester*. The spiritual setting helped to soften his view of the hapless Egidius Pye. The man deserved sympathy. He had written an outstanding play yet had been exiled from its rehearsal. Firethorn wondered if he should have relented and let the lawyer at least watch the piece being slowly put together by the actors. If nothing else, Pye would benefit from the experience. He was still musing on the new play when the vicar reached the climax of his peroration.

'And so,' he declared, eyes raised to heaven, 'when God asks us to open our hearts to him, my friends, what must we answer?'

It was a rhetorical question but it got an instant reply from Firethorn.

'No, no, no!' he howled in despair.

Rising to his feet, he clutched at his body as if in intense pain and staggered out into the aisle. The congregation looked on in horror. Before anyone could catch him, he shivered violently then fell to the floor, seized by such dramatic convulsions that one woman fainted and two had a screaming fit. The vicar was so upset that he had to be helped down from the pulpit by the verger. Firethorn completed his ruination of the sermon with a loud moan of agony that echoed around the church like a death knell. Quite involuntarily, the actor had once again had a remarkable effect on the spectators.

* * *

Word of Lawrence Firethorn's collapse threw the whole company into turmoil. There was no miracle recovery this time. Carried home by neighbours, the actor had been confined to bed with an illness that was way beyond the reach of Doctor Whitrow. All that he had done was to prescribe medicine to ease the pain. Firethorn had grown drowsy and was barely able to keep his eyes open when Nicholas Bracewell, summoned from Bankside, hastened to the house in Shoreditch. Before he fell into a deep sleep, the actor had been insistent that Westfield's Men should depart on the following morning as planned. With or without its motive force, the company had to honour its commitment.

Gloom descended on the actors like a pall. As they gathered at the Queen's Head on Monday morning, they were in a state of disarray. Firethorn was not merely their leader, he was the single biggest reason for the troupe's success. With him, they could outshine any other theatrical company in the land; without him, they were palpably weakened. His absence would take the glow off their welcome at Silvermere. In the new play, in particular, he would be sorely missed. Concealing his own fears, Nicholas tried to fend off questions and still the pessimists.

'When is Lawrence going to join us, Nick?' asked Owen Elias.

'Soon,' said the book holder. 'Very soon.'

'Today? Tomorrow?'

'I can't give you a date, Owen.'

'Is it that serious?' said Hoode.

'He's on the road to recovery Edmund.'

'But he should be on the road to Essex with the rest of us. I know Lawrence. Only plague, palsy or death would keep him away at a time like this. What's wrong with him?'

'He'll be fine,' said Nicholas, raising his voice so that all could hear. 'And he implores you not to be downhearted. We're to go on ahead and he'll follow.'

'Supposing that he doesn't?' said Barnaby Gill, irritably. 'It throws our choice of plays into the melting pot. How can we play *Vincentio's Revenge* without Vincentio? Or *Henry the Fifth* without a king? Changes will have to be made.'

Elias was aghast. 'Surely, *you* don't want to take over those roles, Barnaby?'

'Of course, not,' retorted Gill. 'I recommend that we insert *Cupid's Folly* into the list. *I* carry that piece so Lawrence will not be needed.'

'I've a better idea,' said the Welshman scornfully, 'why not cancel all the plays we chose and give six performances of *Cupid's Folly* instead? Will that content you, Barnaby? Fie in thee!' he exclaimed. 'Lawrence lies sick and all that you can think about is trying to advantage yourself. It's despicable.'

Gill was unmoved. 'It's practical.'

'Practical but unnecessary,' said Nicholas firmly.

'We must have contingency plans, Nicholas.'

'We have them, Master Gill. We leave without him.'

Nicholas clambered up on to the cart to supervise the last of the loading. George Dart and the four apprentices were to travel with him. The rest of the company had brought their own horses except for Owen Elias who had borrowed one from an unnamed lady. Since the husband of the Welshman's earlier benefactor had returned home, Nicholas surmised that he had prevailed upon another of his conquests. It did not matter. The book holder had enough to worry about without speculating on Elias's extraordinary private life. It was the fate of Lawrence Firethorn that dominated Nicholas's thinking. A singularly healthy man had been struck down twice by a mystery illness in less than a week. Whatever was wrong with him?

'It was frightening,' confessed Richard Honeydew, standing beside him.

'Was it?' said Nicholas.

'He stood up in the middle of the sermon and shook all over. I've never heard such a cry of pain. Mistress Firethorn fears that he may die.'

'That's not what she told me,' said the other, anxious to suppress the suggestion. 'She knows her husband better than any of us and assured me that he would be back on his feet in no time at all.'

'The whole congregation prayed for him yesterday.'

'There you are, Dick. That's bound to help his recovery.'

The apprentice was sceptical. 'It hasn't worked so far.'

'Give it time, lad.'

Departures from London were usually occasions of hope tinged with sadness as the members of the company set out on a new adventure, bidding farewell to their wives and children, or their lovers and friends. Emotions of a different kind now prevailed. The shortness of their stay in Essex made for less tearful scenes with their loved ones but there was none of the sense of curiosity with which they invariably set out. A misery verging on despair touched all but a few of them. Instead of delighting in the fact that they were to perform to a select audience in a beautiful country house, they feared that their chances of theatrical triumph had gone before they had even left. Only one thing could have made the scene more depressing and he stepped out of the inn to oblige. Surveying them with hangdog disgust, Alexander Marwood, the egregious landlord who had tried so many times to evict them from his premises, now had the gall to berate them for deserting him and taking a major part of his custom away.

'I deserve better than this!' he said in a voice like a wailing wind. 'What will you find in Essex that I cannot offer you here?'

'Decent beer!' shouted Elias. 'And an audience.'

'Warmer weather will soon come.'

'Yes, Master Marwood, but you'll stay as cold as a block of ice.'

Muted laughter greeted the exchange. The landlord normally provoked scorn and derision among the actors but the sight of him merely depressed them even more on this occasion. He was a symbol of woe, a harbinger of ill fortune. Nicholas decided that it was time to get them on their way, resigned to the fact that he could take them free of the watching Marwood but he couldn't dispel the heaviness in their hearts. After making sure that his passengers and cargo were secure, he got into the driving seat and used the reins to flick the two massive horses into motion. As the cart rumbled noisily across the yard, the rest of the company mounted up and followed it. The clatter of approaching hooves brought them all to a halt. A horse came cantering into the yard before being reined in by its rider. Lawrence Firethorn saluted them with a raised arm and gave a chuckle.

'What's this, you rogues?' he said. 'Do you dare to go without me?'

They had rested at a wayside inn several miles out of London before Nicholas had the chance of a private word with him. Until then, Firethorn had concentrated on trying to reassure his fellows, talking enthusiastically about the performances that lay ahead of them and shrugging off suggestions that he had been seriously ill. Though the apprentices had reported him incapacitated when they left the house earlier, he maintained that he awoke refreshed and restored. He had even claimed that his seizure during the church service was partly a protest against the sustained boredom of the sermon. The actors gradually relaxed, pleased that he was back with them in such patent good health. When they paused at the inn, Firethorn was in such a benevolent mood that he bought them all food and drink at his own expense.

It was only Nicholas Bracewell in whom he really confided the truth.

'Thank you for coming so promptly last night, Nick,' he said.

'It was the least I could do.'

'I'm sorry that I couldn't stay awake longer.'

'So was I,' admitted Nicholas. 'It's so unlike you.'

'I know, I know. I can carouse until dawn as a rule. But not yesterday, as you saw for yourself. I felt as if I just wanted to curl up and go to sleep for a whole month.'

'Why?'

'That's what I want to talk to you about.'

Claiming that he wanted to discuss some aspects of staging the plays, Firethorn had detached the book holder from the others. They sat at a table in the corner. The actor did not want anyone else to guess at his predicament. Seen in profile by the others, he appeared a happy man, talking business with a colleague, and he deliberately peppered his conversation with animated movement and laughter in order to deceive those who might be watching. The substance of his confession was far from comical.

'I'm terrified, Nick,' he said.

'Are you?'

'Can't you see what's happening?'

'Yes,' said Nicholas. 'You've made another wonderful recovery.'

'But from what? Doctor Whitrow didn't have a clue what brought me down this time. Nor did he really explain what prompted that terrible fever last week. The doctor was worse than useless yesterday.'

'He gave you that sleeping draught.'

'That was no cure, Nick. It merely eased the pain so that I was no longer lying there on the rack. When I first woke up, I still felt desperately ill.'

Nicholas was anxious. 'What, then, revived you?'

'I've no idea. The sickness just vanished as if it had never been there. Margery insisted that I stay in bed while she called the doctor but I knew how worried everybody would be by my absence. They needing cheering up,' he said, looking around to distribute a warm grin among the others, 'and so did I.' He turned back to Nicholas. 'You know who's behind all this, don't you?'

'Who?'

'Egidius Pye.'

'That's an absurd idea,' said Nicholas.

'Is it? Have you ever met a man as robust as me?'

'No, I suppose not.'

'Have you ever seen one with the same energy, the same commitment, the same burning love for the theatre and all that goes with it?'

'I don't believe that I could.'

'Then where did it all disappear yesterday? Why did I succumb to that fever last week? These are not natural happenings, Nick.'

'Then what are they?'

Firethorn spoke in a whisper. 'Witchcraft.'

'I didn't think that you believed in such things.'

'I didn't until this happened to me,' agreed the other, 'but I've changed my mind now. I've had to. Remember *The Witch of Colchester*.'

'That's only a play.'

'I wonder. It's turning out to be more of a prophecy.'

'In what way?'

'What happens to Lord Malady when his enemy decides to attack him?'

'A spell is cast and he's . . .' Nicholas paused as he heard what he was saying.

'Go on. Finish your sentence.'

'A spell is cast and he suffers this strange illness. A high fever.'

'Just like the one I had.'

'When he recovers from that,' said Nicholas, going through the play in his mind, 'he upsets Sir Roderick Lawless again and is struck down by a more serious complaint.'

'Just as I was.'

'But there can't possibly be a connection,' argued Nicholas. '*The Witch of Colchester* is no more than a series of words on a page.'

'So is a spell.'

'I put the whole thing down to coincidence.'

'If only *I* could do that, Nick,' sighed the other, 'but I can't. Everything that happens to Lord Malady has so far happened to me. My fear is that there's more to come. What about that scene where my character loses his voice completely?'

'Only for comic effect.'

'It may be comical on stage but it would be a catastrophe off it. This is Pye's revenge,' he said darkly. 'Because I didn't let him watch the rehearsals, he's getting his own back on me by means of a spell.'

'That's ridiculous. Nobody is more eager to see that play acted well on the stage than Master Pye. Why should he disable the one man capable of doing justice to the role of Lord Malady? No,' insisted Nicholas, 'you can rule out the author here and now. He's a kind, gentle, benign fellow.'

'With a passion for witchcraft.'

'Well, yes, that's true.'

'My opinion is that the kind, gentle, benign Egidius Pye has powers over which he has no control. In the act of writing that play, he cast an unintended spell and I'm its principal victim.'

'You're its only victim,' Nicholas reminded him. 'If the play has such danger lurking in it, why wasn't Edmund struck down as well? He's actually amended some of its words and scenes. If anyone would be likely to suffer, it would be him.'

'Edmund Hoode is not a character in the play, Lord Malady is. And I, alas, have agreed to take the role. That means there's more agony in store for me.'

'I beg leave to doubt that.'

'It's as plain as a pikestaff, Nick. I regret I ever agreed to play the part.'

'If you're so worried about it, why not assign it to someone else? Owen, perhaps. He'd lack your fire but he'd be a convincing Lord Malady.'

'No,' said Firethorn bravely. 'I'll not give in. In any case, I love Owen too much to foist a Malady on him that might bring a string of maladies in its wake. All I ask you is this, Nick. Watch over me. If anything happens, call no doctor. Just look to the play. It will be positive proof of what I claim.'

'And what's that?'

'I'm bewitched.'

They were over half a mile away when Isaac Upchard saw them. Swinging his horse round, he galloped back to the place where Reginald Orr was waiting for him. Both men had divested themselves of their Puritan attire to wear nondescript doublet and hose. Orr was breathing hard and resting on an axe.

'They're coming,' warned Upchard.

'How fast?'

'At a walking pace. We've time to finish here.'

'Take over, Isaac,' panted Orr. 'It's almost done.'

Upchard dismounted and took the axe from him. While Orr tethered both horses in the safety of a nearby copse, the young man swung the implement with precision, cutting into the trunk of a tree all but ready to fall. As the last few chips of wood went spinning in the air, there was a loud creak. Upchard pushed hard against the trunk with the flat of his hand then leapt back quickly as the tree was toppled, crashing down across the track and making it impossible for anyone to pass. The two men withdrew to the safety of the copse to watch unseen. Sheaves of dry hay lay at their feet.

It took some time before the little cavalcade came round the bend and started to descend the slight gradient. Driven by Nicholas Bracewell, the cart was leading the way with Lawrence Firethorn and the others riding in pairs behind it. Unaware of what lay ahead of them, they were all chatting happily. It was only when they came right around the bend that they saw the obstacle ahead of them. Nicholas pulled hard on the reins to stop the horses but he was too late. They had already walked past the trap. The hole that Orr and Upchard had dug with such difficulty in the bone hard earth had been covered with branches to conceal it. One of the cartwheels rolled on to the scattered branches and they gave way at once, dropping the wheel so deep into the hole that the cart lurched over at an angle and shed half its cargo and most of its occupants. Bruised apprentices cried in pain as Nicholas struggled to control the neighing horses.

There was more to come. With their way ahead blocked and their cart disabled, Westfield's Men were confronted with another problem. Someone came out of the copse and used a pitch fork to toss sheaves of burning hay at the visitors. Fire seemed to be raining from the sky. Horses reared, men yelled, boys cried and the cartwheel in the hole decided to part company with the axle, sending the remainder of its load on to the ground. The two Puritans rode away in high spirits. They were well pleased with their work. No plays would now pollute their county. Firmly repulsed, Westfield's Men would slink back to London with their tails between their legs.

Chapter Eight

Panic reigned for several minutes. With their road blocked, their horses bucking wildly, their cart disabled and its occupants all thrown to the ground, and their retreat cut off by sheaves of blazing hay, Westfield's Men were utterly confused. The boys cried, Firethorn roared and the animals became even more crazed. Nicholas Bracewell was the first to recover. Tossed from his seat on the wagon when the axle broke, he hit the ground and did a somersault before coming to a halt beside the howling Davy Stratton. He gave the boy a reassuring pat before leaping to his feet to take stock of the situation. Edmund Hoode was having enormous difficulty staying in the saddle as his horse reared madly. Nicholas ran over to grab the reins, holding on until the animal was brought sufficiently under control for Hoode to be able to dismount. The playwright took hold of the reins himself so that Nicholas was free to lend help elsewhere.

Fire was the chief problem. Nobody was actually burnt by the flames but they were causing havoc among the horses. Nicholas ran to the fallen tree, snapped off a branch and used it to beat out the nearest fire. Owen Elias followed his example, jumping down from the saddle, tethering his horse to the cart and snapping off a branch of his own. The hay burnt fiercely but only for a short while. The book holder and the Welshman soon tamed the little circle of fires, stamping out the last of the flames with their feet to leave piles of smoking debris in their wake. The crisis was over. Noise subsided, horses were calmed, apprentices were back on their feet and it was possible to take a proper inventory of the damage.

They had been fortunate. Cuts and bruises had been sustained by all who had been hurled to the ground and George Dart had acquired a spectacular black eye but there were no bad injuries. The company was more shocked than hurt. Several of the properties and some of the scenery had been damaged when flung from the cart but nothing was beyond repair. It was Barnaby Gill's dignity that had been most seriously wounded.

'Is this the kind of welcome we receive in Essex?' he said, surveying the scene with bulging eyes. 'I'll no more of it. I say that we should turn back immediately.'

'Never!' yelled Firethorn, silencing the few murmurs of assent. 'A silly jest is not going to stop us fulfilling our obligations.'

'This is more than a jest, Lawrence,' retorted Gill. 'I might have been killed.'

'No,' insisted Nicholas. 'This was meant to frighten us

away rather than to harm us. Swords or stones would have been used if someone really intended to kill some of us. This was simply a warning.'

'And one that we'll ignore,' insisted Firethorn.

'The best place to ignore it is back in London,' said Gill.

'That would be cowardice, Barnaby.'

'I call it plain common sense.'

'So do I,' intervened Nicholas, keen to stifle the argument. 'Since Master Gill feels threatened by this incident, let him return to the safety of London on his own. We shall miss his genius but there are others in the company who can take over the roles that he vacates. Meanwhile,' he went on, looking around the others, 'the rest of us will ride on to Silvermere where a more cordial reception than this is guaranteed.'

Gill was outraged. 'Someone else will steal my roles?'

'Only until you are ready to rejoin us.'

'I forbid anyone to touch Doctor Blackthought in *The Happy Malcontent*.'

'Somebody must if you desert us, Master Gill,' said Nicholas.

'Yes,' said Elias, realising the book holder's stratagem. 'It's a part I've always coveted, Barnaby. I'll keep it warm for you while you sneak back to London.'

'No!' shouted Gill, horrified at the notion. 'I'll not let you near the role. Besides, how could you play anything at Silvermere when you'll not even get there? This tree is blocking your way completely.'

'It can easily be moved,' explained Nicholas. 'We'll unhitch the horses from the cart and let them drag the tree clear.'

'But our cart is broken. Without that, we have no scenery, costumes or property.'

Nicholas inspected the damage. 'The axle is sound. It's only the wheel that needs to be repaired and that is not beyond our ability.'

'No,' said Firethorn, dismounting from his horse, 'that's a task I'll take upon myself. I was raised in a blacksmith's forge and watched my father prove himself an able cartwright on many an occasion.' He rubbed his hands. 'Let's see if my own skills are still in good order.'

'Are you still here, Barnaby?' teased Elias. 'I thought you were fleeing?'

'We were attacked, Owen,' replied Gill. 'Our lives were in danger. How can you pretend that nothing has happened?'

'Because that's the only way to get our revenge on whoever laid this ambush.'

'And who was that?'

'We'll find out,' said Nicholas, guessing who had tried to scare them away but not wishing to discuss the matter in front of the whole company. 'Meanwhile, there's work to do here for those of us who mean to go on.'

'Yes,' added Firethorn, hands on hips, 'let those who wish to turn their back on us in our hour of need, depart now with my curse upon them. We've suffered worse setbacks than this and always come through. So, my friends, either show loyalty to Westfield's Men and stay or take your miserable carcasses out of my sight.'

Everyone turned expectantly to Gill. Seeing that he had no support, he began to bluster but quickly gave up.

He eventually got down from his horse to indicate that he would stay. Nicholas took charge at once, organising people to gather up the scattered contents of the cart while he unhitched the two horses and, with the aid of ropes, got them to drag the heavy tree aside. Firethorn, meanwhile, addressed the problem of the broken wheel, using the tools they always took with them when on tour and displaying the skills picked up in his father's forge. When the apprentices had gathered wood, Nicholas lit a fire to keep up their spirits then suggested that the actor-musicians might take out their instruments to play some cheerful dances. The shock of the ambush was slowly wearing off. Even the irritable Barnaby Gill was soothed. A sense of camaraderie returned.

Nicholas went off with Elias to search the copse in which their attackers had hidden. The ground was too hard to show hoof prints but they suspected that their assailants had been few in number. Wisps of hay beside a tree showed where the men had concealed themselves to light their sheaves. Broken branches suggested the route they had taken for their hasty departure. It was far too late to pursue them.

'Who the hell were they, Nick?' asked Elias.

'I think we can put a name to one of them, Owen.'

'Can we?'

'Yes,' said Nicholas. 'The person Sir Michael warned us about. Reginald Orr.'

'That malignant Puritan?'

'I believe so.'

Elias was scornful. 'A man of God resorting to violence?'

'I have the feeling that this particular man of God will

go to any extremes,' said Nicholas. 'Actors are vermin in his opinion. They must be put down.'

'Well, he'll have to try a lot harder to put *me* down.'

'Orr doesn't know that yet. He probably thinks he's sent us running all the way back to London. When he learns that we've reached Silvermere and mean to present our plays, he may try to strike at us again.'

'Unless we cut the villain to ribbons first!'

'We need proof before we can accost Reginald Orr,' said Nicholas, 'and we've none at the moment. Until we find some, we must stay our hands.'

'It *has* to be him, Nick,' argued Elias. 'Who else could it be?'

'I don't know. It certainly wasn't a gang of robbers or they'd have closed in when they had us in disarray. No, this ambush was planned, Owen. Somebody knew that we'd be travelling along the road today. Digging that hole and chopping down that tree took time and energy. Nobody would go to such pains unless they were absolutely certain to catch their prey.'

'So what do we do now?'

'Go back to the others to help repair the cart.'

'And then?'

'You can drive it the rest of the way,' decided Nicholas. 'I'll ride on ahead to make sure that there are no more unpleasant surprises awaiting us. I'll take young Davy with me. His short cut through the forest will save us valuable time.'

'As long as he doesn't run off again.'

'Davy won't do that, Owen.'

'Why not?'

'Because he's been too frightened by this ambush. With enemies lurking about, he won't dare to go off on his own.'

They came out of the trees and strolled back towards the others. Westfield's Men had recovered their high spirits. Those who were sorting out the cargo were exchanging merry banter, the remainder were warming themselves at the fire and enjoying the sprightly music that was now being played. Ashamed of his earlier response, Barnaby Gill was declaring his commitment to the company by executing one of his jigs for the amusement of the apprentices. Firethorn was swinging a hammer rhythmically as he worked on the cartwheel, Hoode was rehearsing his lines from *The Witch of Colchester*. The troupe looked less like victims of an ambush than contented travellers who had deliberately made camp beside the road.

Elias was heartened and Nicholas was deeply touched by what he saw.

'They won't stop Westfield's Men,' said the latter, 'whatever they do.'

Sir Michael Greenleaf seemed impervious to the cold. Even though he had taken the precaution of wrapping a cloak around his shoulders, Romball Taylard gave an occasional shiver but his master was untroubled by the low temperature and the gusting wind. The two men were on the top of the tower at Silvermere. Instead of training his telescope on the sky, however, Sir Michael was scanning the horizon in the falling light for signs of his visitors. He stood back and shook his head in dismay.

'There's no sign of them, Romball,' he said dejectedly.

'Perhaps they're not coming today, Sir Michael.'

'They promised faithfully that they would and I take Nicholas Bracewell to be a man of his word. Heavens, they're due to stage their first play tomorrow evening. What am I to tell my guests if I have no theatre company to set before them?'

'Westfield's Men may still arrive today,' said Taylard.

'But they should have been here hours ago.'

'They may have got lost on their way.'

'When they have Nicholas Bracewell and Owen Elias to guide them? I doubt that they've gone astray, Romball. They have Davy Stratton with them, remember. He knows this part of the county as well as anyone.'

'We're assuming that they'll bring the boy, Sir Michael.'

'Oh, they must,' said the old man. 'His father will be in the audience.'

'That's true.'

'Jerome Stratton would be mortified if he did not at least see a glimpse of his son on the stage as Davy sets out on his new career. He's an intelligent lad and may turn out to be a splendid actor.'

'I'm not sure that actors need great intelligence,' opined the steward with the merest hint of contempt. 'They seem to come from all walks of life, with little or no education in some cases. Look at that Welshman who came here.'

'Owen Elias? A brilliant actor, according to my wife.'

'But clearly no graduate of a university.'

Sir Michael laughed. 'Neither am I, Romball,' he said with delight, 'yet I've discovered things that have eluded the most learned men of science at Oxford and Cambridge.

Which of them have my dedication and range of interests? Or, for that matter, my artistic inclinations for, though science is my first love, I don't neglect the arts. It's not only Lady Eleanor who wanted the players here.'

'I appreciate that, Sir Michael.'

'I, too, am an admirer of histrionic skills. Even if you are not.'

Taylard stiffened. 'Me?'

'Come, Romball,' said the other. 'You don't need to dissemble in front of me. For reasons that I can't quite understand, you resent the arrival of Westfield's Men.'

'I deny that charge strongly, Sir Michael.'

'I sense your opposition.'

'It's not for me to approve or disapprove,' said the other smoothly. 'As your steward, I merely carry out your wishes without subjecting them to any kind of moral judgement. My pleasure comes from serving you and Lady Eleanor.'

'Nobody could do it better. What other man would stand on top of a tower in the freezing cold just to keep me company? And there's probably not another steward in England who would put up with the explosions from my cannon and the stench of chemicals from my laboratory. But you've been here too long for me not to get an idea of your own feelings,' said Sir Michael with a wry smile. 'Deny it if you will, I still believe that you have reservations about our visitors from London.'

'I have only one, Sir Michael,' admitted the other, 'and it's nothing whatsoever to do with the actors themselves. It concerns you and Lady Eleanor.'

'In what way?'

'That's already been demonstrated. When you allow plays to be staged at Silvermere, you also invite trouble. The vicar gave you fair warning of it.'

Sir Michael sighed. 'The notorious Reginald Orr.'

'I would hate him to cause any more trouble for you, Sir Michael.'

'Nor shall he, Romball. That turbulent Christian will not be allowed anywhere near the house. Have no fears on our account.'

'I'll instruct everyone to remain vigilant.'

'Yes,' said Sir Michael with a sparkle in his eye, 'and if you still think we're going to be invaded by an army of wild Puritans, you can even mount a man up here to keep watch through my telescope.'

Taylard gave a rare smile. 'There's nobody I dislike enough to put him up here in this weather, Sir Michael.'

'I think it's quite mild today.'

'The lake is still frozen.'

'It won't be when I find a way to smash the ice with cannon balls.'

'Why not leave that task to the servants?' advised the other.

'When science can save them the trouble? It's merely a question of getting the right balance of ingredients in my gunpowder. There's still too much sulphur.' He peered anxiously through the telescope again. 'Wherever can they be?'

'They're obviously not coming, Sir Michael.'

'It will soon be too dark to see anything.'

'Could I suggest that we go back inside the house?'

'We might as well,' agreed the other, giving up. 'We're wasting our time up here. Wait a moment!' he said as Taylard headed for the door. 'Someone's coming.'

'Where?' The steward looked down at the drive below. 'I see nothing.'

'That's because your eyes are not trained like mine. Look over to the left.'

Moving to the edge of the parapet, Taylard shifted his gaze towards the western end of the estate. Figures were slowly coming out of the gloom like so many apparitions. Two riders led the way, followed by a cart and a succession of other riders. Sir Michael was so delighted that he began to wave excitedly at the newcomers even though they could not possibly see him behind the parapet. The steward gritted his teeth and made an effort to sound pleased.

'What a relief!' he said. 'Shall we go down to welcome them?'

Wearied by the delay and worn down by the long ride, Westfield's Men were revived by the sight of Silvermere rising out of the twilight to greet them. The promise of food and shelter even brought a smile to the face of Barnaby Gill. Nicholas Bracewell was at the head of the procession with Davy Stratton. Lawrence Firethorn rode up to join them so that he could introduce his company. Lady Eleanor was the first person to come sweeping out of the house but her husband soon joined her to add his salutations. Firethorn doffed his cap and gave them a token bow from the saddle.

'Westfield's Men are at your service,' he said. 'I am Lawrence Firethorn.'

'We expected you earlier, Master Firethorn,' said Lady Eleanor.

'An unforeseen problem that I'll discuss with you later.'

'Then do so in warmth and comfort, sir,' urged Sir Michael, flapping about at his wife's side. 'Bring the whole company into the house for the time being. The ostlers will look after the horses and take care of your cart. We have a meal awaiting you.'

A spontaneous cheer went up from the company. It was several hours since they had last eaten and the cold was getting into their bones. To be offered such hospitality at Silvermere helped to erase the memory of the ambush that had held them up for so long. A servant led them into the house and along to the kitchen. Nicholas stepped into the hall and saw Romball Taylard standing impassively in a corner. The steward gave him a polite nod. When the rest of the company had gone, Nicholas introduced Firethorn properly to their hosts. The actor gave them a respectful bow.

'We're sorry to keep you waiting,' he said, raising his shoulders in apology, 'but we were attacked on the way here.'

'Dear God!' exclaimed Lady Eleanor. 'Highwaymen?'

'We think not.'

'Was anyone hurt?'

'Happily, no, Lady Eleanor.'

'Then who set upon you?' asked Sir Michael.

'I'll let Nick tell you the tale.'

Taking his cue, Nicholas gave an abbreviated account of what had happened, deliberately playing down the hysteria caused by the ambush. His tentative identification of their attackers was endorsed by Sir Michael Greenleaf.

'It sounds like Reginald Orr's work,' he said without hesitation.

Lady Eleanor was vengeful. 'The man should be put behind bars.'

'He will be, my dear, if we can find evidence to convict him.'

'The main thing is that we got here,' said Firethorn. 'And what a wonderful arena for our art. I cannot tell you how overwhelmed we are with gratitude that you sought fit to invite Westfield's Men to entertain you.'

'It's we who are grateful,' said Lady Eleanor. 'I just wish that your journey here had not been spoilt by this dreadful incident.'

Firethorn flicked a hand. 'A mere distraction, Lady Eleanor. A thousand Reginald Orrs would not prevent us from getting here to honour our engagement. Amongst others,' he said, striking a martial pose, 'I play the role of Henry the Fifth. It will take more than a fallen tree and a few sheaves of blazing hay to deter the hero of Agincourt. Then we have Nick Bracewell here who has been around the world with Drake. Nobody is going to stop a man of his mettle from travelling the much shorter distance from London to Essex.'

'Reginald Orr will be dealt with,' said Sir Michael.

'Unless, of course, it was someone else entirely,' said Nicholas.

His host was adamant. 'It was either Orr himself or some confederates set on by him. He has too much influence

212

over the weaker vessels in his circle. I can only tender my apologies once more. I do hope that it will in no way hinder the performance here tomorrow evening.'

'No question of that,' boomed Firethorn. '*Double Deceit* will make Silvermere ring with laughter. We've arrived safely at our destination and we mean to make a lasting impression on you and your guests.'

Sir Michael beamed, his wife smiled graciously at Firethorn and the actor lapped up their admiration like a cat with a pail of cream at his disposal. Pleased with their reception, Nicholas watched Romball Taylard out of the corner of his eye. Their hosts might fawn over the star of Westfield's Men but the steward took a less favourable view of him. There was such studied hostility in the man's eyes that Nicholas began to wonder if he had been party to the ambush. He turned to answer a question from Lady Eleanor then let Firethorn take over once more. When Nicholas next tried to peep at Taylard, the man had vanished as if he had never been there.

'Do something about him, Michael!' instructed his wife. 'Arrest the man.'

'When enough evidence has been gathered,' he said cautiously.

'Reginald Orr is a menace.'

'He did swear to stop us reaching Silvermere,' Nicholas reminded them. 'What is he going to do when he realises that he failed, Sir Michael? Is he the kind of person who will try to attack us again?'

'Alas, yes,' said Sir Michael. 'Again and again and again.'

* * *

Jared Tuke was a practical man who did not stand on ceremony. When a funeral was to take place at St Christopher's, the gravedigger who was invariably employed was the experienced Nathaniel Kytchen. However, since it was Kytchen himself who had now died, another pair of strong arms had to perform the office and Tuke took it willingly upon himself. He and the deceased had been good friends over the years and he felt a sense of personal obligation. The work was punishing. Frozen earth had to be split with a pick before he could use a spade to any effect. Even on such a wintry morning, Tuke was running with sweat as he stood waist high in the grave. The arrival of Anthony Dyment gave him an excuse to pause.

'How are you getting on, Jared?' asked the vicar.

'Slowly.'

'Not far to go now.'

'Oh, there is,' said Tuke solemnly. 'Nathaniel always went down at least six feet. He'll get no less for his own burial place.'

'As long as the grave is ready for tomorrow.'

'It will be.'

'We shall miss Nathaniel. Who will take over his duties in future?'

'I'll find someone.'

The laconic Tuke used the back of his arm to rub the glistening sweat from his brow. His clothing was soiled, his face reddened by effort. Dyment had a few parish matters to discuss with the churchwarden but decided to postpone them to a time when they were in more appropriate surroundings. The vicar had respected Nathaniel Kytchen but found the old man coarse and unpredictable. Tuke, on the other hand, liked the outspoken gravedigger and would feel aggrieved if he had to talk about the projected repair to the church roof while up to his waist in the grave of a close friend. The vicar was about to take his leave when a figure loomed up out of the gravestones.

'Good morrow!' said Reginald Orr, pointing to the new grave. 'Is that for Nathaniel Kytchen?'

'It is, Reginald,' said the vicar.

'Dig a dozen or so more while you're at it, Jared,' urged the Puritan with a grin. 'We can bury Westfield's Men at the same time.'

'But they're not dead.'

'They are to all intents and purposes.'

'You're not wanted here,' said Tuke, gruffly.

'Except on Sundays,' added Dyment, 'when we never see you.'

'I celebrate the Sabbath elsewhere.'

'You'll be up before the church court again for not attending.'

Orr gave a mocking smile. 'What will they do? Excommunicate me once more? Eviction from a church that I don't believe in is no punishment to me. It's a blessed release. Unless, of course,' he said warningly, 'you'd like me there to comment on the errors in your sermon?'

'There *are* no errors,' said Dyment bravely. 'It's you who are at fault.'

'You wish to talk theology now?'

'No, no. I have parish matters to attend to, Reginald.'

'What is more important in this parish than praising God in the proper way?'

'We do that already.'

'Not in my opinion.'

'That's well known,' grunted Tuke, hauling himself out of the grave. 'Your opinions are leading others astray. They, too, will face the court.'

'Threaten and fine us all you wish,' challenged Orr, 'it will not shift us from our beliefs. God needs no fine churches filled with heathenish idols. Simplicity is the virtue that He appreciates.'

'Simplicity is for simpletons,' said the churchwarden, making a unique excursion into humour. 'Reverend Dyment is our vicar and he practices the true religion.'

'Thank you, Jared,' said Dyment.

Grateful that he had the support of his churchwarden, the vicar was also secretly relieved that Orr no longer attended church. On the last occasion when the Puritan had joined the congregation, he had risen to his feet to contradict some claims made in the sermon. On the previous occasion, he had not even waited for the sermon, charging out of the church with as much noise as he could make and slamming its great oak door behind him. As he looked at their unwelcome visitor, Dyment realised that here was the one parishioner for whom he would gladly dig the grave himself.

'Why have you come, Reginald?' he asked.

'To pass on the good tidings,' said Orr with a sly smile.

'And what are they?'

'Silvermere will not be polluted by a vile theatre company, after all.'

'What makes you think that?'

'I sense that the vermin may have turned back.'

'You sense it,' pressed the other, 'or you *know* it?'

'Let me just say that word reached me yesterday.'

'Then it differs from the word I received only this morning.'

Orr's smile froze. 'What do you mean?'

'A letter from Sir Michael tells me that Westfield's Men arrived safely and are due to perform this evening at Silvermere. I'm invited to attend.'

'They're *here*?' said Orr in astonishment.

'In spite of an attempt to turn them back, apparently.' The vicar watched him carefully. 'I don't suppose that you know anything about that, Reginald?'

Orr was belligerent. 'Are you accusing me?'

'The vicar was asking a polite question,' said Tuke, squaring up to him.

'Then the polite answer is that I've nothing to say on the subject.'

'Sir Michael will pursue you for a proper reply,' cautioned Dyment.

'Let him,' said Orr, unworried. 'What concerns me is the fact that you've been invited to watch this performance at Silvermere.'

'I am Sir Michael's chaplain.'

'All the more reason why you should stop him from walking in the counsel of the ungodly or standing in the way of sinners. Actors are born infidels. They're ungodly sinners who seek to corrupt and defile. Can you, as his chaplain,' he said, jabbing the vicar in the chest, 'condone what Sir Michael is doing?'

'I respect his right to do exactly as he wishes.'

'Even if it vitiates the basic tenets of Christianity?'

'I take a more tolerant view of theatre companies.'

'Then you mean to encourage this degradation?' snarled Orr. 'You reprimand me for not attending church yet you welcome a band of fiends who preach the word of the Devil himself. You're a traitor to your cloth, Anthony Dyment!'

'Rein in your language,' ordered Tuke.

'Why? Does the truth sit too heavily upon your ears?'

'The vicar deserves respect.'

'Well, he'll not get it from me if he watches actors purveying their evil in the heart of his parish. What will you do?' he demanded, returning on Dyment. 'Will you have the courage to spurn this invitation? Or will you feed at the table of Satan?'

For once in his life, Anthony Dyment was lost for words.

Twenty-four hours at Silvermere wrought a complete transformation in Westfield's Men.

The beleaguered company who had arrived at the house, cold, hungry and exhausted, were now happy and alert. Their welcome had been warm, the food excellent, their hosts attentive and their accommodation far better than anything they usually enjoyed when they went out on the road. They found the Great Hall itself inspiring and could not wait to begin rehearsal. *Double Deceit* was one of their most reliable comedies but it called for immense technical precision. Since it was the first play in the sequence, Firethorn was anxious to get it absolutely right in order to create a favourable impression and he drilled his actors throughout the morning and the afternoon. Davy Stratton was given only a brief appearance on stage where he was allowed to join in a general cheer. No lines were assigned to him. Behind the scenes, his responsibilities were much larger.

Nicholas Bracewell made full use of the elements at his disposal, hanging curtains that could be drawn back to reveal the area below the gallery and placing the scores of candelabra in the most advantageous positions. Accustomed to perform outdoors in the afternoon, the company had to adapt to the differing conditions now offered them. Chairs were set out in rows and Nicholas watched some of the scenes from the back row to make sure that everyone was visible as well as audible. All was satisfactory. There were no apparent problems. When the actors gathered in the ante-room that was their tiring-house, morale was high and confidence unlimited. Davy Stratton was the only person who was suffering from nervousness. Efficient during rehearsals, he was now anxious and rather distracted, fearing that he would let his colleagues down on the very first occasion when he worked alongside them. Nicholas sought to reassure him.

'You did wonders during rehearsal,' he said.

'Did I?' replied Davy.

'We could not have got through it without you.'

'But all that I did was to stand there with the various costumes.'

'That's a vital task in this play. Speed is crucial, Davy. If the piece slows down at any point, its momentum is lost and so is much of its comedy. It only works if we do our duty as well as the actors.' He touched the boy's arm. 'Try to enjoy it, lad.'

'I feel sick.'

'So does everyone,' said Nicholas, glancing around the room. 'They just learn to hide it better. But it's not really sickness, Davy. It's excitement. Once the play starts, you'll have no time to worry about a queasy stomach.'

'I like the play. It made me giggle.'

'Let's hope that it has the same effect on our audience.'

Nicholas took the boy with him as he checked the large number of properties required in *Double Deceit*. Those damaged in the ambush had now been repaired and all had been set out in sequence on a long trestle table. The actors, meanwhile, put on their costumes, bantered contentedly or slipped off into a corner for a last rehearsal of their lines. Noise was building steadily in the adjacent Great Hall as the guests filed in to take their places. Judging from the volume of the sound, a sizeable number had gathered to watch the famous company display its wonders. Romball Taylard eventually came into the tiring-house to find out if they were ready. Lawrence Firethorn assured him that they were and sent him back to Sir Michael Greenleaf. He then delivered a short but stirring speech to the company, exhorting them to give of their best. Roused by his words, they took up their positions on stage behind the curtains with increased eagerness.

On a signal from Nicholas Bracewell, the musicians began to play in the gallery and the heavy murmur in the hall quickly died out. Owen Elias then swept out on stage to deliver the Prologue and to harvest the first laughter of the evening. When the curtains were drawn right back, *Double Deceit* began in earnest. Its plot was lifted from a play by Plautus. Two pairs of identical twins were involved in an endless series of merry escapades. Mistaken identities time and again brought howls of mirth from the audience. What made the performance especially memorable was the fact that Lawrence Firethorn and Barnaby Gill each played a pair of twins, leaving the stage as Argos and Silvio of Rome, respectively, only to reappear almost instantly as Argos and Silvio of Florence. Swift changes of costume were vital and Davy was kept busy taking one cloak and hat from Firethorn while handing him replacements, only to give him the original items when he reverted from Florence to Rome again. Standing beside him, George Dart was supplying the changes of costume for Gill, the morose servant to one Argos and the irrepressible jester to the other.

Timing was faultless. Everything was done so expertly that the spectators thought they were watching four actors playing the central roles instead of two. Appreciative laughter never ceased. Some of the bawdry spread blushes among the ladies but the men roared uncontrollably. Subtle innuendo was a form of humour that appealed to husbands and wives with equal success. *Double Deceit* was a triumphant romp, working its double deceit on an audience comprising friends and relations of Sir Michael and Lady Eleanor, some of whom had never seen a theatrical performance before and who were completely enthralled by the novel experience. When Act Five rose to its climax, both sets of twins appeared on stage together for the first time. Owen Elias, wearing a costume identical to that of Firethorn's, looked remarkably like him while James Ingram, dressed to duplicate Gill, was a more than passable imitation.

It was left to Firethorn to deliver the Epilogue, a sixteen-line speech in rhyming couplets that rounded off the play with a mixture of wit and wisdom. Proud of the way that his company had responded to the challenge and delighted with his own double performances, the actor stepped forward to the edge of the stage, cleared his throat and opened his mouth to let the words spring forth. But none came. No matter how hard he tried, Firethorn could produce no more than a faint croak. He clutched at his neck and even poked a finger down his throat but they were futile gestures. What made his predicament worse was the fact that the spectators, assuming his antics were all part of the play, laughed afresh and even applauded when he grimaced as he made one final effort to declaim the elusive Epilogue.

Barnaby Gill eventually came to his rescue. Pushing him aside, the clown did a little dance by way of introduction then invented a couplet to cover the embarrassment of his silent colleague.

'Good friends, let merry servants have their day,
I'll say the words my master cannot say.'

The sixteen original lines now followed, delivered with comic effect by a man who had heard them so often that they were imprinted on his memory. Firethorn was horrified to see his rival stealing his lines and taking a first drink of the applause that burst out. At the same time, however, he recognised that Gill had been their saviour and steeled himself to thank the man when his voice returned. It was baffling. Firethorn was in no pain yet he could not utter a single word. When the company quit the stage, he led them back on again to take their bow, beaming graciously at his hosts who sat in the front row then going through his range of elaborate gestures. Gill could not resist adding insult to injury. As the pair of them came into the tiring-house, he turned to Firethorn.

'Learn your lines, man,' he scolded. 'At least do *something* correctly.'

Nicholas Bracewell knew that the problem was serious. Whatever else he might do, Firethorn would never forget his lines, still less yield up an opportunity for Gill to say them in his stead. Seeing the mingled fury and helplessness in Firethorn's eyes, he swiftly intervened before Gill's mockery provoked Argos of Rome and of Florence to violence. When he took the stricken actor aside, they were joined by Edmund Hoode.

'What happened, Lawrence?' asked Hoode. 'You know that speech backwards.'

Firethorn used a finger to jab wildly at his throat.

'Have you lost your voice?' said Nicholas, getting an energetic nod in return. 'Can you say nothing at all?' A despairing shake of the head came in reply. 'But you had no difficulty at all in the course of the play itself.'

Firethorn tried to explain his dilemma with a series of vivid gestures.

Hoode was bewildered. 'What's wrong with him, Nick?'

'I don't know,' admitted Nicholas, 'but I think he needs a doctor.'

'Nothing like this has ever happened before. Lawrence is invincible.'

'That's no longer the case, Edmund. Or so it seems. First, he has a high fever; then he collapses during the sermon in church; and now this.'

Firethorn nodded his agreement and gesticulated wildly. When other members of the company came over to see how he was, Nicholas waved them away, assuring them that their leader was simply tired and needed a rest. Few were persuaded by the book holder's words. The ebullient actor never tired. Concerned for his state of health, they began to change out of their costumes. Only Gill tried to exploit his colleague's distress. When he had shed the garments he wore as Silvio of Rome, he drifted across to the three men and spoke with a lordly air.

'Lawrence's lapse may yet be turned to good account,' he said, preening himself. 'I think it better from now on if Silvio always delivers the Epilogue to show that the tables have turned and that the master is subservient to the man. What do you think?'

'I think it a monstrous idea,' said Hoode.

'And a singularly inappropriate one,' added Nicholas.

Gill ignored them both. 'What about you, Lawrence? You saw how well they received my Epilogue. Will you give the lines to one who says them properly?'

Unable to speak, Firethorn lurched at Gill with hands outstretched to grab him by the throat. Nicholas and

Hoode restrained him just in time. Gill skipped out of reach and gave a brittle laugh. He was revelling in his moment of triumph. When most of the others had drifted away, Firethorn sat forlornly on a bench, head in hands. Hoode tried in vain to comfort him. Nicholas first supervised the removal of scenery and properties from the stage before returning to his friends. He was about to console Firethorn when Sir Michael came tripping into the room in high excitement.

'Where is he?' he cried. 'Where is that magician called Lawrence Firethorn?'

'Over here, Sir Michael,' said Nicholas.

Their host hurried across to them. 'Oh, sir. Forgive my delay in coming to congratulate you but I was trapped under an avalanche of compliments from my guests. They found the play both hilarious and enchanting. From your pen, I hear, Master Hoode.'

Hoode gave a nod. 'Even so, Sir Michael.'

'Then you, too, deserve unlimited praise. The play and the performance were above reproach. In the dual roles of Silvio, Master Firethorn, you were superb.' The actor smiled for the first time since coming into the tiring-house. 'That device at the end was masterly, sir, pretending to lose your voice like that so that the lowly servant had to deliver the Epilogue. Your gestures and expressions were so wonderfully lifelike.'

His face a mask of anger, Firethorn's gestures were so openly hostile that Nicholas had to stand in front of him to shield him from their host. He smiled gently at Sir Michael and held up both palms in apology.

'Forgive him, Sir Michael,' he said. 'Master Firethorn is fatigued.'

'Hardly surprising after the energy he put into his performance.'

'Would it be possible for him to see a doctor?'

Sir Michael was alarmed. 'A doctor? Master Firethorn is not ill?'

'No, no,' said Nicholas. 'He simply needs a reviving dose of medicine.'

'Then I prescribe a potion of my own devising. It cured my dog's palsy.'

Nicholas was tactful. 'It may not be quite what is called for here, Sir Michael. Five minutes with a doctor are all that is needed. I wondered if perhaps you had such a man among your guests.'

'As a matter of fact, I do,' said the other. 'Doctor Winche.'

'Would he consent to treat Lawrence?' asked Hoode.

'Doctor Winche would insist on it, Master Hoode. The treat would be all his, believe me. He and his wife thought the performance was remarkable. If he has the chance to meet the undoubted star of the evening, Doctor Winche will seize it gladly.'

'Perhaps you could ask him to step in here, Sir Michael.'

'At once, at once, dear fellow,' said their host, scurrying off. 'We can't have Master Firethorn in the slightest discomfort.'

'Ably done, Nick,' said Hoode. 'Lawrence was about to strangle him when he made that remark about the Epilogue. Thank heaven you prevented him or our first performance here would also have been our last.'

Firethorn stood up, pointing a finger and mouthing words that had no sound. Hoode was confused but Nicholas understood what the actor was trying to say to them. He quickly retrieved the prompt copy of *Double Deceit* and brought it over. Taking it from him, Firethorn indicated the title then drew an imaginary line through it, replacing it with four words written invisibly by an index finger.

'What on earth is he doing, Nick?' asked Hoode.

'Telling us to look to another play,' said Nicholas.

'Why?'

'Because that's what caused the loss of his voice.'

'How can a play possibly do that?'

'I don't know but that's exactly what *The Witch of Colchester* seems to be doing, Edmund. You worked on the piece,' Nicholas reminded him. 'Does not Lord Malady suffer a series of strange maladies?'

'Well, yes,' recalled Hoode. 'He's first struck down by a mystery fever, then he collapses for no apparent reason and, when he recovers from that, he . . .' His voice tailed off and he looked back at the patient. 'Are you trying to tell us that you're enduring the same trials as Lord Malady?' Firethorn nodded vigorously. 'But that's incredible.'

'Two of us are coming to believe it, Edmund.'

'Egidius Pye has written a comedy, not woven a spell.'

'Perhaps he's done both without even realising it.'

'No, Nick. I refuse even to countenance the idea.'

Firethorn took him by the shoulders to shake him, peering deep into his eyes. He resorted to mime, first pretending to have a high fever, then falling to the floor and twitching convulsively. Hauling himself back up, he walked around the room as if declaiming a speech then grabbed at his throat with both hands. He ended by thrusting the prompt copy of *Double Deceit* into its author's hands. Hoode looked down at it with misgivings then stared back at Firethorn.

'I still can't accept it, Lawrence. In the play, Lord Malady's woes are wished upon him by his enemy, Sir Roderick Lawless. He engages someone to afflict his rival with various illnesses. Everyone assumes that it's Black Joan, the witch, who has put a spell on him but the real villain is the man who's supposed to be nursing him back to health.'

'Doctor Putrid,' said Nicholas.

'Exactly.'

'A role taken by Barnaby Gill.'

Hoode became pensive. 'I begin to see what you mean. When Lawrence lost his voice this evening, it was Barnaby who gained most. And when Lord Malady is struck dumb in *The Witch of Colchester*, it's Doctor Putrid who reaps the benefit. Can this be so?' he said, arms flailing in disbelief. 'Is the great Lawrence Firethorn, who has triumphed in so many plays, now at the mercy of one?'

Firethorn nodded again then flung himself down in despair on the bench.

Doctor Winche chose that moment to come in with Sir Michael. He was a short, round, bow-legged man of middle years with a rubicund face that was one contented smile. He tugged at his goatee beard then rubbed his podgy hands together.

'This is truly an honour, gentlemen,' he said, beaming

228

at them, 'If laughter is the best medicine, then I'll live to be a hundred.' When he saw Firethorn in distress, his manner changed at once. 'Good gracious!' he cried, swooping on the actor. 'What ails you, sir? Are you in pain?'

'Master Firethorn is very tired, doctor,' explained Nicholas, 'and he's suffering from a sore throat. We'll let you tend him in private?'

'Very sensible,' said Sir Michael. 'Let's step into the hall.'

Nicholas and Hoode went through the door and on to the stage with their host. Hundreds of candles still flickered in the room but two servants were systematically extinguishing the flames now that the audience had left.

Sir Michael was solicitous. 'I hope that his condition is not serious.'

'I'm sure that it's not, Sir Michael,' said Nicholas, careful to divulge nothing more about Firethorn's recent medical history. 'Sleep will work its wonders.'

'And tomorrow, he can rest.'

'Unhappily not, Sir Michael,' explained Hoode. 'Though we may have no performance in here tomorrow, we'll be rehearsing our new play. Actors never rest, I fear. What you see on the stage in two hours is the fruit of much longer time spent in rehearsal. *Double Deceit* is a case in point.'

'A delightful frolic, Master Hoode. My wife chortled with glee.'

'I'm glad that Lady Eleanor was pleased,' said Nicholas.

'Overjoyed, my friend. What comes next?'

'*The Insatiate Duke*. Very different fare, Sir Michael. We follow a sunny comedy with a dark tragedy. In one sense, it's a pity we perform in the afternoon,' he said, watching the servants dousing the candles, 'because we could make great use of shadow with nothing but candelabra to illumine the stage. But no matter.'

'No,' agreed Hoode. 'We usually play the piece in blazing sunshine.'

'You mentioned the new comedy,' said Sir Michael. '*The Witch of Colchester*. That's the one that most appeals to me. Is it a powerful play?'

'Oh, yes, Sir Michael.'

'Too powerful,' said Nicholas under his breath.

They talked on for a few minutes before being interrupted by Doctor Winche who came bustling on to the stage in a more settled frame of mind. His smile returned.

'It's nothing to cause alarm,' he said. 'What Master Firethorn most needs is sleep. His throat is sore yet not inflamed and there's no swelling in the neck. I'll send a potion across to him as soon as I return home.'

'Could you not mix it here, Doctor Winche?' suggested Sir Michael. 'I'm sure that I've all the herbs necessary in my laboratory. That would save time.'

'A great deal of it, Sir Michael. I accept your kind offer. Meanwhile,' he said to the others, 'I advise that you conduct Master Firethorn to his bed. When the poor fellow is comfortable, tell him how much my wife and I enjoyed his performance. Praise is a wonderful medicine. No man can have too much of it.'

He and Sir Michael went off to the laboratory, leaving Nicholas and Hoode with the task of nursing their colleague. Firethorn was still in his costume as Argos when they went back into the tiring-house and they saw no point in getting him out of it until they had installed him in his bedchamber. Nicholas threw a cloak around the patient's shoulders then he and Hoode escorted him slowly towards the side exit of the house. When they came out into the cold night, Firethorn gave a shudder and emitted a soundless cry. They hurried him across to the largest of the three cottages, brushed aside the anxious enquiries of its other occupants and took him upstairs. Firethorn was soon undressed and put into his bed, mystified rather than in any discomfort. When his eyelids began to droop, Hoode nudged Nicholas and they quietly withdrew. Owen Elias was waiting for them at the bottom of the stairs.

'What's laid him low this time?' he asked.

'We don't know, Owen,' replied Nicholas. 'He's been seen by a doctor who advised sleep. Doctor Winche is preparing a potion for his sore throat at this moment.'

'I hope that it works, Nick. Lawrence Firethorn without a voice us like the River Thames without water – a freak of nature.'

'He'll soon recover,' said Hoode.

'And what if he doesn't, Edmund?' said the Welshman.

'Then we do what Barnaby did this evening. Replace him.'

'Only God could replace Lawrence.'

There was a loud banging on the door. Nicholas went to see who was calling.

'That surely can't be Doctor Winche already,' he said, lifting the latch. 'Can he mix his medicines so quickly?'

He opened the door and blinked in surprise when he saw the squat figure of an old woman standing there.

Viewed only in the flickering light of the candles, the visitor had a sinister quality yet he did not sense any menace. She waddled forward so that he could see her more clearly. Dressed in rags and wearing a tattered old cap, she was bent by age and worn down by toil but her eyes had an almost youthful glint in them.

'Did you want something, mistress?' asked Nicholas pleasantly.

'Only to give you this, sir,' she said, offering him a tiny bottle. 'Someone in this house is ill and this potion will cure him if he takes it.'

'But how did you know that we had a sick man here?'

'That's not important. Take the bottle.'

'What does it contain?'

'A remedy.'

Nicholas took it from her, feeling the strange warmness of her hand as it brushed against his own. 'Who are you?' he wondered.

'Mother Pigbone,' she said softly.

Then she drew back into the darkness and was gone.

Chapter Nine

Wednesday was devoted entirely to a rehearsal of *The Witch of Colchester*. The play due for performance on the following afternoon, *The Insatiate Duke*, had been in demand so much the previous year that they knew it by heart and felt confident of staging it after only a morning's work on it. It was the new play that demanded the real attention but they approached it with no enthusiasm. Lawrence Firethorn was not the only person to make the connection between his recurring illnesses and Egidius Pye's drama. Their manager's ordeal mirrored that of Lord Malady and they were not reassured by the fact that *The Witch of Colchester* had a happy ending with its protagonist restored to full health. Before that occurred, the character was due to endure more afflictions. Fear lent a tentative quality to the rehearsal. Superstitious by nature, the actors were highly nervous, picking their way through the play as if each scene was an uncertain stepping stone in a particularly fast-flowing stream.

During a break, Lawrence Firethorn drifted across to Nicholas Bracewell.

'This play is cursed, Nick,' he complained. 'I can feel it.'

'It's brought us good as well as bad luck,' said Nicholas, looking around. 'But for Master Pye, we wouldn't be enjoying the hospitality of Silvermere and the pleasure of rehearsing in this magnificent hall. We'd all be cooling our heels in London, praying for the weather to improve. Whereas here we have work, food, drink, lodging, a fine theatre and a wonderful audience. It's pure joy to work in such conditions.'

'I agree. Acting on this stage was a continuous pleasure. Until I lost my voice.'

'Only for a short while. It's now restored.'

'For how long?' said Firethorn anxiously. 'I feel that a new illness is going to leap out of *The Witch of Colchester* to attack me any minute. The play is a menace.'

'Sir Michael is delighted with our choice of it.'

'Sir Michael doesn't have to take the role of Lord Malady.'

'Other characters in the play are struck down as well as yours,' Nicholas reminded him. 'The two lawyers, for instance, Longshaft and Shortshrift. Master Pye doesn't spare his legal colleagues in the play. Both are stricken yet neither Edmund nor James, who take those parts, have suffered in any way.'

Firethorn groaned. 'I've suffered enough for both of them!'

'Don't be afraid of the piece. It may yet give us our greatest triumph.'

'It may indeed, Nick, but will I be alive to see it?'

Concealing his own fears about the play, Firethorn went off to berate the actors for their lack of commitment to the piece. The voice that had disappeared on the previous evening was now as rich and loud as ever. Nicholas was relieved but still puzzled by his sudden recovery. He called Davy Stratton across to issue his instructions. Given only a miniscule role in the new play, the boy was employed throughout in a series of menial but important tasks. In a piece that involved considerable doubling, he helped actors to change their costumes, held properties in readiness for them when they were about to make an entry and brought on or removed scenery with George Dart whenever the action of the play required it.

'Do you know what you have to do in the next scene, Davy?' said Nicholas.

'I think so.'

'What?'

'Wheel the witch's cauldron on stage.'

'That's the second thing you must do. What's the first?'

'Ah, yes,' said Davy, remembering. 'Help Martin Yeo on with his costume.'

'Think of him as Griselda. That's Martin's name in the play.'

'I'll try but he still looks like Martin Yeo to me.'

'Yes,' said Nicholas sternly. 'I saw you teasing him earlier on. No more of that, Davy. I put you in the cottage with Dick Honeydew and George in order to keep you away from the other apprentices. Don't stir up trouble.'

'It was Martin and Stephen who were mocking me,' claimed the boy.

'Then ignore them. Even in rehearsal, a play needs all our attention. We must work together and not against each other. Do you understand?' Davy gave a penitent nod. 'Good. Let me see you excel yourself as you did during *Double Deceit*.'

'Is that all?'

'No, it isn't,' said Nicholas, wondering why he was so keen to get away. 'This is the first time I've had the chance to speak to you alone and I want to ask you something. Have you ever heard of someone called Mother Pigbone?'

'Of course. Everybody in Essex has.'

'Who is she?'

'A wise woman who lives in the wood beyond Stapleford.'

'Have you ever met her?'

'No, but I think that my father has.'

'Does she sell remedies for strange illnesses?'

'Mother Pigbone does all kinds of things. Some say she's a witch.'

'I thought you didn't believe in witches.'

'I don't but lots of people do.'

'How would I find Mother Pigbone?'

'Ask my father.'

Wishing to resume work, Firethorn waved to his book holder. Nicholas sent Davy off to do his chores and mounted the stage. After checking that all the scenery was in place, he went into the tiring-house to make sure that the actors were in their appointed positions. Full costume was being worn

236

so that they could get used to the frequent changes. Barnaby Gill was adjusting the feather in his cap. Edmund Hoode was composing his features into the solemn expression of a lawyer. Davy Stratton was helping the sullen Martin Yeo into the dress he wore as Griselda, a young woman in the household of Sir Roderick Lawless. Richard Honeydew was in the more striking costume belonging to Lord Malady's wife. Stephen Judd, the other apprentice, was already in the tattered rags of Black Joan. Satisfied that everything was as it should be, Nicholas took his copy of the play into the hall so that he could watch the rehearsal and prompt. He waved to the musicians in the gallery and they played a lively tune to indicate the start of the new scene.

Lord Malady was the first on stage, accompanied by his devoted wife who had nursed him through his latest mysterious illness. It was a clever scene, touching in some ways, yet undeniably comic as well, full of dramatic irony for a discerning audience. When Doctor Putrid entered, the comedy was immediately sharpened as he engaged in a verbal duel with Malady. Leading by example, Firethorn and Gill were putting far more effort into their roles than they had earlier done. Others who joined them on stage also tried to be more positive. All went well until Martin Yeo, in the person of Griselda, had to bend down to pick a discarded flower from the ground. Trained in graceful movement, Yeo was utterly convincing as a young woman as he retrieved the blood red rose. The illusion was not maintained. As soon as he straightened up, he let out such a cry of pain that it made the other actors jump back. Holding his buttocks and yelping madly, he ran in circles around the stage as if his posterior were on fire.

Sympathy was in short supply. Firethorn castigated him for spoiling the rehearsal, Gill added his scorn, Honeydew sniggered, Elias laughed, Judd frowned and Hoode simply gaped in dismay. It was left to Nicholas to offer practical assistance. Leaping on to the stage, he grabbed hold of Yeo, ordered him to stand still then helped him out of his costume to reveal the cause of his agony. A piece of bramble had been cunningly inserted into the material so that it made its presence known when the boy bent over. Extracting the thorns from Yeo's buttocks, Nicholas drew the loudest howls yet from the apprentice. He held up the bramble that had ruined the rehearsal of the scene.

'Davy Stratton!' he called. 'Come out here, lad.'

Reverend Anthony Dyment was in a quandary. As chaplain at Silvermere, he was eager not to offend Sir Michael Greenleaf yet he was equally unwilling to give Reginald Orr grounds for showing further contempt. The invitation to attend *Double Deceit* had caused him immense discomfort. If he went to the play, he would be accused by Orr of making a pact with the Devil; if he refused, it would upset the man who had given him both the chaplaincy and the living at St Christopher's. Compromise was impossible. In the event, he pleaded a severe headache and missed the performance but he was keen to placate Sir Michael and repaired to Silvermere the next day. Admitted to the house, he could hear the voices of the actors in rehearsal in the Great Hall. Dyment was taken by a servant to the room where his master spent so much time. Sir Michael was in his laboratory, mixing some of his new gunpowder and talking to Jerome Stratton.

'Come in, Anthony,' said the scientist, seeing the vicar arrive. 'I hope that you've recovered completely from your headache.'

'I have, Sir Michael,' said Dyment. 'God be praised.'

'Praised indeed. Yours is the second speedy recovery for which we must thank Him. At the end of yesterday's play, Lawrence Firethorn lost his voice and could not utter a word. Doctor Winche could do nothing for him. Then poor Master Firethorn drank a potion and the power of speech returned at once.'

'Amazing!' said Dyment.

'Was this medicine the doctor's concoction?' asked Stratton.

'No, Jerome. It came from a more questionable source.'

'And where was that?'

'Mother Pigbone.'

The vicar was disturbed. 'You'd entrust the health of a guest to her?'

'Mother Pigbone has a reputation as a physician.'

'I'm not sure that it's one I'd trust, Sir Michael.'

'Nor I,' muttered Stratton. 'But the patient is well again, you say?'

Sir Michael beamed. 'Step into the hall and you'll hear him bellowing like a bull.' He switched his gaze to Dyment. 'But I'm so sorry that you had to forego the pleasure of seeing *Double Deceit*. It would have dispelled anyone's headache. My wife and I have never laughed so much in all our lives.'

'I wish I'd seen it myself,' said Stratton.

'Yes, Jerome. It was a pity that business affairs kept you away. You'd have loved it, especially as Davy flitted across the stage at one point. Join us tomorrow and you'll see the company in more tragic vein.'

'I'll be there, Sir Michael. What about you, Anthony?'

Dyment shifted his feet. 'That may be difficult, I fear.'

'You don't have any qualms about watching a play, do you?' said Stratton.

'Not at all. I appeared in more than one while an undergraduate at Oxford.'

'But they were usually in Latin,' noted Sir Michael, wiping his hands on a piece of cloth. 'And always on some religious theme. Westfield's Men present drama of a more immediate nature. They show the weaknesses of man and hold him up to ridicule. *Double Deceit* was an hilarious sermon on the eternal follies of the human condition. It would have given you great amusement, Anthony.'

'Perhaps so, Sir Michael, though I'm not entirely persuaded that a man of the cloth *ought* to be amused in that way.'

'Laughter is good for the soul, man.'

'That depends on what kind of laughter it is.'

'You're beginning to sound like a sour-faced Puritan,' said Stratton. 'Everyone is entitled to enjoyment and that's what a theatre company offers.'

'I'll take your word for it, Master Stratton.'

'Jerome has no worries at all about Westfield's Men,' remarked Sir Michael chirpily. 'If he had, he wouldn't have apprenticed his own son to them.'

'Quite,' said Stratton.

'To watch them at work is a profound education, Anthony.'

'I'm sure that it is,' said the vicar, 'but not everyone accepts that view. It's one of the reasons I called this morning. Sir Michael. To give you fair warning.'

'Of what?'

'Further trouble from Reginald Orr.'

'That rogue!' said Stratton angrily. 'We should drive him out of Essex.'

Dyment pursed his lips. 'That's the fate he wishes on Westfield's Men, I fear. When I spoke to him yesterday, he was in buoyant mood, assuring me that they would never even get as far as Silvermere. Master Orr was deeply upset to learn that they'd already done so.'

'That's because he probably arranged that ambush for them,' said Sir Michael. 'Did he say anything to that effect, Anthony?'

'He was careful to give nothing away.'

'Have him arrested on suspicion, Sir Michael,' advised Stratton.

'It's not as simple as that, Jerome.'

'The man is a danger.'

'That's why I came to warn you, Sir Michael,' said Dyment. 'If one thing fails, he'll try another. Keep your house well guarded. Protect your players.'

'I'm doing just that,' replied Sir Michael. 'And the players are extremely good at protecting themselves. They'll not be scared off by a fanatic like Reginald Orr.'

'He disapproves of plays.'

'Orr disapproves of *everything*,' said Stratton harshly.

'That's his business,' said Sir Michael, 'until he commits a crime, of course, when it becomes mine. I did warn him. If he comes up before me again, I'll impose the stiffest sentence that I can.'

'He ought to be hanged, drawn and quartered.'

The older man was tolerant. 'For holding some extreme views about religion? Come now, Jerome. We must live and let live. Orr is a nuisance but he doesn't deserve the punishment we reserve for treason. Well,' he continued, smiling at the vicar, 'since you missed *Double Deceit*, I insist that you watch one of the other plays.'

Dyment trembled. 'Must I, Sir Michael?'

'It's the least you can do. Give them the blessing of the church.'

'And give yourself a treat in the bargain,' said Stratton.

'I'll think about it,' promised the vicar.

'No prevarication,' said Sir Michael. 'I want a firm commitment now. My wife was deeply upset that you refused our invitation, albeit because you were indisposed. Do you intend to disappoint her again, Anthony?'

'No, no, of course not.'

'Good. Which play would you like to see.'

'Come tomorrow to see *The Insatiate Duke*,' said Stratton, touching his arm. 'It's a swirling tragedy that will make your blood run cold.'

'Tragedy is not to my taste.'

'What about history? They play *Henry the Fifth* on Saturday.'

'I have to take another burial service then.'

'In that case,' decided Sir Michael, 'you'll have to see *The Happy Malcontent*. It's another boisterous comedy, I hear, and it will be certain to brighten up your day. It's settled, Anthony. I'll expect you here to sit beside me and watch the piece.'

'When will it be performed, Sir Michael?'

'On Sunday.'

Dyment's legs almost melted beneath him.

Meals were served to the company in the main kitchen at Silvermere. The actors were encouraged to eat heartily and drink as much ale as they wished. Most of them rolled off to bed that night in a contented frame of mind. The rehearsal had been successful, the new play was taking shape and Lord Malady had survived intact. Pleased to have gone through the whole day without mishap, Lawrence Firethorn was nevertheless unhappy. As he sat with Nicholas Bracewell and Edmund Hoode over the vestiges of his meal, he had a different source of complaint.

'We should have left Davy Stratton in Shoreditch,' he said rancorously.

'Margery wouldn't have thanked you for that,' said Hoode. 'The lad caused enough trouble for ten apprentices when he was there.'

'But look what he's done since he's been here, Edmund.'

'Boyish high spirits,' suggested Nicholas.

'That's not what I'd call them,' growled Firethorn. 'That jest with the bramble was only one of many. Did you know that he put damp straw in Martin's bed last night and a handful of salt in Stephen's drink this morning? Dick

Honeydew is the only one who's escaped his villainy. The boy needs to be soundly beaten.'

'I shook him until his teeth rattled and warned him that we'd send him back to London if we have the slightest trouble out of him again. I don't know what got into Davy today,' confessed Nicholas. 'That piece of bramble must have been agonising.'

'We should have stripped the lad naked and thrown *him* into a bramble bush.'

'That would've been too cruel, Lawrence,' said Hoode. 'Nick did the right thing. He chastised Davy, made him apologise to Martin then watched him like a hawk for the rest of the day. Sending him off to bed early was a just punishment.'

'Not in my eyes. Do you know what I think?'

'What?'

'I may have been wrong about *The Witch of Colchester*. Perhaps it's not the play that's bringing all this misery down on me.'

'I'm certain that it isn't,' said Hoode.

'Coincidence can't be ignored, Edmund.'

'But that's all it is – pure coincidence.'

'No, it isn't. When did our problems start?'

'When you sent Master Pye on his way,' said Nicholas.

'No, Nick,' argued Firethorn. 'They started the moment we took Davy Stratton into the company. He caused problems in my house, ran away from you in the forest, tried to escape again when you spent the night at Silvermere and is now up to his old tricks again. It's not the play I should fear, it's that little rascal.'

'Make allowances for his age.'

'Yes,' said Hoode. 'Davy is still finding his feet.'

Firethorn was bitter. 'I'll cut them from beneath him if we have any more of these antics. Davy Stratton is the reason that I've been struck down three times in a row. He's been sent to torment me,' he went on, pursuing the logic of his argument. 'There's malevolence in that boy, I sense it. I thought that he might be an asset to the company but he's already indentured elsewhere.'

'What do you mean?' asked Nicholas.

'He's the Devil's apprentice.'

Firethorn emptied his cup of ale and rose to his feet. Nicholas did not try to contradict him. Though he took a less critical view of Davy Stratton, he was troubled by the boy's behaviour. Even after he had been expressly told not to tease Martin Yeo, the newcomer had played a nasty trick on him. Nicholas would brook no disobedience. He had given Davy such a severe reprimand that the boy had burst into tears, fearing that he would lose the friendship of the one person in Westfield's Men he respected above all others. A partial reconciliation had been achieved between them but Nicholas still felt hurt and let down. He wondered why someone who had been so well-behaved a guest at Anne Hendrik's house was now so obstreperous.

The three men left the main house and strolled across to the cottages in the darkness, guided by the candles that burnt in the windows ahead of them. After an exchange of farewells, Firethorn and Hoode went into the cottage they shared with Elias and Ingram. In the adjacent lodging,

Nicholas had elected to look after two of the apprentices, Davy Stratton and Richard Honeydew, as well as George Dart. Rowland Carr and Walter Fenby, both sharers, were also under the same roof. The first thing that Nicholas did was to take a candle to make sure that the boys were safely asleep. Opening the door of their room, he was pleased to see both Davy and Honeydew slumbering quietly in the same bed. At their feet, talking to himself in his sleep, was the exhausted Dart. A sense of peace hung over the room. Looking down at his young companions, Nicholas gave a paternal smile.

Weary himself, he did not undress completely to get into the empty bed under the window. He feared reprisals. Martin Yeo would seek revenge on his own behalf as well as on that of his friend, John Tallis, and the best time to strike back at Davy was at night when the apprentice was off guard. Even the presence of Nicholas in the chamber would not stop someone with enough determination and Yeo certainly had that. When he went to bed, therefore, Nicholas remained half-dressed, leaving the shutters slightly ajar so that he could catch any sounds of entry below. If anyone tried to sneak into the room, he would be ready for them. An hour passed before he went off to sleep, another before anything disturbed him. The creaking of a door then brought him awake. It came from the direction of the stables. When he heard the frightened neighing of a horse, he was out of his bed at once.

Grasping his sword, Nicholas crept downstairs in the dark, moving as silently as he could so that he did not disturb anyone. When he let himself out of the cottage, he heard further noises from the stables. The open door suggested an intruder. At first, he thought it might be Yeo, gathering up an armful of filthy straw to scatter over Davy by way of retaliation but several horses were now disturbed enough to neigh their protest. Nicholas decided that the intruder was there for a more serious purpose than merely getting revenge on a wayward apprentice. If he was trying to steal a horse, he had to be apprehended. Sword held in front of him, he slipped in through the open door and peered into the gloom. The spark gave the man away. As he set light to a pile of fresh straw, he revealed his hiding place in a corner.

'Stop!' yelled Nicholas, darting across at him.

'Who are you?' grunted a voice.

The intruder was surprised but not easily overpowered. Before Nicholas could reach him, he took an armful of straw and hurled it into his face, using the momentary confusion to buffet his way to the door. Fire was taking hold now and frenzy was starting to spread among the horses. Nicholas grabbed a pail of water to douse most of the flames then stamped out the rest with his feet. As soon as that was done, he sprinted through the door in pursuit of the footsteps he could hear on the drive. Anger lent wings to his heels. His quarry moved fast but he had left his horse some distance from the stables and was soon panting madly. Pausing to rest against a tree, he stayed there until he realised that someone was after him. The man set off again, blundering through the undergrowth until he found the clearing where he had tethered his mount. Before the rider could even get his foot in the stirrup, however, Nicholas came charging at him.

'Stay there!' he ordered, holding his sword point against the man's neck.

But his adversary acted swiftly again, using a dagger to parry the sword then kicking powerfully with his right foot. Nicholas suffered a glancing blow on the thigh and staggered back. When the man aimed a second kick at him, he caught the foot and twisted it hard until he let out a yell of pain. As the intruder fell to the ground, Nicholas struck at the hand holding the dagger and opened up a gash in his wrist. An even louder yell came as the man released his weapon. Nicholas dropped the sword and flung himself down on the figure who now was writhing on the ground in the dark. Sitting astride him, he began to pummel away with both fists but the fight was almost immediately curtailed. A second rider came out of the shadows and used a cudgel to belabor Nicholas. Dazed by blows to the head, the book holder lost all his strength and was pushed away roughly by the man beneath him. The second rider dismounted to help his confederate into the saddle of his own mount. By the time that Nicholas was able to stagger to his feet, both men were galloping off into the darkness.

The commotion brought several people running from the cottages and the main house. Nicholas soon found himself surrounded by lighted candles and curious faces. Firethorn pushed his way through his friend.

'Are you hurt, Nick?' he said, supporting him by the arm.

'A little,' conceded the other.

'What happened?'

'Somebody tried to frighten us away again.'

The nocturnal assault accomplished part of its objective. The fire might have been put out in the stables but the flames of doubt continued to crackle in the minds of the company. On the following morning, the rehearsal of *The Insatiate Duke* was slow and half-hearted. Reminded that they had enemies, the actors kept looking over their shoulders and wondering where the next attack would come from. The sight of their book holder was usually a reassurance but it was now visible proof of the desperation of their unknown foes. Face covered with bruises and head wrapped in a piece of linen, Nicholas had taken a lot of punishment. If the strongest and most resourceful man in the company had been subdued, they reasoned, what hope did the rest of them have?

Sir Michael was highly sympathetic. Flanked by his wife and his steward, he came into the hall at the end of the rehearsal to offer his apologies and to enquire after the condition of the wounded book holder.

'This is appalling!' he said, staring at Nicholas's bruises. 'I invited you here as my guests and you've twice been the target of a vicious attack.'

'It's not your fault, Sir Michael,' said Nicholas.

'But it is, dear fellow. My wife and I are distraught.'

'We are,' confirmed Lady Eleanor, wringing her hands. 'We're shocked beyond measure. This kind of thing has simply never happened at Silvermere before.'

'I did warn Sir Michael,' said Taylard piously. 'When there is such opposition to the arrival of a theatre company, it might have been wiser to turn them away.'

'No, Romball!' exploded Sir Michael with uncharacteristic vehemence. 'I'll not give in to anyone. Westfield's Men are more than welcome here. I'll gladly bear any blows that come in their wake.'

'The blows fell on someone else,' noted his wife, gazing sadly at Nicholas. 'Do you really feel well enough to get out of bed, Master Bracewell?'

'No, Lady Eleanor,' said Nicholas with a grin, 'but if I'm not there, you'll have no play this afternoon and your guests will be bitterly disappointed.'

'You're so brave!'

'I suspect it's more a case of folly than bravery.'

'And loyalty,' added Firethorn, joining the group. 'A bang on the head will not stop Nick Bracewell from steering us through another performance. But he cannot be expected to patrol the stables every night, Sir Michael,' he added, confronting his host. 'What we would like to know is if you've arranged for a proper guard to be set?'

'Romball has the matter in hand,' said Sir Michael.

'Yes,' said the steward officiously. 'Two men will watch over the stables and the cottages throughout the night. They'll be relieved at regular intervals so that the pair on duty are always fresh and alert.'

'How will they be armed?' asked Firethorn.

'With sword and dagger.'

'Give them each a musket from my arsenal,' ordered Sir Michael.

'I don't think they'll attack again at night,' said Nicholas, 'because they know we'll be ready for them. But it's a comfort to have armed men on patrol.'

'What about the villain who tried to burn down the stables, Sir Michael?' said Firethorn seriously. 'Do you have any idea who it was?'

'Not yet, Master Firethorn,' replied Sir Michael.

'What about this mad Puritan, Reginald Orr?'

'He'd certainly be capable of such villainy,' argued Lady Eleanor.

Taylard was suave. 'Yet he'd hardly be capable of running so fast away from the stables, Lady Eleanor, and of getting the better of Master Bracewell in a fight. Reginald Orr is not a young man. He's strong but far from lithe.'

'Then he's not the fellow I wrestled on the ground,' decided Nicholas. 'He was young, strong and quick. I had him beaten until I was cudgelled from behind by his confederate but I meted out some punishment of my own. Search for a man with a twisted ankle and a wounded wrist. Yes,' he went on, pointing to his face, 'and with some bruises like these. I know I drew blood from his nose.'

'I still think that Reginald Orr is involved in some way,' said Lady Eleanor.

'That will emerge in the fullness of time, my dear,' said her husband. 'I've sent word to the constable to question him closely on the matter.'

'I'd like to put a few questions to him myself,' said Firethorn ruefully.

Sir Michael raised appeasing hands. 'Leave all that to me, Master Firethorn. The only thing you need to worry about is your performance this afternoon. We'll hold you up no longer. All that I can do is to offer you my sincere apologies and to assure you that no other setback will occur while you're at Silvermere.'

Gathering up his wife and his steward, the old man backed out of the Great Hall.

Firethorn watched them go with mixed feelings before putting an affectionate arm around the book holder's shoulders.

'How do you feel now, Nick?' he asked.

'My head is still pounding a little.'

'You took some severe blows.'

'I look forward to giving some in return.'

'Would you like us to summon Doctor Winche?'

'I'm not that bad,' said Nicholas.

'But the doctor might be able to give you something to ease the pain.'

'If I wanted a potion, I'd not look to Doctor Winche.'

'Then where would you go?'

'To whom else?' said Nicholas with a smile. 'Mother Pigbone.'

Mother Pigbone used the broken half of a broom handle to stir the mixture in the wooden pail. It gave off a pungent odour that merged with a compound of noisome smells that already pervaded the kitchen in her hovel. When she was satisfied that the food was ready, she lifted up the pail and carried it into the garden. An elderly woman of medium height, she had a plump body and a pleasant face that was always lit by a quiet smile. She wore ragged clothes, stained by a dozen differing hues, and a dirty head clout. Though she had no children of her own, there was a motherly quality about her that was quite endearing. Shuffling to the end of the little garden, she chuckled when she heard a series of grunts ahead of her.

'Yes, yes, Beelzebub,' she cooed. 'It's coming. I haven't forgotten you.'

The pig was housed in a makeshift sty that seemed hardly solid enough to contain such a large animal. Leaning over the fence, she poured the contents of the pail into the rudimentary trough. Snout deep in the food, Beelzebub began to eat it, emitting an array of slurping sounds that were punctuated by grunts of satisfaction. Mother Pigbone leant over to pat the bristled head of the huge black boar. She was so busy talking to him that she did not hear the approach of a rider.

'Mother Pigbone?' asked a voice.

She turned to look up at the man in the saddle. 'Yes, sir?'

'I believe that you can help me.'

The performance that afternoon was extremely competent rather than inspiring. It held the audience throughout but it fell short of the high standards usually attained at the Queen's Head. Lawrence Firethorn played the title role in *The Insatiate Duke* with the blend of physical energy and emotional power that were synonymous with his name but few members of the cast were able to hold their own against him. As the wise Cardinal Boccherini, Edmund Hoode was less impressive than he normally was in a part he had helped to shape to his own talents. The play itself was written by Lucius Kindell, a young author who had needed Hoode's guiding hand to complete his drama. It featured Cosimo, Duke of Parma, a man of such insatiable desires that he took his pleasures ruthlessly wherever he chose. When Cosimo turned his lecherous gaze upon the beautiful Emilia, the Cardinal did everything he could to persuade him to spare the girl but the Duke would not listen. Rather than submit to his demands, Emilia, as played with affecting pathos by Richard Honeydew, took a fatal dose of poison. After her death, Cosimo learnt that she was, in fact, the child he had fathered on a woman at the Milanese court. The Duke had, in effect, killed his own daughter and bitter recrimination followed.

Barnaby Gill provided the comic relief in a heavy tragedy and made the Great Hall resound with laughter. It was the relationship between Duke Cosimo and Emilia that really fascinated the spectators, however, and made them shudder with horror or sigh with regret. Edmund Hoode, in the robes of a Roman Catholic cardinal, managed to win over a Protestant audience with his innate decency. Westfield's Men used the available space to dramatic effect. At the suggestion of Nicholas Bracewell, some of the more intimate scenes were played in the minstrels' gallery and he devised a spectacular death for the Milanese ambassador, a role taken by Owen Elias. Stabbed in a fit of anger by the Duke, he fell backwards over the balcony and dropped into the waiting arms of four actors carefully stationed below. It was a breathtaking moment and drew a full minute of applause. Elias was back on stage within minutes as a Venetian spy.

The problems did not begin until Act Four. It was then that Davy Stratton had two separate entrances. The apprentice was a servant without a single line to speak but he nevertheless made an impact. In a scene where he was required simply to hand a silver chalice of wine to the Duke, he managed to drop it and provoke unintended laughter. Nicholas put it down to nervousness but Firethorn took a harsher view. Storming off at the end of a scene, he hissed in the book holder's ear.

'If Davy does that again, I'll strangle him!'

'It was an accident,' said Nicholas.

'He did it deliberately.'

'Davy apologised as soon as he came offstage.'

'What use is an apology when he's already ruined a scene?'

'It won't happen again.'

'It had better not, Nick.'

Before he could chastise the boy, Firethorn had to surge back on stage. He imposed his control over the audience once again and kept it throughout the remainder of the act until Davy entered once more. All that the boy had to do was to hand him a scroll so that the Duke could unfurl it and read it. Davy trotted in, bowed obsequiously to his master, and took something from his belt. Instead of giving Firethorn a letter, however, he handed him a large carrot. Pretending that it was an error, he swiftly retrieved it and gave him the scroll instead but the damage had already been done. More laughter burst out. Davy saw the murderous look in Firethorn's eye and fled the stage, bumping into George Dart, who was entering with a tray of food, and hitting him to the floor. There was another eruption of mirth. The dramatic tension patiently built up in the scene was completely vitiated.

When the boy finally came offstage, Nicholas grabbed him by the neck.

'What do you think you're playing at?' he said angrily.

'I'm sorry,' whimpered the boy.

'That was no accident. You're doing this on purpose.'

'No, I'm not.'

'Don't lie to me, Davy,' said Nicholas before signalling Cardinal Boccherini back on stage. 'What you did was unforgivable. You'll not go out there again.'

'But I've three entrances to make in Act Five,' said Davy.

'Your contribution to *The Insatiate Duke* has finished, lad. Go back to the cottage and wait there till we come. I'll make sure that nobody comes near you until Master Firethorn has had a stern word with you.'

The boy ran out sobbing but Nicholas had no sympathy for him. Instead of a compliant servant, they had a rebel on stage and there was no place for him in a tragedy that had to be played with high seriousness. The unscheduled humour that Davy had injected into the play left Firethorn in a towering rage but he exploited it well, working himself up into such a fury in the final scene that the audience was genuinely frightened of him. He then broke down in tears with such moving sincerity over the corpse of his daughter that they forgot his long sequence of evil deeds and actually shared his pain. The insatiate Duke appeared a sad, lonely, suffering, tragic figure. At the supreme moment in the play, however, Firethorn was once again thwarted but it was not by an apprentice this time.

When he delivered his last line, he plunged a dagger into his own heart then collapsed across the body of his daughter. A profound silence should have ensued, during which both corpses were carried away with regal dignity. Even at the Queen's Head, notorious for the turbulence of its spectators, everyone was struck dumb with pity at the sight. The shocked silence was not maintained at Silvermere. No sooner had the two bodies been hoisted on to the shoulders of those about to bear them off than a woman's cry rang out with awful clarity. The husband seated beside her had collapsed in a heap on the floor. Consternation spread throughout the entire hall. Seething with anger, the dead Cosimo came back to life to open a jaundiced eye in order to survey the unhappy scene. Dozens of people had leapt to their feet and a loud murmur grew in volume. In one second, an anonymous member of the audience had eclipsed two hours' dramatic expertise from Westfield's Men.

Lowered to the ground in the tiring-house, Firethorn was fuming. Such was the commotion in the hall that he did not know whether to lead out his company to take a bow or remain sulkily out of sight.

'O injurious world!' he yelled. 'It'll drive me mad, Nick!'

'Someone has been taken ill,' said Nicholas.

'Yes, his name is Lawrence Firethorn. I have the sweating sickness.'

'Will you not take your bow?'

'Would anyone notice if we did?'

'Sir Michael will expect it.'

'Then he shouldn't have arranged for one of his guests to fall off his chair at the very moment when I was being borne off to the mortuary.'

'There!' said Nicholas as desultory applause filtered through from the hall. 'They want to acclaim you. Take your due.'

'Follow me, lads,' ordered Firethorn, looking around the room. 'Let's see if we can milk something from them at least.'

Hiding his annoyance behind a broad smile, he strutted back on to the stage with the company on his heels. Sir Michael and Lady Eleanor set an example by rising to their feet to clap their hands hard but they had few imitators. Applause was polite but subdued. The tragedy being played out in the middle of the hall was claiming much more attention. After only two bows, Firethorn decided to cut his losses and beat a hasty retreat. Once in the tiring-house, he made straight for the book holder.

'Where is he, Nick?' he demanded.

'Who?'

'Davy Stratton. The Devil's apprentice. This is his doing.'

'You can't blame him for what just happened out there,' said Nicholas.

'I blame him for *everything*. From the instant he came to us, Davy's brought nothing but strife. Look what he did to me on stage!' he wailed. 'The rascal handed me a carrot instead of a scroll. I was supposed to read a message not eat a vegetable. Davy's wilful. He set out to mar my performance.'

'Nobody could ever do that.'

'No,' said Gill spitefully, walking past, 'you do it so well yourself, Lawrence.'

'Let me at him,' snarled Firethorn. 'Bring Davy over here.'

Nicholas shook his head. 'I ordered him back to the cottage so that he could do no more damage. Before you censure him, I suggest you calm down a little.'

'Calm down! When that imp tries to ruin my reputation?'

'Davy knocked me flying,' moaned George Dart.

'He trod on my robe,' complained Hoode.

'And spilt some of that wine over me,' said Elias.

'Wait your turns,' said Firethorn vengefully. 'I want the first go at him.'

Nicholas did his best to placate him but he was inconsolable. After the success of *Double Deceit*, they had faltered and Firethorn wanted a scapegoat. Nothing was more important to him than the integrity of his performance. To have it threatened by a mere apprentice was unpardonable. Nicholas let him fulminate. The Great Hall, meanwhile, was being rapidly emptied. When he peeped through the curtains, he saw a small group of people clustered around the fallen man. Doctor Winche was kneeling beside him. From the attitudes of the others, Nicholas realised that the situation was serious. He went back into the tiring-house where the actors were getting out of their costumes in a mood of resignation. It had been a fraught afternoon for them. A meal awaited them in the kitchens but they went off to it without alacrity.

Firethorn was the last to change out of his costume.

Nicholas stayed close, anxious to keep him away from Davy Stratton until his hot temper had cooled. He was still angry with the boy himself but felt it more important to probe the reasons for his bad behaviour instead of simply punishing it. Firethorn read his thoughts.

'You'll not keep my hands off his hide this time, Nick.'

'I'll not try,' said Nicholas. 'He deserves rebuke.'

'I'll rebuke his buttocks until they glow with pain.'

'That may not be the best way to treat the lad.'

Firethorn bridled. 'You're surely not suggesting that I overlook his treachery?'

'No,' said Nicholas. 'He must be made to understand how serious his lapses were. We'll certainly keep him offstage from now on even if his father is in the hall to watch him. In fact, I'm wondering if that was the trouble.'

'What?'

'The presence of Jerome Stratton out there. When he handed the boy over to us, the father was all smiles and benevolence but there's no love lost between him and Davy. Could it be that he wanted to embarrass his father by his naughtiness on stage?'

'Who cares about his father, Nick? He embarrassed *me*.'

'I know,' sighed Nicholas.

'Nobody does that with impunity.'

'There could be another explanation.'

'Davy is a little demon – that's the explanation.'

'Is it? I think we're forgetting the death of his mother. That's still fairly recent. It must have upset the boy deeply,' said Nicholas thoughtfully. 'I noticed how drawn he was to

Anne when he stayed with us in Bankside. She treated him like a son of her own and he showed real affection towards her. Could it be that Anne resembles his mother in some way?'

'No,' retorted Firethorn. 'His mother was some foul witch and the child was fathered on her by the Devil himself. He's the progeny of Satan and there's no room for him in Westfield's Men.'

'But a contract was drawn up and signed.'

'I repudiate it!'

'Do that and Master Stratton will bring an action against us.'

Firethorn was contemptuous. 'I don't care a fig for Master Stratton! As for that little brat he foisted on to us,' he said, grabbing a walking stick that had been used in the play, 'I'll see if I can beat some manners into him with this.'

Before Nicholas could stop him, he stalked off towards the door but his exit was blocked by the arrival of Sir Michael Greenleaf. Their host was disconcerted.

'Thank heaven I've caught you, Master Firethorn,' he said with relief. 'I wanted a private word with you before you go. First, dear sir, let me congratulate you on your performance as Cosimo, Duke of Parma.'

'It was abysmal,' said Firethorn bluntly.

'It deserved an ovation. I'm sorry that you didn't get one.'

'One of your guests decided to steal my applause from me.'

'Not intentionally, I promise you.'

'How is the man, Sir Michael?' asked Nicholas solicitously.

'That's the second thing I have to tell you,' replied the old man. 'The news is desperate, I fear. Robert Partridge – for that's his name – collapsed and died in our midst. That's what robbed you of your due reward, Master Firethorn. I can only apologise. Don't blame Robert Partridge for the interruption. It was beyond his control.'

Firethorn was saddened. 'Then I take back what I said, Sir Michael.'

'What was the cause of death?' said Nicholas.

'That's the curious thing,' said Sir Michael. 'At first sight, it looked as if the poor fellow had succumbed to a heart attack and Doctor Winche gave that as his opinion when he examined the body just now. But I have my doubts.'

'Why?'

'Robert Partridge was not young but neither was he old. Indeed, he was very robust for his age and had no symptoms of a weak heart. He was a successful lawyer who was seen out riding at a gallop this very morning. Yet he drops down dead in the middle of the Great Hall.'

'If only he could have waited another two minutes!' said Firethorn.

Nicholas turned prompter. 'You say that you have doubts, Sir Michael.'

'Yes,' confessed their host. 'Far be it from me to contradict Doctor Winche but my researches as a scientist have given me certain insights. I can read dead bodies as other men read books. When I looked at Robert Partridge, I don't believe that I was staring at a man who died of heart failure. His face was contorted, his skin a strange colour and his hands bunched tightly. It was a sudden death and an agonising one. Then there was the strange smell on his breath. That's what really convinced me.'

'Of what?' said Nicholas.

'I think that he may have been poisoned.'

Firethorn angered again. 'Do you mean that he was poisoned deliberately so that he'd wreck the crowning moment of the whole play?'

Sir Michael shrugged. 'I could be wrong, of course.'

'Supposing that you're not,' said Nicholas.

'Then we have to face a hideous possibility,' admitted Sir Michael, running a hand across his brow. 'Robert Partridge was murdered.'

Firethorn fell silent as his mind grappled with the tidings. Making his excuses, Sir Michael withdrew to comfort the grieving widow and to attend to the large gathering of friends who had been badly ruffled by the incident. Firethorn lowered himself to a bench as he brooded. Nicholas sat beside him. The actor suddenly clicked his fingers.

'Did you hear what he said about the victim, Nick?'

'Yes,' replied Nicholas. 'The man's name was Robert Partridge.'

'His profession is the crucial thing.'

'He was a lawyer.'

'Exactly!' said Firethorn. 'Just like Shortshrift in *The Witch of Colchester*. And what happens to Shortshrift?' he asked, eyes enlarging. 'He's poisoned! We're back to Egidius Pye again. No wonder Lord Malady was spared this time. It was somebody else's turn to suffer.'

Nicholas was unconvinced. 'It's far too early to make that assumption.'

'I told you that the play was cursed.'

'Then why didn't Master Partridge die in the middle of it and not at the end of *The Insatiate Duke*? It's just one more unfortunate coincidence.'

'Fever, collapse, loss of voice, murder. All four happen in that order in Pye's damnable play. Yes,' he went on, getting to his feet in alarm, 'and the next thing is that Lord Malady goes blind. How can I act if I can't see?'

'The blindness is temporary,' said Nicholas, rising to soothe him, 'and it occurs in the pages of a play and not in reality. Stop confusing the two.'

'But they're joined indissolubly together, Nick.' He reached a decision. 'Cancel the play. We'll have no witch of Colchester on these boards.'

'We must. Sir Michael has insisted.'

'All that he insists upon is a new piece. We set Pye's work aside, put a tried and tested old comedy in its place, brush off its cobwebs and swear it's never been performed before. Sir Michael won't know the difference.'

'Lady Eleanor will,' warned Nicholas. 'She's watched us many times at the Queen's Head. So has Master Stratton. We'll not fool them. Besides, *The Witch of Colchester* has been advertised. Cancel it now and there'll be repercussions.'

'They can't be any worse than the repercussions we'll have if we retain it. Take pity on me, Nick,' he implored. 'Aren't fever, collapse and loss of speech enough for me to endure? Will you wish blindness upon me as well?'

'That's not what I'm doing.'

'Keep the play and we keep the curse that goes with it. A plague on Egidius Pye!' he roared. 'He's written a comedy that just killed this poor fellow, Robert Partridge.'

'But he didn't,' insisted Nicholas, 'don't you see? You're confusing fact and invention again. Master Partridge is no character in the play. If a lawyer was to die by poison in the way it occurs in *The Witch of Colchester*, then it should have been James Ingram for it's he who takes the role of Shortshrift. Yet James was in excellent health when he left us a while ago. How do you explain that?'

Firethorn was baffled. He sat down again and tried to work it out. Nicholas watched him with mild exasperation, fearing that the actor might make a decision that would make them all suffer. It was some time before either man became aware that they were not alone. Framed in the doorway, too shy to speak, was Richard Honeydew. He waited until Nicholas finally caught sight of him.

'Dick,' he said, turning to the boy, 'what are you doing here?'

'I've something to tell you,' replied Honeydew nervously.

'Well, spit it out, lad,' ordered Firethorn. 'We've lots to do before we turn in for the night. It includes giving that friend of yours, Davy Stratton, a sound beating.'

'But you can't do that, Master Firethorn!'

'Try to stop me and you'll feel the weight of my hand as well.'

'What's the trouble, Dick?' said Nicholas gently. 'You're shaking all over.'

'I did wrong,' admitted Honeydew. 'I know that you sent Davy to the cottage and forbade any of us to speak to him but I felt sorry for him. While we were all eating in the kitchen, he was alone over there. So I . . .' The apprentice bit his lip before continuing. 'So I took some food across there for Davy.'

'It sounds to me as if you deserve a thrashing alongside him,' said Firethorn.

'That's what I came to tell you, Master Firethorn. Beat me, if you wish, but you won't be able to lay a finger on Davy.'

'Why not?' said Nicholas.

Honeydew was crestfallen. 'He's run away.'

Chapter Ten

The search for Davy Stratton was swift, thorough and entirely fruitless. Led by Nicholas Bracewell, three of them combed the stables, the cottages and the immediate environs. The boy had vanished, taking his meagre belongings with him and leaving behind no clues as to where he might have gone. Opinions about his disappearance varied. Lawrence Firethorn was at first delighted, Nicholas was very disturbed and Owen Elias occupied a middle position between them, relieved that Davy was not there to cause them any more trouble yet concerned for his safety. It was late afternoon as the trio stood outside the stables to review the situation.

'No question about it,' said Elias. 'Davy has gone.'

'Good riddance!' said Firethorn.

'The lad is our responsibility,' Nicholas reminded them. 'We can't have him wandering about the countryside in weather like this.'

'That's not what he's doing, Nick,' said Elias.

'How do you know?'

'I don't but it's what instinct tells me. Consider this possibility. Davy didn't run away from us. Supposing that he ran *to* somebody else?'

Nicholas was dubious. 'Well, it certainly wasn't his father, Owen. Master Stratton is still here. All the boy had to do was to stay at Silvermere if he wanted his father.'

'Jerome Stratton is the last person he wants.'

'I'm not surprised,' said Firethorn. 'I wouldn't want that slimy merchant for a distant cousin, let alone a parent. On the other hand, I suppose that he ought to be told that his son's absconded yet again.'

'No,' said Nicholas, thinking hard. 'Keep him ignorant for the time being. The boy can be retrieved without any recourse to Master Stratton.'

'But he knew where to find him last time,' observed Elias. 'They caught the lad on foot in the woods because they were looking in the right place.'

'Where had Davy been in the meantime? That's the critical question, Owen, and I'm inclined to agree with you. The boy might have had a destination nearby,' concluded Nicholas. 'Who did he go to see that day and why?'

'I've no idea, Nick.'

'Nor I,' said Firethorn, 'and I don't care. He's flown the coop and that's that. Why should we bother to retrieve someone who's been such a damnable nuisance?'

'Because we have to,' said Nicholas reasonably. 'Davy Stratton is ours and we can't disown him, whatever antics he may get up to. Since he misbehaved so badly today, it might suit us to have him out of the way but he's bound to Westfield's Men by contract and must return sooner or later. This is no blind dash for freedom,' he went on. 'Davy has a refuge in the vicinity. Someone is looking after him.'

Firethorn was bitter. 'Good luck to them!'

'One thing is certain,' said Nicholas, glancing at the stables. 'The lad's on foot. He didn't take one of the horses. That means the place he's heading for can't be too far away. He's had a good start on us but it might be worth giving chase. This light will hold out for another hour or so. I'm going after him,' he decided on impulse. 'Will you bear me company, Owen?'

'Gladly,' said the Welshman.

'But you don't know which way he went,' Firethorn pointed out.

'Towards the village, at a guess,' said Nicholas, gazing in the direction of Stapleford. 'That's where the nearest habitation is. Perhaps he has friends there. He certainly doesn't have any at Holly Lodge, his old home.'

'Who on earth would want to take in a mischievous wretch like Davy?'

'We were all capable of mischief at that age, Lawrence,' said Owen with a grin. 'You may hate the lad at the moment but you liked him at first. So did we all. Remember that and join in the hunt for him.'

'No. I'm more likely to attack Davy than coax him back.'

'Stay here, then.'

'Meanwhile,' suggested Nicholas, 'don't let this upset the rest of the company. They've taken enough blows as it is. Find some simple explanation for Davy's absence.'

'Yes,' said Elias. 'Nick is right. Show no anxiety or it will spread like wildfire. Dick Honeydew knows the truth of it but will keep it to himself. The others can be told that Davy is visiting relations in the area.'

'What are they called?' asked Firethorn. 'Lucifer and Belial?'

Elias laughed but Nicholas had already gone into the stables to saddle one of the horses. The other two men followed him and the Welshman began to tack up his own mount. Looking around, Firethorn heaved a sigh of relief.

'I suppose we should be grateful he didn't try to burn this place down,' he said.

'The boy is waggish,' argued Nicholas, 'and not destructive. He'd do nothing like that to harm us. We've still to find the man who did try to set fire to the stables last night.' He rubbed his head gingerly. 'He has a friend I'd like to meet again as well.'

'I'll be there to watch your back next time, Nick,' said Elias.

'Thank you, Owen.'

'What am I supposed to do while you're gone?' asked Firethorn.

'Carry on as if nothing has happened,' advised Nicholas.

The actor was scornful. 'Oh, that will be very easy. Nothing *has* happened,' he said with heavy sarcasm. 'Our performance was ruined, a member of the audience was poisoned and one of apprentices has taken to his heels. It's the kind of happy, normal, uneventful day that we always have.'

'You've forgotten something, Lawrence,' said Elias.

'Have I?'

'You've gone through another whole day without an illness.'

'Blindness is still to come,' moaned the other. 'I've that to look forward to.'

'While you still have eyes to see,' mocked the Welshman.

He and Nicholas finished saddling their horses and led them outside. Both men were armed. After a few parting words with Firethorn, they mounted up and set off. Nicholas took them in the direction of the village, glad that the weather was milder and that the frozen track had started to thaw at last. Since dusk would not be long in coming, they rode side by side at a brisk canter, eyes peeled for any glimpse of the fugitive. Davy Stratton was nowhere to be seen. Stapleford was fairly close but there was no guarantee that the boy had gone there. They might well be heading the wrong way altogether. Seeing the bleak landscape around them, Elias began to have doubts.

'It's like searching for a needle in a cartload of hay,' he said gloomily.

'Davy has to be tracked down.'

'Where do we start, Nick?'

'At the first house we come to.'

'We can't knock on every door in the village.'

'Yes, we can,' said Nicholas. 'You never know what we might find.'

Isaac Upchard was still in pain. His wounded wrist was smarting and he felt a sharp twinge whenever he put any weight on his right ankle. A black eye, a bruised chin and a broken nose were further souvenirs of his nocturnal visit to Silvermere. Feeling very sorry for himself, he was perched on a chair in Reginald Orr's house, grimacing wildly. His friend was unsympathetic.

'It was your own fault,' he said coldly. 'You made too much noise.'

'I could hardly see in the dark, Reginald.'

'All that you had to do was to set light to some straw.'

'That fellow was on me before I could start the blaze.'

'Yes,' said Orr. 'If I hadn't been there to help you out, he'd have overpowered you for certain. You failed, Isaac. Miserably.'

'Not for want of trying.'

'We had the perfect opportunity to put this theatre company to flight. Burn down those stables and we'd have scattered their horses halfway across the county. Westfield's Men wouldn't have dared to stay at Silvermere a moment longer.'

'According to you,' recalled Upchard with another hideous grimace, 'they'd never even get there.'

'I thought we'd turned them back for sure.'

'That's not so easily done, Reginald. They're too determined. The one who attacked me was as strong as an ox. If the others are like him, nothing will stop them.'

'Oh, yes, it will,' said Orr quietly.

'What do you mean?'

His companion was brusque. 'Never you mind. The important thing now is to cover our tracks. You can't stay here any longer, Isaac. It's far too dangerous.'

'But I must,' said Upchard, indicating his face. 'I can't be seen abroad in this state. And how do I explain this wound on my wrist?'

'You won't have to explain it if you go to ground for a while. Sir Michael has set a search in motion. I've already had a visit from the constable,' said Orr with disdain, 'but, luckily, that oaf could not detect a crime if it happened right under his big nose. I quickly disposed of him. But others may come in his wake, Isaac, and they may not be as easily turned away as a brainless constable. Whatever happens, you must not be found under my roof.'

Upchard was hurt. 'Would you turn me out?'

'Only for your own good.'

'For *your* good as well, Reginald.'

'I'm not thinking of myself here,' said the other. 'The simple fact is that I'm bound to come under suspicion. I spoke out boldly against this vile theatre troupe and told the vicar in so many words that I'd fight to keep them at bay. They're certain to question me again,' he predicted, 'but they've no evidence to tie me to that escapade last night at Silvermere. With you, Isaac, it's a different matter.'

'Is it?'

'Your attacker *knows* that he wounded you, man. You bear his marks upon you. If they catch you here, they'll have the evidence they need to arrest us both.'

'But I'd swear that you had nothing to do with it.'

'Your word might not be enough to save me.' Orr stood over him. 'Do you want me to be imprisoned when we're just starting to win converts to our sect? My presence here is vital, Isaac. If I leave, the others will soon fall away.

You understand that. I'm the only one who can keep them together.'

'I know.'

'Then do as I say. Leave after dark and hide until you recover.'

'Where?'

'I've friends near Maldon,' said Orr, moving to sit at the table. 'I'll write them a letter to explain. They'll take good care of you.' He put a scrap of parchment in front of him and reached for his pen. 'Tell them no more than you have to, Isaac. All they need to know is that you're running from persecution.'

'It's more than that,' complained Upchard, pulling a face. 'We ambushed the company and tried to set fire to some stables. They're serious crimes.'

'Necessary evils to drive out a darker malignancy.'

'That's not how the court will look at it.'

'Only if you're brought to trial,' said Orr petulantly, 'and there's no chance of that if you do as I tell you. Now, let me compose this letter.'

Upchard struggled to his feet. 'Must I ride all the way to Maldon?'

'As soon as it's dark.'

'Let me spend another night here, Reginald.'

'No! It's out of the question.'

He was about to explain why when there was a rapping noise at the door. Upchard twitched guiltily. After putting a finger to his lips to advise silence, Orr nodded towards the kitchen. His visitor limped off into the adjoining room and shut the door behind him. Another rap was heard. Orr rose to his feet and crossed to open the door. He looked into the bruised face of Nicholas Bracewell and saw the bandage around his head. Owen Elias was standing beside his friend.

'What do you want?' asked Orr gruffly.

'We're looking for a missing boy,' said Nicholas.

'He's not here. I live alone.' He tried to close the door in their faces but Elias put out a hand to stop it. 'I've no business with you, sirs. Away with you.'

'Not so fast,' said Elias, noting his Puritan attire. 'Would you happen, by any chance, to be Master Reginald Orr?'

'What if I am?' came the defiant reply.

'I've a feeling we met before on the road.'

'Not to my knowledge, sir.'

Nicholas took over. 'My name is Nicholas Bracewell and this is Owen Elias,' he said. 'We're members of a theatre company visiting Silvermere.' Orr's face darkened. 'I understand that you object to our being there, Master Orr.'

'Very strongly.'

'So what have you done to stop us?' challenged Elias.

'Nothing outside the law.'

'You weren't involved in an ambush a few days ago?'

'No, sir!'

'Yet you were heard swearing to keep us out of Essex.'

'I'll not bandy words with you,' said Orr contemptuously. 'In my view, actors are nothing but rats who gnaw away at everything that's decent and wholesome.'

Elias grinned provocatively. 'He likes us, Nick.'

'You and your kind should be wiped from the face of the earth.'

'That's a harsh judgement, Master Orr,' said Nicholas calmly, 'and it's not one shared by Sir Michael Greenleaf. He and Lady Eleanor are good Christians yet they see no harm in letting us into their beautiful home. Would you wipe Sir Michael and his wife from the face of the earth as well?'

'Good day to you,' snapped the Puritan but he was again prevented from shutting the door by Elias's strong hand. 'Let go at once, man.'

'Not until you tell us where you were last night,' warned Elias.

'I'm not answerable to you.'

'You're answerable to the law of the land,' said Nicholas, 'and the constable will be asking the same question that my friend just put to you.'

'He's already done so,' sneered Orr, 'and I sent him packing. I was here in my house last night and did not stir from it. So, Master Elias,' he added, glaring at the Welshman, 'may I be allowed to close my own front door?'

Nicholas nodded his assent and Elias stepped back. The door was firmly shut.

Vexed in the extreme, Lawrence Firethorn tried to assimilate all the facts in order to make sense of them. Since their arrival in Essex, his company had been ambushed, his voice had deserted him at an embarrassing moment on stage, the stables adjacent to their sleeping quarters had been a target for arson, his new apprentice had deliberately tried to spoil the afternoon performance and a member of the audience had died in time to rob them of their curtain call. Set against those disasters, the flight of Davy Stratton might be seen as a bonus rather than an additional crisis. When he applied calm thought to the problems, however, Firethorn saw that he might have been leaping to conclusions. The death of an anonymous spectator had not been foreshadowed in Egidius Pye's play even though the victim was a lawyer. What worried him was Sir Michael's suggestion that the man might have been poisoned. Had he been murdered in order to disrupt *The Insatiate Duke?* Did the company have an enemy inside Silvermere?

To learn more about the sudden death of Robert Partridge, he walked back to the house to seek out its owner. Sir Michael was in the entrance hall, talking with an agitated Doctor Winche. Lurking in the background, inevitably, was Romball Taylard. The actor ignored the steward and hurried across to the others.

'Forgive me for interrupting you, Sir Michael,' he said with a gesture of apology, 'but I simply had to hear the latest news.'

Sir Michael smiled sadly. 'The guests have all departed, Master Firethorn, as you see. Apart from those who are staying under my roof, of course. In the circumstances, they felt that they wanted to get away.'

'That's understandable but my real concern is for the unfortunate victim.'

'Robert Partridge's body has been removed to the mortuary,' said Winche. 'I'll be able to give it a proper examination there.'

'Were you able to confirm death by unnatural means, doctor?'

Winche registered surprise. 'No, Master Firethorn. Why should I?'

'Sir Michael had the impression that the man may have been poisoned.'

'It was only an impression,' stressed Sir Michael.

'There was no hint of poison,' said Winche firmly. 'Robert Partridge died by natural means. It may seem unusual for an apparently healthy man to suffer heart failure but it does happen, especially in winter.'

'Sir Michael spoke of a strange smell on the victim's breath.'

'Doctor Winche explained that,' said Sir Michael. 'There was nothing sinister in it, according to him. It could be put down to the rich food on which he dined before coming to the play. I'm sorry if I misled you Master Firethorn. I'm an experimental scientist rather than a physician. My true skill lies in astrology. Indeed, I have better news for you on that score,' he said with inappropriate glee. 'When I read the constellations last night, I thought I detected joyful events for Westfield's Men.'

Firethorn spoke through clenched teeth. 'Your astrology may be as inexact as your medical knowledge, Sir Michael. We've seen no signs of joy as yet.'

'It will come, dear fellow, it will come.'

'I'll believe it when I see it.'

'Well, I must be off,' said Winche. 'I need to visit the mortuary.'

'Before you go, doctor,' said Firethorn, detaining him

with a hand, 'do I have your word that there were no suspicious circumstances surrounding this death?'

Winche detached his arm. 'None, Master Firethorn.'

'Then what provoked the heart attack?'

'*You* might be partly to blame, sir.'

'Me, doctor?'

'I fear so,' said the other with a frown. 'This is no criticism of your art, Master Firethorn, quite the reverse, but the fact is that you gave such a powerful performance as Duke Cosimo that we were all swept along by it. I'll confess that you had my own heart pounding in the final scene when I thought you were about to ravish Emilia.'

'That goes for me, too,' said Sir Michael. 'I was throbbing with emotion.'

'A worthy tribute to an actor's skill.'

'Thank you, doctor,' said Firethorn. 'But I still don't see that I'm to blame.'

'You may not be, sir, but you may unwittingly have contributed to his death. Robert Partridge was a man of high passion. Your performance would have worked on his emotions as it did on ours. It's not inconceivable that, at the very height of the tragedy, he could take no more. In short, his heart burst with pity, Master Firethorn.'

'Spectators are not in the habit of dying during my performances.'

'This was a special case,' said Sir Michael.

'A very special one,' agreed Winche. 'If any poison was involved, it was administered on stage by brilliant actors. *The Insatiate Duke* was so affecting that it took hold of Robert Partridge and shook him until he died.' He moved away. 'And now, you must excuse me. I promised his widow I'd examine the body properly as soon as I can.'

Firethorn was silenced for a moment but not altogether convinced.

'What sort of man was the deceased, Sir Michael?' he asked.

'Robert Partridge was an able lawyer with a good reputation.'

'Was he a popular man?'

'Lawyers are never popular,' said Sir Michael with a wry smile. 'They're rather like undertakers. An unappealing necessity.'

'Did he have anything to drink before he came into the hall?'

'Romball would be able to tell you that,' said his host, indicating the steward.

Taylard glided forward. 'I believe that Master Partridge enjoyed a cup of wine just before the performance,' he said easily, 'but so did most of the guests, including his wife who sat beside him. Nobody else was struck down so the death could not possibly have been the result of poison or the house would be littered with bodies.'

'One is quite enough,' said Firethorn sharply. 'Particularly when it falls to ground during the climax of the drama. If there's one thing I abhor as an actor, it's bad timing.'

Sir Michael sighed. 'Yes, I do hope this will not cast a blight over the other plays. Perhaps it's just as well there's no performance tomorrow. It will give people a day to get over the shock. The same goes for you, naturally, Master Firethorn.'

'I'll admit that it was a blow to our self-esteem.'

'An unintentional one.'

'Everything will soon improve,' said Sir Michael confidently. 'My telescope rarely lets me down. It's in the stars. Westfield's Men are on the verge of triumph.'

'Really?' said Firethorn. 'How many heart attacks will I provoke next time?'

Stapleford was only a small village but their work still took over an hour. By the time they had finished, darkness was beginning to close in. They rode on to a nearby hamlet but their enquiries drew nothing from the inhabitants there except blank looks and a shake of the head. Nobody had seen Davy Stratton or could give them any information about his whereabouts. Nicholas Bracewell and Owen Elias mounted their horses yet again.

'We can do no more today, Nick,' said Elias resignedly.

'Then we search again tomorrow at first light.'

'You may have to go without me. Lawrence needs me for rehearsal.'

'I'm needed as well,' said Nicholas, 'but finding Davy is more important than having me there to prompt actors. I'm certain the lad can't have gone far afield.'

'Well, he didn't come this way or somebody would have seen him.'

'True enough.'

'We've spoken to everyone here and in the village,' said Elias as they set off at a trot. 'Including that egregious Reginald Orr.'

'You and he will never be brothers, Owen.'

'Why not?' joked the other. 'Welshmen are puritanical by nature.'

'Then you must be the exception to the rule.'

'What did you make of the fellow?'

'Master Orr was exactly as they described him,' said Nicholas. 'Strong-willed and fanatical. But he wasn't the man I fought at Silvermere last night.'

'Are you sure?'

'Completely sure. He's too old.'

'That doesn't mean he wasn't involved in some way.'

'Oh, I agree. There were daggers in his eyes. Reginald Orr is certainly capable of setting fire to a stable but I think he'd have preferred to have us inside it at the time.'

'Why was he so keen to close the door in our faces?'

'You heard what he said about actors.'

'There was more to it than that, Nick. He was hiding something.'

'Or somebody.'

'Do you think we should go back there?'

'He won't open his door to us a second time.'

Aware of a marked drop in temperature, they pulled their cloaks around them and rode on through the dusk, speculating on the whereabouts of their missing apprentice and on the relationship between the boy and his father.

'Do you think he'll come back of his own accord?' said Elias.

'Not this time, Owen. He'll be too scared to face us after this.'

'Davy can't stay on the run for ever.'

'No,' said Nicholas, 'but we may have to accept that

he's not for us. We can't keep an apprentice who's so keen to escape.'

'That's not what he did in London, Nick. I know that he caused merry hell in Lawrence's house but he didn't actually run away from there. Nor from Bankside, for that matter, when he spent time with you and Anne.'

'Davy would have been lost in London,' explained Nicholas. 'It's a big city, full of strangers. Where would he go? He needed us to bring him back to Essex. That's why he was on his best behaviour at the end. So that we wouldn't leave him behind.'

'You think that he planned this latest escape?'

'I'm certain of it. Davy was biding his time. I think that he deliberately created havoc during the performance so that I'd send him away in disgrace. It was the one time when none of us could watch him and he took full advantage of it.'

'The cunning little devil!'

'He has an old head on young shoulders.'

'It won't stay on there for long if Lawrence gets his hands on the lad.'

'That's why I want to reach the boy first. To get the truth out of him.'

'I think that we already know it, Nick. You said it a moment ago.'

'Did I?' asked Nicholas.

'Yes. Davy is not for us.'

They continued on their way until they got with a couple of hundred yards of the village. A rider then cantered towards them out of the darkness. Seeing them approach, he reined in his horse and swung it off the track as if waiting for them to pass. They were too far away to pick out more than his outline. Elias's hand went straight to his sword.

'Another ambush?' he said.

'I think not, Owen. Someone just doesn't want to be seen.'

'Davy, perhaps?'

'He has no horse.'

'What's to stop him stealing one?'

The two them maintained the same pace to give the impression that they would carry on into the village. When they reached the point where the other rider had veered off, however, they took their horses into the bushes after him.

'Is that you, Davy?' called Nicholas.

'Where are you lad?' shouted Elias.

But the rider was no fleeing apprentice. He was a well-built young man in black attire and hat. Head down to conceal his face, he kicked his horse into a gallop and shot between the two of them, buffeting Elias across the chest with his forearm. Taken by surprise, the Welshman was knocked from the saddle and let out a roar of pain as he hit the ground. Nicholas did not stop to help him. Spurring his own horse, he went off in pursuit of the phantom rider. If the man had such a pressing reason to keep away from them, Nicholas wanted to know what it was. Caution was thrown to the wind. The man rode hell for leather along the track, ignoring the bushes that flapped against his legs and the stinging caresses of overhanging branches. Nicholas was equally scornful of safety, urging his horse on and sensing the importance of catching his quarry. The lead was gradually cut back. Glancing over his shoulder, the rider winced audibly. When Nicholas got even closer, he could hear gasps of pain.

They did not deter him. With a last spurt, his horse drew level with the other and allowed him to grapple with its rider. The man was strong but he cried in protest when Nicholas took firm hold of his bandaged wrist. It was all the proof that the book holder needed. He was struggling with the same man who had tried to set fire to the stable. Holding the reins in one hand, he swung the other arm with full force against the man's head, making him reel in the saddle. Nicholas slipped his feet out of the stirrups and flung himself hard at his adversary. Both fell heavily to the ground and rolled over a couple of times. Their horses continued to race on. Nicholas raised a fist to deliver a punch but he did not need to overpower his victim. The man had been knocked unconscious by the fall. His hat had blown off. There was enough moonlight for Nicholas to see his handiwork on the face of Isaac Upchard.

Owen Elias arrived a minute later, sword flailing vengefully in the air. He brought his horse to a halt and looked down anxiously at the two bodies on the ground.

'Are you hurt, Nick?' he said.

'No, Owen.'

'Do you need any help?'

'We do,' said Nicholas, panting. 'Find the horses for us.'

Among the guests who remained at Silvermere when the bulk of the audience left was Jerome Stratton and he joined the others for a banquet that evening in the Great Hall. The rows of chairs had been cleared and a massive table set in the middle of the room. A sumptuous meal was lit by a series of silver candelabra. Sir Michael was a generous host and Lady Eleanor an assiduous hostess but they could not entirely dispel the shadow that hung over the occasion. Yards from where they were sitting, a man had died during the performance of a play. It affected even the most voracious appetites. Slowly, however, the mood of sadness was replaced by a muted jollity. Stratton even felt able to make light-hearted remarks about the deceased.

'It's a dreadful loss for his wife, I grant you,' he said to Sir Michael in an undertone, 'but the rest of us may gain. No more huge legal bills from Robert.'

'He was ever an expensive gentleman,' agreed Sir Michael.

'Expensive and unbelievably tardy. The two went together, of course. The longer a case took, the more money he made. The Partridge coat of arms should have been a giant snail carrying a huge bag of gold.'

'Don't speak ill of the dead.'

'It's not censure, Sir Michael. I admire any man who can make money so well.'

'Yet you and Robert had profound disagreements, as I recall.'

'That was purely a business matter,' said Stratton airily. 'I always liked him.'

'So did I. Acute mind. A subtle advocate.'

'Too subtle for his own good sometimes,' murmured Stratton.

Romball Taylard suddenly appeared at Sir Michael's shoulder to whisper in his ear. The old man was torn between pleasure and astonishment. He leapt up at once.

'Do excuse me, ladies and gentleman,' he said, moving away, 'I'll not be long.'

'What's happened?' asked Lady Eleanor.

'I don't know,' said Stratton, 'but it must have been important.'

'Nothing is more important than entertaining guests properly. I'll give my husband a reprimand when he comes back,' she said, smiling to show that it was not a serious threat. 'Enjoy yourselves, my friends!'

A more convivial spirit was now taking over. Putting aside the death that marred one play, the guests began to discuss the others that had been commissioned for their entertainment. Lawrence Firethorn's name was spoken with relish but other actors earned acclaim as well. Ladies were universally delighted with Barnaby Gill and his comic dances while Richard Honeydew's portrayal of Emilia gained an ambiguous popularity among the men. Sir Michael was away for some time. When he finally returned, he sat beside Stratton again to confide him.

'One of the rogues is taken,' he said proudly.

'Taken?'

'By that remarkable Nicholas Bracewell. The stout fellow not only saved the stables from being burnt to a cinder last night, he's captured the man responsible.'

'Who was he, Sir Michael?'

'Isaac Upchard.'

'Upchard? He's one of Reginald Orr's cronies.'

'Yes, Jerome. And our recalcitrant Master Orr may yet be charged as his confederate. Isaac Upchard, apparently, swears that his friend was not implicated but he may tell a different tale when I have him under oath in court.' He gave a dry laugh. 'It's a shame that Robert Partridge is not here to question him at the trial. He could tear any man to shreds with vicious skill.'

'Yes,' murmured Stratton.

'We've something to celebrate,' said Sir Michael, reaching for his wine. 'One villain is now behind bars and another may soon join him.'

'I'll drink to that, Sir Michael.'

'Nicholas Bracewell is the man to toast, though perhaps we should couple his name with that of Davy Stratton.'

'Davy?'

'Your son achieved a small victory up there on stage, Jerome. He brightened up our afternoon for an instant. He introduced some mirth when we most needed it. You must be very proud of the boy.'

Stratton forced a smile. 'I am, I am, Sir Michael.'

'And so you should be.'

Davy Stratton did not dare to approach the house until it was dark. The long walk had been interspersed with bouts of running and he needed time to recover before he made one final effort. He had travelled light, carrying nothing more than a change of clothing in the satchel that was slung across his shoulder. It was cold under the trees and he blew on his hands to keep them warm, stamping his feet at the same time. Only when he felt confident of being unobserved did he creep towards the house and make his way furtively around to the back. Shutters were closed in the upper rooms but candlelight spilt out through the slits in the wood. The climb was a test of his bravery. The stone wall was hard, cold and slippery. It offered little help. Davy inched his way upward, afraid to look down as he groped for each new hand hold, fearing discovery at any moment.

It was a nerve-racking ascent with no promise of success at the end of it but Davy drove himself on nevertheless. When he reached the room he wanted, he clung on to the eaves while he adjusted his footing. He then tapped quietly on the shutters. There was no response. He was filled with dread that the bedchamber was empty and that he might be marooned on the roof for hours. Unsure of his purchase and exposed to the biting wind, he could not stay there indefinitely. The prospect of a fall returned to haunt him. When he made the mistake of looking down, he felt giddy. Davy tapped on the shutters again and was relieved to hear movement inside the room. A new fear troubled him. What if the wrong person opened the shutters? Or what if they were flung back so violently that they knocked him off the wall? He clung on to the eaves more tightly and waited.

The shutters were unbolted and one side pushed tentatively ajar. A face peeped out until it saw a small boy, shivering violently and hanging there in desperation.

'Davy!' said an alarmed voice. 'What ever are you doing out there?'

The meal served in the kitchen at Silvermere could not compare with the banquet in the Great Hall but it was eaten with far more relish. Westfield's Men were thrilled to hear of the capture of Isaac Upchard and of his incarceration on a charge of arson. Praise for Nicholas Bracewell was unstinting. Owen Elias embroidered his own part in the arrest to garner some plaudits but it was the book holder who was the true hero. The fall from his horse had left Nicholas with several new bruises by way of mementos but no bones had been broken. Seated between Lawrence Firethorn and Barnaby Gill, he was typically modest about his exploit.

'The man gave himself away,' he explained. 'If he'd ridden past us and tipped his hat in greeting, neither Owen nor I would have turned a hair. Because he acted so suspiciously, we were put on our guard.'

'But how did you know he was the villain who tried to burn down the stable?' asked Gill. 'You could hardly recognise him in the gloom.'

'You can recognise panic in any light.'

'Yes,' said Elias. 'The rogue knocked me from the saddle as he went past.'

'Are you sure it wasn't too much drink which did that?' teased Firethorn.

'Never!' denied the Welshman over the mocking laughter. 'I could drink a barrel of beer and still ride bareback to the top of Mount Snowdon.'

Gill was irritable. 'Let Nicholas finish.'

'I was there as well, Barnaby,' said Elias.

'Fetching the horses. Yes, we've heard.'

'Owen came along at just the right time,' said Nicholas, shielding his friend from further derision. 'I couldn't have done it without him. We pinioned Master Upchard then hauled him off to the constable.'

Firethorn frowned. 'That's the only bit that worries me. These country constables are even worse than our London watchmen. You only get to hold the office if you've one eye, one arm, one leg, one tooth, and one foot in the grave.'

'How many testicles, Lawrence?' asked Elias, chuckling.

'Three,' retorted the other, 'so you can apply for the post tomorrow.'

'Is the prisoner safely under lock and key?' asked Gill over the merriment.

'Yes,' said Nicholas. 'The constable is elderly but he knows his job and has put Master Upchard in a cell from which he'll not escape. I doubt that he'd have strength to do so. I landed on top of him when we fell to the ground.'

'We should have buried him where he lay,' said Elias.

Nicholas was pleased to be able to bring back such heartening news. It cheered the whole company. Firethorn had said nothing to them about the flight of their new apprentice and the story of Upchard's capture diverted attention away from Davy Stratton. With unlimited ale at their disposal, the actors caroused for hours before they began to peel away. Gill was among the first to leave.

'A word in your ear, Nicholas,' he whispered to the book holder. 'Give that young scamp fair warning from me. I'm the clown in this company. If Davy tries to steal a laugh from me on stage again, I'll cut him into pieces and feed him to the ducks.'

As the kitchen slowly cleared, Nicholas was left alone at

the end of the table with Firethorn. The actor was able to confide his worries about the death of Robert Partridge. He recounted in detail the conversation with Sir Michael and Doctor Winche.

'I felt that the doctor was lying, Nick.'

'Why should he do that?'

'I've no idea but he wouldn't even discuss the notion that the man had been poisoned.' Firethorn bristled. 'He had the nerve to suggest that *I* was responsible for the man's heart attack. Duke Cosimo overexcited the fellow, that was his claim.'

'A strange diagnosis for a doctor to make.'

'Yet he cured me when I lost my voice so he's a competent physician.'

'I'm sure that he is,' said Nicholas, 'or he would not enjoy Sir Michael's confidence. But we must remember that it was not his medicine that brought back your voice. It was a potion from this Mother Pigbone.'

'He called her a local wise woman.'

'How many doctors rely on such an unusual source?'

'None that I know of, Nick.'

'I'd like to meet this Mother Pigbone at some point,' said Nicholas. 'She must be an extraordinary woman if she can win the trust of someone like Doctor Winche. As to his diagnosis, he may have been simply trying to ward off panic.'

'In what way?'

'Sudden death like that is always disturbing. To announce that the victim had been poisoned would have spread even more alarm and distressed the widow beyond bearing. Perhaps that's why the doctor concealed any hint that the death might be by unnatural means. Besides,' added Nicholas, 'he only examined the man in the hall when he had a small audience around him. How could he make a proper diagnosis there?'

'It was impossible,' said Firethorn, finishing his drink. 'The doctor was anxious to make a fuller examination of the corpse. It's been removed to the mortuary.'

'Here at Silvermere?'

'I believe so. It's at the rear of the family chapel.'

Nicholas ran a meditative finger around the rim of his tankard. 'Do you think that we should pay our respects to Master Partridge?' he said at length.

'Why?'

'He might tell us something that Doctor Winche is keeping from us.'

'But he's stretched out on a slab.'

'I've looked on death more times than I care to remember,' said Nicholas a pained expression, 'and it has many guises. When I sailed with Drake around the world, we lost a large number of men. Some were drowned, some killed by hideous accidents on board, a few perished at the end of a rope. Others died of fever, scurvy, fatigue, sweating sickness, eating strange fish or even drinking their own infected urine when fresh water ran out. You can tell by a man's face if he died happily or not.'

'Say no more,' decided Firethorn, reaching for a candle. 'Let's introduce ourselves to this lawyer. I can ask him if he enjoyed my performance.'

Nicholas smiled. 'Don't expect an answer.'

They left the kitchen and made their way along a passageway. Having been given a tour of the house on his first visit, Nicholas knew how to find the chapel. It was in the east wing of the property, close to the private apartments of Sir Michael and his wife. The mortuary was at the rear of the chapel, a small, stone-flagged chamber that was reached by a flight of steps. Nicholas and Firethorn went slowly down the steps and opened the door. A candle burnt inside the mortuary, casting a pale glow over the corpse on the marble slab. Herbs had been scattered to sweeten the atmosphere but the smell of death and damp was still paramount. Holding his own candle, Firethorn took it across to the body of Robert Partridge and held it close to his head. Nicholas peeled back the shroud to reveal the tortured features of the deceased. He studied the face carefully before pulling the shroud back further in order to look at the torso and arms. Stripped naked, the corpse was still in an attitude of torment.

'Is *this* what I did to him?' whispered Firethorn.

'Not without help from someone else,' said Nicholas. 'I think he was poisoned.'

'That was Sir Michael's feeling.'

'He may be a sounder physician than Doctor Winche.'

'Or simply a more honest one.'

Nicholas pulled the shroud back over the face of the cadaver and they turned to leave. Both of them started when they saw a tall figure standing in the doorway. In the wavering light of the two candles, they saw the expression of cold anger on the face of Romball Taylard. They had not heard him arrive and had no idea how long he had been there. The steward's voice was heavy with disapproval.

'This is private property,' he said.

Firethorn gave a shrug. 'We got lost.'

Mother Pigbone sang quietly to herself as she put another log on the fire and adjusted the iron pot that hung above the flames. It was early morning but she had been up since dawn to feed Beelzebub before getting her own breakfast. The black boar was not merely an agreeable companion for her. It gave her warning of the approach of strangers. When she heard a series of loud grunts from the sty, she knew that somebody was coming. Wiping her hands on her grubby apron, she went outside to see who it was. The rider was following the twisting path through the woods before he emerged into the clearing. He came to a halt in front of her hovel and looked down at her.

'Mother Pigbone?' he asked.

'Yes, sir.'

'Then I offer you greetings and thanks,' said Nicholas Bracewell, touching his hat politely. 'I belong to a company of players who are performing at Silvermere. When one of our number was struck down, you supplied a potion to recover him.'

'I believe that I did,' she said cautiously, peering at his bruised features. 'Have you come for medicine on your own account, sir? I can see that you need it.'

'It's information that I seek.'

'Would you not like some ointment to take away the pain?'

Nicholas dismounted. 'No, thank you, Mother Pigbone.

I'm more interested in the concoction you gave to my friend.'

'Did it work?'

'Extremely well.'

'Then you've no complaint.'

'None whatsoever,' he said pleasantly. 'In fact, Master Firethorn, the patient whose voice you brought back, asked me to pass on his congratulations. He's indebted to your skills.'

'So is half the county,' she replied complacently.

'May I ask what was in the potion you gave him?'

Mother Pigbone cackled. 'Ask all you want, sir,' she invited, 'but you'll get no answer from me. My remedies are all secret. If I gave them away, people would use them to medicine themselves and I'd lose my custom.'

'How much custom does Doctor Winche bring you?'

'That's between me and him.'

'Does he come here regularly?'

'I didn't say that.'

'He obviously trusts you, Mother Pigbone.'

'More than I trust you, sir,' she said, folding her arms with suspicion. 'What brought you here at this time of the morning?'

'I was curious to meet you.'

'Well, now that you've satisfied your curiosity, you may ride on.'

'In a moment,' he said, meeting her stare. A loud grunting noise took his gaze to the little garden. 'You obviously keep pigs.'

'Just one, sir. Beelzebub.'

'A fearsome name.'

'He's a fearsome animal. Beelzebub is my guard dog. When I have unwelcome visitors, I let him loose on them. Nobody stops to argue when they see an angry boar coming at them.'

'A *black* boar, by any chance?'

'Beelzebub is as black as can be, sir. Why do you ask?'

'It's an odd coincidence,' he said, thinking of *The Witch of Colchester*. 'A character in one of our plays keeps a black boar. But I didn't come here to discuss our repertoire with you. I wanted your advice.'

She was circumspect. 'About what?'

'Poisons.'

'You want to buy one, sir?'

He watched her closely. 'Could you provide it if I did?'

'I didn't say that.'

'But you'd have the means to make poison, I suspect.'

'Some herbs can save, others can kill.'

'Would you prepare a compound that could kill?'

'I work to save lives, sir,' she said defensively, 'not to take them.'

'What if someone wanted to get rid of rats or other vermin?' he pressed. 'Surely you'd have something you could sell to them?'

'I might.'

'Then that same poison could be used on a human being.'

'Not with my blessing, sir,' she said vehemently. 'If I did sell rat poison – and I'm not saying that I do – it would be solely to poison rats. I can't be called to account for what use it was put to when it left here. I made a potion for your friend but I had no means of stopping it from being given to a horse or a cat instead.'

'I'm not here to accuse you, Mother Pigbone,' he assured her. 'I merely wanted to establish how well you knew Doctor Winche and to ask about poisons.'

'Then you've no need to linger, have you?'

'No, I suppose not.'

'Unless you want some ointment for those bruises,' she said, softening her tone. 'You must've taken a lot of punishment to get those. Who cracked open your head?'

'I wish I knew.'

'You've clearly not had a happy time since you came to Essex.'

'It's not been without its pleasures. Meeting you is one of them.'

Mother Pigbone cackled again. 'Your flattery comes twenty years too late for me or I might invite you in for refreshment. If you could stand the smell, that is. Most people can't. They have the gall to complain that Beelzebub stinks. What else is a pig to do?'

Nicholas was glad to be leaving on a less hostile note. Hauling himself back up into the saddle, he gave her a smile of gratitude then pretended to have an afterthought.

'You're rather isolated out here in the woods,' he observed.

'That's the way that Beelzebub and I prefer it.'

'Visitors would only come for a special reason.'

'Yes,' she admitted. 'Like you, sir.'

'Have you had many callers recently? Apart from Doctor Winche, that is.'

'That's for me to know and you to guess.'

'Then my guess is that somebody may have come here to buy some poison from you, Mother Pigbone. From what I hear, there's nobody else in this part of the county who could supply it. It had to have come from here.' He looked down at her. 'Did it?'

'Ride on, sir.'

'Did it?' he repeated.

Mother Pigbone turned on her heel and walked around to the sty at the bottom of the garden. When she unhooked the gate, the black boar came charging straight out with its mouth open and its teeth glinting. Nicholas did not wait to be formally introduced to Beelzebub. He had his answer and rode swiftly away.

Chapter Eleven

The euphoria of the previous night had entirely disappeared. During the rehearsal next morning, Westfield's Men were sluggish and jaded. Having celebrated the fortuitous capture of Isaac Upchard, they had now learnt of the flight of Davy Stratton and it unsettled them deeply. Two of the apprentices, Martin Yeo and Stephen Judd, rejoiced in the news and hoped that their young colleague would never return but Richard Honeydew was so upset by the loss of his friend that he was hopelessly distracted. Some actors were merely depressed by the news, others were extremely irritated. When work was so scarce, they felt utterly betrayed that someone should run away from the company and imperil their chances of giving good performances, all the more so since his disappearance meant that they also incurred the far more serious loss of their book holder. Nicholas Bracewell had never been missed more painfully.

'You idiot! Consumption take thee!'

'Yes, Master Firethorn.'

'Stupidity, thy name is George Dart!'

'If you say so.'

'Use what little sense you have!' shouted the actor. 'Are you deaf?'

'No, Master Firethorn.'

'Blind?'

'No, Master Firethorn.'

'Then employ those ears and eyes to good purpose for once,' railed Firethorn, looming over Dart in the Great Hall as if about to strike him. 'We're rehearsing Act Two, Scene Three, you imbecile, so do not try to prompt us with Act Three, Scene Two open before you.'

Dart quailed. 'I'm truly sorry.'

'Is there *nothing* you can do properly?'

'I don't yet know the play well enough to prompt, Master Firethorn.'

'How can we master the lines if you feed us the wrong ones?'

Dart was a proving a feeble substitute for the book holder. Promoted to the role of prompter, he sat with a copy of *The Witch of Colchester* in his lap, wondering from time to time if he even had the right play, let alone the correct scene. So chaotic was the rehearsal that most of the lines spoken seemed to bear little resemblance to those penned by Egidius Pye. They were devoting another full day to the new comedy even though Edmund Hoode's chronicle play, *Henry the Fifth*, would be staged on the following evening. The latter was a known quantity and well within their compass. *The Witch of Colchester,* by contrast, was taking them into uncharted territory. Fresh hazards greeted them every inch of the way.

Barnaby Gill was among the first to voice a shrill protest.

'I thought that there was a dance at some point,' he said.

'We moved it to the end of the scene,' said Firethorn impatiently.

'Why wasn't I told, Lawrence?'

'You just have been.'

'I prefer my jig where it is.'

'The decision has already been taken.'

'By whom?'

'Edmund and me.'

'But you can't just change things to suit yourselves.'

'It suits the play, Barnaby,' said Firethorn irritably, 'and not us. Believe me, if I wanted to suit myself, the only dance you'd execute would be at the end of a rope as you were hanged from that gallery.'

'That's a monstrous suggestion!' howled Gill over an outburst of laughter.

'Then stop pestering me, man.'

'I demand to have my jig restored.'

'We'll cut it out altogether if you keep holding up the rehearsal.'

'This is impossible!' said Gill, stalking towards the door. 'I'll talk with my feet.'

'They can't say their lines any worse than you, Barnaby.'

'A pox on this play!'

As Gill flounced out, there was more sadness than amusement among the company. Fierce rows between the two men were normal events but they rarely occurred with such venom and both parties were quickly reconciled by the tactful intercession of Nicholas Bracewell. Dart was no peacemaker. Whoever else took on ambassadorial duties, it would not be the assistant stagekeeper, too terrified of both men to approach either in the spirit of harmony. In the event, it was Hoode who volunteered to take on the difficult assignment. He sauntered across to Firethorn.

'You'll have to go after him and apologise, Lawrence,' he said.

'Never!'

'How can we rehearse without Barnaby?'

'We can't rehearse *with* him when he's in this mood.'

'You were the one who made him choleric.'

'He was born choleric, Edmund,' snarled Firethorn. 'God's blood! Why on earth did we give the part of Doctor Putrid to him?'

'Because it fits him like a glove.'

'Putrid by name and putrid by nature.' He waved a peremptory hand. 'I'll not say sorry to that freakish homunculus.'

'Then at least let me convey your apologies to him, Lawrence.'

'It's Barnaby's apologies that need to be conveyed to me.'

'Do neither of you have the grace to give way?'

'No, Edmund. It would be a sign of weakness in me and a sign of humanity in Barnaby. Forget the wretch,' he ordered, walking to the centre of the stage. 'We'll continue the rehearsal without him.'

'Act Two, Scene Three?' asked Dart, flicking the pages.

'No, George. Act Three, Scene Two. Since we lack our Doctor Putrid, we'll move on to the Lord Malady's confrontation with Longshaft and Shortshrift.'

'I can't seem to find it.'

'Well, look more carefully, you dolt!'

'Is it the scene with the witch?'

'See for yourself, you lunatic!'

When Dart eventually found the correct page, he sat on a stool at the front of the stage to watch the action and prompt accordingly. He was soon employed. Hoode and Elias had mastered their roles as the two lawyers but Richard Honeydew had only an approximate recollection of his lines as Lord Malady's wife. He tripped over them so often that Dart ended up reading out the majority of his part. Firethorn was enraged. Storming onstage to upbraid the apprentice, he was so incensed that he did not see a wooden chest that had been incorrectly set for the scene. Instead of laying hands on the gibbering Honeydew, he fell headlong over the chest, knocked Hoode on to his haunches in the process, lost his wig, dropped his walking stick and broke wind uncontrollably.

Egidius Pye chose that inopportune moment to enter the hall by the main door.

'I could stay away no longer,' he said breathlessly. 'How does my play fare?'

Nicholas Bracewell could hear the argument clearly. As he tethered his horse to a yew tree in the churchyard, the voices came ringing through the open door. He had no difficulty in identifying the rasping tones of Reginald Orr.

'Do you intend to go there or don't you?' he demanded.

'That's a matter between me and my conscience, Reginald.'

'Attend a play and you *have* no conscience.'

'Sir Michael has invited me,' explained the vicar. 'It's a courtesy to accept.'

'And if he invited you to jump off the top of your church or drown in the lake at Silvermere, would you still show him the courtesy of accepting?' Orr was roused to a pitch of anger. 'Are you a priest or a mere sycophant? Do you do everything your precious Sir Michael tells you? Or do you have the courage to take a moral stand?'

'I'm taking one against you at this moment, Reginald.'

Nicholas removed his hat and entered the church. 'Am I interrupting?' he enquired, sensing that the vicar needed to be rescued. 'Ah, Master Orr,' he went on, smiling politely at the Puritan. 'We meet again though I never thought to encounter you in such a place as this.'

'Ordinarily, you would not,' grunted the other. 'It's a Popish temple. But you're a heathen, sir. I wouldn't have expected you to venture onto consecrated ground.'

'St Christopher is the patron saint of travellers.'

'Not when they travel in the name of Satan.'

'Lord Westfield is the banner under which we ride.'

'Then he, too, is a child of hell.'

'I'm so pleased to see you, Master Bracewell,' said Anthony Dyment, coming down the nave to greet him, 'albeit sad to see you in such a condition. Look at your poor face! Sir Michael has told me of your bravery. You're to be congratulated. Thanks to you, a dangerous man is in custody.'

'Isaac Upchard is innocent,' asserted Orr.

'He tried to burn down the stables at Silvermere,' said Nicholas.

'You're mistaken, sir. I'll depose that Isaac was with me at the time when this outrage is supposed to have taken place. He slept at my house.'

'I should imagine that he needed to after the punishment he took. We had a fight in the dark. I twisted his ankle and cut his wrist with my sword. Isaac Upchard still has the limp and the wound that I inflicted.'

'In the dark. When you could not be sure that it was him.'

'There's evidence enough.'

'Not to my way of thinking.'

'Nothing is to your way of thinking, Reginald,' said the vicar, bolstered by the presence of Nicholas. 'So I'll thank you to stop causing an affray in the house of God and go about your business.'

'Keeping you on the straight and narrow path *is* my business.'

'The vicar is entitled to watch a play, if he chooses,' said Nicholas.

'Not when it sets such an appalling example to the rest of the parish. I don't expect you to understand,' sneered Orr. 'You're one of them, steeped in sin and wallowing in corruption. But some of us have the zeal to fight you.'

'Is that what Isaac Upchard was showing the other night? Zeal?'

'Isaac is a man with spiritual values.'

'So am I!' insisted Dyment.

'Then why surrender them for a seat at a playhouse? You're a Judas, sir!'

'That's slanderous talk.'

'It's also unbecoming language to hear inside a church,' said Nicholas, moving to the door. 'Perhaps we should take this argument outside, Master Orr.'

'I'll not argue with you,' said the other, brushing past him. 'You've sold your soul to the Devil and I'll not have you near me for a second longer.'

He went out of the door like a gust of wind and a restorative silence followed. The vicar was patently harassed. After first closing the door to ensure privacy, he turned wearily to his visitor.

'I'm very grateful to you, Master Bracewell,' he said. 'You saved me from being harangued though that's not the only reason he came here this morning.'

'Why else? Surely not to take Communion?'

Dyment gave a hollow laugh. 'Hardly. You're far more likely to find Mother Pigbone ringing the church bell than to see Reginald Orr kneeling before me. No, his real purpose in coming was to engage me to speak up on behalf of Isaac Upchard in court. The two of them treat their vicar with utter contempt but they're not above using my good opinion if they can secure it.'

'Can they?'

'No, Master Bracewell.'

'Did you refuse to vouch for Isaac Upchard?'

'I simply said that it was not my place to do so. That's when he began to shout.'

'I heard him from churchyard.'

'Puritanism has powerful lungs.'

'Oh, we've discovered that, sir.'

'I'm sure, I'm sure. Still,' said the vicar obligingly. 'How may I help you? I take it you've come for advice of some sort?'

'I have,' replied Nicholas. 'Our new apprentice, Davy Stratton, has run away.'

'Saints preserve us!'

'We believe that he's still in the locality.'

'Sir Michael made no mention of this when I saw him earlier.'

'We've deliberately kept him unaware of the situation and will continue to do so. It's our problem and not Sir Michael's. Please say nothing to him.'

'As you wish,' said Dyment uneasily. 'What of Jerome Stratton?'

'He, too, is ignorant of the boy's flight.'

'But he's Davy's father. He must be told.'

'The lad belongs to Westfield's Men now. We're *in loco parentis*. Our aim is to find Davy quickly so that nobody is any the wiser about his disappearance.'

When he explained his reasons for believing that the apprentice was still in the neighbourhood, Nicholas drew a nod of agreement from the vicar. The latter was duly impressed at the number of places he had visited.

'You've been very thorough,' he said admiringly.

'I was in the saddle at dawn.'

'Riding in one big circle around Silvermere, by the sound of it.'

'I wanted to know if there's anywhere that I missed,'

said Nicholas. 'I wasn't able to follow every path I came across.'

'You seem to have explored most.' Dyment pondered. 'But I didn't hear any word of Oakwood House in that list you gave me?'

'Oakwood House?'

'Yes, it's on the other side of the forest and well hidden by trees. You could ride within a hundred yards and not even know that it was there.'

'Who lives there?' wondered Nicholas.

'Clement Enderby and his wife. Good, honest, upstanding Christians.'

'Is Davy related to them in any way?'

'No, and he'd have little reason to go there either. Clement Enderby was just one more person unlucky enough to fall out with Jerome Stratton. There have been a number of them over the years, I fear. Well,' he said, recalling the death that had occurred at Silvermere. 'Robert Partridge was another. For some reason, he and Master Stratton became sworn enemies. That was not the case with Master Enderby but he somehow found himself on the wrong side of our friend at Holly Lodge.'

'A less than friendly friend, it seems.'

'Davy was forbidden to go anywhere near Oakwood.'

'Why should he want to do so?'

'To play with the children there.'

Nicholas pursed his lips reflectively. 'How would I find the house?'

'Follow, me I'll point the way,' said the vicar.

Dyment took him outside, relieved to see that Orr was

no longer on church property. The violent argument with the Puritan had upset him and he was still jangled. When he had given Nicholas precise directions, he wished him well.

'Is there anything else I can tell you?' he offered.

'There is one thing, as it happens,' said Nicholas casually. 'How well do you know Doctor Winche?'

'As well as anyone in the parish. A vicar and a doctor have to work closely together. Where medicine fails, prayers can sometimes succeed. Doctor Winche and I have sat beside a lot of beds together in our time.'

'He seems a very able man.'

'One of the best in the county.'

'Yet he resorts to Mother Pigbone in an emergency.'

'So do many people,' admitted the vicar with a sigh. 'Mother Pigbone has rare gifts, there's no denying it but they smack too much of sorcery for my liking. But I'm in a minority, no question of that. If a respected doctor finds her potions helpful, there's no better advertisement for them.'

'She keeps a black boar called Beelzebub.'

'Had it been named Matthew, Mark, Luke or John, I'd view her more kindly.'

He walked with Nicholas to the waiting horse. 'Before you go, perhaps you could give *me* some advice.'

'Willingly,' said Nicholas.

Dyment was embarrassed. 'It concerns the dispute you overheard in the church.'

'I won't breathe a word about that to anybody.'

'That's immaterial, Master Bracewell. I need your help, not your discretion. The plain truth of it is this,' he went on, blurting it out. 'Reginald Orr caught me on a very raw spot. Sir Michael has not merely invited me to watch a play at Silvermere, he's more or less insisted that I go. As his chaplain, I can hardly refuse but, as vicar here at St Christopher's, I find it more difficult to accept.'

'Do you fear that your congregation would disapprove?'

'Eyebrows would certainly be raised.'

'Then why tell them you're going to Silvermere? It's a personal matter.'

'Some of my parishioners are bound to see me there.'

'Then you can raise your eyebrows at *them*,' countered Nicholas, producing a sudden giggle from the vicar. 'They can hardly censure you for something that they themselves are doing. When are you bidden to the house?'

'That's the problem,' said Dyment. 'On Sunday.'

'Ah. I see your quandary.'

'Do theatre companies in London flout the day of rest?'

'They do, I fear, yet not in any shameful way. Westfield's Men do not play on the Sabbath because we're under city jurisdiction but our rivals in Shoreditch and Bankside open their doors regularly. If people are not allowed to work, they argue, then they're entitled to be entertained.'

'But entertainment *is* work, Master Bracewell.'

A deep sigh. 'None of us would gainsay that.'

'So what am I to do?' asked Dyment, washing his hands in the air. 'Stay in the safety of the church and risk insulting Sir Michael? Or come to a play and leave myself open to moral condemnation?'

Nicholas smiled. 'Why not simply repay a compliment?' he suggested.

'Compliment?'

311

'Regardless of what Master Orr might think, actors are not outlandish heathens. When you take matins on Sunday, you'll find Master Firethorn and the entire company joining you for worship. We're Christian souls. So,' continued Nicholas, untying the reins from the yew tree, 'you can do unto us as we do unto you.'

'I don't follow.'

'Since we'll come to see you performing in church on Sunday morning, it's only fair recompense for you to watch us at work that same afternoon.' Nicholas saw the look of dismay on his face. 'Forgive my glib suggestion. It was not meant to offend.'

'Oh, I'm not offended,' said Dyment. 'Far from it. There's a comforting logic to your argument. But I don't think that it would persuade Reginald Orr.'

'Is he likely to be at Silvermere on Sunday?'

The vicar rallied. 'No, Master Bracewell. Whereas I have a legitimate reason to call at the house for I always take a private service in the chapel. If I happen to dally long enough to peep into the Great Hall, who can blame me?'

'Nobody. I hope that you enjoy the play.'

Nicholas mounted his horse and thanked the vicar for his help. He rode off at a brisk trot, following a track that led in the direction of the forest. Eyes on the way ahead, he did not notice the tall man who stepped out from behind a tree after he went past.

Reginald Orr was positively smouldering with hatred.

Lawrence Firethorn was horrified to see the author. When Egidius Pye had arrived at Silvermere without warning, the actor had stared at him as if seeing a ghost. Nobody was less welcome at that moment. Given the suffering that the play had already inflicted on Firethorn, his first impulse had been to flee from the man who wrote it but Pye's meek and apologetic demeanour kept him there. Edmund Hoode had introduced the newcomer to the company and suggested that they prove themselves worthy of presenting *The Witch of Colchester*. Put on their mettle and aware how badly they had worked that morning, the actors made an effort to vindicate themselves. A small miracle occurred. Not only did they rehearse one of the most difficult scenes in the play without a single blemish, their momentum carried them on until the end of Act Three. Watching them sulkily through the window, Barnaby Gill had been so impressed that he had rejoined the others to take his place on stage and complete the final scene with one of his jigs.

Pye was overjoyed and clapped his hands until his palms were stinging. With the author's praise still ringing in their ears, the company went off to the kitchen for their midday meal. Firethorn and Hoode lingered in the hall with the lawyer.

'Extraordinary!' said Pye. 'Quite extraordinary!'

'You liked it?' asked Firethorn.

'I adored every moment, sir. I could not believe you've done so much to the piece in so short a time. As for the play itself,' he said, turning to Hoode, 'your touch has been magical. Your name should be placed alongside my own as co-author.'

'No,' insisted Hoode, taking care to stand outside the range of Pye's bad breath. 'That would be unjust. Take all the credit, sir. The play is essentially yours. I've added little enough but been proud to be associated with such an accomplished piece of work.'

'Thank you, Master Hoode!'

'The whole company, as you saw, was inspired by the play.'

'Their performance was faultless.'

'And what of mine?' asked Firethorn, fishing for individual praise. 'Did I bring out the best in Lord Malady?'

'It was a revelation!'

'I missed nothing of the humour in his plight?'

'Neither the humour nor the pathos. You were sublime, Master Firethorn.'

The actor beamed with false modesty. 'I always strive to please an author.'

'You delighted this one, sir!'

'Which of my scenes excited you the most?'

'All were equally wonderful,' declared Pye. 'You were Lord Malady to the life!'

'Yes,' said Firethorn, his smile vanishing at once. 'That's something I need to speak to you about, Master Pye. When I agreed to take on the role of Lord Malady, I did not expect him to pursue me so relentlessly.'

'I don't understand, sir.'

'Neither do I.'

'Let me explain,' said Hoode quickly, hearing the ire in his friend's voice. 'In the course of your play, Master Pye, the villainous Sir Roderick arranges for Lord Malady to be spellbound. He is struck down by fever, then convulsions and even loses his voice. All three things happened to Lawrence in real life.'

Pye was shocked. 'Never!'

'They did,' said Firethorn ruefully. 'I thought the play bewitched.'

'Lawrence suffered grievously,' said Hoode.

'That was not the end of it, Edmund. Tell him about the lawyer.'

Hoode nodded sadly and explained how the final moments of *The Insatiate Duke* had been interrupted by the sudden death of Robert Partridge. In spite of assurances from Doctor Winche that the man died from a heart attack, he added, the use of poison could not be ruled out. Pye was both disturbed and chastened by what he heard. He seemed to withdraw into himself like a snail seeking the refuge of its shell. Firethorn did not let him escape.

'What's going on, Master Pye?' he demanded.

'I don't know,' mumbled the other.

'You know *something*, man. I can see that.'

'I might do and I might not.'

'Stop talking like a lawyer.'

'But that's what I am, Master Firethorn.'

'Not when you take up your pen. You turn into something ever nastier.'

'There must be some explanation,' said Hoode, using a gentler tone to coax the truth out of Pye. 'No sooner did Lawrence take on the role of Lord Malady than he began to be afflicted by these horrendous diseases. What prompted you to invent the spells that are used in your play, Master Pye?'

'I didn't invent them,' confessed Pye.

'Then where did they come from, man?' asked Firethorn.

315

'A witch.'

'A *real* witch?'

'So it now appears.'

'Then I *have* been at the mercy of some evil spells.'

'Not intentionally, Master Firethorn,' said Pye sheepishly. 'And the spells did not last long. You recovered quickly each time.'

'That's no consolation. I was in torment. Fever was bad enough, collapse in the middle of church was even worse but there's no humiliation to compare with being robbed of my Epilogue in *Double Deceit* by Barnaby Gill. A plague on your witchcraft!' he roared. 'You filched my voice from me.'

'Yet it was soon restored,' noted Hoode.

'Do you recall how, Edmund?'

'By a potion from Mother Pigbone.'

Pye was puzzled. 'Who is Mother Pigbone?'

'Another witch, I'll warrant!' Firethorn was livid. 'What's the use of a play that turns me into a permanent invalid? I thought that Davy Stratton was the devil's apprentice but I see that his true name is Egidius Pye.'

'All may yet be well,' said Pye, trembling under the onslaught.

'It had better be, sir. I don't relish being blinded.'

'Then we change the spell that's used to blind you in the play.'

'What of the others?' asked Hoode.

'We alter each one to take the sting out of them all. When I began to write the play,' admitted Pye, 'I thought witchcraft arrant nonsense that was only fit for derision.

Then I met a woman who claimed to be able to conjure up evil spirits and began to have doubts. She had strange powers that unnerved me. You've met her as Black Joan in my play where I made her a much more likeable character than she is.'

'Did she tell you how to cast spells?'

'Yes, Master Hoode, and charged me handsomely.'

'It was money well spent,' growled Firethorn. 'Her witchcraft was deadly.'

'We don't know that, Lawrence,' said Hoode. 'It may just be that the play made such a profound impression on you that you imagined the afflictions of Lord Malady.'

'Imagined!'

'You *became* the character.'

'How can anyone imagine fever, convulsions and a lost voice? That's nonsense! You saw me on that stage, Edmund. Do you believe I'd let Barnaby poach my Epilogue if I could possibly stop him? I was in despair.'

'If the play is to blame,' said Pye, 'I offer you my abject apology. It clearly has a power that reaches out from the page. Let me amend the lines here and now. I'll render the spells harmless then you'll have no fear of blindness.'

'What must I suffer in its place?' said Firethorn sourly. 'Impotence?'

'Lord Malady's complaints will be confined to the play.'

'How do you know?'

'It stands to reason.'

'Not when we're dealing with witchcraft. That defies reason.'

317

'Give me the play,' said Pye, 'and I'll remove its venom.'

'You're too late to do that for Robert Partridge.'

'We're not sure that there's any connection between his death and *The Witch of Colchester*,' said Hoode. 'The deceased just happened to be a lawyer.'

'Who was poisoned just like the lawyer in the play.'

'Are you certain of that?' asked Pye.

'Nick Bracewell is and he's seen the effects of poison before.' He rounded on the playwright. 'You were supposed to have written a comedy, sir, not a stark tragedy.'

'Blame the witch, sir, and not me.'

'I blame you for purchasing her spells.'

'Her sorcery was limited,' said the other. 'There's no way that her incantations could have brought about the death of a member of the audience. If the gentleman was poisoned, as you claim, it was done by human agency.'

Firethorn threw up his arms. 'Who would want to do such a thing?'

'Someone determined to bring us down, Lawrence,' said Hoode.

'We've too many enemies to name.'

'I think we can put a name to this one. He's desperate enough to arrange an ambush for us and to set someone to burn down the stables. Master Pye is innocent of those charges. The man I'd accuse is that rabid Puritan.'

'Reginald Orr?'

'He'll do anything in his power to expel Westfield's Men.'

'Anything?' said Firethorn quietly as he was seized by

a dreadful thought. 'Is there no crime to which he'll not stoop? Do you think he would even try to murder our book holder?'

Oakwood House was over five miles from Silvermere. When he eventually found it, Nicholas Bracewell realised why he had missed it on his earlier ride through the area. Situated on the far side of the forest, the house was set in a hollow and encircled by a protective ring of oak trees that blocked it from view. The place was old and rambling but kept in good repair. Thatch had given way to slate on some roofs. Wood had been replaced by brick in the most recent addition to the property, a series of outbuildings. Clement Enderby was evidently a man of substance with a fondness for his home. Even in its winter garb, the formal garden that fronted the house was a remarkable sight. Smoke curled up from every chimney. The place looked warm and welcoming.

When Nicholas dismounted, he first stole a glance over his shoulder, convinced that he had been followed for some part of the journey. Nobody was in sight. He decided that he was mistaken and rang the doorbell. When the visitor asked to see the master of the house, he was invited into a little hall with a fire burning brightly in its grate. Portraits hung on every wall and he was still scrutinising them when Clement Enderby came out to meet him. Enderby was a broad-shouldered man in his forties with the manner and attire of a merchant. Having been brought up in a merchant's household, Nicholas recognised the telltale signs at once. Enderby winced when he saw his visitor's injuries. After introducing himself, Nicholas explained the purpose of his visit.

'Bless me!' said Enderby with alarm. 'Young Davy has gone astray?'

'I wondered if he might have come here,' said Nicholas.

'Why should he do that?'

'I understand that he used to play with your children, Master Enderby.'

'He did, sir,' admitted the other, face darkening. 'But that was some time ago when his father and I were on speaking terms. Jerome Stratton was a friend of mine once even though we are rivals in business. Yet he suddenly announced that his son would never come here again and that my children were no longer welcome at Holly Lodge.'

'Did he give no reason?'

'None that made any sense.'

'Might not Davy be defying his father on purpose in coming here?'

'He might,' said Enderby, 'but that's not the case. It would be a wasted journey on the lad's part because my children are not even at Oakwood House. My wife has taken them to visit their aunt and uncle in Chelmsford.'

'I see.'

'They'll not be back until tomorrow and I'll hold them to that.'

'Will you, Master Enderby?'

'Of course,' replied the other with a chortle. 'We've been invited to Silvermere to watch *Henry the Fifth*. How often do we get a chance out here to see a famous theatre company from London? Sir Michael is keeping open house while you're here.'

'His hospitality has been overwhelming.'

'I'm sorry that Davy Stratton has not found it to his taste. But, then, I'm rather surprised that the lad has been apprenticed to you in the first place. I'd assumed that he'd follow his father into trade.'

'Not all sons of merchants wish to ape their fathers, Master Enderby.'

'Mine do,' said Enderby firmly. 'I made sure of that.' His eyes narrowed. 'It will be interesting to see how Jerome Stratton greets us at Silvermere. He's sure to be there.'

'By that time, we hope to have Davy back in harness.'

'Did you have any forewarning of his disappearance?'

'A little,' conceded Nicholas. 'He hasn't taken to the life. Davy's been fretful and picked fights with the other apprentices.'

'That doesn't sound like him. Whenever he was here, Davy always behaved very well. It was my own sons who had to be schooled for rough play. Poor lad! He must be so unhappy to run away from you like that.'

'It's upset us all, Master Enderby.'

'What does his father say?'

'He knows nothing about it yet,' said Nicholas, 'and there's no reason why he should if we can retrieve Davy. The one certain fact is that he's not gone home to Holly Lodge. I don't think Master Stratton would be too pleased to see him.'

'No, Jerome could be very strict with the lad.'

'So I gather. But I'll trespass on your time no longer, sir. Davy is not here, alas, so I'll have to continue my search elsewhere.'

'How are you finding things at Silvermere?'

'We've no complaints at all, Master Enderby. Sir Michael has seen us like old friends. He could not have done more for Westfield's Men.'

'Romball Taylard is the man to thank.'

'Yes, we've seen rather a lot of the steward.'

'He runs the household superbly,' said Enderby. 'Taylard is not the most appealing individual but he knows how to control his staff. Anyone who has worked at Silvermere is a cut above the ordinary servant. Well,' he added, tossing a look over his shoulder. 'Kate is a perfect example.'

'Kate?'

'Katherine Gowan. One of my own servants here. A splendid young woman. She was employed at Silvermere for a while then she moved to Lincoln. When she wanted to come back to the area, I offered her a post at once and have never regretted it. Silvermere leaves its mark upon people.'

Nicholas gave a pained smile. 'I fancy it will do that to us, Master Enderby.'

'Good luck with your search.'

'Thank you.'

'I hope to see young Davy back on stage tomorrow,' said Enderby, opening the front door. 'What can we expect from *Henry the Fifth*?'

'Stirring words and hard-fought battles.'

Enderby grinned. 'Those may occur if I bump into Jerome Stratton.'

'Has he always been so truculent?'

'It's got worse since the death of his wife. That changed everything.'

Nicholas bade him farewell and went out to his horse. Though he had not found Davy, he had learnt facts about him that helped him to understand the boy a little better. He rehearsed them in his mind as he rode through an avenue of trees past the neat lawns with their rectangular flowerbeds and well placed statuary. Nicholas noticed for the first time that the ice in the fountain had melted in the midday sun but all that concerned him was where Davy Stratton had spent a cold night.

When he reached the forest, he had the sensation once more that he was being watched. He could hear no sound of pursuit and wondered if his imagination was playing tricks on him. There was one way to make sure. Instead of looking behind him, he waited until he came to a thick outcrop of bushes that would obscure him from anyone on his tail. Swinging his horse around, he waited for several minutes in his hiding place. It was all to no avail. The only sounds that disturbed the forest were those of the birds. Nicholas pressed on, kicking his horse into a canter along the winding path. Sunshine was slanting in through the branches above him. He was in the heart of the forest when the attack came and it caught him off guard. As he came round a bend and slowed his horse to cross a little stream, there was a sudden explosion only yards away. The horse reared in fright, lost its footing and staggered violently. Nicholas was unseated and thrown into the water. Pulling out his dagger on instinct, he stood up to defend himself but nobody came. Hoofbeats departed at speed among the trees but he could not be sure in which direction they went. What was clear was the fact that he had just had a fortunate escape. Someone had trailed him in order to ambush him.

After reclaiming his own horse, he tethered the animal securely while he went to investigate. The loud report could only have come from a musket. If the ball had missed him, it must have spent its venom elsewhere. He began a long, lonely, painstaking search, first working out where his attacker had been when he fired the shot then trying to guess at its likely trajectory. He poked among bushes, studied the trunks of trees and felt along the ground. It was taxing work but his patience was eventually rewarded. The musket ball had passed perilously close to his head and embedded itself in the mossy interior of a hollow yew. Nicholas used the point of his dagger to dig it out. Aimed at his skull, it soon lay in the palm of his hand. It was a valuable clue.

Mother Pigbone emptied the food into the trough and watched with satisfaction as Beelzebub guzzled it down. She leant over to pat him on the back then played fondly with his ears. Without warning, the boar suddenly raised its head and exposed its teeth.

'Is someone coming, Beelzebub?' she asked, listening hard. 'I'm getting old. Your hearing is so much better than mine.' She soon picked up the drumming of hoofbeats. 'Yes, another visitor. As always, you're right.'

The animal remained alert until the rider brought his horse to a halt. Beelzebub then relaxed and addressed himself to his meal once more. Mother Pigbone grinned.

'A friend this time, is it?' she said. 'Good. No need to let you out again.'

As she turned around, she saw a familiar figure waddling towards her on bow legs, his face pale and lined with anxiety. He touched his hat in a token greeting.

'Good day, Mother Pigbone.'

'And to you, sir. What can I do for you this time, Doctor Winche?'

When they resumed their work in the Great Hall, the company continued to work well. It was almost as if Egidius Pye's arrival had lifted a cloud from them. It soon descended again. Nicholas Bracewell returned without their missing apprentice and there was general disappointment. Lawrence Firethorn was grateful that the book holder had come back unharmed. Calling a break in the rehearsal, he took Nicholas aside to hear the details of his search. Owen Elias joined them.

'No luck at all?' said Firethorn.

'None so far,' admitted Nicholas. 'I'll do a wider sweep this afternoon and I'd value your company on the ride, Owen.'

'Gladly,' said the Welshman.

'But we can't spare Owen,' said Firethorn. 'Why do you need him, Nick?'

'Because I'd prefer to stay alive.'

Nicholas told them about the attempt on his life in the forest. Both men were outraged. Elias wanted to ride off immediately in search of the would-be assassin but Firethorn took a more cautious view.

'I think that both of you should stay here,' he said anxiously.

'When someone has tried to kill Nick?' asked Elias. 'We need to catch the villain and string him up from the nearest tree.'

'But we don't know who the man is.'

'I think we do, Lawrence. A name is easily put to him.'

'Perhaps too easily,' observed Nicholas.

Elias was adamant. 'It simply has to be Reginald Orr.'

'Does it, Owen?'

'That would be my fear,' said Lawrence, 'and it's the reason I'd prefer the pair of you to remain at Silvermere where it's safe.'

'There was no safety here for Robert Partridge,' Nicholas reminded him. 'If my guess is right, he was murdered under this roof. And we can't just wash our hands of Davy. The search for him must continue.'

'That lunatic Puritan is the man we should be searching for,' said Elias, waving a fist. 'Heavens, Nick, the man tried to shoot a hole through your head.'

'Did he?'

'Why else was he lurking in the forest?'

'To give me a fright, Owen. Yes,' he said, holding his hands up to stifle the protest he saw coming, 'I know that you disagree but I've had time to reflect on it during the ride back. Reginald Orr is an enemy who's vowed to chase us out of Essex. And, as it happens, he and I exchanged hot words when we met at the church earlier.'

'That's all the evidence you need, Nick!' urged Elias. 'You provoked him.'

'Into a rage, perhaps, but that does not mean he became an assassin. I've met the man twice now and seen him breathe fire at us. Master Orr may be an awkward Christian but he's a Christian nevertheless and that might stay his hand.'

'It didn't stay his hand during that ambush,' noted Firethorn.

'We've yet to prove his involvement in that.'

'What about the attempt to burn our stables? You caught Orr's confederate in the act. Thanks to you, Isaac Upchard is rotting in a cell.'

'Rightly so, Lawrence,' said Elias. 'Reginald Orr should join him there.'

Nicholas was patient. 'Let me make my point. The ambush and the fire were both attempts to scare us off. No attempt was made to kill any of us. Look at me,' he said, indicating the bandage on his head. 'When I was cudgeled to the ground, I couldn't defend myself. If they'd wanted to kill me, they had the chance there and then.'

'They were too eager to get away, Nick.'

'Yes,' said Firethorn. 'Since then, you've given Reginald Orr a stronger motive to want you dead. You not only arrested his friend, Isaac Upchard, you'll be the principle witness against him. What are the chances of guilty verdict against him if there's no Nicholas Bracewell to speak against him in court?'

'Whoever fired that musket was trying to kill you,' asserted Elias. 'I think that we should lay violent hands upon him before he tries again.'

'What of Davy?' asked Nicholas.

Firethorn was blunt. 'Better a missing apprentice than a dead book holder.'

'We can't just abandon the lad.'

'Davy is the one who abandoned *us*, Nick.'

The argument continued for a long while until Nicholas finally persuaded them to accept his advice. He and Elias were to continue the search. Before doing that, however, Nicholas had someone else to see.

'Saddle your horse, Owen,' he instructed, 'I'll join you in a while.'

'Where are you going?'

'To see a man about a musket ball.'

Sir Michael Greenleaf was standing on the top of the tower, cleaning the lens of his telescope with a cloth. The breeze made the wisps of hair on his uncovered head dance in all directions. He was too absorbed in his work even to notice the arrival of two people. Romball Taylard cleared his throat to attract his master's attention. Sir Michael looked up and gave Nicholas a warm greeting.

'Have you come to take a peep through my telescope?' he said, patting it gently.

'No, Sir Michael. I need your advice.'

'Then my advice is to come up here at night when the stars are out. I'll show you how to read them. The portents for Westfield's Men are excellent.'

Nicholas had doubts on that score but he suppressed them. Instead, he glanced at Taylard who was hovering meaningfully in the background. He did not wish to have a private discussion with Sir Michael while the steward was present.

'I'd value a word alone with you, Sir Michael,' he said pointedly.

'Feel free to speak in front of Romball. I've no secrets from him.'

Nicholas was firm. 'But I have, I'm afraid.'

'Then I won't intrude,' said Taylard politely. 'I've more than enough work to keep me occupied elsewhere. The visit of Westfield's Men has placed extra burdens on us all.' He gave a faint nod. 'Please excuse me.'

Nicholas waited until the steward had shut the door behind him before he spoke.

'What I have to say is strictly confidential, Sir Michael,' he warned.

'Of course, dear fellow, of course.'

'There are two things I need to raise with you, neither particularly pleasant.'

'Dear me!' said Sir Michael. 'I hope you have no complaints.'

'None at all.'

'I told Romball that Westfield's Men were to have everything they wanted.'

'And we have done,' said Nicholas gratefully.

'The one thing we could not legislate for was that unfortunate business during *The Insatiate Duke*. I know that it ruined the final moments of the play and I offer my apologies. We had no idea that Robert Partridge would be struck down by a heart attack.'

'I'm not certain that he was, Sir Michael.'

'No?'

'It's the first matter I wanted to discuss,' said Nicholas. 'You may remember telling us that your first impression was that the victim had not died from natural causes at all. You spoke of poison.'

'Too hastily. Doctor Winche overruled me.'

'Then perhaps he spoke too hastily as well.'

'What do you mean?'

'The case interested us, Sir Michael. It's not every day that someone drops down dead during one of our performances. Master Firethorn and I decided to pay our respects to the victim. I hope that you don't think it presumptuous of us,' said Nicholas, 'but we entered your chapel without asking permission.'

'It's always open to my guests.'

Nicholas told him what they had found in the mortuary, explaining his own familiarity with death by poisoning and calling into question the doctor's diagnosis.

Sir Michael was shocked. 'Doctor Winche is an experienced physician.'

'Everyone makes mistakes.'

'Well, yes, I know. It's what I did when I first saw the body.'

'Your opinion is supported by my own, Sir Michael.'

'Then why do we differ from Doctor Winche?'

'Who knows?' replied Nicholas. 'Perhaps we are both in error. All I ask is that you take a closer look at the victim with me now.'

'But that's impossible, my friend.'

'I merely wish to point out the signs that I detected.'

'You're too late,' said Sir Michael. 'The body of Robert Partridge was removed from here first thing this morning. He lives in the parish of St Margaret's. Since the church is big enough to have its own mortuary, that's where he's been taken. Doctor Winche was here to supervise the transfer of the cadaver.'

'I see.'

'He takes his duties very seriously, Master Bracewell.'

Nicholas was not sure that the man's duties involved the removal of a dead body from one mortuary to another but he said nothing. Sir Michael's faith in Doctor Winche was clearly unshaken. The whole subject needed to be postponed.

'What's the other matter you have to raise with me?' asked Sir Michael.

'It concerns this,' said Nicholas, opening the palm of his hand to disclose the musket ball. 'It was fired at me earlier today.'

Sir Michael was startled. 'By whom?'

'I wish I knew.'

'Where did the shot occur?'

'A few miles away. In the middle of the forest.'

'May I see it?'

'Please do, Sir Michael,' said Nicholas, passing it to him. 'There can't be too many people in this part of the county who possess a musket. You have several in your arsenal and are clearly an expert on firearms.'

'They've always fascinated me.'

'When I was at sea, I was trained in the use of a musket so I know how unreliable they are. Even over short distances, aim is sometimes difficult.'

'That fact may have been your salvation, sir,' said Sir Michael, holding the musket ball to his eye to study it. 'This would have killed you outright.' He looked across at Nicholas. 'What were you doing in the forest?'

'Returning from Oakwood House.'

'You had business with Clement Enderby?'

'Yes,' said Nicholas, careful not to divulge the full details. 'Davy Stratton went across there this morning to visit Master Enderby's children who are old friends of his. When the lad was late returning, I went in search of him but Davy had already come back to Silvermere by another route so my journey was in vain.'

'And almost fatal.'

'So it seems.'

'How did you find Clement Enderby?'

'In good spirits, Sir Michael, and looking forward to the performance of *Henry the Fifth* tomorrow. He was delighted that you invited him to Silvermere. He spoke very well of someone who used to be in service here.'

'Oh? Who was that?'

'A young woman called Kate, I believe.'

'Ah, yes,' said Sir Michael. 'Katherine Gowan. We were sorry to lose her. My wife, especially. But the girl upset Romball in some way and she had to go. I never interfere in disputes between my steward and his staff. That would be foolish.' He handed the musket ball back to Nicholas. 'My eyes are not what they were, Master Bracewell. Look closely. Do you see any marks upon it?'

'What sort of marks, Sir Michael?'

'Three dots in the form of a triangle.'

'I can see one, I think,' said Nicholas, peering at the ball. 'And there's a trace of a second. If there was a third, it was scraped away when the ball hit the tree.' He licked a finger and rubbed. 'There are certainly two dots. I can see the second clearly now.'

'As I suspected.'

'Do you know what sort of musket fired it?'

'Only too well,' admitted Sir Michael, tugging nervously at his beard. 'That musket ball was made here in one of my own moulds. We mark all ammunition with three dots when the molten iron starts to harden.' He took a deep breath. 'I regret to tell you that you came close to being killed by one of my own muskets.'

'Who has access to them?'

'Nobody but myself. As you saw, they're kept under lock and key.'

'Somebody must have got into your arsenal.'

Sir Michael paled. 'They didn't need to, Master Bracewell. I've just remembered. I lent a musket and some ammunition to a friend when he was overrun with rabbits. He borrowed the weapon to control their numbers.'

'And who was this friend, Sir Michael?'

'I hesitate to say his name.'

'Why?' pressed Nicholas. 'Who was it?'

'Jerome Stratton.'

Chapter Twelve

Nicholas Bracewell used the journey to Holly Lodge to discuss the implications of his discovery. His nagging suspicion about Jerome Stratton had been confirmed. Riding beside him, Owen Elias was difficult to shift from his original opinion.

'I still think that Reginald Orr is involved somehow,' he asserted.

'No, Owen. I can't accept that.'

'Can you accept that he might have attacked you with a cudgel the other night?'

'Easily.'

'The difference between a cudgel and a musket is not that great.'

'It is,' said Nicholas.

'Both can be used to kill.'

'Only in the wrong hands. If it *was* Master Orr who hit

me – and we've yet to unmask him as the culprit – then he did so simply to set Isaac Upchard free rather than to knock out my brains. I absolve him completely of the charge of shooting at me.'

'Well, I don't, Nick.'

'How would he get hold of a musket?'

'Sir Michael is not the only man in Essex who possesses them.'

'He's the only one with distinctive markings on his ammunition,' said Nicholas. 'He took me to the arsenal again and showed me his supply of musket balls. Each one had the same triangle of dots.'

Elias was scornful. 'I'm not interested in Sir Michael's little triangles. All that I'm concerned with is the single round hole that someone tried to put in your head. And my guess is that it was Reginald Orr who pulled the trigger himself or who set someone else on to do it.'

'I disagree, Owen.'

'What if he and Jerome Stratton are confederates?'

'That's unthinkable. They'd loathe the sight of each other. Can you imagine someone like Orr approving of the way that Master Stratton makes his money? And I hardly think that Davy's father would consort with a Puritan. No,' said Nicholas, 'they live in different worlds.'

'Different worlds, maybe, but they share the same code.'

'Code?'

'If something stands in your way, remove it.'

'That's certainly what Master Orr tried to do to us,' conceded Nicholas.

'And what better way to do it than to take our book

holder away?' said Elias. 'Remove you and Westfield's Men totter. From the moment you caught Isaac Upchard, you were a marked man, Nick. Orr is thirsting for your blood. There's a sequence here,' he argued. 'The ambush, the attack on the stables and that shot in the forest.'

'You've missed out the death of Robert Partridge.'

'It was murder. We both know that.'

'Do you lay that at Reginald's Orr feet as well?'

'Of course. He'll do anything to disrupt our performances. I believe that that lawyer was deliberately poisoned so that he'd die during the play. We were fortunate that it happened when it did and not earlier in the action. Orr is to blame,' he said, smacking his pommel with the flat of his hand. 'I'd stake my fortune on it.'

'You don't have a fortune, Owen.'

The Welshman chuckled. 'I'd forgotten that.'

'You also forgot to explain how the poison was administered,' said Nicholas. 'Reginald Orr is not allowed anywhere near Silvermere. How did he sneak in there to give the fatal draught to Robert Partridge and why select a harmless lawyer as his victim?'

'Lawyers are never harmless. Look at Pye.'

'You've not answered me. Master Orr would get into the Palace of Westminster more easily than into Silvermere.'

'He must have a friend in the house.'

'I doubt if he has a friend in the whole county apart from Isaac Upchard. You've met him, Owen. He's more skilled at making enemies than friends.'

The Welshman was unconvinced. He still believed that their trail would lead eventually to the inhospitable Puritan on whom they had called before. The two friends agreed to differ and rode on. It was a fairly short journey to Holly Lodge. As they trotted up the drive, Nicholas issued a caution.

'Say nothing about Davy running away from us.'

'If that's what actually happened, Nick.'

'We know that it was.'

'Do we? Suppose that he's been kidnapped by Reginald Orr?'

'Davy went of his own accord. You can't blame everything on Master Orr.'

'Oh, yes, I can. He probably had a hand in the Spanish Armada as well.'

Nicholas laughed and reined in his horse. When they knocked at the door, they were invited into the hall. Jerome Stratton was highly displeased to see them. He already had one visitor at the house and could spare little time for any others. When he came out of the parlour, he left the door faintly ajar.

'What are you doing here?' he demanded, strutting over to them. 'I hope you haven't come here to tell me that Davy has fled from you again.'

'No, Master Stratton,' said Nicholas.

'Good.'

'If he did run away, we'd not look for him here.'

'He's your responsibility now. Davy is off my hands, thank heaven. So,' he said, feet astride, 'why are you bothering me again?'

'It's about a musket that you borrowed from Sir Michael Greenleaf.'

337

Stratton gaped. 'The two of you came all this way to reclaim a musket? What an extraordinary errand to perform! If Sir Michael is so eager to get it back from me, why not send one of his servants?'

'Because it's rather a special weapon, sir,' said Elias.

'Special?'

'It was used to fire at Nicholas in the forest.'

'That may or may not be true,' explained Nicholas. 'Someone shot at me earlier today. The musket ball missed me but I was able to retrieve it. Sir Michael identified it as having come from his own moulds.'

'So?' said Stratton. 'You're surely not alleging that *I* fired that shot?'

'Did you, sir?'

'Of course not.'

'You borrowed the musket to shoot rabbits, I understand.'

'Did you mistake Nick for one?' asked Elias sarcastically.

'No, I did not,' retorted Stratton, flaring up, 'and I resent the suggestion. You've no right to come here hurling wild accusations at me. It's slanderous.'

'Could I see the weapon, please?' said Nicholas quietly.

'Why?'

'Because I might be able to tell if it's been fired recently.'

'You'd be wasting your time.'

'Let me be the judge of that.'

'This is a matter between Sir Michael and me.'

'I may be unwittingly involved.'

'You're not, I promise you.'

'Show me the weapon and I'll know for certain.'

'If you insist,' said Stratton, realising that it was the only way to get rid of him. He summoned a manservant and snapped an order that sent him scurrying off. 'The musket hasn't been fired for weeks because it's completely jammed. It's far too dangerous to use. You can take it back to Sir Michael with my compliments.'

'Do you have any other firearms in the house, sir?' said Nicholas.

'Would I need to borrow one if I did?'

'What about the supply of musket balls? Are they intact?'

Stratton exploded. 'I've better things to do than to spend my time counting a bag of musket balls. If someone shot at you, it wasn't me though I'm beginning to have some sympathy with the marksman.'

'Don't you dare to insult Nick,' warned Elias, 'or you'll answer to me.'

'Are you threatening me in my own house?'

'No, Master Stratton,' said Nicholas in a more conciliatory tone. 'And we didn't come here to accuse you, sir, merely to establish certain facts.'

'Well, here's one that you can establish,' said the merchant as his servant returned to hand him the musket. 'See for yourself. The weapon is useless.'

Taking the musket from him, Nicholas needed only a moment to see that it was damaged. He considered the possibility that Stratton had deliberately put it out of action after firing at him but dismissed it instantly. The man might be angry with him but he had no real motive to kill him. Since his son was now a member of Westfield's Men, it was in Stratton's interests to safeguard the company rather than to murder one of its members.

Nicholas gave the musket to Elias. Out of the corner of his eye, he thought he saw the door of the parlour inch open a little.

'Where exactly did this attack take place?' said Stratton.

'In the forest,' replied Nicholas. 'I was returning from Oakwood House.'

'Oakwood? What took you there?'

'Private business. Though your name did come into the conversation.'

Stratton was sour. 'I'm sure that it did. Clement Enderby wastes no opportunity to run me down. You'll get no endorsements for me at Oakwood House, sir, and none at all at Holly Lodge for Enderby.'

'Yet it was not always so, I hear,' probed Nicholas.

'That's our affair.'

'According to Master Enderby, you and he were friends at one time.'

'I thought you came to Essex to stage some plays,' said Stratton, 'not to listen to the local tittle-tattle. Be about your business, the both of you.'

'We've not finished here yet,' said Elias. 'The local tittle-tattle has it that you and Robert Partridge were not exactly brothers-in-arms either. Is that true?'

'Your question is offensive.'

'Then give me an offensive answer,' taunted Elias.

'What Owen was intending to say,' interrupted Nicholas, silencing his friend with a glance, 'was that there's been a new development. It appears that Master Partridge may not, after all, have been the victim of a heart attack.'

Stratton shrugged. 'But that was Doctor Winche's verdict.'

'We have reason to believe otherwise, sir. Poison was used.'

'Poison!'

'It's conceivable that he may have been murdered.'

'But that's a ludicrous notion. Who would possibility want to murder him?'

'Someone who fell out with him,' said Elias levelly.

'Oh, I see,' said Stratton, surprise turning to anger. 'You're going to accuse me of that as well, are you? What did I do? Put a supply of poison in the end of the musket and fire it down Robert Partridge's throat?'

'Nobody is accusing you of anything, Master Stratton,' said Nicholas gently.

'Then be so good as to leave my house.'

'At once, sir. We apologise for this intrusion.'

'Let it be the last you ever make on my property.'

Before Elias could deliver a tart rejoinder, Nicholas hustled him out. When they mounted their horses, the Welshman was still holding the musket. He held it up.

'It's a pity it's out of action, Nick, or I'd have put a ball between his eyes.'

'Jerome Stratton was not my assassin,' said Nicholas.

'I'd willingly be his.'

'He'll still repay watching, Owen. Did you hear the way that he talked about Davy? When he first brought the lad to London, he played the doting father but not any more. He's obviously glad to get rid of the boy.'

'I'd like to know why.'

'So would I,' said Nicholas, 'and there's another question that intrigues me.'

'What was that?'

'Who was listening to us from the parlour?'

It was all that Lawrence Firethorn could do to keep the company together during the rehearsal that afternoon. Deprived of his book holder, shorn of the actor who played the key role of Sir Roderick Lawless and deserted by his latest apprentice, he was finding it hard to concentrate. Egidius Pye's presence, an unlikely boon at first, became an intense irritation to them all. It was not long before tetchiness crept in. George Dart was a convenient whipping boy.

'George!' bellowed Firethorn.

'Yes, sir?'

'You're getting worse.'

'Am I?'

'Dreadfully so. I begin to fear for your sanity.'

'I'm doing my best, Master Firethorn,' said Dart, deputising as prompter.

'Well, it's nowhere near good enough. What is Master Pye to think when he sees his wonderful play ripped to shreds by the galloping incompetence of its prompter? When you say the lines,' continued Firethorn, exposing him to the ridicule of the company, 'we can't hear them. When we hear them, we can't understand them. And when we finally do understand them, we realise that they're from entirely the wrong scene in the play.'

'I went astray, sir.'

'You were *born* astray, George.'

Cruel laughter broke out as Dart once again bore the brunt of Firethorn's abuse. When another break in rehearsal was taken, it was Barnaby Gill who came to Dart's aid.

'It's unjust to single George out for condemnation,' he said.

'Yes, Barnaby,' returned Firethorn. 'You certainly deserve your share.'

'Why?'

'You're completely out of sorts this afternoon.'

'It's you who should take most of the blame, Lawrence. You hardly got through a speech without a stumble. Lord Malady's malady is forgetfulness.'

'And yours is spite.'

'I'm entitled to point out your mistakes.'

'Not when you make far more yourself, Barnaby.'

Gill stood on his dignity. 'What mistake did I make?'

'Entering the profession of acting.'

'At least I did enter it,' said the other haughtily. 'You stumbled into it like a drunken man falling through the door of a leaping house. My mistake was in joining Westfield's Men while it had someone like you in it.'

Firethorn inflated his chest. 'I'm not *in* the company, I *am* the company.'

Edmund Hoode was poised to intervene before hot words provoked one or other of them to stalk out for effect but his placatory talents were not needed. The door of the Great Hall opened and Anthony Dyment came scurrying over the oaken floor.

'I need to speak to Nicholas Bracewell,' he said.

Firethorn rolled his eyes. 'So do we all, sir.'

'Is he here?'

'Alas, no, as you would have seen from the carnage upon this stage.'

Introductions were perfunctory. The vicar did not linger over the niceties.

'Where might I find him?' he asked anxiously. 'Is he still searching for your missing apprentice?'

'Keep your voice down,' said Firethorn, looking around to make sure that nobody else heard the visitor. 'Do not voice it abroad, sir. When Nick confided our little problem to you, he expected you to be discreet not to preach a sermon on the subject.'

'I'm sorry, Master Firethorn. My lips are sealed on that matter. But if you know that he called at the church, you'll also know that he fell foul of Reginald Orr.'

'Who does not?'

'An apt question, sir.'

'Has the bellicose Christian been making threats against Nick?'

'Worse than that, I fear.'

'Oh?'

'He's gone strangely quiet.'

'Then perhaps God has taken pity on us all and whisked him up to heaven before his time. Is this all your news?' teased Firethorn. 'A noisy Puritan has been silenced?'

'Two noisy Puritans, Master Firethorn.'

'Two?'

'The other one's name is Isaac Upchard.'

'The very same rogue who tried to serve us charred

horse meat for breakfast. Nick caught him setting alight the stables then captured him later in the day. You can forget about Upchard,' Firethorn assured him. 'He's languishing in a cell and wishing he'd never heard of Westfield's Men.'

'But that's the whole point, sir,' said the vicar. 'He isn't.'

'You mean that he's *glad* we happened to cross his path?'

'Far from it, Master Firethorn.'

'Your words confuse me, sir. Could you try them in English, please?'

'Isaac Upchard is languishing in a cell no longer,' declared Dyment. 'That's why I had to warn Nicholas Bracewell. The prisoner has escaped and he was last heard vowing to get his revenge on your book holder.'

'The devil take him!'

'The constable thinks that Master Orr may have devised the escape but there's no proof of that. When the prisoner slipped out of his cell, the constable was fast asleep.'

Firethorn was scathing. 'Are such imbeciles ever truly awake?'

'He's begun a search for the fugitive.'

'What comfort is that supposed to bring?'

'None, sir. I share your dismay.'

'Rural constables are as much use as a hole in the road.'

'Officers of the law are difficult to find.'

'This one should have been left where he is. I'm surprised the oaf didn't give the prisoner the key to his cell before he went off to sleep. Are there no clues? Is there no indication of where Isaac Upchard went?'

'He's disappeared into thin air.'

'What of Reginald Orr?'

'He, too, has vanished from sight. It's deeply troubling.'

'Yes,' said Firethorn with a worried frown. 'Thank you for coming to warn us. Nick should certainly be told but I've no idea where he is. Luckily, he has Owen Elias at his side. They make a formidable pair when armed.'

'My fear is that Upchard may somehow waylay them.'

'He'll be no match for either of them.'

'Don't be fooled by Puritan garb,' said the vicar.

'It always makes me laugh.'

'Before he was converted to his peculiar faith, Isaac Upchard was a soldier who fought in Holland. He's been trained to fight, Master Firethorn. That's why I was so eager to raise the alarm. Nicholas Bracewell must be alerted,' he stressed. 'Upchard is a dangerous enemy, skilled in the use of sword, dagger and musket.'

Firethorn started. Taking the vicar by the shoulders, he pulled him close.

'Did you mention the word "musket"?' he said.

'What sort of a woman is Mother Pigbone?' asked Owen Elias. 'Motherly or pig-like?'

'A little of both,' said Nicholas.

'I'll play on her emotions and charm the truth out of her.'

'Not even *your* skills could charm this lady, Owen. Mother Pigbone is no tavern wench with a bright smile. She's more seasoned in the ways of the world.'

'Why, so am I, Nick.'

'It may not be a meeting of minds.'

Elias grinned lecherously. 'Who cares about minds?

She's a woman, isn't she? That's all I need to know.'

'Not quite,' said Nicholas. 'Beware of Beelzebub.'

'Is that the black boar you told me about?'

'He's very fond of Welsh beef. If you value your legs, keep clear of him.'

After leaving Holly Lodge, they headed in the direction of Stapleford. Nicholas was anxious to speak to Mother Pigbone again, to probe the nature of her relationship with Doctor Winche and to find out for certain if she had sold poison to someone earlier in the week. It was not a reunion he looked forward to with any pleasure. Elias offered to spare him the ordeal altogether.

'Let me go alone, Nick,' he volunteered.

'Why?'

'Where a gentleman like you failed, a roisterer like me might succeed.'

'But I didn't fail, Owen. I touched her on some raw spots, that's all. Before I could elicit the truth from her, she turned Beelzebub loose on me.'

'He can't be any more frightening than Lawrence Firethorn on the rampage.'

Nicholas smiled. 'There are similarities, I grant you.'

They caught the first whiff of Mother Pigbone's lair when they were almost fifty yards away and its pungency steadily intensified. Loud grunting noises showed that Beelzebub was aware of their approach. When they reached the house, Mother Pigbone ambled out to size them up, combining surprise and disgust when she saw Nicholas.

'You dare to come back, sir?' she sneered.

'Nick enjoyed his own visit so much,' said Elias,

dismounting and doffing his hat to her with a flourish. 'And I can see why, Mother Pigbone. I'm delighted to meet you. My name is Owen Elias, actor with Westfield's Men.'

'Then go back to them.'

'Will you not invite us in?'

'No, sir,' she said. 'Leave while you can or I'll set Beelzebub on you.'

Elias raised the musket. 'Please do,' he challenged. 'He won't be the first boar I've shot dead. Go on, Mother Pigbone. Let him out and you'll be able to dine off pork for a month.'

She wilted. 'What do you want?' she asked, backing away.

'Some honest answers for a change.'

'I won't speak to you, sir.'

'Then talk to Nicholas instead,' said Elias, pretending to aim the musket at her. 'And be sure to tell the truth or my finger may slip on the trigger.'

'There's no need to threaten Mother Pigbone,' said Nicholas, touching the barrel of the musket to lower it. 'I'm sure that she understands the seriousness of the situation. All that I wish to do is to put two very simple questions to her.'

'What are they?' grunted the old woman.

'You've heard them both before.'

'Shall I jog her memory, Nick?' asked Elias.

'No, no. Mother Pigbone will oblige me in time. She's an intelligent woman. She'd much rather talk to me here than face the same questions in front of Sir Michael Greenleaf when he dons his robe as a Justice of the Peace. Which is it to be?' he asked, dismounting to stroll across to her. 'A polite conversation here at your home or a more thorough examination by a lawyer?'

'I've done nothing!' she protested.

'Apart from setting that wild beast on Nick,' said Elias.

'Beelzebub is not wild.'

'I wouldn't let him curl up in *my* lap.'

'Leave this to me, Owen,' said Nicholas. 'Mother Pigbone knows the law. I fancy she's had many brushes with it over the years. She's aware of the penalty for withholding evidence. Aren't you, Mother Pigbone?'

She glared at him, transferred her hostility to Elias then looked towards the sty.

'Ask your questions,' she said at length.

'What sort of dealings do you have with Doctor Winche?'

'I sell him a potion or two.'

'To kill or cure?'

'To cure,' she said defiantly. 'That's where my skill lies. Whatever they may say about me, I'm no witch. I don't cast spells. But I know the trick of lifting them. That's why I was able to give a voice back to your friend,' she boasted, hands on hips. 'Doctor Winche had no medicine for that complaint. I did. That's why he turned to me.'

'Does he often turn to you?'

'No.'

'Why not?'

'He has no need.'

'But other people come in search of remedies?'

'It's how I live.'

'Are any of these people bewitched?' asked Nicholas.

'They believe they are and that amounts to the same thing.'

'Why do they call you Mother Pigbone?'

Elias wrinkled his nose. 'I can tell you that, Nick.'

'Let's talk about the poison.'

'What poison?' she said.

Nicholas met her gaze. 'The one that Sir Michael Greenleaf will ask you about if you come before him in court. If you'd rather discuss it under oath, you can. But a lawyer will be more ruthless than I am and squeeze you hard until the truth comes out of you like pips from an orange.' He gave a cold smile. 'Do you understand, Mother Pigbone?'

There was a long pause. 'I may have sold poisons in the past.'

'To whom?' mocked Elias. 'Bored wives who want to kill off their husbands?'

'To people who want to get rid of vermin.'

'I know a few husbands who'd fit that description.'

'This is no place for levity, Owen,' scolded Nicholas. 'A man's life was taken against his will. The least that we can do is to find out why. Do you want his widow to go to his funeral thinking that he simply had a heart attack?' His eyes flicked back to Mother Pigbone. 'When was the last time you sold a poison?'

'Some time ago.'

'This week? Last week? Be more precise.'

'I can't be.'

'Then you'd better come with us,' he said brusquely. 'This crime took place under Sir Michael's own roof so he's

350

more than willing to issue a warrant for your arrest. Lock up your house, Mother Pigbone,' he ordered. 'You may be away for some time.'

'No!' she cried.

'I've tired of your lies. Come on.'

'Wait!' She pushed away his hand as he tried to reach out for her. 'If I tell you what I know, will you go away?'

'Yes,' said Elias, 'before we die of the stink.'

Nicholas held his ground. 'I'll tolerate no more evasion. We're talking about murder here, Mother Pigbone. If you deliberately provided the poison to kill Master Robert Partridge, then you're an accessory.'

'I didn't, I didn't!' she yelled. 'I swear it.'

'Then what did you do?'

She hung her head. 'Supply a compound to a gentleman.'

'For what purpose?'

'To kill off rats, he said. Or I'd not have sold it to him.'

'When was this?'

'Two days ago.'

'What was the man's name?'

'I don't know, sir. I've never seen him before.'

'Have you any idea where he lives?'

'None whatsoever. Spare me, please,' she begged, taking his arm. 'You know everything now. He bought what I sell. That's all there is to it. I didn't even get a proper look at the man because he kept his hat pulled down over his face.'

Nicholas stepped back. They had learnt all that they were going to from Mother Pigbone. After issuing a stern warning that they might return, he rode off with Elias. When they were well out of her earshot, Nicholas turned his friend.

'You threatened to shoot her boar,' he said.

'I had to, Nick.'

'But that musket is broken.'

'*We* know that but Mother Pigbone didn't.'

'What would you have done if she'd set Beelzebub on to you?'

'Run like hell,' confessed Elias with a laugh. He became serious. 'You really scared her with that talk about a warrant for her arrest. It forced the truth out of her.'

'Part of the truth, Owen. My guess is that she and Doctor Winche work more closely than she was ready to admit. Why a doctor should fall back on the remedies of a wise woman I don't know but there's some connection between them.'

'Do you think it was the doctor who bought that poison?'

'No, it was a stranger. I believed Mother Pigbone on that score.'

'Was it the same poison that killed Master Partridge?'

'In all probability.'

'Then why did Doctor Winche say the man died of a heart attack?'

'I don't know,' said Nicholas thoughtfully. 'The answer may lie in this odd friendship he has with Mother Pigbone.'

'Do you remember what he said when he brought that potion for Lawrence?'

'Yes, Owen.'

'The doctor said it came from the house of last resort.'

'Mother Pigbone.'

'I wouldn't touch any of her foul concoctions.'

'Don't disparage them, Owen. She helped to bring back a lost voice.'

'Yes, but she silenced another one for ever.'

'Not deliberately,' said Nicholas. 'I think that Mother Pigbone sold that poison in good faith to get rid of vermin. She didn't know how it would be used.'

'Didn't know and didn't care.'

'Oh, I think she cared a great deal. If it was used to kill a human being, it could easily be tracked back to her. Mother Pigbone wouldn't want that. But what really puzzles me is why Doctor Winche didn't recognise the signs of poisoning when he examined the dead body.'

'He must be incompetent.'

'No,' decided Nicholas, 'there's another explanation, I feel. Could it be, in some obscure way, that he was trying to protect Mother Pigbone?'

'Why should he do that?'

'It's one of many things we need to find out, Owen. But we mustn't lose sight of our main task. Hunting for muskets and searching for a source of poison are important, I know, but there's another mystery to solve first.'

'Yes,' said Elias with a sigh. 'Where is Davy Stratton?'

When he heard footsteps on the staircase, he dived swiftly back into his hiding place beneath the bed. Davy Stratton waited with apprehension. Discovery would be a disaster for him. When the latch was lifted, he closed his eyes tightly and prayed that nobody would look under the bed. His fears were imaginary. The visitor did not even come into the room. Something was pushed hastily inside before the door

353

was shut again and the footsteps retreated. Davy relaxed. When he opened his eyes again, he saw something that made him crawl out of his refuge at once. Bread and cheese were lying on a wooden platter. Snatching it up, he sat on the bed and began to eat his first meal of the day. It tasted good. Davy was content. He felt wanted.

Sir Michael Greenleaf was poring over a table in his laboratory when his visitor arrived.

'Ah, come in, Doctor Winche,' said the old man. 'You find me, as ever, trying to explore the farthest horizons of science.'

'What are you working on now, Sir Michael? Your new gunpowder?'

'No, dear fellow. My mind is turning to the manufacture of more peaceful substances. I'm trying to create a liquid that burns brighter than any candle yet lasts much longer.' He rubbed his hands together. 'I intend to fill Silvermere with light.'

'You already do that.'

Sir Michael beamed at the compliment and Romball Taylard, standing at his master's elbow, allowed himself a whisper of a smile. When the old man stepped away from the table, the steward began to clear things up after him.

'I got your message, Sir Michael,' said Winche.

'Good of you to come so quickly.'

'There was a hint of urgency in the missive.'

'Quite so. I felt that the matter had to be resolved once and for all.'

'What matter, Sir Michael?'

'It's this business of Robert Partridge's sudden death.'

'But that needn't cause you any more concern,' said Winche. 'The body has been removed to St Margaret's church and a date for the funeral has been set.'

'The poor fellow died in my house, doctor.'

'An unfortunate coincidence.'

'Not according to Nicholas Bracewell.'

'Oh?'

'He and Master Firethorn viewed the body when it lay in my mortuary and they reached a conclusion that, I must confess, flitted across my own mind.' Sir Michael pursed his lips. 'They feel that Robert Partridge might have been poisoned.'

'That's quite out of the question.'

'Is it?'

'I examined the body with care.'

'So did they, Doctor Winche.'

'But only in the dark,' said Taylard, easing into the conversation. 'They went into the mortuary without permission. When I found them there, they were giving the body a very cursory examination with the aid of a single candle. What could they see with that?'

'An admirable point,' said Winche, smiling with gratitude. 'When I visited the mortuary, I had candelabra set up so that I could inspect the corpse properly. And even then, the light was inadequate.' He gave a laugh. 'I could have done with some of that magic liquid you're working on, Sir Michael. Better illumination was needed.'

'Nicholas Bracewell seemed so certain,' recalled Sir Michael.

'Why should it even concern him and Master Firethorn?'

'Because the death occurred during their play.'

'Does that mean they're entitled to become physicians in my stead?'

'Of course, not.'

'Then why do they question my judgement?'

'There's another aspect of this, Sir Michael,' said the steward. 'They had no right to sneak into your private chapel. How would Master Partridge's widow feel if she knew that two complete strangers had been staring at his corpse? It's indecent.'

'And wholly unnecessary,' added Winche with an edge to his voice. 'Exactly how long has this Nicholas Bracewell been practicing medicine?'

'He sailed with Drake,' explained Sir Michael, 'and saw a lot of death aboard, including those poor souls who died of food poisoning.'

'Is that what he thinks Robert Partridge did? Ate some weird fish from the Pacific Ocean and died in agony? The man had a heart attack, Sir Michael,' he affirmed. 'Brought on by overwork. Robert pushed himself too hard.'

'That's true.'

'I thought he looked unwell when I saw him before the play.'

'So did I,' agreed Taylard. 'He also drank more wine than the other guests.'

'Yes,' said Sir Michael. 'Robert was always fond of his wine.'

Winche chortled. 'I don't blame a man for that. I enjoy a cup of Canary myself. But over-indulgence can be dangerous.' A thought nudged him. 'Nobody likes a drink more than actors. After their performance, I daresay they went off to celebrate.' He turned to the steward. 'Were wine and ale laid on for them?'

'As much as they wanted,' said Taylard.

'What state were the two men in when you found them in the mortuary?'

'Drink had certainly been taken, doctor. I smelt it on their breath.'

'There we are, then, Sir Michael,' said Winche. 'On one side, you have the opinion of a doctor who has seen dozens of people struck down by a heart attack. On the other, you have the ludicrous claim of two drunken men who stole into your mortuary on impulse and examined the body by the light of a candle. Whom do you believe?'

'When you put it like that,' said Sir Michael, 'I obviously trust *you*.'

'Thank you.'

'Yet Nicholas Bracewell seemed so convinced.'

'Mistakenly.'

'So it appears.'

'Robert Partridge has been a patient of mine for years. I knew what to look for.'

'I accept that, doctor, but, as you know, the possibility of poison did occur to me as well. That strange colour in his cheeks.'

'Too much wine.'

'That might explain it, I suppose.'

Winche was categorical. 'Robert Partridge died of a massive heart attack.'

'You should be grateful to hear that, Sir Michael,' said Taylard quietly.

'Grateful that a guest of mine died, Romball?' asked the old man.

'No, that was regrettable. It was a dreadful thing to happen. But since it did, Sir Michael, surely it's better that Master Partridge died from natural causes rather than by any other means.'

'Be more explicit, man.'

'The visit of Westfield's Men means a lot to you.'

'And even more to my wife.'

'To you and to Lady Eleanor. Both of you, Sir Michael, have gone to immense pains to offer entertainment to your friends.'

'Wonderful entertainment!' said Winche.

'Everyone accepts that,' continued Taylard, his face expressionless. 'But ask yourself this, Sir Michael. How many of your friends would choose to come to the remaining plays if they thought that one of your guests had been poisoned here?'

It was a sobering idea and it made Sir Michael shudder.

Lawrence Firethorn decided that it was time to assert his authority. When they came back empty-handed to Silvermere, he told Nicholas Bracewell and Owen Elias that their place henceforth was with the rest of the company. They could not be spared again.

'But we haven't found Davy Stratton yet,' said Nicholas.

'Nor will you,' said Firethorn. 'He's done enough damage to us already. I'll not have him robbing us of our book holder any longer. To be honest, I don't care if we never see hide nor hair of him again.'

'He's tied to us by contract, Lawrence,' said Elias.

'So are you, Owen, and I'm enforcing that contract.'

'What if his father learns that Davy has given us the slip again?'

'I'm afraid that he'd show scant interest,' admitted Nicholas. 'You heard the way that he talked about his son earlier on. He's effectively disowned him.'

Firethorn glowered. 'So have I.'

Nicholas gave him a terse account of their travels that afternoon but the actor was only concerned with his own woes. The rehearsal of *The Witch of Colchester* had ended in bitterness and confusion. Late into the evening, Firethorn still bore the scars.

'Forget the musket in the forest,' he ordered. 'Ignore a miserable lawyer who might have been poisoned. There's murder enough in Westfield's Men to keep the pair of you occupied.' He pointed a finger as he reeled off the names of his intended victims. 'I plan to put a hundred musket balls into Egidius Pye. I mean to tip a hogshead of poison down Barnaby Gill's throat. And, as for that mooncalf, George Dart, I'll shoot, poison and bury him alive in cow dung. The three of them have *tormented* me.'

Nicholas and Elias listened patiently while he rid himself of some more bitterness. The three men were seated at a table in the kitchen, eating a meal with those members of the company brave enough to stay within Firethorn's range. Pye cringed over his food at the table farthest away from them, Gill conversed with Edmund Hoode in a corner and the embattled Dart hid behind a side of beef that swung from a hook and hoped that nobody could see him. It was only when he had finished his recriminations that Firethorn thought of another reason why his companions should stay at Silvermere.

'Isaac Upchard has escaped,' he announced.

'How?' said Nicholas.

'The constable went to sleep and his prisoner walked calmly out. The vicar brought the news because he was so anxious to warn us. Upchard is a vengeful man. He'll be on your trail, Nick.'

'I'll be ready for him.'

'No, you won't. You'll be here in the safety of Silvermere, doing the job for which we pay you and saving George Dart from an early death.'

'This is Reginald Orr's work,' said Elias. 'He must have set his friend free.'

'So the vicar thought but there's no proof. And if it's left to the local constable to find it,' said Firethorn gloomily, 'there never will be.'

Elias was rueful. 'I knew that we hadn't heard the last of Reginald Orr.'

'He'll not bother us if we stay here, Owen, and that's what we'll do. There'll be no more expeditions for you or Nick. Everywhere but Silvermere is out of bounds.'

'I fear for young Davy,' said Nicholas.

'He was the one who chose to run away.'

'I'd hoped to widen the search still further tomorrow morning.'

'No!' said Firethorn, banging the table with his fist. 'You

won't stir an inch from here. We've a large audience coming to see us in *Henry the Fifth* tomorrow. I refuse to rehearse a single line with that mumbling fool, George Dart, as our prompter. We need to have the play in good order.'

'I agree,' said Nicholas with reluctance. 'It's the least we owe Sir Michael for his hospitality. For tomorrow's play, he's offered to loan me gunpowder for some of our alarums. That should keep the spectators awake.'

Firethorn was soulful. 'I don't mind them sleeping, Nick, as long as none of them drops down dead on me. Henry the Fifth is supposed to kill the French, not the audience.'

They finished their meal then drifted back to their lodging with the rest of the company. A row of torches burnt in front of the cottages. Two men were on duty with muskets over their shoulders. Romball Taylard was giving them instructions. When he saw the actors coming, he turned to explain.

'Sir Michael wants the guard maintained,' he said, indicating the men. 'Word has reached us that Isaac Upchard has escaped from custody and we don't wish to take any chances.'

'Post as many sentries out here as you wish, Master Taylard,' said Firethorn. 'I'm in favour of anything that will help the company slumber in safety.'

'You'll have no problems tonight, sir.'

The steward bade them farewell and strode towards the house. The approach of a rider made him halt. Nicholas paused to watch the lone horseman coming up the drive, wondering who could be calling so late. It was difficult to identify the newcomer until he dismounted from his horse to talk with Taylard. His profile and gait were distinctive and Nicholas recognised him at once. It was Jerome Stratton.

The reputation of Westfield's Men had spread quickly and people came from some distance to watch the first of three performances on consecutive days. Sunday would bring them *The Happy Malcontent* whose wild antics would be offset by the sad grandeur of *Vincentio's Revenge* on Monday. For those who flocked to Silvermere on Saturday evening, however, *Henry the Fifth* was in store. History, comedy and tragedy were set to form a memorable experience over three days. Dozens of guests converged on the front entrance at the same time and the household servants were deployed in large numbers to welcome them and to offer them light refreshment. Diverted by the activity in one part of the building, nobody noticed the arrival of two uninvited guests at the rear of the property. Clad in black and taking advantage of the failing light, they slipped in through a back door and searched for a hiding place.

Lawrence Firethorn was in a buoyant mood. Rehearsals had been uninterrupted, the new stage effects had worked superbly and the company had recovered much of its spirit. A fine stage and a full audience beckoned. Since he no longer had to fear being attacked by a mystery illness, Firethorn was able to concentrate on his kingly duties. When he was costumed in his robes of office, he put the crown on his head and called the company around him in the tiring-house. His voice was low but moving.

'Friends,' he said, letting his gaze roam around their faces, 'we've had our setbacks. I'll be the first to admit that. But they are behind us now and you must banish their memory from your minds. Everything is now in our favour. We may have a few enemies in Essex but we have many admirers and the hall is full of them.' He raised a finger. 'Listen!' he told them. 'Can you hear that expectant buzz? Can you sense that anticipation? They are won over before we even step out on that stage. And there's other news I have to tell you that will gladden your hearts. We have the best friend of all in the audience this evening.'

'What's her name?' asked a grinning Elias.

'I talk of our patron, Lord Westfield.'

'Then I resign my claim to Barnaby.'

'Did you hear what I said, Owen?' continued Firethorn, quelling the sniggers from the apprentices. 'Sir Michael and Lady Eleanor deserve sterling performances from us. Lord Westfield demands something more. Are we going to make him proud to lend his name to the company?' Affirmative calls came from all sides. 'Then let's buckle on our armour and carry our weapons with bold hearts. We're not just going to win the Battle of Agincourt out there, we're going to conquer that audience as never before.' He drew his own sword to hold it aloft. 'Onward!'

Nicholas Bracewell could see the effect that the words had on them. Though they had heard Firethorn many times, he still had the power to inspire. With the solitary exception of George Dart, a diffident actor, everyone was straining to get on stage to attest their worth. Even the mild-mannered Edmund Hoode was roused.

'I feel that I could win a battle single-handed, Nick,' he said.

'Well, I don't advise it,' replied Nicholas. 'In the role of the Dauphin, you have to be on the losing side. Win the battle and you fly in the face of history.'

'Did you know that Lord Westfield was out there?'

'Not until just now.'

'Lawrence is a sly old fox. Trust him to keep those tidings until they'd be of most value. The whole company has been cheered.'

'They need to be lifted. It's a full-blooded play that calls for lots of energy.'

'We'll make Silvermere shake to its foundations.'

Nicholas smiled then made a swift tour of the room to check that all was well. Musicians were dispatched to the gallery and actors took up their positions. As well as playing five different characters, Dart was responsible for the various properties used and he stood nervously beside the table where they were laid out in order. The heavy murmur in the hall faded away as the musicians came into view. Given their signal, they struck up some introductory chords then Owen Elias stepped out to deliver the Prologue. *Henry the Fifth* was by no means the best of Hoode's plays but it told a familiar story with vivid clarity and offered its eponymous hero a magnificent role. Firethorn seemed to grow in size when he made his first appearance as the king and gasps of wonder came from the ladies in the audience. Dashing, peremptory and undeniably regal, he dominated the stage even when Barnaby Gill, providing ripe comedy as a reluctant soldier, shared it with him. Long before the end of Act One, the company had achieved its desired effect. The audience was utterly enthralled.

It was during the next scene that Nicholas had the first hint of trouble.

'There's someone lurking behind the gallery, Nick,' whispered James Ingram.

'Are you sure?' said Nicholas.

'I could hear them moving around when I delivered the Herald's speech.'

'But nobody is supposed to be up there until the siege.'

'That's why I thought you should know.'

Ingram went off to change into the costume of the Governor of Harfleur and left Nicholas in a quandary. Controlling the play from behind the scenes, he could not simply slip away to see if there were intruders behind the gallery. On the other hand, he could not run the risk of disruption, especially as the play was approaching one of its most dramatic points. The siege required a number of effects that had been carefully rehearsed. Nicholas was needed to coordinate them. Yet nobody else was free to investigate the warning from Ingram. The book holder acted on impulse.

'George!' he called.

'Yes?' said Dart, scurrying across to him.

'Did you see the way that I lit that gunpowder this afternoon?'

'With a spark. It made such a wondrous bang.'

'You've got your own chance to make a wondrous bang now,' said Nicholas, pointing to the crucibles of powder. 'I have to go for a minute or two. If I'm not back in time, light the touch-powder in the first crucible.'

'But I don't know how!' cried Dart, unequal to such a demand.

Nicholas did not hear him. He was already making for the stairs that led to the gallery. When he reached the top, he saw the glow of candelabra that illumined the stage. The play continued with unabated fury below him. Attired in armour, Henry was trying to rouse his men for another attack on Harfleur, stirring up such a spirit of patriotism in the hall that some voices were urging them on. Nicholas was involved in another battle. It was against an enemy he barely glimpsed in the room on the other side of the gallery. He was trapped. Since he could only get to them by passing in full view of the audience, he had to stay where he was, wondering who the shadowy figures were and what they intended to do. He soon found out.

Having made their way into the little room that led off the gallery, Reginald Orr and Isaac Upchard were biding their time until they could interrupt the play to maximum effect. They chose the siege of Harfleur but the real hero of the hour on this occasion was not Henry the Fifth but the unarmed George Dart. At the very moment when the two Puritans dashed out on to the gallery, the assistant stagekeeper did as he was told. Unsure which of the three crucibles of gunpowder to ignite, he struck sparks madly and contrived to set off all three simultaneously to produce an explosion that took actors as well as audience by surprise. The report was deafening. When Orr and Upchard emerged from their hiding place, therefore, they were completely obscured by billowing smoke. The huge banner that Orr unfurled, proclaiming the sinfulness of all plays, was hidden from view and the musket that Upchard fired to gain attention was unheard in the general pandemonium.

Nicholas could just see enough to spring into action. He felled Orr with a relay of punches then squared up to his companion. Upchard swung the musket viciously at him and Nicholas had to duck under it. He dived for his adversary's legs and brought him crashing to the floor. Upchard groped for the dagger at his belt but Nicholas gave him no time to reach it. Seizing the fallen musket, he used its butt to pound him hard. Upchard's groans were drowned out by the sounds of warfare on the stage. Orr was not finished yet. Dragging himself up, he grabbed Nicholas by the throat and squeezed hard, yelling at the top of his voice. Nicholas gave him more reason to yell, jabbing the musket into his groin then hurling himself on to the man as he fell back. The fight was over. Before he could land another punch, Nicholas and his opponents were dragged out by strong hands. The victorious Lawrence Firethorn stepped over them to take up a commanding position in the centre of the gallery.

'Out of my way!' he boomed. 'I've just taken Harfleur!'

By the time that the noise had subsided and the smoke cleared, Henry the Fifth was seen in an attitude of triumph atop the city walls, ready to deliver his victory speech. Spontaneous applause broke out. Down in the tiring-house, two dazed Puritans were being bound and gagged by Nicholas so that they could take no further part in the drama.

Dart was apologetic. 'I set off all the gunpowder by mistake,' he said.

'You saved the day, George,' said Nicholas happily. 'Congratulations!'

* * *

The play surged on to be met by an ovation at its close. Even their patron, who had seen it many times before, rose to his feet to acclaim them. What stuck in the minds of the audience was the brilliant recreation of the siege of Harfleur when ordnance filled the field and three soldiers were dimly seen fighting for their lives on the gallery. Instead of ruining the performance, Orr and Upchard had merely enhanced it. Far from expelling the actors, they had unintentionally joined their ranks. When both men had been arrested and taken off, Nicholas was able to relax at last. A major threat to the company had been decisively removed. Upchard's possession of a musket singled him out as a possible assassin in the forest. Danger seemed to be over.

Celebrations were in order. The actors were in a state of high excitement and Nicholas was as ready as any of them to make his way to the kitchen. He felt that he had earned his supper and was keen to toast the success of the company. Arm around George Dart, he followed the others down the corridor. Clement Enderby intercepted him.

'One moment, my friend' he said. 'Might I have a word with you?'

'Of course,' replied Nicholas. 'Go on ahead, George.'

Dart went off to the kitchen and left Nicholas alone with Enderby.

'There's no need for me to tell you how much I enjoyed the play. It was truly astonishing. Westfield's Men gave us the most exhilarating event we've had in Essex for many a year. It was a priceless gift,' said Enderby, eyes sparkling. 'I think that you deserve one in return.'

'A gift?'

'His name is Davy Stratton.'

'You know where he is?'

'We brought him with us but nobody else knows that he's here. I felt it wrong to spring him on you when you were just about to mount your performance.'

'How is Davy?' asked Nicholas anxiously. 'Is he hurt in any way?'

'No, Master Bracewell. I left him at your cottage. Come and see.'

Nicholas found it hard to contain his curiosity but Enderby would give no further explanation. He took his companion out through a side door of the house and across to the cottages. Candles burnt in the lodging used by Nicholas and the others. When the two men went into the parlour, Davy was sitting on a chair in the corner. He looked sad and uncomfortable.

'Good even, Davy,' said Nicholas.

'Good even,' murmured the boy.

'Where have you been?'

'At Oakwood House.'

'Why?'

A woman stepped out of the shadows. 'He came to see me, sir.'

'This is Kate,' introduced Enderby. 'Katherine Gowan, as she was known when in service here. She was very unhappy about coming back to Silvermere.'

'I was, sir. But I want what's best for Davy.'

She glanced across at him and Davy responded with a wan smile. Nicholas looked first at the attractive young woman in front of him, then across at the boy, then back at Katherine Gowan. In the space of a few seconds, he began to understand a great deal. Enderby came forward to reclaim Davy.

'Talk to Kate alone,' he advised. 'Some of it's not for Davy's ears.'

He took the boy into the kitchen and shut the door after them. Nicholas could see how uneasy and embarrassed the woman was. He invited her to sit down then took the stool beside her. Katherine searched his eyes for reassurance.

'Davy said that I could trust you,' she said.

'I'm his friend, Kate.'

'That's what he told me.'

'He didn't tell me about you,' said Nicholas softly. 'I had no idea that his mother was still alive.'

The woman blushed and lowered her head. It was minutes before she could speak. Nicholas was patient, sensing the effort that it was taking her, wondering how he could make it less of a trial. He attempted to coax the words out of her.

'He went to you, didn't he?' he asked. 'When he ran away from us in the forest that first time, he wanted to be with you.'

'I told him it was wrong, sir. I made him go back.'

'And this time?'

She gave a shrug of defeat. 'I tried to hide him in my room but it was no use. Davy couldn't stay at Oakwood House forever. Master Enderby is a kind man. He's been good to me. I couldn't keep the secret from him.'

'When did Davy find out himself?'

'When I came back to Essex, sir. I was sent to Lincoln to

work, far away, so that nobody would know. Davy was to be brought up in a fine house. I could never give him that. It seemed right for him. I was in disgrace, sir,' she said quietly. 'I had to agree.'

'But you came back eventually.'

'He was never out of my mind.'

'Did you keep in touch with his father?'

'No,' she said firmly.

'Did he want you to come back?'

'Oh, no!'

'I can see now why Master Stratton stopped the boy coming to Oakwood House.'

'But he's not the father, sir.'

'Isn't he?'

'I'd not let him near me, sir,' she said with spirit. 'He's a harsh man.' She bit her lip. 'It's a long story and I don't know it all myself. What little I do know makes me ashamed of my part in it.'

'Why?'

'It was a cruel thing to do to any woman, sir. It was wicked.' She became wistful. 'And it was a terrible thing to do to Davy as well, God forgive me.'

'What happened?' asked Nicholas, taking her hand. 'I'll not sit in judgement on you. Davy obviously loves his mother so much that he'll do anything to be with her. You came back in order to be near him, didn't you?'

'Yes.'

'And that's why Master Stratton stopped him coming to Oakwood House to play with his friends. He packed the boy off to London to keep him out of the way.'

'It hurt Davy so much, sir. To be separated from me.'

'It must have been agony for you as well.'

'Oh, it was. I'd had years of it, wondering where my son was and how he was faring. I could stand it no longer. I knew that he could never be mine but I wanted to be close to him somehow.'

'How did he come to be at Holly Lodge in the first place?'

She took a deep breath. 'You have to remember that this took place a long time ago. I may not have all the details right but this is what I recall.' Nicholas could feel her hand trembling. 'Master Stratton's wife was desperate to have children and she was heartbroken when she had two stillbirths. Her husband didn't want her to go through the ordeal again. I can understand that. When she conceived again, he feared the worst.'

Nicholas was ahead of her. 'The third child was stillborn.'

'Yes, sir, but she was never told. The dead baby was taken away and she was given a live one in its place, thinking it was her own.' She lowered her head. 'My son, Davy, had been born a few days earlier. They took him from me.'

'They?'

'Doctor Winche and the midwife.'

'Where was the baby delivered?'

'In a cottage on the other side of Stapleford,' she said, distressed at the memory. 'They hid me away until my time came then I was sent off to Lincoln to start a new life.'

'And did Master Stratton's wife ever learn the full facts?'

'No, sir. She loved Davy as her own son, poor woman. But he was a bad father. As soon as his wife died, Master

Stratton turned on Davy. Then he heard that I'd been taken on at Oakwood House and looked for a way to get rid of him altogether.' A pleading note sounded. 'I didn't come back to cause trouble, sir, truly I didn't.'

'How did Davy find out that you were his mother?'

'He defied his father and sneaked off to play with Master Enderby's sons. Davy saw me at the house. There are some things a woman can't hide, sir. Davy soon guessed. We were drawn together. He came whenever he could slip away.'

'Let's go back to the birth itself,' he said gently. 'You told me that the baby was taken from you by Doctor Winche and the midwife.'

'That's right, sir. Mother Pigbone.'

Nicholas was shocked. '*She* helped to bring Davy into the world?'

'Mother Pigbone was much younger then and kind to me at first.'

'But what about the legal side of things?' asked Nicholas. 'Two people can't lose their own child and simply reach out for someone else's. A doctor is supposed to record all stillbirths. How was it hushed up?'

'I'm not sure.'

'Davy must be Master Stratton's heir yet he's not legally his son. Were no questions asked at the time? How were you persuaded to part with him?'

'They forced me to sign a document, renouncing my claim to Davy. Everything was to be kept secret. Doctor Winche knew a lawyer who arranged it all.'

Nicholas guessed his name. 'Robert Partridge?'

'I couldn't tell you that, sir. They kept me out of it.' She turned to him in quiet despair. 'What's going to happen to Davy, sir? He's apprenticed to your company, I know, but his heart is not in it. He hates being taken away from me. Will you force him to go back to London with you?'

'It's not up to me, Kate. It's something we'll have to discuss very carefully. But there are other things to be resolved first,' he said, rising to his feet. 'Thank you so much for what you've told me. I can see how much it's cost you.' He pointed to the kitchen door and smiled. 'Go back to your son.'

'But there's something I haven't told you, sir.'

'Is there?'

'The name of Davy's father.'

'I think I know that.'

Jerome Stratton was furious. He stamped around the room and waved his arms wildly. During an acrimonious debate, his voice was the loudest and most bitter.

'Why on earth wasn't I told about this earlier?' he demanded.

'Because you would've tried to stop me,' said Romball Taylard.

'That's certainly true.'

'I wasn't party to this either,' said Doctor Winche defensively. 'Romball acted of his own accord and I had to cover for him.'

Stratton rounded on the doctor. 'You're as much to blame as him. Why didn't you tell me the full truth when you called at my house? Damnation!' he exclaimed. 'You were there yesterday when Nicholas Bracewell told me that poison had been used to kill Robert Partridge. You assured me that he was wrong.'

'What else could I do, Jerome? This has to be kept quiet.'

'How?'

'Quite easily,' said Taylard, trying to take control of the discussion.

The three men were in the steward's private apartment. While the other guests were still mingling down below, Stratton and Winche had slipped upstairs for an urgent conference with Taylard. Alone of the spectators, they had not enjoyed the performance.

'All that we have to do is to stick together,' insisted Taylard.

'We can't do that if you keep me in the dark,' growled Stratton.

'There was no need for you to know. If that meddling Nicholas Bracewell had not interfered, this whole business would have blown over. Robert Partridge would have gone quietly to his grave and,' he said pointedly, looking from one man to the other, 'nobody in this room would have mourned him.'

'That's certainly true.'

'Yes,' added Winche. 'Robert was becoming a problem.'

'He won't bother us any more,' said Taylard smoothly. 'His secrets will be buried with him. I thought to kill two birds with one stone. That's why I procured the poison from Mother Pigbone. You know how fond Robert was of wine. He drank so much of it before the play that he didn't notice when I slipped a powder into his cup.'

'But *why*?' asked Stratton.

'And why not forewarn me?' bleated Winche.

'What were you trying to do, man?'

'Disrupt the performance in the middle,' said Taylard, 'and stop it in its tracks. That would have taken the shine off Westfield's Men. Who would want to come to see them play when they heard about a violent death in the audience? Their visit here might have been brought to a premature end. But,' he added with a curl of his lip, 'Robert Partridge had a stronger constitution than I bargained for. The poison was too slow to take effect. By the time he fell, the play was almost over.'

'Yes,' said Winche irritably, 'and I was left in the awkward position of lying about the cause of death.'

'It's not the first time you've done that, doctor,' Taylard reminded him. 'We'd have got away with it if Nicholas Bracewell hadn't poked his nose in.'

'He knows too much.'

'That's why I tried to silence him as well.'

Stratton was appalled. 'It was *you* who shot at him in the forest?'

'Killing him is the one sure way to evict the company from Silvermere.'

'But you didn't succeed, Romball,' said Winche anxiously, 'and the fellow's still on our tail. He's been hounding Mother Pigbone about the poison.'

'I want no part of this,' declared Stratton, heading for the door. 'I can't condone murder. You two can dig yourselves out of this hole on your own.'

Winche took his arm to stop him. 'You're in this with us, Jerome.'

'Not any more!'

Stratton flung him aside and stormed out of the room, leaving the door wide open. Winche began to lose his nerve. He moistened dry lips with his tongue.

'We're done for, Romball,' he decided. 'I'm going to make a run for it.'

'No!' shouted Taylard.

'The truth is going to come out.'

'Not if we get rid of Nicholas Bracewell.'

'How can we possibly do that?'

'I was about to ask the same question?' said Nicholas, appearing on cue in the doorway. 'I was hoping to find you here, Master Taylard. I wanted to talk to you about your son – Davy Stratton.'

'You see?' cried Winche in alarm. 'I told you that he knows too much.'

Nicholas smiled. 'I know everything.'

Taylard reacted with speed. Grabbing hold of the doctor, he pushed him hard in the direction of Nicholas. The collision gave him vital seconds to make his escape into the bedchamber. Nicholas went after him but found the door locked. He tried to force it with his shoulder. When it would not give way, he snatched up a stout chair and used it to pound away at the door. When the lock finally sprung open, he dashed into the room only to find that Taylard was not there. Cold air blew in through an open window. Nicholas ran over to it and was just in time to see a tall figure, making his way across a flat section of the roof towards the tower. He did not hesitate. Clambering through the window, he picked his way carefully across the slippery surface. Taylard disappeared through a door in the side of the tower. By the time that Nicholas reached it, the steward was several yards above him, struggling towards the edge of the parapet with a cannon ball in his hands. Had the stone missile hit him, Nicholas's head would have been smashed to a pulp but he just managed to dodge it, flinging himself through the door as the cannon ball crashed down through the roof.

Taking out his dagger, he went up the dark stairs with great caution. Taylard was waiting for him at the top with another cannon ball in his hands. Nicholas put his head through the doorway then withdrew it quickly. A second missile passed within inches of him. Before the steward could grab a third, Nicholas darted out on to the top of the tower. Taylard backed away and the two men circled each other slowly.

'Now I can see why you didn't want us here,' said Nicholas. 'The last person you wished to see at Silvermere was your own son.' Taylard tried to make for the door but Nicholas cut off his retreat. 'Katherine Gowan has explained it to me. When she was a servant here, she made the mistake of letting you into her bed. She was soon carrying your child. Like the considerate father you are, Master Taylard, you not only turned her out, you even stole the child from her.'

'It was for her own good.'

'That's not what Kate says.'

'She should never have come back to Essex.'

'There are lots of things that should never have happened,' said Nicholas, jabbing the dagger at him when he tried to move in. 'You shouldn't have bought that poison from Mother Pigbone. You shouldn't have murdered Robert Partridge. You shouldn't have shot at me in the forest. Yes,' he continued, still circling his prey, 'it had to be you, Master Taylard. Who else would have the key to Sir Michael's arsenal? You took one of the muskets and came after me, didn't you?'

'Yes!'

'Well,' said Nicholas, tossing his dagger to the floor, 'I'm still here.'

He spread his arms to invite attack. Taylard responded at once, hurling himself at Nicholas to grapple with him, forcing him back towards the doorway. Nicholas had a firm grip and slowly exerted his strength. Unable to get the better of him, Taylard tried to kick and bite his attacker but that only annoyed him the more. With a sudden burst of energy, Nicholas threw him violently to the ground and stood over him. The steward groped around until he found the discarded weapon. Leaping to his feet, he waved the dagger at Nicholas to keep him at bay. The fight was no longer on equal terms. Taylard manoeuvred him around until Nicholas had his back to the parapet. The lunge finally came. Nicholas was ready for it. He managed to grab the wrist that was holding the dagger and he twisted the weapon free. When it clattered to the floor again, Taylard seemed to go berserk, gathering all his reserves of strength to seize Nicholas and force him steadily backwards until he was up against the parapet.

At the highest point of the house, the two men struggled for their lives. Taylard was spurred on by desperation

379

but Nicholas had the greater willpower. He was not only fighting on behalf Westfield's Men, he was avenging a small boy and a discarded mother as well. It lent him additional strength. When he felt the cold stone against his spine, he moved sharply to his left and tugged the steward with all his might. Romball Taylard's momentum was his own undoing. He was pulled irresistibly forward. Instead of pushing Nicholas over the edge of the parapet, he was flung into the void himself and fell through the darkness with a cry of terror before hitting the ground below.

The performance of *The Witch of Colchester* exceeded all expectations. Westfield's Men were eager to add their own greetings on Sir Michael Greenleaf's sixtieth birthday and they achieved an excellence that surpassed even that shown in *Henry the Fifth*. The Great Hall at Silvermere was packed to capacity to view the phenomenon. Lawrence Firethorn gloried in the role of Lord Malady, able to control his recurring illnesses now instead of being at their mercy. As his arch enemy, Owen Elias revelled in the part of Sir Roderick Lawless while Barnaby Gill clowned his way expertly through the role of Doctor Putrid. Edmund Hoode and James Ingram drew much laughter as a pair of calculating lawyers. Solid support from the rest of the company made the premiere of Egidius Pye's play the crowning event of their visit and the embattled author was in the audience to weep with gratitude all the way through it.

The occasion was not without sadness for Sir Michael. His joy was tempered with regret. Those who had come to celebrate his birthday surrendered to the magic of the play but it had a deeper resonance for him. The waddling figure of Black Joan reminded him of Mother Pigbone and the death of Shortshrift gave him another jolt as he recalled the poisoning of another lawyer in that very hall. Westfield's Men could not be blamed for the unsettling coincidences with which their comedy abounded. In exposing the wickedness of Romball Taylard, the trusted steward, Nicholas Bracewell had drawn the poison out of Silvermere itself and that alone justified the visit of the company. The one person whom Sir Michael and Lady Eleanor had hoped to see on the stage was instead seated beside Clement Enderby and his family. Davy Stratton was entranced. The devil's apprentice was marvelling at the work of accomplished masters of their trade.

Thunderous applause broke out when the play ended. Firethorn beamed at his troupe as they gathered around him to reap the reward of their hard work. He struck the pose that he had used to such effect as Lord Malady.

'Praise is the best medicine of all,' he announced. 'Take as much as you can get.'

The company came out to clapping and cheers that went on for several minutes. The acclaim did not end there. Though they had come as guests of Sir Michael, more than one spectator wanted to express his thanks in monetary terms. Firethorn graciously accepted the bounty. When they later counted their takings, Westfield's Men learnt that they had made a handsome profit. It helped to erase some of the harsher memories they might have taken away from Silvermere. While birthday celebrations continued in one part of the house, the company had their own banquet in the kitchen. It was a fitting way to end their stay in Essex.

Dawn found them loading their cart for the long trek back to London. Nicholas checked that nothing was left behind. Elias strolled across to pat him on the shoulder.

'Your cargo is a little lighter now, Nick,' he observed.

'Yes,' said Nicholas. 'We leave with one less apprentice and that may prove a gain rather than a loss. Since he was not legally the boy's father, Jerome Stratton's contract with us was null and void.'

'That lousy merchant broke the law in other ways as well.'

'He'll answer for that, Owen.'

'So will Doctor Winche and Mother Pigbone.'

'Yes, they were all involved in the conspiracy but the real villain was Romball Taylard. It was so ironic,' he commented, gazing across at the house. 'Master Stratton apprenticed Davy to us in order to get rid of him yet the lad's first engagement as an actor was at Silvermere. Injustice came home to roost.'

'How will the lad fare?'

'Very well, I'm sure. Master Enderby showed great kindness in taking him in.'

'Every boy should be with his mother.'

'Nonsense!' said Firethorn, coming to join them. 'Believe that and we'd never get a single apprentice. Theatre is the best mother of all, Owen. Have you so soon forgotten what happened on that stage last night? She suckled us delightfully.'

After giving the order to mount up, Firethorn hauled

himself into the saddle and led his company past the main door of Silvermere. Sad to see them leave, Lady Eleanor and her guests were standing on the steps to wave them off but there was no sign of their host. Firethorn doffed his hat in a gesture of farewell then took the cavalcade around the perimeter of the lake. Seated beside Nicholas on the cart, Egidius Pye was still bubbling with pleasure at the success of his play.

'Thank you, thank you!' he said effusively.

'It's we who should thank you for a wonderful play,' said Nicholas.

'I'll be a lawyer no more. You've changed my life.'

No sooner had he spoken than there was an ear-splitting explosion behind them. Standing beside the smoking culverin that had been winched to the top of the tower, Sir Michael Greenleaf looked on as his cannon ball described a gentle arc through the air before landing in the middle of the lake. The last of the ice was shattered and the departing actors were covered with spray. From his lofty eminence, Sir Michael had added his individual tribute to them.

The Wizard of Silvermere had perfected his new gunpowder at last.

If you liked *The Devil's Apprentice*,
try Edward Marston's other series . . .

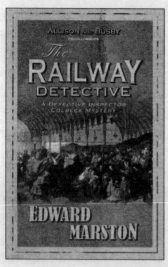

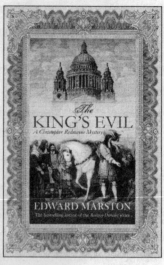